Addy,
Be the Light.
J.P. Mulroy

BRIDE TREE

JP ROBINSON

SECRETS OF VERSAILLES II

Copyright © 2018 JP Robinson
All Rights Reserved

Logos Publications
PO Box 271
Lampeter, PA 17537

ISBN 13: 978-0-9997793-0-9
ISBN 10: 0-9997793-0-3

Printed in the United States

Scripture taken from the New King James Version®. Copyright © 1982 by Thomas Nelson. Used by permission. All rights reserved.

This is a work of fiction. Names, characters, businesses, places, events, locales, and incidents are either the products of the author's imagination or used in a fictitious manner. Any resemblance to actual persons, living or dead, or actual events is purely coincidental.

Dedication

To the heroes whose struggles in the great battle for truth inspire us still today.

Prologue

Apostolic Palace, Vatican City, Italy 1770

"He is ready, Your Holiness."

Pope Clement XIV tilted his red-capped head to one side. "Is he?" The pontiff continued to contemplate the agony reflected on the face of the suspended Christ-figure before him. Clement wore a simple mottled gray garment, more like the habit of a twelfth-century monk than the elaborate vesture typically worn by the Successor of the Prince of the Apostles.

"Is he indeed... ready?" His voice was hoarse and low, like a man who spoke but was not sure if the world was ready to hear his words. He tore his gaze away from the imposing statue that loomed above his head and, with a soft sigh, turned around to fix his eyes upon the young man who now stood before him. Cardinal Rezzonico, the man who had first spoken, placed his hands protectively on the boy's head as the pope stepped forward.

"Fabio. Twelve years of age. Twelve years of training—one for each disciple." Clement placed his hands underneath the soft flesh of the boy's chin. "Abandoned by a mother who did not want you. I gave you a home and I prepared you to do God's work." He tilted the boy's face upward and sighed again. "Now, I am sending you to your death."

Rezzonico sucked in his breath. "You cannot know that Your Holiness. Fabio may well survive his mission." He drew the young man still closer into the folds of his protective embrace, almost as a mother would her child.

Clement gave a noncommittal nod. "That is true. You *may* survive but, should your mission require your death, are you prepared to die, my young Fabio?"

1

Dark eyes, that had seen more hardship in twelve years than most men saw in a lifetime, stared up at him with smoldering intensity. Then the youth's chin jerked downward in a decisive nod.

"Good... that is very good." Clement patted Fabio's shoulders, his fingers touching boyish muscle hardened beyond its years by rigorous combat training. "There is strength here. It may be that these shoulders carry the destiny of the Mother Church."

He bent low and stared into Fabio's eyes. "Why do you live?"

The boy spoke swiftly, the oft-repeated answer spilling from his mouth like water pouring over the edge of a cataract. "I live for the glory of God and the glory of his holy Church."

"To whom do you owe your full allegiance?"

This also was expected.

"To the man whom God ordains to sit on the throne of Saint Peter."

Clement nodded, pleased. *Cardinal Rezzonico has done his work well.*

He stepped back and asked a question that the boy could not expect. "What is it you desire most?"

Fabio blinked several times before answering. His eyes flicked past the pope to the massive cross that protruded from the stone walls around them.

"I wish to be made a saint." He touched the Franciscan rosary of seventy-two beads that dangled around his neck. Like all his clothes, it had been dyed obsidian black.

"High aspirations indeed." The pontiff pursed his lips. "But not out of reach." He stooped and put his face inches from that of his prodigy. "Sainthood can be granted only to those whose actions mirror the greatness of the prize. You know what you must do?"

The onset of adolescence coupled with the momentous nature of the moment made Fabio's voice crack. "I will overthrow the government of France, Holy Father."

"Excellent Fabio." Clement arched an eyebrow. "Now let us test your knowledge of the French language." This last statement was said in French which Fabio had learned since childhood. "Let me give you a parting gift of wisdom." He straightened with a groan. "You must remember that nothing is as it seems. This is a fundamental principle in the world of men." Clement gestured toward the life-sized crucifix. "God disguised as a man."

He pointed to his simple tunic. "The Vicar of Christ dressed as a common priest." The finger singled Fabio out. "A highly-trained servant of the Church who appears to be a mere boy. Everything deceives so that it may better proclaim the truth. *Tu comprends?*"

Fabio nodded his understanding.

The pope steepled his fingers as he paced in front of his silent audience.

"I will make our position perfectly plain." He cleared his throat. "The Kingdom of France is quickly straying—no, *running*—from the path of righteousness. Reason and politics undermine the influence of the Church. Our armies are not strong enough to invade France, leaving us with only one option: to destroy her government from within. Any envoy sent from Rome would arouse suspicions at King Louis's court of Versailles. But a child? You may succeed where we would surely fail."

He fell silent for a moment, then continued. "The penalty for not reclaiming our place of prominence would be to lose control of France and, ultimately, the rest of Europe. Already the feuds between Catholic monarchs cause many to lose faith. If left unchecked, France's growing defiance will influence others to succumb to the will of Satan."

He paused and cast a shrewd glance at the boy. In the wrong hands, the secret he was about to divulge could ignite a war. Then the cardinal's words echoed in Clement's mind. *He is ready.*

The pontiff nodded once, then continued. "Over a century ago, Pope Clement IX saw the evil brewing under the reign of Louis XIV and tried to curb its rapid growth. Unfortunately, the plot to assassinate the Sun King failed and Rome has silently watched the cultural center of Europe slip into the darkness of unfettered heretics."

Unable to stay still, the pope resumed his pacing. "Like his forefathers, the King of France prefers science to Scripture. He is too weak to crush underfoot the serpent that is polluting his Eden."

Clement raised a clenched fist toward the vaulted ceiling. "Therefore, it falls to Rome to destroy the wicked one. It is our task to rip out the tares that will choke the wheat if left unfettered. This time we will not only bring down a king. No, we will destroy the entire Bourbon dynasty!"

His face flushed and a thin sheen of sweat dotted the creases of his furrowed brow. "As we speak, the pangs of hunger, fear and uncertainty tighten like the coils of a serpent around the hearts of the French, stifling their hope of a better future. French is stagnated into three social groups: the peasants, the middle-class *bourgeois*, and the nobility. If we sow the seeds of rebellion, the peasant rabble and the *bourgeois* will unite against the upper echelon of society. The government will collapse from within and our venerated clergy in France will usher in a new era—one controlled by Rome."

The pontiff grabbed the boy's shoulder. "Maria-Antonia of Austria is soon to marry the *dauphin,* Louis Capet, who will be the next King of France. If we succeed, he will be the last Bourbon to rule." He swept the child into a sudden embrace and held him close to his chest.

"Fabio, Fabio." His voice was a low murmur. "You must be the autumn wind which sweeps away the dead leaves that cling to the gnarled branches of the tree. You will go to France and live on the streets. Homeless, you will endure eighteen years of solitude. You must become one of the people, surviving by the strength of your will and the cunning of your mind alone.

As our Lord began his ministry in the thirtieth year of his life so, in your thirtieth year, will you strike for the glory of God." Clement's grip tightened but Fabio did not flinch.

"As Christ gave a new name to Simon calling him Peter the rock, so I give you a new name. Alexandre, the name of a conqueror. For you will destroy an earthly kingdom so that the kingdom of God may rise in France and, from France, spread throughout the world."

He succumbed to a violent fit of coughing. Rezzonico rushed forward but the pontiff waved aside his assistance.

"This illness comes and goes." He wheezed and coughed again. "I may not live to see your mission completed boy, but you must finish it. Complete it for the Church who has sheltered you. Complete it for the chance to achieve eternal glory."

The glint of unshed tears shone in Fabio's eyes. "I will not fail you, Holy Father." He gripped his rosary. "I swear it."

Clement mopped his brow with his sleeve. He took a deep breath and continued. "In addition to sainthood there may be other, more temporal rewards that await you. When the Bourbon lineage is destroyed, I will place a worthy man as absolute ruler under the authority of the Church. Prove to me that you are worthy and you will receive your reward." He clapped his hands twice and Fabio bowed low.

"Go with God, my son." He traced the pattern of a cross in the air and Fabio left the hall without another word. "Go with God."

Cardinal Rezzonico closed the door then turned back to his master, the mask of a protective mother dropping with the speed of a headsman's axe.

"You are not seriously considering making *him* the ruler of France?" Scorn dripped like acid from his thin lips. "It will take twenty, maybe thirty years for Fabio... for *Alexandre* to accomplish his mission, *if* he succeeds. But surely you have considered that no ruler of Europe will accept a puppet of Rome on the throne of France! Even the clergy of France would balk, especially the Jesuits who already hold you in contempt."

Clement pressed his lips into a thin line. "When this is over, if the boy survives, you will kill him yourself. History must never bear witness to the true force that lay behind the fall of the Bourbons."

He paused and turned toward the crucifix, mesmerized by the painted blood that dripped from the nail-pierced palms of Christ. "Serve me well Rezzonico, and it may be you who sits on the throne of France."

⚜

"What are we doing here?" Philippe whispered in French to his father, the Duke of Valence. He craned his twelve-year-old neck in a vain attempt to see over the dense crowds that were massed inside Whitefield Chapel.

"Quiet my son." His father's gray eyes flickered over the bystanders whose bodies pressed against them. Then he stooped and whispered in the child's ear. "No French here today, son. English only when in England. We're safer that way."

He straightened and said in a louder tone, "This is history in the making. Perhaps it is only coincidence that we were visiting relatives in England during Reverend George Whitefield's funeral, but I do not wish to miss this opportunity to hear the renowned John Wesley speak."

Philippe crinkled his brow. He didn't know who George Whitefield was, but the name of the Protestant preacher *Wesley* was often whispered in hushed undertones as though he were the devil himself. "But Father, why would you want to hear Mr. Wesley? Isn't he a heretic? We are Catholics. And why are we disguised?" He tugged the edge of the plain garments that covered his father's expansive belly.

Again, the Duke bent to his son's ear. "We *are* loyal Catholics. That is why we do not want anyone to know who we are. I have heard how this John Wesley is turning England upside down." He shrugged. "I do not want to miss the chance to see him in action. One must know one's enemy. Now, no more questions!" He rested his broad palm on his son's thin shoulder.

At that moment, a low murmur swelled among the crowd. A man, robed in black, with a nose that reminded the boy of an eagle's beak, strode to the vaulted platform which jutted over the heads of the crowd. Wavy, shoulder-length white hair framed a strong face. Even from this distance Philippe could feel the sorrow and resolve that emanated from the man. This was him! This could only be John Wesley.

Without preamble, the preacher began to speak:

"Let me die the death of the righteous, and let my last end be like this man's." His voice, sonorous and powerful, rumbled over the audience. "How many of you join in this wish?" The young soul of Philippe de Valence trembled. *I wish it!*

"Perhaps there are few of you who do not wish it, even in this numerous congregation. May this wish also rest upon your minds—to be 'where the wicked cease from troubling, and where the weary are at rest.'"

Again, Philippe felt something churning within him. Fear of what would happen to him when he died mingled with a longing for some positive assurance of entering Paradise. The thought struck him that this man had walked from heaven, like an angel, to speak to him. But why would God send a heretic to him?

Papa's priest assures me that I will be saved. I am good, I recite my catechism and am kind to others. There is no need to worry.

Wesley's voice cut through his thoughts like a fiery sword. "The man who lies before us was convinced that we 'must be born again' or outward religion would profit us nothing."

What is this? The wood flooring beneath Philippe's feet seemed to shake. He gripped his father's arm as his eyes darted around the crowd. If the ground was indeed trembling, no one but him appeared to notice. Perhaps it was the preacher's words that had unhinged the foundation of his faith. *Nothing? All my prayers mean nothing?* His heart cried out for answers as the reality of what he was hearing sank into his mind.

"It is not enough to say that all men are *sick* of sin." Wesley raised a fist. "No, we are all *dead* in trespasses and sins. We are all guilty before God and are liable to death both temporal and eternal."

Philippe's heart clenched within him. Fear. It was raw, ugly fear. His mind conjured up images of red, writhing demons who tortured his skin with blazing pitchforks while he begged in vain for them to stop. He could not—he would not—spend eternity in hell.

"What can I do?" He whimpered the words in agony. Philippe felt as though the multitudes around him had all disappeared. He had never heard anything like this. Wesley's words were sharp arrows that penetrated an invisible target: his immortal soul.

"Christ was wounded for our transgressions, he was bruised for our iniquities. *He* bore all our sins in his own body upon the tree. He was delivered for our offenses and was raised again for our justification."

Is there hope? Philippe's mind screamed at the preacher. *Can I earn my way to heaven?*

He buried his face in his hands, forgetting his father's presence and the thousands around him. Images of his sins flitted through his mind. Although the list of his wrongs would be considered trivial by most, the God that Wesley described would not overlook even one transgression. Each memory pressed down on him like a mountain of despair, crushing him beneath its weight.

"It is not by works, lest any man should boast," Wesley's voice thundered to the young and trembling soul before him. Then his tone gentled. "But by faith alone."

The evangelist laid emphasis on the final word and, in that moment, the fountains of Philippe's understanding broke open. With understanding came faith—the simple faith of a child that could move a mountain of fear.

The church cannot save me. Neither could he escape hell by his good deeds. The price of salvation had already been paid by a man who had hung on a tree, bleeding and dying because of *him*. Tears streaked down his face and he sniffed, trying in vain to stop the waterfall of emotion that threatened to bury his soul with its intensity.

"Conscious then of your own wants and of God's bounteous love, who gives liberally and upbraids not, cry to Him that works all in all for a measure of the same precious faith!" Wesley hammered the pulpit with his fist. "Cry!"

And Philippe did cry. His thin reedy voice bounced off the soaring walls and up to heaven's gates. Curious heads jerked around at this unexpected interruption. Philippe lurched forward, crying, laughing, and screaming, as joy, wonder and fear surged within him like geyser erupting toward the heavens. His father's flailing arms grasped at his coat but the Duke's fingers caught only empty air. All Philippe knew was that he had to go forward. Like a drowning man he reached out, desperate to make his way past the crush of the onlookers who separated him from this messenger of God whose words had changed everything. The crowd parted.

"Who is he?"

"What's going on?"

The whispers grew but he was oblivious to them. Wesley had stopped preaching and watched the young man make his way forward as though he was used to this sort of spectacle. Perhaps he was.

Philippe bypassed the coffin and threw himself to his knees. He didn't know how to pray. His catechism seemed insufficient to the task of expressing the needs of his soul. He didn't know what God wanted but he knew that he wanted God.

He lifted his arms. "Save me, please save me!"

A tender but firm hand squeezed his shoulder and he looked up into the sparkling eyes of John Wesley. The evangelist had come down from his pulpit to help a soul that yearned to be lifted into the presence of God. "He died on the tree to redeem a bride for his name's sake. His love is greater than your fear. Do you believe this?"

Philippe jerked his head up and down. He didn't understand everything the man said but he believed it.

"Grace is given to you, young man." Wesley's smile was warm and genuine. "Believe that Christ takes you unto himself."

They were simple words but they brought with them a peace that the boy could not explain. "I, I won't go to hell?" It seemed too simple to be true.

Wesley responded with a question. "Do you truly believe he died for your sins?" His eyes bored into those of the young man before him.

"Yes!" Philippe grabbed the preacher's flowing robe. "I do."

"Then how can God condemn what his son has already saved?"

Wesley pulled him to his feet. Philippe's heart flooded with light. Joy replaced fear; assurance conquered uncertainty.

"Son?" The voice was his father's but it was hesitant... almost foreign. Philippe stood up from the altar, glowing with the effect of what had just transpired. His father stared at him, slack-jawed. Philippe ran forward, throwing his arms around him and murmuring, "*Oh Papa.*" He lapsed into French. "It is wonderful, so very wonderful!"

Wesley looked at the display in silence. "I ask you all," he spread his arms wide as the beginning of another smile tugged at the corner of his mouth, "what better tribute could there be to the life of Reverand Whitefield than this?"

She is coming. All of France was talking about it. The cathedral bells had heralded the news for days. Marie-Antoinette, the future queen, was even now *en route* to Versailles. Marie-Antoinette, the woman that he was going to kill.

It was said that she would stay in Rheims and, from Rheims, she would travel to Versailles where the heir to the throne awaited her arrival. *He'll be waiting a long time.* The boy sniggered as he pushed another branch out of his way and stole along the forest path. Instead of an eager bride, the prince would be confronted with a pale corpse.

The boy had made the three-day journey from Arras to Rheims in only two. His twelve-year-old legs had carried his thin frame along country roads late into the night. With each step, his father's words drummed through his mind without reprieve. *Death steals everything, boy. Everything but your name.*

His father's breath had reeked with the stench of stale beer while his blood-shot eyes bored deep into his son's skull. Then he had gripped the back of the boy's stubby neck. *Make our name to be remembered. Become so powerful that the whole world will tremble when they hear it whispered.*

Then his father had lurched to the door, slammed it shut, and walked out of his son's life forever.

Abandoned by his father while still grieving the loss of his mother, the boy had taken his younger siblings to his relatives in Arras, France. That had been six months ago. The loneliness of those six months had transformed an idealistic child into a potential murderer.

His eyes narrowed as he broke through a copse of trees and spied the towering cathedral which had consecrated the kings of France for almost a thousand years. "I did it!" His whoop rang out across the clearing. "I reached Rheims just like I told Augustin I would." The thought of his younger brother made his throat tighten.

"Don't go." Augustin had pleaded with him two nights ago, just as he prepared to sneak out of their bedroom window.

"I have to do this, Augustin." He had gently detached his brother's small hand from his black coat. "Father told me that a name is the only thing that outlives us. Look at how quickly mother died! It could be the same for us, Augustin."

"But this is not what Father would have wanted." Augustin's small face, pockmarked by pre-pubescent acne, crinkled into a pale ball. He was about to cry.

"How do you know what Father would have wanted?" Frustration had tinged the boy's voice. It was time to go. "I'm the eldest and I know best! Something has to be done to make sure that our name is remembered forever." He laid his hand on Augustin's shoulder and took a deep breath. "Cook says that 'Father always was a man of extremes.' Maybe if I kill this foreign queen, Father will see that I can make our name great and will come back to us."

Tears had blurred the boy's eyes and he dashed them away with the back of his hand. He was angry at his father for leaving, angry at his own weakness in crying, angry at God for taking their mother and letting all this happen in the first place.

"Augustin, this is our chance to get Father back. Don't you see?" He had tapped the wooden handle of the rusty meat cleaver which protruded from his belt. He had stolen it when Cook's back was turned. "We'll show Father that we're worthy of him and he'll come home again."

Augustin had stuck his thumb in his mouth and nodded. "If it will bring Father back." Unshed tears had glistened in his eyes as he lifted a small hand in a gesture of farewell and watched his older brother disappear into the night.

Now the young assassin's face hardened as he glared at the royal entourage that wound its way through the city below him. "I will do it, Father. For you." The angular lines of his cheeks slanted upward beneath the mop of his brown curls. "For *Maman*. I will become the master of life and death. The world will never forget our name."

Marie-Antoinette, future Queen of France, gazed out of her carriage at the royal entourage that prepared to complete the final stage of the journey from Rheims to Versailles. She had been travelling for twenty-one days, and every inch of her pampered fourteen-year-old body pleaded for an end to the trip. That would not happen of course. She would arrive in two more days. Just in time for her royal wedding. Marie sighed.

She had plenty of company: fifty-seven carriages, one hundred seventeen footmen, and three hundred seventy-six horses from her home country in Austria had been joined by a myriad of courtiers from France. A small army surrounded her. Not that there was any danger, of course. All of Austria loved her and it was only natural that her French subjects would love her also.

"What's not to love?" She pulled a pearl-encrusted mirror from one of the drawers built into the wall of her carriage and stared at her reflection. A powdered, oval face with cheeks that were still rounded from childhood looked back at her.

The image blurred in her mind for a moment and her face was replaced by that of her mother. Lines, created by the weight of the crown, became more prominent as her mother's words echoed in her thoughts. *Be so good that the people of France will think I have sent them an angel.*

"I will, Mama." Marie whispered the promise. "I will make you proud." The mirage—more a memory than her imagination—disappeared but as it did, Marie became conscious of another presence in the carriage. The princess-bride slowly tore her gaze from the mirror only to be confronted by twin pools of dark intensity set in the angular face of a boy her age. Smudges of dirt accentuated the dark circles that lay underneath his disconcerting amber eyes. In his hand, he held some sort of metal knife.

A scream built up inside her but, anticipating her reaction, his free hand shot out and clamped down over her mouth. He pressed himself closer as she struggled to free herself. He was quite strong for such a small boy.

"Shh, Princess." He shifted closer and the stench of dried sweat and manure burned in her nostrils. She wriggled again, desperate to free herself from this walking chamber pot.

"Don't scream." He tightened his grip on the knife. "I will take my hand away if you promise you won't scream." Her head bobbed up and down. After a moment, he released his hold.

She scooted to the opposite end of the carriage and pressed her body against its wall of plush satin. *How did he get in here?*

"It was quite easy really." The boy glanced down at his smooth hands then back up at her face. "Getting into your carriage, I mean."

Her face paled. Was he a sorcerer with the ability to read minds?

"It's quite amazing how one can be so alone while surrounded by so many people." His right cheek twitched as he spoke. "All the guards thought I was just another errand boy. Only one, an Austrian, bothered to question me when I came close to the carriage. I told him that I had been ordered to empty your chamber pot." He spread his hands. "And here I am. No one knows my true purpose."

Marie found her voice. "What is that purpose?"

He paused and looked down as his cheek twitched again. She found the reaction quite revolting.

"I don't know... now," he said at last. "At first I came here to kill you but..." He broke off, as though distracted, and stared at her. His empty hand reached out and fingered a ringlet of her golden hair which had come undone in her short struggle. "You are quite beautiful you know." He pressed his lips against her hair. "So very beautiful."

Marie was a statue, struck dumb by his audacity. Then she jerked away from his grubby paw.

"You're mad!" Royal pride vanquished her fear and anger arose like an awakened dragon. "How dare you touch me?" Her fingers tightened on the mirror that lay unnoticed on the seat beside her. In one smooth motion, she lifted and smashed it against his face. His hands flew upward in a vain effort to protect himself and he released his hold on the cleaver in the process.

Shards of glass bit into his cheek below his eye causing blood to stream down his face. "What right have you to call me beautiful? You filthy brute!" She spat on him. "Am I some *bourgeoise* on whom you can make advances? Do I look like a woman of the streets? Like your mother?"

He shrank back, screaming, and she slammed the broken mirror against the side of his head again. "I am the betrothed wife to your sovereign, peasant. Respect me. Fear me. But never insult me by making me the object of your affection!"

Dimly her outraged mind registered three things:

One: alarmed voices were coming closer to the carriage which meant help would soon arrive.

Two: The boy had meant to kill her. *Why?*

Three: He too had heard the noise and, despite his fury and pain, he was intelligent enough to throw himself to the door of the carriage, pry it open with bloody fingers and drop to the ground.

"My mother?" He pivoted on his heel. "A woman of the streets?"

His bloodied face looked demonic. "I swear to you," he lifted a trembling finger, "one day, Marie-Antoinette, you too will quake at the sound of my name." He slammed the door behind him, lurched away and slipped into the entrance of a nearby barn.

Once out of sight, the boy lost no time in pulling the hood of his shirt over his head to conceal the blood that still flowed from the cut under his eye. He peeked out in the direction of the outraged princess. A crowd of servants and soldiers swarmed around the carriage and he saw a few heads turning toward him. Quickly he pressed his thin frame against the side of the door, slipped outside and around the corner of the barn.

Rheims was a heavily populated city with a constant flow of travelers. The city's population had swelled slightly as visitors made the journey toward Versailles to be spectators at the upcoming nuptials. It was this natural disguise of ten thousand tourists which had allowed him to slip undetected into Marie-Antoinette's presence. It was this very thing that would allow him to leave Rheims and make the long journey home to Arras.

Why didn't I do it when I had the chance? He struck his small fist against his thigh. But he knew the answer. To kill her would be to crush an irreplaceable jewel. The clear skin, golden hair and bright eyes of the Austrian princess had blinded him for a few fatal seconds and, in those moments, he had lost the critical element of surprise. That would not happen again.

Father would be disappointed in me. His steps lengthened as he slipped around a shop corner and waited, peering over his shoulder to ensure that he had not been followed. *Now he'll never come back.*

"I will make her remember our name." His nerveless fingers tightened until the knuckles of his fists went white. "I swear that before I die, the queen and all of France will bow before the name of Maximilien Robespierre!"

Part One

Twenty years later

Chapter One

January 1789. Sixth Precinct, Paris

Paris was angry. Viviane de Lussan could feel the fury fermenting inside the deprived souls that lined the cobblestone streets like yeast ferments in a corked bottle of wine. Soon the bottle would explode into a million fragments, but it would be red blood, not wine, that flowed in the heart of the city.

French society was a complex system of three highly stratified social classes, called Estates that were relics of an antiquated feudalistic order. The clergy comprised the First Estate, the nobility made up the Second Estate while the unfortunate Third Estate—the largest class and most heavily taxed of the three—was composed of peasants, urban workers and upper-class merchants known as *bourgeois*.

She pressed her face against the open window and stared at the squalor around her, then covered her nose with a plain cloth handkerchief as the stench of five hundred thousand unwashed bodies assaulted her nostrils. The Third Estate bore the twin burdens of heavy taxes and limited rights while the clergy and nobility enjoyed the privileges of tax-free wealth and power. Constant hunger, years of poor harvests, and a high cost of living had caused many of the poor to cast jealous eyes on the extravagant lifestyles of the nobility and some members of the clergy.

"It's quite a sight, Madame Viviane, isn't it?" Olivier, her driver shouted down to her from his perch in front of the carriage. "I don't imagine you see much of this in Lussan?"

Olivier was responsible for transporting her from her mother's simple cottage in Lussan to the royal palace at Versailles where her cousin, Duchess Gabrielle de Polignac, had invited Viviane to join her. Her mother's parting words drummed through her mind like the muted hoofbeats of the horse that pulled her carriage. *Make a better life for yourself, Viviane. No matter what it takes.*

After seeing the misery of the citizens of Paris, Viviane realized that she had indeed been blessed in her small village. While living conditions in Lussan had been difficult at best, nothing she had ever seen in her entire twenty-five years could have prepared her for the misery and pent-up fury that virtually oozed out of every puff of wind in Paris.

"*Non*, monsieur, home is nothing like this." She swept a stray tendril of her blond hair out of her eyes as she shouted to be heard over the rattling of the carriage wheels on the snow-covered cobblestones. Her driver edged the travel-stained carriage down the narrow streets, narrowly missing a swarm of ragged urchins whose bare feet sloshed through icy puddles as they dashed about in the falling evening shadows.

One of the children lingered behind the group, struggling to keep pace. He turned and glimpsed her peering face then came to an abrupt stop. Yellowed sleeves, attached to a grimy tattered shirt, were rolled down below his elbows in a futile effort to ward off the winter cold. Wild black hair sought to escape the prison of a faded beret atop his head. He coughed twice. His pinched cheeks bore mute testimony to the hunger that he faced but it was not until Viviane looked at his feet that she understood why this child could not run with the others.

"Stop!" She pounded her fist against the wooden frame of the carriage door. "Stop, I said!"

Olivier pulled hard on the reigns but, before the carriage stopped rolling, Viviane shoved the door open and dropped into the street.

"Madame!" Olivier's voice rose in panic. "*Attendez!*"

But Viviane's eyes were glued on the boy with the missing leg. He stood still, gazing up at her. As she hurried forward, Viviane jerked her money pouch from a pocket in her homespun dress. She fumbled with the short drawstring, knowing before her slender fingers slipped inside that there were only two coins remaining.

She reached him at last, breathless. He leaned upon a makeshift crutch, his right leg severed below the knee. His long pant leg fell limply onto the muddy street. They stood in the intersection of the crossroads staring at each other until she held out the two coins.

"Here." She took his hand and placed the *livres* in his grubby palm. "Take it. Take it with my blessing."

The boy dipped his head and opened his mouth as though he wanted to speak but was unable to find a voice. *He was mute!* The revelation came as a shock. How could nature be so cruel that this child should be deprived of both speech and his leg? A strangled cry came from the boy's mouth and he clenched his fist over the coins as tears spilled out of the corners of his eyes.

"It's alright." Viviane dropped to her knees and pulled him close. He reeked of sewage and rotten fish, but she did not care. "It's alright. I understand." She repeated the words as he laid his greasy head against her shoulder.

"Madame!" It was Olivier's voice that shattered the emotional intensity of the moment. "Please, Madame Viviane, we must leave at once. It is not safe for you to be here."

He gripped her arm and dragged her from the unknown child who wiped his nose with a dirty fist. The carriage waited about twenty yards away. Olivier's eyes darted around at the grim faces that peered out from the shadows as he edged forward.

Wiping tears from her own eyes, Viviane turned around, not trusting herself to look back.

"Please," Olivier pushed her forward. "Do not do such a foolish thing again." He opened the carriage door. "Paris is a dangerous place, especially for those with wealth."

"But Olivier," Viviane stooped as she entered the coach, "I have no wealth. My last two coins were given to that poor boy."

Her driver slammed the door shut. "Believe me, these days it does not matter. You ride in a carriage while they walk. In the people's eyes, you are rich! We go, *non?*"

Olivier's last words were lost in the thunderous clatter of another coach that careened down the road they had just left. Viviane had just seated herself when she heard the scream.

It's him.

"No!" She jerked open the door and threw herself outside of the carriage, evading Olivier's desperate grasp. Her heart told her what she would find before her eyes registered the truth.

There.

He lay in broken pieces on the crossroads, squirming in muted agony. She rushed to his side, ripping the air with her cries. Over her shrieks came the mocking laugh of the aristocratic driver who had not bothered to see the damage caused by his reckless driving.

"Peasant trash!" The slurred words of a man who had drunk too much alcohol bounced off the sodden tenement walls.

"Please, please be alright." Every instinct insisted that her prayer was futile. Missing a leg, the boy had not been able to escape the furious pace of the drunken aristocrat's horses and his useless voice had only been able to scream out his pain. His body convulsed in a desperate last attempt to keep life within his veins. Blood spurted out from his nose and crushed chest while glistening shards of bone protruded through his torn clothes. The silver coins lay unnoticed in a muddy puddle near his outstretched fingertips.

"No!" Viviane sank to her knees. "No, no."

A crowd had begun to gather, drawn by the noise and by the rumor that an *aristo* had killed the child. Germain. She heard them shout his name.

His blood ran down her hands and discolored the faded gray of her dress.

"Uhh…" Germain made a superhuman effort to turn his head toward Viviane.

"Shh." She caressed his unruly blood-stained curls. "It's alright, I promise." She rocked back on her heels and kissed his forehead.

"Uhh…" They boy bared his teeth in an attempt at a smile, placed his left hand in hers, and died.

"Let me through, let me through!" A young woman elbowed her way through the throng until she stood opposite Viviane. Long black curls swirle around her storm–gray eyes, framing her square jaw.

"Germain?" She pushed Viviane away from the body. "Take your hands off my brother, aristo!" She spat on Viviane's feet and laid a trembling hand on Germain's pale, still body. She breathed deeply but shed no tears and, when she looked at Viviane again, her beautiful face was contorted with fury.

"This is what *they* do to *us!*" She stabbed her finger in Viviane's face. A murmur of agreement rippled through the crowd.

"What?" Viviane recoiled, shocked. "I didn't—"

"They feed on our labor, ridin' around in fancy carriages." The woman sneered at Viviane and began to pace in a slow circle around her. "*They've* got nice clothes to wear." She grabbed the front of Viviane's arm and roughly pulled her so the crowd could clearly see her dress. "And *we* dress in rags!"

"That's right Salomé!" The lone voice was joined by a chorus of others.

"Make the aristo wretch pay!" another called out. Viviane felt a twinge of real fear.

"Please, you mustn't think I had anything to do with this." She held up her hands before her face. "I'm innocent. I just—"

"Innocent?" Salomé cut her off with a hard slap. "You're rich!"

"That's crime enough!" The crowd hooted and jeered as their frustration found an unexpected scapegoat.

A woman shoved Olivier forward with a screech. "This one's with her."

"Take this pike." A man thrust the spear-like weapon in the air. "Let's see how pretty she looks without a head!"

Olivier stumbled forward. "Please, the king is expecting us. You must let us go!"

It was the wrong thing to say.

Salomé rounded on him, her eyes alight with malicious evil. "The *king?*"

To the crowd, "We've caught ourselves a royal!" She bowed before Viviane, twirling her fingers in a mock salute. "She's got friends at the court of a king who ignores the sufferin' of his own people!"

She shoved her face inches from Viviane's. "My brother—the only family I had left—is dead because of your kind." Her lips pulled back in a snarl. "I think there's been enough cryin' in our part of town."

She turned back to the crowd whose bloodlust was now at fever–pitch. "I say it's time the aristos learned the meaning of pain. I say it's time we made 'em pay!"

"Yes, yes!" The mob surged forward. Someone grabbed Viviane's arms and wrenched them behind her back.

"No." She writhed in his grasp. "Don't do this!" Her voice was lost in the thunder of hate that surged from the crowd. "Stop! Please stop!"

"Shut her up." Salomé pointed with the knife.

Viviane tried to fight back, tried to escape, but her arms were bound behind her back and a dirty cotton shirt was shoved between her teeth.

She was going to die.

A few burly men lifted her off her feet and threw her onto a loading-dock that rose a few feet above the heads of the people. Someone pressed a rusty knife into Salomé's waiting palm.

"Salomé, Salomé! Pay, pay, make 'em pay." The cry became a pulsing chant that reverberated off the squalid buildings.

"Pay, pay, make 'em pay!"

Salomé swung herself lightly onto the dock. "We'll send her precious head to the king in a basket!" She thrust the knife into the air.

The murderous crowd howled its approval.

Viviane was gagged but she swung her head to the right just in time to see Olivier's bulky body as it was heaved up next to hers.

The coachman trembled as he met her gaze. "W-we should not have stopped."

Tears ran in fresh waves down Viviane's cheeks. "I'm sorry." She tried to apologize but only a wordless garble came through the cloth that forced her lips apart.

Two muscular men shoved Olivier to his knees. Salomé stepped behind him, and twirled the knife in her right hand.

"Pay, pay, make 'em pay!" The crowd was lost in wild abandon, chanting and cheering as the executioner took her place.

"Shall we make 'em pay?" Her voice somehow made itself heard above the thunderous cacophony of sound.

"Make 'em pay!" Her captivated audience roared in delight.

"For Germain!" She screamed the words as she placed the cutting edge of the knife along the tender flesh underneath Olivier's chin. Then, in one smooth motion, she slit his throat. A geyser of blood spurted over her pale fingers and pooled onto the wooden boards beneath her feet.

Viviane's scream was a garbled moan.

"They will pay!" Salomé spread her bloodied arms wide as through embracing her admirers.

"They will pay!" The ecstatic throng echoed her cry as she pushed the twitching body over the edge of the dock with her foot into their waiting arms. Within minutes the mob had ripped the head from the corpse, trampling flesh and bones into the grimy earth.

Salomé turned to Viviane who stared at her with wild eyes. "It's your turn, love." She crooned the words as if they were part of a song. "It's your turn to pay." She crooked her bloody finger. The two men brought Viviane forward and made her kneel in the dark puddle of blood. Olivier's blood.

The executioner bent low and whispered in Viviane's ear. "All the money in the world can't bring back my brother, love. And all the money in the world can't save you from death... or from me!"

The iron taste of fear made Viviane choke. What should she do if she only had seconds to live? *Pray. I should pray.*

Her lips twitched uselessly. *God, help me. I'm too young to die.* She was too frightened to close her eyes. She shook her head at Salomé, willing her to put down the knife. The vengeful rebel smiled and tightened her grip on its hilt.

Salomé stalked behind her.

Viviane felt her heart plummet.

She saw the stained blade descend before her eyes. She felt Salomé's hand jerk her head backward. She heard the shouts of the crowd as they bayed like rabid dogs for her death.

"Are you ready to pay the price, aristo?" The sharp edge of the blade bit into her throat.

"Pay, pay, make her pay!"

The knife dug in deeper and she felt the first trickle of blood begin to stream down her throat. Salomé spread her legs apart and—

"Stop this at once!"

A commanding voice rang out over the tumult and Salomé jerked her head toward the intruder. Her eyes fell on a tall, dark-haired man who casually straddled a white horse. Behind him, twenty mounted men-at-arms held drawn swords at the ready.

"I said," he thrust a finger toward Salomé, "stop this travesty at once!"

A hush enveloped the mob. Viviane did not dare move.

"You there! Woman with the knife. Let that poor creature go."

"Stay out of this, aristo!" Salomé's voice ripped through the night air. "What do you care of what we do?"

She appealed to the crowd. "Shall we make her pay?"

Only a trickle of voices answered.

A few former rioters glanced between her and the newcomer and his men. Muttering imprecations under their breath, first one, then two and then a few more slipped away until only a handful remained.

Salomé trembled, keeping one hand on the dagger at Viviane's neck. "I'll slit her throat."

"I would not do that if I were you." He rode closer, his stallion closing the gap between them in seconds.

"Who are you and why should I care what you think?"

A benign smile crossed the intruder's face. "I am Philippe, Duke of Valence, *Prince du Sang,* and cousin to the King of France. One word from me, and my men will end your life before you can say 'Hail Mary.'"

He pressed closer and then he lowered his voice. "Believe me, Madame, I also want change for the people of France. However, spilling the blood of your countrymen—rich or poor—is too high a price."

Philippe held out his hand.

Salomé tightened her grip on Viviane's hair. "I-I could kill you instead."

"You could." The prince patted the neck of his snorting stallion. "But you're too smart to throw your life away."

Salomé looked down. By now the crowd had completely disappeared.

She grimaced as she lifted the edge of the blade from her victim's neck and shoved it into the cloth belt that encircled her waist. "One day," she brandished a fist, "the people of Paris will ignite a flame that not even you will be able to put out."

Philippe tilted his head to one side. "But today is not that day."

Salomé did not answer, but shoved a trembling Viviane into his arms, leapt off the back of the dock, and disappeared into the night.

He had watched the drama unfold on the stage as he held back, cloaked in the deepening shadows. Blood from the carriage driver's shredded arm seeped into the worn cuff of his pants. Alexandre crouched and dipped his fingers in the small, dark puddle that pooled below it as the enraged Salomé leapt from the dock.

What were the odds that he would again cross paths with his nemesis, Philippe de Valence, after so many years? And the woman! He shook his head, trying to clear his thoughts. *Such an uncanny resemblance...*

Alexandre straightened. It could not be coincidence that drew Philippe, himself and a woman whose face was an exact replica of his lost love together in one fateful night. "It is a sign. The sign for which I have long waited." He curled his bloodied fingers into fists, savoring the taste of anticipation. "After twenty long years, my time has come."

Chapter Two

January 1789. Café Procope, Paris

M aximilien Robespierre slowly tilted his glass of watered wine and sipped at the contents as his amber eyes flickered over crowd that loitered in the Café Procope. He was waiting for his brother Augustin, a lawyer like himself, to join him. No doubt he was out in the streets, trying to gain support for the coming revolution.

Violent protests had become common throughout the country as the deprived lower classes refused to cow before the profligate nobles and the sanctimonious clergy. It was only a matter of time until the winds of revolution swept the Bourbon dynasty away like the chaff it was.

Violence. Robespierre stroked the faded scar that ran from his right eye to the bottom of his pale cheek. Two decades had passed since he had failed to kill the young queen. His first attempted act of violence had set the course for the rest of his life.

Some would call him talented. He had become an educated lawyer who had endeared himself to the common people of Paris by refusing bribes and defending the rights of the urban workers.

Some would call him ambitious. Despite his youth—he was only thirty-two years old—Robespierre had successfully campaigned for the privilege of representing the French people before King Louis XVI himself. He would be one of six hundred ten representative voices that would unite to bring radical reform the government of France.

Some would call him successful. But Robespierre knew this to be a lie. He took the glasses off his face, wiped the corners of his eyes and then fingered the rough edges of the scar once more. Twenty years had not completed the healing of his face nor removed the scar from his heart.

Heart? He barked out a dry laugh. It was a disturbing sound, not unlike the warning rattle of a serpent's tail. A lanky *bourgeois* who lounged in the corner started at the idiosyncratic noise but glanced away when Robespierre's tawny eyes came to rest upon him. *My heart was ripped from my chest when Father left us all to rot.*

He was no longer the idealistic boy of twelve. Time and experience were the masters of disillusionment. Robespierre knew that the father who had disappeared would never return. The silent tears that he had cried into his pillow as a child had long since dried, leaving behind a rabid hunger for vengeance against the one person still within his reach. She was the woman whose beauty enthralled him. She was the noble whose callous disdain infuriated him. She was the queen whose throne made her unreachable. She was Marie-Antoinette.

Salomé sensed rather than saw that she was being followed. *The prince?*

She pushed the unlikely thought from her mind. She had willfully taken roads that passed through ominous dark alleys. The path she had walked would confuse a homing pigeon.

Whoever it is must know Paris as well as I do. The thought was quite disturbing. Only other members of the underworld knew Paris as she did. If she was being followed by one of them, it could be for no good reason. She trotted forward a few more paces, threw herself into the shadows of an open doorway, then glanced around while loosening the dagger that she had tucked into her waistband. Patches of moonlight glinted off the dark, churning waters of the Seine River which cut through the heart of the city. She retreated further into the gloom.

The footsteps came closer but much more slowly. Salomé felt the hard handle pressing into the flesh of her skin. It was odd how awkward the blade now felt in her hand, as though one solid puff of wind would knock it from her fingers. The rage that had consumed her earlier had been replaced by an emotion that she disliked in others and despised in herself: fear.

Crunch... crunch... crunch. The sound of boots on snow stopped and the broad, black-cloaked shoulders of a tall *bourgeois* suddenly blocked her view of the moonlit Seine. *Now!* Salomé leaped forward and pressed the sharp edge of the blade against the man's ribs.

"Who are you?" She tried to mask the irregular rhythm of her heart by hardening her voice. "Never mind that, just tell me why you're followin' me or I'll gut you like a fish!"

"I will not answer either question, Salomé. Not until you put the knife away."

The stranger was much too calm. His lack of emotion increased her uneasiness.

"You are in no position to argue." She licked her lips. It did not surprise her that the arrogant fool knew her name. The crowds had howled it over and over before the prince's untimely interference. She jabbed the knife against his side. "Answer me or I will slip this knife into your ribs and throw your body in the Seine!"

"If you do that," his voice was cool, almost detached, "then you will die with me." It was only then that she felt the hard edge of a blade press against her own abdomen. Salomé glanced down. It was a mistake but it was one that she could not resist making. Without a discernible motion, the stranger had drawn a long-bladed stiletto and had placed its tip just above her navel!

Although his back was still turned, the man sensed her motion. Whirling with the speed of a viper, he slapped the blade from Salomé's hand, lifted his own knife to her throat and pressed her body against the frame of the door in which she had waited a few moments before.

She started to struggle but bit back her stream of epithets when her attacker lifted a finger and increased the pressure on the blade.

"Shh." He pursed his lips. When she fell silent he stared at her for long moments, as though trying to decide if he knew her.

"What?" She glared at him, her chest heaving. "Never seen a woman before?"

His eyes roved over her body. She was used to looks of lust. Her low neckline and trim figure often lured weak-minded men into her arms. But this was different.

"You look like someone I knew," he said at length.

"And you look like a gutter rat!"

He arched an eyebrow. "Shouldn't you be asking my name?"

"I don't care about your stupid name!" She began squirming again, more angered by her helplessness than she was afraid of his knife.

"I am Alexandre."

She stared at him. "Is that supposed to mean somethin' to me?"

"If I take this away will you run?" He gestured to the knife in his hand with his left palm. "Or can we talk?"

"You have nothin' to say that I want to hear."

His teeth glinted white under his black wavy hair. Alexandre eased the pressure off her throat, then slipped the knife into a sheath that she could not see. "Then Salomé, feel free to go your way."

She crinkled a brow. "You were not sent to kill me or," she swallowed, "worse?"

Alexandre's laugh was bitter. "Believe me Salomé, if I wanted you dead, the fish would already be feasting." He turned away and gazed at the dark water that swirled underneath the Saint-Michel bridge.

Salomé's instincts warned her to flee, to run from this man who spoke so easily of her death, but found that she could not. *I'll just listen. No harm comes from listenin'.*

"And what is it that you want?" She retrieved her knife but stayed about ten paces away from him.

"Revenge for your brother's death." He spoke over his shoulder, uttering the words as casually as though he spoke of buying bread.

Salomé looked down at the boot-tramped snow. She mourned her brother's death but life on the streets of Paris had replaced her heart of flesh with one of stone. "You never knew Germain. What's his death to you?"

Alexandre spun on his heel, his dark eyes now glinting with anger. "His death is the latest proof that society as we know it *cannot* continue! The carriage driver who stole his life is but one of an entire race of privileged people who can never know what it means to give a week's pay for one loaf of bread."

His voice softened and he stepped closer, gently laying a hand on her shoulder and looking deep into her eyes. "They don't know what it means to have to sell their bodies just to stay alive."

Salomé flinched. The night air suddenly seemed much colder than it had a few moments before. "Look, Alexandre, nothin' is going to change."

"You're wrong Salomé. I saw the crowd tonight. You were their voice, crying out against the injustices that have been heaped upon us. The people of Paris are ready to rise and shake off the chains of oppression. They just need someone to follow!"

Salomé expelled a deep sigh and shook her head. "Today I killed a man. I wanted to kill the girl too, not because I was truly angry about my brother's death but because..." Her voice trailed off and her eyes shifted to the river that slid by.

"Because I was jealous of them. I was jealous of *her*." She glanced back at him, feeling tears prick the back of her eyes.

"She's got everythin'." Salomé spat on her numbed hands and rubbed them together quickly. "I can't choose who I sleep with or how I earn my livin' but *she* does. I'll never have a home of my own, but *she* can ride in a carriage and live in a king's palace! Why? Because of who our parents were. Does that sound like God's justice?"

"Then help me bring God's justice on a sinful king who ignores the needs of his people," Alexandre said through gritted teeth. "In your line of work, you must have come across some influential men who are eager for change. Introduce me to them. With me at their side, their cause will not fail."

"What makes you so sure?" Her eyes flickered over him. "Who are you exactly?"

He spread his hands wide, the beginnings of a smile tugging at the corners of his mouth. "Nothing more than a humble instrument of God."

Salomé stamped her feet and quickly came to a decision, more from cold than because she believed that he could get anything done.

"There is someone." She jerked her head to her left. "Tonight, he'll probably still be at the Café Procope."

Alexandre nodded. "His name?"

"It's best if I take you." Salomé jerked her head to one side. "Follow me."

She started to walk away but swung back toward him, fingering the knife that she had tucked into her belt. "Just not too closely."

Alexandre's teeth flashed again as he dipped his head in a bow. "As you wish."

⚜

Maximilien Robespierre leaned against the back of his wooden seat. A faint smile pulled at his mouth as his brother, Augustin, scowled at him from across the table. Augustin's sallow, moon-shaped face was sharply divided by a prominent nose and thin lips. Now, those lips twitched in irritation. A chessboard lay between them and, despite the dim light and rising tobacco smoke that swirled within the café, it was obvious that Augustin's queen was in mortal danger.

"I see that your service to France's impoverished masses has only sharpened your hatred of the monarchy." Augustin tapped his index finger against his temple.

"You know my motto Augustin," Robespierre placed his pawn diagonally adjacent to his opponent's queen. The monarch in question was now hopelessly caught between his pawn and the reach of his knight. "*Liberté, égalité et fraternité*. Liberty, equality and brotherhood. One day I will write this message on the heart of every man in France."

Augustin shrugged as he dolefully eyed the board. "And if the monarchy does not agree with your message?" He edged his king one square closer to his queen, hoping that Robespierre would be distracted by the comment and would not notice the small change.

"If the queen does not listen to the message of the common man," Robespierre gestured to his pawn, "then she will be forced to hear the message preached by those who carry swords." Swiftly advancing his knight, Robespierre eliminated Augustin's queen from the game.

Augustin sighed then arched an eyebrow at his brother. "Are you certain that your fight against the monarchy is for France... and not for yourself? Is it justice or revenge that you seek?"

Robespierre became deathly still and, in a surge of panic, Augustin realized that he had overstepped his bounds. "I-I mean..." he fumbled for a way to redeem himself. "Well, it's just that you've never forgotten how she scorned you and—"

His brother's voice cut through his babble like the razor-edge of a blade. "All that I have done, all that I am doing, and all that I will do is for the people of France." He thrust his finger in Augustin's face. "Never forget that."

"Yes, of course. I apologize." Augustin cleared his throat. He knew his brother loved him, but Robespierre buried emotions like a child hiding a hoard of candy. One never knew that he was angry until he chose to lash out at the most unexpected of times.

Robespierre continued. "Has the girl that mocked me and slandered our dead mother's good name become a queen worthy of our devotion?" He locked eyes with his brother.

"No, she has not." Augustin tilted his head. "It is common knowledge that the queen spends lavish amounts of money amusing herself with extravagant parties and dresses while the masses starve in the streets. She has gone so far as to create a peasant village on the palace grounds, so she and her ladies-in-waiting could pretend to be milkmaids!" He ground his teeth together. For far too many in France, being a peasant was not a game—it was a grim reality.

"Has she, a foreigner, been in *any* way, an example of morality?" Robespierre's voice was rising but he didn't seem to notice. Augustin glanced around uncomfortably as heads began to turn in their direction.

"Calm down Maximilien." He leaned forward and spoke in a hushed undertone. "No need to yell."

"No need?" The fury in Robespierre's tone was so tangible that Augustin blanched. Robespierre stood to his feet, planted his fists on either side of the now-forgotten chess board and placed his face inches away from his brother's. "She holds orgies in the palace of Versailles; she degrades the honor of France; she *slanders* our mother's good name and you say there is no *need*? The shame of her harlotry should be spread across the land!"

The conversations around them had stilled and, in the sudden silence, it was as though Robespierre had shouted the words.

⚜

"Perhaps I can be of service." A male voice spoke up from behind the incensed lawyer.

Robespierre maintained a habit of sitting opposite a low-hanging oblong mirror in the Café Procope, so that he could see those who passed behind him without being observed. Now, he did not turn to acknowledge the speaker, but glanced up from his bent position at the reflection in the mirror.

His first impression was that he had been approached by some sort of human wolf. Black wavy hair spilled over a pale brow. Gray eyes that hinted at dangerous secrets straddled a narrow nose that protruded over a scruffy beard. His well-worn clothes were all black and his gaze was fixed on the mirror into which Robespierre himself looked.

"And you are?" Maximilien Robespierre straightened.

Instead of answering, the stranger strode to where Augustin sat. "May I?"

Augustin ceded his place, a curious light in his eyes.

The intruder glanced at the board and shook his head. "I always found God's ways to be beyond my understanding." He sat while keeping his eyes on the board. Then he glanced up at Robespierre. "Please, sit!"

The lawyer complied. "Who are you?"

"God." His opponent chuckled as he picked up his bishop and aligned it diagonally with Robespierre's king. "God gives a strong king a foolish, weak son who weds a woman that only increases everyone's misery. Check."

Robespierre shook his head, confused. "I'm sorry, did you say that you are... God?" He slid his king into the corner of the chessboard. *Safe!*

His rival chuckled, if the low growl could truly be called a chuckle. "The only way to save the country is to destroy the woman." His rook eliminated Robespierre's queen. "But to do that, you need to make someone she trusts betray her."

Robespierre glared at the board. In two moves, this irritating stranger who considered himself God had forced his king into a trap and slaughtered his queen! He frowned, tugged at his chin then smiled as inspiration struck.

"So, if betrayal is in your blood then you are *not* God but Judas." He moved his knight in for the kill. One more turn and it would be—

"I suppose it is all a matter of perspective," came the reply. "If you were the one being betrayed, then yes, I suppose I would be Judas." He slid his other bishop toward Robespierre's king.

"However, if I were to save your life, then I suppose that I would be God to you—or at least his representative." He leaned back in the tall chair and folded his hands across his lap. "That, my friend Robespierre, is checkmate."

The lawyer felt his heart plummet as he saw the clever trap into which he had fallen. His king had been forced into a corner while his opponent had subtly used the power of his bishops to prevent him from escaping.

"You see," the stranger lowered his voice. "No matter who it plays against, the Church always wins."

Robespierre could stand it no longer. He rose to his feet, hand outstretched. "Please sir, your name."

"His name is Alexandre." At the sound of the female voice, the murmur of conversation that had sprung up again experienced a second death. While women were not expressly forbidden from the café, tradition had made it a male-dominated center.

Robespierre pivoted on his heel and, for the second time in only a few seconds, his heart sunk.

"It's Salomé!" a voice rang out. Word had quickly spread about the violent encounter led by the fiery prostitute. First one, then two, then dozens of men who had come to the café to exchange ideas, play chess and discuss the current political climate stood to their feet, saluting her with thunderous applause.

Her blue eyes sparkled, and she lifted her arms to acknowledge their acclaim.

"Salomé, Salomé!" The shouts reverberated throughout the shop. Her long black hair swayed as she made her way toward the reticent lawyer.

"Ah, Salomé. How unpleasant it is to see you again." The taciturn lawyer wrinkled his nose as though the sight of her was somehow odious.

"Believe me, Maximilien, the sight of you doesn't make my heart sing for joy either," she said saucily. "But Alexandre," she pointed a shapely finger at the victor of the chess match, "feels that by combining efforts we can change France for the better."

She moved to stand behind Alexandre. "Alexandre, meet Maximilien Robespierre, known to most of Paris as *l'Incorruptible*. They may know him as incorruptible," she winked at Robespierre as her tongue slid over her lips, "but I know him to be a man like any other."

"That was one moment of weakness, Salomé, in a lifetime of fortitude." Robespierre did not blush, but his knuckles went white as he gripped the back of the chair. "There is no need to mention it again. Ever."

Augustin cleared his throat and caught his brother's eye. He jerked his head toward the crowd of curious spectators.

Robespierre straightened his gray jacket and faced the crowd. "Thank you for your support of citizen Salomé, a woman whose courage and resilience inspires us all. Now if you please gentlemen, as you were..."

He waited until the low murmur of conversation resumed then both he and Augustin took their places around the table.

"Now, Monsieur Alexandre—"

"Just Alexandre."

Robespierre hid his irritation at being interrupted. "Now, *Alexandre*, no more games. Tell me simply: what is it that you want?"

Alexandre leaned forward. "I want to help you overthrow the Bourbon dynasty."

"There are many who, like me, dream of a republic governed by virtue instead of a tyrannous despot that is ruled by his own greed." Maximilien pursed his lips. "What can you do to help our cause?"

"I will gain access to Queen Marie-Antoinette's private life. Her secrets will become your secrets. Once they are yours, they will belong to the public—to the people of France."

Robespierre's nostrils flared. "The queen, you say?"

"Yes."

"And how will you, a *bourgeois*, gain access to her secrets? Is she so bored with the king that her taste runs to commoners?" A thin smile creased Robespierre's face.

Alexandre did not join in his sordid humor. "Salomé almost killed a woman tonight who was traveling with her carriage driver to Versailles. 'The king is expecting us,' the driver said just before he died. The woman must be of some importance for the king to expect her arrival. Her clothing was worn, so she is obviously a *bourgeoise* yet she was travelling to Versailles. Why?"

"I don't know." Robespierre shrugged.

"But I want to know," Alexandre tapped the table with his finger. "She must be connected to the queen, as we all know that Louis does not entertain lovers. I will find this newcomer, earn her trust and, through her, gain the information we need."

"Oh, yes." Salomé placed her fingertips on Alexandre's muscled shoulders. "I like the way you think."

Robespierre's kept his face rigid. "How will you gain access to her?"

Alexandre leaned back in his chair, squaring an ankle over one knee. "The king's gardener, Claude Richard, has been forced to reduce his staff due to the national financial crisis. I'll ask him to hire me and offer to work for experience and not silver."

"And how will you earn your bread, the cost of which is not cheap I might add?" This question came from Augustin who had said nothing until this moment.

Alexandre's eyes settled on him. "That is my affair."

Thoughts raced through Robespierre's mind like ants around their hill. *Can I trust this man?* It was no secret that he wanted a constitutional monarchy or, better yet, no monarchy at all. His goal was to have a republic and, as such, he had earned many enemies. Could Alexandre be an assassin hired by the queen? He rejected the thought. If so, he would have killed him when his back was turned and tried to escape, not sat down for a game of chess.

All the same, his statement that the Church always won hinted at a larger purpose behind his offer to help. Robespierre despised the Church, but he could not deny that this man could be an asset.

He cleared his throat, his decision made. "I admit that I underestimated you." He pointed at Salomé. "Take the woman. It would be better if you and I are not seen together. If you need to contact me, send her. I am not a rich man by any means, but I will advance you a few *livres* to allow you to rent a home together until you find employment."

Salomé's hands flew to her hips. "Am I a horse that you can make go where you please? What if I am not willin' to go with him?"

Robespierre rose, threw a small sack of coins on the table and slung his overcoat around his shoulders. Augustin followed suit.

"You will go, Salomé." He threw a flat glare in her direction. "You will always follow the money because you are a whore. Thanks to your untitled birth, that is all you will ever be."

He nodded at Alexandre, tapped his brother's sleeve and stepped into the darkness that held Paris in its grip.

Chapter Three

January 1789. Château de Versailles

Viviane lurched upright as streams of warm daylight caressed her face. The lingering rays illuminated the vast boudoir in which she slept. She blinked several times as her mind struggled to absorb the lavish display of opulent wealth that surrounded her. *Where am I?*

Fragments of the preceding night's horrors flashed through her mind. The dead crippled boy. Olivier's murder. Salomé's jealous fury. The unfeeling edge of the knife against her skin. Viviane squeezed her eyelids shut and clutched the silken bedsheets against her chest. She wished that she could close the eye of her mind to the memories but, while she had escaped Salomé's clutches, there was no way to escape herself.

She remembered little of her journey to the *Château de Versailles*. Olivier's last words had drummed through her mind without reprieve the entire way. *We should not have stopped.* Images of his battered body and her own narrow escape had blotted everything else from sight. Her brow crinkled as her thoughts fell upon the man who had saved her. *What was his name?* The trauma of those climatic moments had driven it from her mind.

Viviane rose from the large canopied bed, placing her feet on a cushioned, two-step footstool. Her eyes darted around the room. Golden cherubs, melded into the base of candelabras the height of her shoulders, raised thick white candles toward an ivory rectangular ceiling that was framed by an intricately carved crown molding. She padded toward an ivory armoire that stood next to a matching dressing table, hesitated, then reached for the handle. She caught her breath as the parting doors revealed a series of elaborately decorated gowns. *Who could afford such luxury?*

"Viviane?"

She jumped as a low, refined voice called to her from outside the room. Viviane slammed the armoire doors together, then spun around. She started to move forward but came to an abrupt halt as she caught a glimpse of her reflection in a gilded mirror that graced the embossed, turquoise walls. Dark half-moons shadowed her eyes which were still red from tears. Her hair lay in tangled curls around her head.

She pivoted to the right as two sharp raps sounded on the immense ivory and gold double doors. They swung open to admit three female servants. The women barely glanced at Viviane, but scurried to either side of the door and curtsied deeply when a woman of regal bearing glided into the room.

"Viviane?" The woman threw a look of curiosity in her direction.

"Cousin Gabrielle?" Viviane caught her breath at the sight of her beautiful cousin. Clouds of dark hair had been meticulously sculpted into rolls embellished with strings of pearls and gray powder. Perched atop the massive conglomeration was a miniscule golden throne which was secured by a green *aigrette* or tufted feather.

She hesitated then stepped forward, unsure if her cousin was truly hiding beneath the mountain of silk and golden thread that formed her *robe de cour*. "Gabrielle de Polignac, is it really you?"

"Of course, Viviane, who else would it be?"

A sudden surge of joy made her rush forward but Gabrielle checked her advance by extending an impervious hand. Viviane froze, enthusiasm yielding to an awkward sense of embarrassment.

Gabrielle turned to the maids who had remained in position by the door. "Leave us."

The women curtsied again and exited the room in silence.

When the door had closed behind them, Gabrielle pulled her cousin into a restrained embrace.

"How do you fare dear Viviane?" A frown crossed her brow. "I heard all about your horrible experience. You are not hurt?"

A flicker of pain pierced Viviane's heart. "No, not physically. I was saved by a man..." She frowned trying to concentrate. "I can't recall his name. He—"

"I *cannot* remember his name," Gabrielle said.

Viviane's forehead puckered. "What?"

"Your words were, 'I *can't* remember his name.'" Gabrielle held a warning finger before her face. "You should have said 'I *cannot* remember his name.'"

Viviane stared at her, nonplussed. "But that's how I speak! I have always said, 'I can't.'"

The aristocrat sighed. "You are no longer a country bumpkin in Lussan, Viviane. You cannot allow yourself to speak like a commoner! These things matter at Versailles. One wrong word and your status could be ruined."

She took her cousin by the arm and guided her to a door-sized window that allowed access to a balcony whose iron rails were emblazoned with a golden sun. Gabrielle did not open the door but gestured outdoors. The snow could not hide the beauty of the massive courtyard that sprawled out in elegant spirals of white-covered bushes and arched stone.

Viviane's shook her head, awed at the sight. Her family had received an occasional letter from Gabrielle after she and her husband had gone to live at Versailles—the center of France's power and primary residence of King Louis and his wife, Queen Marie-Antoinette—but nothing in her fortuitous cousin's letters had prepared her for this!

An image of the squalor she had witnessed in the streets of Paris and the crippled boy, Germain, flashed before her. *Had he ever seen a space so large in his short life?*

Gabrielle's voice intruded on her thoughts. "It is much better in the spring, when thousands of tulips and jasmine spread all over, but still it is quite lovely."

She followed Viviane's gaze and pointed toward a massive building that dominated the southern horizon. "We call that building the Orangery. Each winter, over one thousand orange and citrus trees are placed inside and remain there until spring."

"I must see it!" Genuine enthusiasm warmed Viviane's voice.

"But of course." Gabrielle sniffed and patted her nose with a silken handkerchief. "I had forgotten that you have always been the little cousin who loves getting her hands dirty." She touched Viviane's arm. "Life here is beautiful, but it is also dangerous."

A soft smile played at the edges of her mouth, but Viviane noticed that it did not reach her eyes. "Especially now that the commoners of France entertain the ridiculous notion that they also have rights." Gabrielle eyed her cousin speculatively. "Perhaps you share that view?"

"Why should I?" Viviane shrugged.

The smile left Gabrielle's face. "Well, unlike my husband Jules and myself, your branch of the family is associated with the lowest class in France, so it occurred to me that you might share the rabble's opinions in certain matters."

Viviane cringed. Gabrielle had always been blunt, focusing on the pursuits of her own designs rather than the feelings of others.

"What of it?" Her chin raised a fraction of an inch. "I understand that, although you and Jules had a noble title, both of your families fell on hard times and couldn't—*could not*—maintain your extravagant lifestyles." She pointedly eyed the elaborate hairdo.

Gabrielle glared at her. "If you must know, my hairstyle is called '*le pouf*.' I have had my coiffeur add a small throne to show my unwavering support for the king and queen in these turbulent times."

She patted Viviane's arm. "That is the way we play the game, *chérie*. If you wish to win, then you must learn from the best. That would be me."

Gabrielle turned from the window, her long skirts swishing as she stepped lightly toward the door and motioned for Viviane to follow. Her cousin complied, lost in a whirlwind of humiliation and curiosity.

Gabrielle cracked open the door and peered into the adjoining room. "Good. The room is empty. Come."

They passed into a spacious outer chamber whose walls were not of wood but of white marble over which portraits framed in gold, depicting generations of the Bourbon royal family, hung suspended from gilded chains.

Viviane, lost in the enthralling beauty of her surroundings, became vaguely aware that Gabrielle was speaking. She had stopped and stood before the portrait of a woman with a heart-shaped face and powdered hair which was shaped, like Gabrielle's, into an elaborate *pouf*. Instead of carrying a throne, however, this woman's hair boasted a detailed wooden replica of a battleship.

"That is the queen, Marie-Antoinette." Gabrielle's voice was a reverent whisper. Viviane hurried over to her cousin, nearly tripping on the long fabric of her nightgown.

Gabrielle turned away from the portrait. "For me, she is not only a queen but a friend." She made a wide sweep of her hands. "All that you see is mine."

Viviane's eyes widened. "How is that possible?"

"The queen." Gabrielle flipped open a jeweled fan that dangled from her wrist and flitted it before her face. "Her kindness to those she considers her friends is nothing short of overwhelming. When Jules and I arrived at Versailles, she chose to pay off our debts and gave thirteen rooms of this castle to me. Only a few years ago, my husband was named a duke and I was proclaimed a duchess."

Viviane folded her arms across her chest. "Why exactly did you invite me to live here? I have nothing to offer."

Gabrielle's violet eyes darkened. "You understand how vital the queen's friendship is to Jules and myself?"

"Yes, but what does that have to do with me?"

Gabrielle snapped the fan shut with a flick of her wrist and leaned forward. "I need you to ensure that in these times of turbulent politics, everything continues as it has up to this moment." She took a deep breath. "That is why I have asked the queen to appoint you her *dame d'honneur*."

Viviane felt the blood drain from her face. "Me? A lady-in-waiting to the Queen of France? Gabrielle, that's... that's not possible!"

"That *is not* possible." Her cousin's voice hardened. "And you are wrong Viviane. It is not only possible, it has been done. Although you are *bourgeoise* you do have a trace of nobility in your murky bloodline."

She coughed delicately. "The queen, graciously acceding to my request, has overlooked the *bourgeois* strain in your blood and chosen to justify her decision by focusing on the more distant ties that bind your family to the crown."

Gabrielle took Viviane's moist palm in her own. "This is an office of high rank. You will be with her always. You will be the woman who accompanies her on her private outings. You will know her every secret."

Viviane grappled with this information. A niggling inner voice warned her that Gabrielle's actions had not been motivated by pure generosity. "How... how does this help you?"

A tight smile slipped across her cousin's lips. "Naturally, I would expect you to offer me a small gesture of appreciation. You will be close enough to the queen to know her very thoughts. You will be the eyes that see the letters I will be unable to access."

Viviane recoiled from her cousin. "I will not spy for you!"

"Spy?" Gabrielle crinkled her nose. "You misunderstand me, cousin." She linked arms with her relative, strolled over to an ivory chair whose cushion was splayed with intricate designs of flying cherubs, and sat down while motioning for Viviane to do likewise.

"Viviane, you must understand that France is reeling from a civil conflict. Angry mobs have been known to attack the king's men. You also almost fell victim to an assassin's knife."

Viviane's eyes dropped as she remembered the feeling of helpless panic caused by the edge of Salomé's blade.

Gabrielle squeezed her hand. "Every loyal subject must do everything possible to protect the throne. I am concerned that the queen does not fully comprehend the passions of the rabble. As a *bourgoise*, you are better able to... well... understand their kind."

"And you think I can better understand *my* kind, by spying on the queen?" Viviane was scandalized. "You do realize that I could be killed for doing that?"

"No, my dear." Gabrielle dismissed her cousin's concerns with a casual wave of her hand. "All I want is for you to be in a position where you can do what is best for the queen. Observe her letters and note who requests audiences with her. If you should discover anything that you feel is hazardous to her well-being—or that she plans to take away any of the benefits given to Jules and myself—you must inform me."

Viviane was younger than Gabrielle, but she was no fool. "By the queen's well-being, you mean your own."

Her cousin did not hesitate to respond. "The queen's welfare *is* my welfare."

Viviane idly traced the swirling pattern on the cushion with her finger. "If there is trouble, why should I not simply warn the queen herself?"

Gabrielle threw her an amused look. "Tell the Queen of France and Navarre that you, a servant from the backwoods of Lussan, feel that she has chosen to meet with the wrong person?" She threw back her head and laughed. "That is not how things are done, child. In time, you will understand."

Viviane bristled. "Children grow up quickly in my world."

Gabrielle's laughter died on her lips. "Oh, believe me my dear, I know. Sometimes they even think they can outwit their parents. Of course, that is never the case."

She changed the subject. "Speaking of parents, how is your mother, my dear Aunt Ariadné? I have not heard from her since your father's tragic death."

Viviane's shoulders slumped as memories flooded her mind.

It had been her fifth birthday and all of France was celebrating her birth. At least that was what her father, Gilbert de Lussan, had said. Later, she had learned that France rejoiced because the new queen, Marie-Antoinette had married the dauphin Louis XVI. The festivities would be closed by an enormous display of fireworks in the public square of Paris. All clergy, nobles and commoners were invited to attend and her father, ever eager to show his love for his only child, had insisted that they not miss the event.

"We must go, Ariadné," he had declared to her mother. "Our princess cannot miss such a historic event. Imagine... fireworks!" And so, they had joined the streams of travelers who flooded the roads like monks on a pilgrimage for the six-day journey to the heart of Paris.

The night of her birthday Viviane had gaped in awe as blazing balls of noise, smoke and fire exploded in the ebony skies. Bronze dolphins, attached to pyramids and colonnades, had spouted cascading rivers of multicolored flame as over three thousand rockets banished the darkness in a blazing display of glorious light.

Her father had swung her up onto his broad shoulders. They were hemmed in on all sides by a massive throng of spectators that were cordoned off by the carriages of the wealthy in the rear.

Suddenly, a gust of wind had blown a spark from one of the glowing cylinders and a set of rockets had burst into a gigantic ball of flame.

"Look father!" Viviane had chirped pointing ahead at the brilliant orb. "Isn't the sun so pretty?"

Like Viviane, many had thought the explosion was part of the artist's design, but those closest to the center had quickly recognized the detonation for what it was—an unplanned fire.

Viviane closed her eyes as Gabrielle's words ripped open the scab on a twenty-year-old wound. Panic had descended like a living thing among the crowd, stripping away reason and leaving only the raw will to survive. Those in front had scrambled away from the combustion while those in the rear were caught between the flailing hooves of the maddened horses, the impenetrable fence made by thousands of carriages, and the sea of humanity which swept away all those in its path, leaving behind a swath of broken bodies.

Seeing what was happening, her father had taken her down from his shoulders and passed her to her mother.

"Ariadné," he had gasped, the fingers of flame reflecting off his pale face. "If we separate we have a better chance of surviving. Take her and go home! I'll join you there." He had kissed her mother as Viviane had reached out with her girlish arms. Just before their hands could connect, the surge of the crowd had ripped them apart.

"Papa!" She could still remember the terror in her wails. "Papa, where are you?"

"Come child!" Her mother had grabbed her outstretched arm and pushed against the throng in the opposite direction. They had been swept along a narrow street that lay to the side of the square. Everywhere the masses trampled each other underfoot, each one seeking a way to escape the maw of death.

Her mother, Ariadné, had stumbled into an open door and had pulled Viviane in with her. They had waited through the night, trembling as hundreds rushed by. Screams had filled the air, piercing their hearts with numbing pain. When the somber light of a gray dawn had at last broken the horizon, they had made their way through the bloodied streets, hoping against hope that they would not see the face of her father among the fallen.

But hope had proven to be a fickle god. In fleeing the fire behind them, the mob had forced others forward, causing hundreds to drown in the Seine River's dark depths. At the edge of the water, floating among the reeds, they had found the broken corpse of her father.

Viviane's eyes flickered open. "*Maman* is alive. She found work as a laundress for the village. We had no other way of earning bread after father... was taken." She fell silent for a moment. "No matter how difficult it is to pay the butcher or the baker *Maman* is always cheerful, confident that God will save her somehow."

"You see Viviane." Gabrielle leaned forward. "If you are not willing to do as I ask for my sake, do it for the sake of your mother. No doubt she is hoping that you will improve your station in life. How will that happen if revolutionary madmen destroy the very woman to whom we both owe all our material benefits?"

Viviane wavered as her mother's words echoed in her mind. *Make a better life for yourself child. No matter what it takes.*

She resisted the temptation. "No, I am sorry but I cannot. Mother would never approve of this. God would not approve."

Gabrielle moved closer. "God would expect you to honor your mother's wishes. What says the Scripture?" She frowned, struggling to remember the forgotten text. "Honor your father and mother so you can have a happy life."

"So that your days may be lengthened." Viviane shook her head in despair. She was not overly religious but Ariadné had ensured that her daughter at least knew the Ten Commandments.

"Right. That." Gabrielle flicked away an invisible piece of lint from her dress. "Think of this as your service to your family—a sacrifice to God himself."

Viviane mulled the proposal. "It's too dangerous Gabrielle," she said at length. "You are asking me to spy on the Queen of France!"

Gabrielle shook the closed fan at her. "No Viviane, never that. I am asking you to protect the queen. Protect her from the mobs and from herself." Her eyes narrowed. "You and I are family. We do not abandon each other to the wolves! Should anything go wrong, I will personally take full responsibility. On that you have my word."

Viviane considered this. She had been close to Gabrielle as a child, but the woman who stood before her was different... very different. Gabrielle had offered little reason for trust but perhaps all she needed was the opportunity to pick up where they had left off as children. Besides, her cousin was right. Her future was as tied to the queen as was Gabrielle's. *Could it really be that wrong to protect my future?*

"Alright." Viviane released a breath that she didn't know she had been holding. "I will keep my eyes open and nothing more. If the queen were even to think that I am abusing her confidence, you will explain everything, telling her that I did this on your behalf to protect *her* interests."

Gabrielle's eyes widened. Her smile became so broad that Viviane almost believed it was genuine.

"Are we agreed?" Her voice was tight.

Gabrielle rose with a rustle of silk and lace. "I will have my servants prepare you for your audience with her imperial majesty Queen Marie-Antoinette this afternoon. It appears that I have chosen wisely." She turned and glided to the door.

Irritation tinged Viviane's voice as she stood to her feet. "Are we agreed?"

Gabrielle placed her hand upon the golden handle and looked back, a bemused expression on her face. "But of course, my dear." She shrugged. "Whenever have we disagreed?"

⚜

"Ridiculous! Just ridiculous! The little urchin should be grateful for what I've done for her. Instead she *haggles* with me over a simple favor."

Jules de Polignac arched a thick brown eyebrow as his wife, Gabrielle, slammed the heel of her hand on the small wooden writing desk that occupied a corner of her spacious apartment. He had hoped to find her in a more amorous mood. After all, they had reason to celebrate did they not? The sea of debt that had threatened to drown his family had been parted by the queen's generosity; the ghastly cost of living at court had also been subsidized by the liberal monarch and recently—Jules smiled at the thought—he had been granted the title of Duke, again due to Marie's friendship with his wife.

Jules cleared his throat. Gabrielle always locked her emotions in an iron cage of self-control, only letting anger show when she felt it would help her win whatever game she was playing. Today, however, it appeared that she was on the brink of an emotional collapse.

The thought gave him pause. Was it truly anger that provoked this outburst or was it fear? He stroked the bushy sideburns that engulfed his cheeks.

"Did your cousin Viviane refuse to help us then?"

Gabrielle spun toward him.

"No, but the ingrate hesitated, Jules, she hesitated!"

He sighed as a sense of relief swelled in his chest. "Oh, there is nothing to worry about then." He took her in his arms, confident that the problem was solved. Now his beautiful Gabrielle would relax, smile and make love to him after he told her about the thousand *livres* he had won in a card game with the king's brother, the Count of Artois.

He was to be disappointed.

"You don't understand." Gabrielle wriggled out of his embrace, forgetting her stigma against improper speech in heat of her emotion. "All of this," she gestured to the elaborate furniture that surrounded them, "all of it has been given by the queen. With a *snap* of her royal fingers everything that we have received can be taken away."

Jules shrugged. "Marie-Antoinette loves you Gabrielle. Since our arrival at Versailles *you* have been her closest friend. The king himself feels that you have a calming influence on his wife. Has she said anything that worries you?"

"It is not what she says Jules, it is what *they*, the peasant rabble, say that worries me." Gabrielle tossed her decorated head toward the window. The sudden motion sent the precariously perched throne crashing to the floor. It shattered into a hundred jagged pieces. The couple watched in silence, gripped by a dark sense of foreboding.

It was Gabrielle who spoke first. "I-it means nothing, I'm sure. The pomade must be melting. I will have the coiffeur come up with a more durable design next week." She gripped his green and navy silken waistcoat.

"Jules, I fear that, under pressure from the mob, Marie will take away all that she has given us." The panic in her eyes alarmed him. "I can't go back to a life of financial uncertainty Jules, not after knowing the pleasures that wealth can bring. I can't, do you hear me?"

He patted her arm, more frightened by her attitude than by anything that Marie-Antoinette would do. "Don't be afraid, my love." He placed a quick peck on her powdered cheek. "Viviane has agreed to monitor the queen's actions and, if anything is amiss, she will warn you."

"She had better." Gabrielle gritted her teeth. "Or I will make my cousin regret her betrayal until the day she dies."

Jules's only answer was a thoughtful glance at the throne that lay broken at their feet.

Chapter Four

January 1789. Château de Versailles

Alexandre trudged down one of the monumental twin staircases, known as the Hundred Steps, which led to the entrance of the king's massive indoor garden called the Orangery.

Obtaining employment from the king's gardener, Claude Richard, had been easier than expected. Claude was more than happy to find someone willing to work without pay. No doubt the man thought his sanity was suspect, but Alexandre had been told to report to Bernard de Jussieu, overseer of the palace gardens, in the morning.

He shoved his hands in his pockets. The frigid temperatures mirrored his cold joy at having successfully been accepted as part of King Louis's body of servants. "It is always easier to destroy from within than without."

His fingers found little warmth in the threadbare black *manteau* which served as both overcoat and blanket in the night. Alexandre did not mind the cold, but he did object to the wolfish hunger that gnawed at his belly. *Whatever doesn't kill me will only make me stronger.*

The purse of coins given to him by Robespierre had secured lodging in the clapboard hovel that he and Salomé would call home for a few months, but the remainder could not cover the cost of one loaf of bread.

Bread—the staff of life—had become the most expensive commodity in Paris. Many in the city would die tonight for lack of it. He gripped the black rosary that hung underneath his rough cloth shirt, drawing a measure of comfort from the worn, smooth beads.

Salomé had told him she would have the money they needed by the time he returned to their cottage tonight. He did not doubt she would succeed. Poor harvests and the soaring cost of grain may have made Paris's poor more miserable, but the wealthier men of the city had not been deprived of their lust. When he had rounded the corner, the raven-haired siren had already lured one victim into her embrace.

Salomé. Alexandre forked his fingers through his slick black hair. She was so like his lost love Juliette that at times he could barely stand the pain of looking at her. Her involvement in this affair had been as unexpected as the newly formed alliance with Robespierre.

His brow furrowed. To Alexandre, Robespierre was another weapon in a growing arsenal. The desire to overthrow the monarchy linked them together but Alexandre knew that the enigmatic lawyer's vision of France left little room for the Church. As such, he was an enemy—a useful one to be sure—but an enemy all the same.

The Orangery soared upward before him, as though declaring to all passerby that it embraced the will of heaven. It was an immense sand-colored cube, embossed with detailed stone columns and soaring arches. As his eyes swept over the lavish expression of wealth, Alexandre could not escape the unexpected sense of destiny that swelled within him. It was as though his life had been formed for this moment. With each step that he took across the snowy courtyard, a memory of the past twenty years sprang to fresh life in his mind.

Crunch. He had been abandoned at the age of twelve—left by the men Pope Clement had commissioned to bring him to Paris. He recognized now that his period of solitary existence had been an extreme test proposed by a mind used to bending others to its will. If he did not have the stamina to survive adolescence alone in a violent city, he would not have the ability to destroy the House of Bourbon. Cold, and with no more than six silver *livres* to his name, Alexandre had made his home in the labyrinth of rat-infested sewers that intersected beneath the city.

Crunch, crunch. His mind flew to Philippe de Valence. Bile rose in Alexandre's throat at the thought of the young prince who had once been his closest friend. Philippe had convinced his father that it was their Christian duty to feed the poor. Under normal circumstances, Philippe's father would have dismissed his son's idea out of hand, but something had happened to Philippe in England that had left the aged duke terribly shaken.

He had stopped their carriage and chosen Alexandre from the surging masses because the boy appeared to be about his son's age. He had given his servants instructions to "feed the poor devil for a week" at their nearby Château de Saint-Cloud. Later that afternoon, the Duke's scornful head steward had ushered Alexandre to the castle and an ecstatic Philippe had remained with him. One week became two, then three. In the end, Alexandre and the young prince developed an unexpected bond of friendship.

Alexandre had soon realized that Philippe's friendship was largely due to a desire to resolve the growing problem of starvation in Paris. Philippe's father, the Duke of Valence, only tolerated the urchin because he had no desire to deprive his unsociable son of the one person he considered a friend.

Alexandre scooped up a handful of the snow. "Friend." He crushed the snow between his fingers. "As true a friend as Judas!"

At first Alexandre had been eager to turn the Duke's unexpected kindness to his own advantage, knowing that the House of Valence was part of the king's own family. But, as the years flowed by and Philippe's kindness continued unabated, Alexandre had begun to wonder if all members of the French aristocracy were as corrupt as he had been led to believe.

Juliette... Alexandre stumbled on a loose stone as the memory of her face blotted everything else from sight.

On his eighteenth birthday, he had met Juliette. She was the daughter of the prune-faced head steward, but it was obvious that she had inherited her mother's looks. Her glossy black hair glistened as it tumbled about her shoulders. Her eyes, the color of a stormy sky, had made a prisoner of his heart. But Juliette's beauty was surpassed by her ardent passion for revolution. It was her relentless love of liberty that had pushed Alexandre to ask her to abandon the prison of Saint-Cloud and run away with him.

His feet slowed to a standstill. He closed his eyes, lost in the pain of his past. Juliette had agreed, her love for Alexandre and his idealistic principles overriding her desire for her father's approval. Alexandre had entrusted his secret to Philippe, certain that his friend would never betray him. That had been his fatal mistake.

Alexandre's face turned to stone. It had taken twelve agonizing years to develop a plan capable of destroying not only Louis, but also his renowned cousin, Philippe de Valence. Now, he was ready. A thrill of anticipation swept through him.

He began walking again as he neared the small door by which gardeners entered the Orangery in the winter months.

Crunch. Crunch. Crunch. P'tit Jean. It was the name of the first man—a musclebound, overgrown boy, really—that he had killed. P'tit Jean had led a ragtag gang of teenage thieves and castaways which roamed the sewers, going above ground only to steal what they needed to survive.

He had encountered the group on his third night in the gutters. Smaller in size and close to starving, Alexandre had appeared easy prey to the bully. He had not expected Alexandre to fight like a soldier. In the end, P'tit Jean lay face-down in a puddle of filth while Alexandre, surrounded by the dead man's awed followers, claimed both the former captain's knife and position as head of the *Moustiques*.

The word meant "Mosquitoes" and that is exactly what Alexandre created over the next twelve years. The Moustiques were an invisible network of seventy-two men and women who no longer hid in the shadows of the sewers, but mingled undetected among the varied echelons of Parisian society.

The excesses of the nobility made them the natural target for the organization's rage. Scattered throughout the kingdom of France, they started the rumors that fed public discontent with the Bourbons. Some of the newer recruits, who had never known life in the gutters, held positions of high social standing. Others, who had been with him from the beginning, had worked their way into the various political parties that fought for reform. Some organized violent protests and disseminated pamphlets that viciously attacked both king and queen. It did not matter that more than half of what was printed was not true. For Alexandre, the ends always justified the means.

Crunch. Crunch. His mind shifted to the note he had received from Rome yesterday afternoon just after Salomé had launched her own little rebellion. A smile tugged at his lips. The fact that Rome knew where to find him confirmed his long-held suspicions that at least one of his men had been planted by the Holy See to ensure that their agent did not falter in his commitment. Alexandre could easily imagine the penalty for failure.

The note had born no name. Someone had slid it under the door of the small flat that he had occupied.

To everything there is a season.

He had recognized the handwriting as the author had undoubtedly known he would. Cardinal Rezzonico's message was the final proof that his conclusion in the square had been correct. The time for revolution had come.

Chapter Five

May 1789. Château de Versailles

Marie-Antoinette, Queen of France and Navarre, stared at her reflection as she contemplated the contrast of the black, diamond-strewn silk of her dress against her fashionably pale skin. Her brow furrowed. Then, a sudden burst of giggles erupted from her painted lips. "It is so exquisite that I will have Louis order me another twenty—each in a different color!"

The queen was surrounded by a small entourage of her ladies-in-waiting and Geneviève Poitrine, who was nurse to her son Louis-Joseph.

"What do you think of it Gabrielle?" Marie turned to Gabrielle de Polignac who stood to her left.

"*C'est magnifique.*" The woman stepped back as Marie spun in a slow circle. "It is the perfect gown for this evening's spring ball."

"The king was quite furious with me, you know." Marie smiled, and placed her hands on her hips. "Monsieur Necker, our detestable Minister of Finance, told him that it was already my ninety-fifth dress for the year." She groaned. "I, the Queen of France, am persecuted by that wretched man because I have an acute sense of fashion—a gift he evidently lacks."

She glanced sidelong at Viviane. "And what does my chief lady-in-waiting say of my latest acquisition?"

Gabrielle reclaimed the monarch's attention with a flick of her embroidered fan. "What did you tell the king, Your Grace?"

"The king?" Distracted, Marie-Antoinette turned back to her friend. A sly grin slid over her face. "I flitted my lashes and told him that if it upset Monsieur Necker so much to see me well-dressed, then I would be sure to order another hundred before midsummer's eve!"

She swung toward her son's nurse. "Have you ever seen Monsieur Necker when he is enraged, Geneviève?"

"Fortunately, Your Grace, I have never been close to the Minister of Finance," Geneviève said.

"Well," Marie puffed out her cheeks for a moment. "His rotund face becomes a particular shade of red that makes me think of a plump tomato." She held her breath until her face turned red, then let it out in a *whoosh*. "I would love to see the tomato explode someday!" Apart from Viviane, Marie's laughter was echoed by the women around her.

"So, you have not said, Viviane." Marie returned to her original thought, glancing at the hitherto silent young woman. In the months following her formal introduction to court, Viviane had quickly risen to the challenges that her role as *dame d'honneur* presented and had installed herself as an essential part of the queen's inner circle. She handled Marie's schedule with a dexterity that allowed the queen more time to pursue her private passions.

"What is your opinion of my latest *robe de cour?*" The queen turned back to the mirror. "Will my beauty be evident despite the mask I will wear tonight?" She laid her hand against her chest and sighed. "You know that the Marquis de Lafayette will be present, and it is essential that he notice no other woman but me."

Viviane hesitated.

"Well?" Marie-Antoinette prodded.

Viviane paused again before answering. "I think that the Queen of France will look beautiful in anything she chooses to wear."

"Ah!" Marie glowed and smiled at her reflection. "I must agree with you."

"However," Vivian continued, "when word of the evening reaches the common people, might not your enemies take the purchase of this gown as an opportunity to criticize you?"

Her gaze dropped to the ivory tiles beneath their feet. "I am only a simple *bourgeoise*, but I know that many in the city struggle to find bread each day." She pointed to the gown. "Is such an elaborate display of wealth truly in the queen's best interest?"

There were six frozen statues in the room. The silence that filled the room was so complete that the queen heard the blood surging in her temples. Marie was the first to recover. She spun on her heel toward Viviane.

"Bread?" Marie's brow crinkled. The thought of not having enough bread to eat was simply laudable. "No bread?"

She laid a slender finger over her mouth. "Poverty bores me, Viviane. If the dirty little peasants have no bread, then," she shrugged, "well, let them eat cake!"

A smattering of polite laughter again swept through the gaggle of women but it was swallowed up in a surge of silent anticipation.

Marie regained her composure and turned back to the mirror, mind churning. Her audience was waiting. Like piranhas, they waited in vicious silence for her to lash out at Viviane. Then they would follow her lead, tearing into the *dame d'honneur* with their words if not their teeth.

Her face tightened. "Leave us!"

The command from the queen was unexpected but everyone hurried to obey—everyone but Viviane.

⚜

Viviane knew that as *dame d'honneur,* she was to remain with her sovereign unless ordered to depart by the king or another member of the House of Bourbon. The first three months of her stay at Versailles had been spent learning court protocol and the intricacies of her new role.

She knew that each word at court was analyzed a thousand times by those who heard it. Within the hour, her supposed criticism of the queen would reach the king's ears. By sunset, all three thousand people living in Versailles would know that she, a *bourgeoise* herself, had reprimanded the queen. Speculative eyebrows would rise among the nobles, and Versailles's populace would wonder where her true loyalties lay.

And the queen? Viviane knew that she had mortally insulted a woman whom she did appreciate. But instead of appearing infuriated at her tactless remark, Marie appeared... pleased.

"Thank you." Smiles wreathed Marie's face. She sat on a plush divan, whose fabric was embroidered with roses, and patted the space next to her.

"For what?" Viviane's heart tumbled wildly in her chest as she sat down.

"For vindicating my choice." Marie nodded. "I was right to choose you."

There was an unusual atmosphere around the queen. Marie emitted a new air, a feeling that—

"I did not ask you to be my closest companion because Gabrielle recommended you, but because you possess what I need to win my struggle."

Clarity struck Viviane's mind. The queen had discarded her aura of frivolity. Viviane shook her head. "What fight, Your Grace?"

Marie-Antoinette lifted her chin. "The battle that I am fighting for my throne, for my family," she took a deep breath, "and for my life."

Viviane gasped. "What do you mean?"

Marie looked away, making the diamond-encrusted pearls of her earrings sway. "Since you joined my service I have believed that you are a woman that I can trust. Over the past five months, I have observed your character and see that you are honest—a quality worth more than gold to me." She twisted one of the many rings that glittered on her fingers. "I should wait for more proof I suppose, but the forces that conspire against me grow stronger by the hour. I find myself compelled to trust you."

Marie closed her eyes for a moment. "France is ruptured by many factors, one of which is myself. Yes, the people hate me because I am Austrian. Many still remember the last war between France and my country and find it hard to trust a foreigner."

Her brown eyes flickered open. "It is true that they loathe me because they feel I spend their taxes with wild abandon. But the true source of their hatred stems from one man: Maximilien Robespierre."

"The lawyer?" Viviane did not understand. "That is no secret. Everyone knows that he preaches reform."

"Lawyer." Marie's face twisted as though she had just swallowed a mouthful of rancid meat. "He is behind the lies that tarnish my name."

Viviane arched an eyebrow. "Is it all lies?"

Marie flushed but evaded a direct answer. "I believe that this Robespierre is the same man who tried to kill me on my way to Paris twenty years ago."

Viviane nodded as understanding began to dawn. The story of the queen's assault while *en route* to her wedding was well-known. There were many who wished that the boy-assassin had succeeded in killing the girl-bride. "France would've been richer!" was the consensus.

Marie glanced at her manicured nails. "In three days, the king will convene a meeting of representatives from all three estates. Louis mentioned that Robespierre's name is on the list. When I see him, I will know if it is he."

She grabbed Viviane's hand. "This lawyer's influence has already caused riots throughout the country. 'Madame Deficit' the people call me. Can you imagine?"

Her nostrils flared. "He is the architect of my pain—this Robespierre. It is he who is my enemy!" She pressed her long fingernails into the edge of the divan. "I rejected him years ago, and now his wounded pride is driving the kingdom to the brink of anarchy."

"Isn't there something the king can do?"

"The king!" Marie scoffed as she shook her head. "All Louis sees in me is a wayward woman who is obsessed with foolish whims. I was fourteen when we married, just a girl really, and the court of France felt like a prison. I found ways to entertain myself while my husband practiced politics. By the time I began to understand just how heavy a weight the crown can be, I had already earned the reputation of an adulteress who rules her husband."

"Then show him the truth." Viviane's voice was insistent. "Why continue the pretense? If the king knows that you truly care about his kingdom, and if you share your suspicions about Robespierre, surely he will take the appropriate measures."

Marie's smile was sad. "I have worn the mask for so long that I am afraid it has fused with the woman underneath. Besides, you do not understand the vagaries of nobility. Should I change my lifestyle now, the peasants will claim my reforms as a victory and, by consequence, the royal family would lose the support of those loyal to us. Those near the throne would consider any such change as a weakness. They would seize this as an opportunity to gain power or even overthrow the Bourbon line."

She shook her head. "Maybe when this is over I will be escape the prison that I have built. Maybe someday Louis will see the real woman beneath the mask." She held Viviane's gaze. "But not today. In public, I will be the untroubled queen. In private, I will wage my war. That is why I have chosen you."

"I-I do not understand."

"You are a *bourgeoise*. You understand the thoughts of the commoners... as you demonstrated moments ago."

Viviane flushed. "I meant no disrespect my Queen."

Marie ignored her comment. "I have placed my deepest secret in your hands. Now, will you help me?" Her intense gaze probed Viviane's eyes. "I could command your obedience, but what I propose is so precarious that I must know that you are doing this of your own will."

Marie's words brought Gabrielle's request to the forefront of Viviane's thoughts. In truth, she had seen nothing worth sharing with her cousin but it was also true that, over the course of five months, her aversion to her cousin's request had grown more intense. The crack in their relationship had widened into a canyon due to her rising influence with the queen. Gabrielle hated competition and that was exactly what Viviane had become.

No man can serve two masters. Her mother had often quoted that passage. Now Viviane realized that the time of decision had come. When forced to choose between a queen and a duchess, there was no reason to hesitate.

Viviane inclined her head. "How can I be of service, Your Grace?"

Chapter Six

May 1789. Outskirts of the Versailles Estate.

Simon scowled in mock anger as Alexandre, his commanding officer and leader of the clandestine order called the Moustiques, sauntered out of his cabin's sagging door. Alexandre's message inviting him to the cottage he shared with Salomé had come as a surprise, given the leader's penchant for secrecy. His invitation could only mean that trouble was coming. Simon sniffed the air in appreciation. He liked trouble. Trouble was good.

"Have you come to send me back to hell, brother?"

"To hell?" A grin split Alexandre's narrow face. "I pity the devil who lets you in!"

Simon roared with laughter and clasped Alexandre in his arms. He had been accepted into the Moustiques shortly after Alexandre became its leader. They shared a bond, not only because Simon was also Italian, but because he was as devoted to the Church as Alexandre himself. Alexandre had shared his vision of a France controlled by Rome and Simon had sworn to bring this worthy goal to fruition.

For over a decade he had helped Alexandre extend the unseen influence of the order until their reach included minor governing officials, wealthy but untitled *bourgeois*, and the teeming masses of France's poor.

"I'm surprised to see that you're not soft and fat from all the food in the king's palace." Simon jabbed Alexandre's stomach. "I hear that Louis eats so much he can hardly roll out of bed!"

"Nothing distracts me from my mission Simon." Alexandre's gaze sobered.

His friend nodded. "That is what I kept tellin' myself but I still can't understand why you risk exposure by bringin' me here, to the place you share with your woman." Simon jerked a thumb toward the shack.

"She is a tool, nothing more." Alexandre narrowed his eyes and crossed his arms. "You know that my heart will forever be closed to any woman but Juliette."

Simon pursed his lips. "Why did you send for me?"

"There's a woman that I need to meet. Philippe de Valence brought her to Versailles about five months ago. She is the reason I chose to infiltrate the palace."

"I am confused." Simon frowned and cracked all ten fingers at once. "You ignore a beautiful woman livin' in your home but go chasin' after the guest of a man you despise?" He lapsed into Italian. "*Sei pazzo, amico mio*! You're crazy, my friend!"

Alexandre sighed. "I will explain in due time, Simon. I don't need your advice or your criticism. I simply need a horse, hat, sword, and mask fancy enough to get me into the palace."

Simon shrugged. "That's it? Our men will have it here in three hours."

"One." Alexandre held up a finger.

"One hour." Simon saluted. He turned to go but paused midstride. "Get whatever revenge you want, Alexandre. Just be sure it doesn't cost us France."

⚜

Robespierre looked again at the papers that he clutched between sweaty fingers, but the words made as little sense to him now as they had three hours ago. Frustrated, he threw the sheaf onto his bed. It was a detailed list of the grievances and demands that the people of France wanted him to voice to the king. He would need to be familiar with them to better represent his constituents at the upcoming meeting of the Estates General in three days. While he knew that he should read the cumbersome document, other thoughts crowded his mind. *She* crowded his mind.

He flopped onto the edge of his narrow bed and glanced around at the sparse furniture. His eyes fell on a small dagger with which he opened letters. He clutched it between his fingers, relishing the sense of power it provided.

"Twenty years and I can still hear the music in your voice." He let his obtuse head drop between his hands. "Twenty years and your scent still lingers in my nostrils." His face tightened as darker memories surfaced. "Twenty years and I still feel your scorn. It's there... in my head and I cannot get it out." He gripped a clump of his hair near his forehead and pressed the sharp edge of the knife at its base.

"'Respect me,' you said." His grip tightened. "'Fear me,' you said." He pulled still harder, clenching his teeth against the pain. "But never insult me by making me the object of your affection!"

His last words were a mangled cry of rage and agony as the mass of hair yielded to his fury and the cutting edge of the knife. Robespierre felt the burning sting of his self-inflicted head wound and stared at the gruesome clump of hair and skin that dangled from his right hand.

"Maximilien?" It was his brother Augustin who called from the other side of the door. "Maximilien, what is it?" He burst into the room to find his brother seated on the bed, a stream of blood flowing from a gash in his scalp.

"Dear God, help us!" Augustin grabbed a handkerchief and sprang toward his brother. "What's wrong?"

Robespierre stood up slowly, pushing his brother away. "Wrong Augustin? Nothing is wrong." He smiled and held up the bloody scalp. "Blood. That is the way to deal with the pain. Do you understand?"

Augustin glanced away from the macabre sight.

"Yes." Robespierre purred as he lifted the mass to the level of his eyes. "It does take getting used to but oh, how liberating it feels." He stepped closer to Augustin who backed away, his eyes darting from the dagger in Maximilien's clenched fist to his face.

"Brother? Maximilien? What are you doing?"

Robespierre stopped and dangled the scalp next to his sibling's face. "I am relieving the pain, Augustin. In three days I will meet with the king. I know that he will refuse our demands. Then the people of Paris will rise as one man. Blood will flow. *Her* blood will flow. Then the pain will end."

Augustin's eyes widened. He stood as one frozen, except for the trembling of his lips. "A-are you sure b-brother?"

"Are you with me?" Maximilien fixed his piercing amber eyes on his brother. "To the death?"

Augustin glanced away and swallowed. "Yes brother." Beads of sweat broken out on his forehead. "To the death."

Chapter Seven

May 1789. Château de Versailles

Versailles is on fire! That was Viviane's thought the moment she stepped off the rose-strewn marble staircase and entered the Hall of Mirrors, just behind the queen. Light beamed from every corner, setting the massive hall ablaze. Immense golden chandeliers, encrusted with costly glass, cast a fiery glow on both the arched frames of the glass windows that formed one side of the ballroom and the hundreds of mirrors that surfaced the walls on the opposing side. The chandeliers, floating inches above the heads of the thousands of revelers who had gathered to celebrate the onset of spring, blazed in spectacular competition with opulent massive candelabras that were spaced about every ten feet the entire length of the hall.

Viviane's breath caught in her throat at her first glimpse of a royal masquerade. A sea of masks, whose colors could rival a rainbow's kaleidoscopic spectrum, surged and ebbed around the massive floor. The dancers moved in intricate harmony with the lively *minuet*, played by a virtual army of court musicians whose music seemed to fuse with the very air she breathed. The bodies of the dancers twirled in a series of memorized patterns, dazzling her with their skill.

She ran moist hands over a vivacious scarlet gown that clung to her trim figure, then realized that the sweat might damage the luxurious fabric. The garment was a gift from the queen's own closet that the royal seamstresses had managed to adjust in time for the evening's entertainment.

The gown itself was a treasure. Diamonds, sewn into its sleeves and across the bodice, caught the light of the thousands of candles, making it appear that she was surrounded by a cloud of shimmering light. Marie had presented the dress to her this afternoon as a token of her appreciation for Viviane's "unsurpassed devotion." While the sight of the dress had robbed Viviane of speech, a quiet voice in her mind persisted in decrying it as a bribe and not a gift at all.

A hush rolled over the crowd. The musicians stopped their performance as they noticed the queen's presence.

"Marie-Antoinette, Queen of France and of Navarre!"

A smattering of insincere applause followed the proclamation. Marie covered the awkward moment by gesturing for the entertainment to continue. After a collective bow in her direction, the musicians and dancers resumed their intricate marriage of motion and music. Viviane eyes widened as she took in the performance. She knew that each handhold had been memorized by both men and women. To misstep would be a stain on the offender's public image.

One tall dancer, wearing a long azure waistcoat with golden trim, broke away from the crowd and made his way toward the queen. His eyes roamed over her and Marie threw a coquettish smile in his direction. Viviane knew that this man was the celebrated war hero, the Marquis de Lafayette.

"The sight of your loveliness, my Queen, reminds me why I left America and returned to France." His voice, no doubt accustomed to shouting commands on the battlefields, was now gentle and seductive. "Nothing there could compare to the glory my eyes now behold."

"Be careful, *mon général*." Marie tittered and flitted her fan before her powdered face. "Much more and you will provoke our king to jealousy."

She inclined her head toward her husband, an overweight monarch whose hooded eyes and short neck reminded Viviane of a stuffed owl. Louis's throne had been transferred from the Apollo Salon and placed on a raised dais for the evening's festivity. It was to be a joyful occasion, but the king's dour expression was more appropriate for a funeral than for a ball.

"Some things," Marie lowered her voice to a suggestive whisper, "must only be said… in private."

Viviane stared at the queen, her jaw slack. If Marie's flirtation was all an act, then she played the part to perfection. The Marquis bowed again, the tips of his ears turning pink. "I am only too willing to render whatever service you require, my Queen."

The innuendo was blatant but Viviane found the voluptuous atmosphere rather liberating. The strict moral code of her mother's rustic world seemed repressive when compared to the glamorous environment that surrounded her. Her spine tingled. She had entered a new phase of life, one free of her mother's watchful eye. Versailles was the cultural center of Europe and here, pleasure was the only rule.

"You have never seen anything like it, I am sure."

The voice that broke into Viviane's thoughts made her start, but she recovered by fluttering her brocaded fan in front of her face. She slid masked eyes to her left. A tall, muscular man wearing a brilliantly white costume, tastefully accented with sequins of gold, stood next to her. A short sword dangled at his waist and his white half-mask could not conceal the warm amusement that sparkled from his dark brown eyes.

"Your pardon, Monsieur, but have we met?" She bit her lower lip. Had he noticed the quaver in her voice?

Marie-Antoinette turned at the sound of the stranger's voice. A thin band of black gauze constituted her mask, but it did nothing to hide the naked hostility in her eyes. Her rigid posture revealed that this man, whoever he was, held no favor from the queen.

"Ah, Philippe, so it is true after all." Marie's habitually cordial tone now had the warmth of a snow-covered rock.

"What is true, Your Grace?" Philippe bowed.

"*L'habit ne fait pas le moine.*" The queen raised her chin while quoting the proverb. "The clothing does not make the monk. You dress like one of us now, yet I hear that you gallivant in the streets, espousing ideas that threaten the very foundation of our kingdom."

Philippe smiled. "I see that our queen has not only mastered our language but has also drawn on the fountain of France's wisdom." He gestured toward Viviane. "This is your new *dame d'honneur?*"

Marie jerked her chin downward in a stiff nod. "Madame Viviane de Lussan."

Philippe bowed. Then turning to the queen, "Forgive, if only for one evening, this wretched rogue the beliefs that offend you and allow me the honor of introducing your head lady-in-waiting to the court."

Marie hesitated a moment. "I must join the king, so she is yours for the evening." She held up a warning finger. "Philippe. Do not corrupt her."

"As you wish."

With a swirl of her skirts, Marie-Antoinette and the remainder of her serving women huffed off to join King Louis on his raised dais. Philippe turned to Viviane who fiddled with her fan.

"Let me introduce myself properly." His warm voice washed over her. "I am Philippe, Duke of Valence, cousin to the king and royal Prince of the Blood." His lips twitched in a faint smile. "I saved your life."

⚜

Alexandre leaned against a marble pillar, near one of the domed glass windows that had made the Hall of Mirrors renowned throughout Europe. His eyes narrowed as he watched Philippe, lead the queen's lady-in-waiting around the dancers to a quiet corner in the hall. He had no trouble identifying his childhood friend. Despite the mask and the years that had come between them, the surge of hatred that moved within him like a wild beast left no room for doubt.

Rage made him want to slit Philippe's throat here and now, but years of discipline held his anger in check. He calmed himself by mentally rehearsing the facts of Philippe's life.

One: He was the cousin of King Louis XVI. Should Louis and his two sons die, it would be Philippe who stood to wear the crown.

Two: At age twelve, Philippe had gone to England with his father. There he had been influenced by the itinerant Protestant preacher John Wesley. Alexandre grimaced. He hated the Protestant faith and despised those who fell prey to the lies spawned by its leaders. How a Prince of France could have been so deceived, he could not understand. It proved the extent to which the monarchy had degraded itself. Surely it was God's will to rid the kingdom of such fickle vermin!

While Philippe had never officially left the Church, he began espousing ideas that were at odds with its core ideologies. At first, his late father had attributed the boy's newfound theories of salvation by faith and reluctance to participate in religious rites as some sort of rebellious adolescent phase. But the rebellious boy grew into a stubborn man and his inflexible beliefs had sparked an irreparable rift within the royal family.

Three: Due, in part to his twisted faith, Philippe had often urged his cousin, King Louis, to moderate his lifestyle and attend to the needs of his people. Some believed that Philippe was sincere while others, like Alexandre, were convinced that he was simply trying to win the support of the people in a strategic bid for the throne. Whatever his reasons, Philippe's vocal defense of the common man had earned the admiration of most of Paris populace—and the sworn enmity of Marie-Antoinette.

The red wine turned to gravel in his mouth. Alexandre sneered as he considered his next move. The woman with Philippe was obviously the same one that Salomé had almost executed. Philippe had never been one to mingle with the fairer sex, but it made sense that he would seek out the woman whose life he had saved. Still, there was something about the way he carried himself around her that hinted at something more significant than idle companionship. Alexandre's calculating mind began to analyze the prince's posture, drawing on Rezzonico's lessons on subconscious physical reactions that revealed hidden emotions. Parted lips, hands that refused to stay still and his constant fidgeting indicated that he was nervous.

Nervous? It seemed incongruous with the man he knew. *Why?* Realization struck him with the suddenness of a summer storm. Philippe was attracted to the girl!

At first, Alexandre almost laughed from sheer incredulity but, the more he thought about it, the more he realized how plausible the idea was. He knew Philippe better than anyone alive. The man had never married but a woman like *this*—a stunning beauty of a lower social class, impetuous and full of life—that would be the kind to draw him.

Yes. Alexandre stroked his chin as the physical signs continued. Philippe was leaning forward now, head nodding as he listened with rapt ears to whatever the woman was saying. Perhaps the prince himself was not aware of his budding attraction but the signs were unmistakable.

A twisted smile snaked across his face as he emptied his chalice and tossed it to a passing servant. Alexandre touched the beads that hung beneath his ivory costume, cast a mental prayer to the Virgin and stepped out of the corner. It was time for the game to begin.

⚜

Philippe stared at the graceful creature that sat across from him. Such poise! And from a *bourgeoise*? Her blond hair in graceful waves to the small of her back and the scarlet of her dress subtly accented the jade of her hypnotic eyes. *How did I not notice her beauty that night in Paris?*

As a man who stood close to the throne, Philippe had been exposed to countless women, some beautiful and others not. Most had sought only the wealth and power that he could provide. Until this moment, nothing had persuaded him to go beyond a casual greeting. But tonight, something had changed. He could feel a subtle shift in the rhythm of his heart whenever their eyes met. It was something he could not begin to comprehend, let alone explain.

"I never had an opportunity to thank you for saving my life." Viviane's cheeks reddened. He found her discomfort enthralling. They sat on the plush stools that lined the ballroom floor where couples now whirled in a slow waltz.

"It was not that I did not *want* to thank you," she lowered her eyes, "it is just that I had forgotten your name."

Philippe laughed, causing bystanders to turn in their direction. In his peripheral vision, he noticed a few female heads wagging in unison behind half-open fans.

"We've just given the court gossips something to ponder." He inclined his head and covered his mouth with one hand, mimicking a gossiping woman. "Why is a prince enjoying the company of the queen's new lady-in-waiting who, I have heard, has a penchant for criticizing the royal family *and* forgets the names of those who save her life?"

"Now you are mocking me." Viviane fumbled with her fan.

"Not at all, Madame." Philippe lowered his hand and leaned toward her. "In fact, I find myself intrigued by a woman who is compassionate enough to stop her carriage in a terrible district of Paris to help an orphan."

She glanced at him, smoothed a fold in her skirt, and spoke in an uncertain tone. "How do you know about that?"

"I returned the next day and spoke to a few who witnessed the debacle."

"You, a Prince of France, went into that place alone?" Her eyes widened and she licked her lips. "They could have killed you!"

Her concern was touching.

"It is alright." He squeezed her hand then released it. "Sometimes I mingle with the common people, dressed as one of them. How else will I truly know what they think?"

He shrugged. "Unfortunately, no one would tell me where to find the woman who almost killed you. It is for the best. Any attempt to bring her to justice would exacerbate the tension between the crown and the people of Paris. Her arrest would transform her into a sort of martyr."

Viviane's eyes shifted to the queen who sat next to her husband. "Forgive me if I am too bold," she looked at him again, her expression pensive. "But why does Her Grace dislike you?"

He hesitated before answering. "Our perspectives on the essentials of life are radically different. For example, she believes that God is confined to a specific church whereas I feel that God seeks a relationship with every individual, regardless of their creed."

Viviane frowned. "You are a Protestant?"

"Would you think less of me if I said I am?" Though spoken gently, the words carried a hint of rebuke. For a moment Viviane remained silent and shifted in her seat.

"When my father died in the stampede of Paris," a faraway look crept into her eyes, "I blamed God. I thought that I would never pray again. My mother and I were destitute."

"How did she survive?"

"She became a laundress in Lussan." Viviane twisted a tendril of her shimmering hair.

"And then?"

"One Christmas, the priest from a nearby village read a passage from the Scripture. 'To everything there is a season; a time to be born,'" her voice fell to a whisper, "'and a time to die.'"

She shrugged. "My father died on my birthday. At that moment, everything made sense. I realized that this was a test of my faith and that I needed to keep on believing."

"Go on." Philippe rested his chin in his palm.

Viviane took a deep breath. "Instead of hating the Church, I drew comfort from its rituals. Knowing that my works can make me acceptable to God brings me a sense of peace. If am good enough, someday I might see my father again."

She folded her arms across her chest. "I-I am sorry. I have said too much."

"No," Philippe said. "You have shared a part of your soul and for that I thank you. We are more alike than you might think."

It was Viviane's turn to laugh. "A prince and a laundress's daughter? The only thing we have in common is our language!"

Philippe smiled. "The difference between absolute truth and a mortal lie is only one word misrepresented. The difference between noble and *bourgeois* is even less than that."

"I can see why some would find your opinions objectionable." Viviane's brow furrowed. "What do you mean?"

The smile faded from Philippe's face. "Like you, an event in my childhood forever altered the way I see the world. The social classes and rules that we have established do not reflect God's laws. The clergy fail to live by every word that Christ left us; the nobles fail to show the compassion God requires."

He passed a hand over his brow. "Will a man gain access to heaven because of his church affiliation?" Philippe shook his head. "You speak as though your deeds can earn you God's mercy but I believe that my deeds do not earn God's forgiveness for if they could, why did Christ have to die?"

He gestured at the swirling masses. "If I truly believe in Christ then my works should show my faith. As such, I have asked my cousin to modify his treatment of his subjects. He has not listened, but suspects that I am trying to win favor with the people to claim the crown for myself. My views have alienated me from most of my family, especially the queen."

"I see." Viviane pursed her lips.

"Do you?" Philippe gazed at the scarlet mask that veiled half of her face. No one had ever claimed to understand the loneliness his beliefs engendered. The possibility that she might indeed identify with the pain of his past stirred his emotions. "Madame de Lussan..."

"Yes?"

A question burned in his throat, but though a prince, he hesitated to voice it. The truth was that he longed to see her face. The partial view of her face was like a droplet of water on the tongue of a man dying of thirst. It was torture.

"Will you..." He fell silent. To unmask herself during the ball was taboo. Any spectators could easily draw the wrong conclusions. Yet he needed to see her again. To drink his fill of the beauty that radiated from her skin. To drown in the depths of the twin emerald lakes of her eyes. The words slipped out before he could stop them. As he spoke, Philippe knew that he had crossed an unspoken line, but he felt no regret. Only a tingle of anticipation.

"Will you remove your mask?"

⚜

The question was so unexpected that, at first, she was sure she had misunderstood. "What did you say?"

"Your mask, will you remove it?" Philippe motioned toward her face. "I would like to see you as you really are."

Nervousness seized her. It was not that she had anything to hide. What unnerved her was the distinct impression that, if she unveiled herself at this precise moment, she would open a very personal window into her soul.

A slight tremor shook her hands. A part of her wanted no pretenses between herself and this man whose words wrapped themselves around her mind, but reason resisted the thought of exposing herself to him while those around remained hidden in a world of mystery and deceit.

Philippe saw her hesitation. "Here let me go first." He lifted the corner of his visor and flipped it upward.

He was not overly handsome, but every aspect of his face depicted a part of his character. A strong jaw, accented by a subtle beard, provided the impression of determination. His aquiline nose spoke of a noble birth and his dark eyes seemed able to rip through the curtain of time. They were eyes that penetrated the facade of what she now was and exposed the truth of what she could become.

Her hands drifted to the edges of her own mask, her heart threatening to rip its way out of her chest. *Thud.* She touched the edge of the satin. *Thud.* Her fingers curled to lift it off her face. *Thud.* She tugged at its edges—

"May I request the honor of this dance, Madame?"

The sinuous voice ripped both Philippe and Viviane out of the magnetism of the moment. They pivoted as one toward the intruder. A tall dark-haired man who shared both Philippe's height and build stared down at Viviane. He wore ivory and his hand rested with easy familiarity upon the hilt of a sheathed sword. Unlike Philippe, whose mask had barely covered his eyes, this man's mask extended from his dark hairline to his lips, leaving only his eyes, mouth and strong chin visible.

"Would you honor me with this dance?"

Viviane looked at Philippe who said nothing, but pinned the intruder with his gaze.

"I-I am no dancer, Monsieur." She felt flattered that in the space of only twenty minutes, two men vied for her attention but was unsure how to respond. Despite his mask, the stranger's gaze held a mysterious allure that she found darkly appealing.

"Do I not know you, sir?" Philippe rose, placing himself between them.

The intruder bowed and replied with a flourish of his plumed hat. "With regret, I cannot claim such an honor." He straightened and stepped around Philippe. "Now, I am sure that a man of your greatness will not begrudge me a few moments with this portion of heaven that has come down to earth."

His gaze shifted to Viviane. "As to dancing, I will teach you everything you need to know." He extended his arm.

Viviane's gaze alternated between the two men. She could sense Philippe's disapproval but, prince or not, what right did he have to dictate the terms of her evening? Even now, couples swirled around the floor and, while her mind conjured up nightmarish images of herself falling on her face, this stranger's aura of confidence bolstered her own courage.

The tantalizing prospect of pressing her body close to his was exhilarating. *What would Maman say?* She squelched the unwelcome thought. At the moment, home was far away and so were its litany of rules.

Viviane rose and placed her hand in his. "If you insist." She tried to mimic the queen's seductive tone. "But I warn you, you will soon tire of this poor student."

He studied her masked face before replying. "One would sooner tire of life than of you."

She turned back to Philippe with a curtsy. "If Your Grace will excuse me, I will soon return."

Without another word, the mysterious man led her away from Philippe and into the swirling heart of the masquerade.

⚜

The musicians had struck up a lively *contredanse* and Viviane gave a mental sigh of relief. It was a relatively uncomplicated folk dance that was common among in country towns such as Lussan. The royal court had adopted it years ago as a carefree respite from the more complex official dances. A line of female dancers stood across from a line of men. The couple at the end of the line danced down to the beginning of the group and their place was taken by the couple to their left. The dance was simple but allowed the waiting couples a few moments for idle chatter.

Her eyes flew to the man whose well-muscled arm curled around her waist. She was grateful for his support as her legs felt like they had turned to wet straw.

"What is your name, Monsieur?"

"Alexandre." He motioned for her to move in front of him.

"Are you from Paris?" They took their place at the beginning of the line and Viviane noted that about five other couples had positioned themselves to their right on the dance floor.

"Yes," Alexandre slipped his hands behind his back. "But you are not."

She stiffened. "And what makes you say that?"

The dance had begun, and they shifted to their right as the first couple began spinning in a tight circle while moving down the line.

Alexandre tilted his head to one side. "You have an exotic beauty that, like a breath of fresh air, tells everyone you meet that you are not of this crammed city."

"Monsieur, surely you exaggerate." Viviane twisted her hands together. *Exotic?* No one had ever described her with such bold charm.

"Please, I am only Alexandre."

Viviane lowered her eyes. Alexandre certainly did not *seem* offensive. In fact, his words touched a part of her soul that, until this moment, she had not known existed.

"What is your name?" He stepped closer and she inhaled the clean scent of earth and trees. Then it was their turn to dance and she curled her sweaty palms into tight balls. Alexandre held out his left arm and she stepped into the embrace, placing her right palm against his. The lively music soon loosened her muscles and, as they circled down the dance floor in a series of pirouettes, a warm glow spread through her body. She told him.

"Lussan." Alexandre nodded as she spun underneath his arm, the long scarlet tail of her gown coiling around her ankles. She leaned backward into his caress as they slid forward in unison. Again, the scent of earth filled her nostrils, sending warmth radiating through her body.

"Then you are like me, a *bourgeois*," he said.

She started, lost her timing and almost tripped over his feet. Alexandre leaned over and caught her in his arms, working the action into his own movement so that the entire near-catastrophe seemed rehearsed. *Smooth. So very smooth.*

"I'm sorry." Viviane felt her chest heaving. He was bent over her, his lips inches from her own. *What would it be like to kiss him?* The thought flooded her mind and she pushed herself upright.

"*Au contraire*, it is I who must apologize for startling you." Alexandre's voice was calm and low.

Everything about him is just... smooth. For the second time that evening, she found herself intrigued by a stranger. While it was unusual for a *bourgeois* to attend a royal ball, it was not against the law, provided the citizen met the dress code. And he certainly did that!

Viviane's eyes roamed over his body. She was drawn by the dark atmosphere of raw masculine power that radiated from each movement he made. Her head barely crested his shoulder giving her a sense of security. He held himself erect with a confidence that was not often seen among the *bourgeois*. His motions were deliberate, and his words as musical as the sounds that perfumed the air of the ballroom.

You are an exotic beauty... Sparks slid down her spine turning her world into fire.

"Our turn again."

"Oh!" She had been caught staring.

They spun in a series of mini-circles working their way around the dance floor and she looked at the other guests, the painted ceiling, the floor—anything but Alexandre who continued to smile at her, appearing unfazed by a woman ogling him.

"What is your role at Versailles?" She groped for something to say, trying to cover her embarrassment.

"I care for the plants of the king in the Orangery."

Her ears pricked up. "You are a gardener?"

"I work *for* the gardener." He pulled her to him. "I have for several months."

"Is it dangerous for you, as a Parisian *bourgeois*, to work for the king?"

He shook his head. "There are protests but not all of us Parisians are violent. Most hope for simple changes on the part of the king. Others like Maximilien Robespierre anticipate more radical action." She caught her breath as she whirled away. *Robespierre?* Her conversation with the queen rose fresh in her mind.

"Do you know him... this Robespierre?"

He hesitated and let her twirl into his arms before answering. "In a manner of speaking, yes."

Viviane wanted to press the issue, but Alexandre abruptly changed the topic.

"Have you ever seen the Orangery?" The dance pulled them apart but only for a moment.

"No," Viviane said when she was back in his arms. "The queen's schedule leaves little time for frivolities." She wasn't sure if her heavy breathing was from the exertion of the dance or the man whose touch electrified her.

"I would not call pursuing your passion a frivolity." Alexandre's eyes slid to her own.

"And you think that gardens are a passion of mine?" The words were wrapped in a burst of laughter that escaped her lips as he swung her off her feet and spun her in a tight airborne circle.

"I know it," he said when her feet were once again on the ground.

Alexandre was a mystery—a mystery that grew more intriguing with every passing second. If truth be told, he was right. She had been devoted to horticulture in Lussan and sorely missed the peace that came from feeling the dark soil beneath her bare feet. The fact that Alexandre had not only somehow guessed this but was also connected to one of the greatest orangeries in Europe piqued her interest even further.

They had just completed the second-to-last round when, instead of dancing back to their place in the line, Alexandre took the lead and spun outward toward a less populated corner of the hall.

"What are you doing?" Viviane gasped as she peeked over her shoulder, certain that every eye would be upon them. No one appeared to have noticed.

"Come with me."

"What?" She stepped back, increasing the distance between them. "Come where?"

"Let me show you the Orangery." Alexandre squeezed her hand, the glowing firelight of the gilded candelabra playing games of light and shadow over his masked face. "Its beauty is best seen by moonlight."

Viviane froze. *I shouldn't.*

"Thank you, Alexandre but I cannot. The queen—"

"The queen is royalty." He cut off her protest. His voice softened and he ran his gloved thumb lightly over her chin. "She is not from our world and cannot understand us. She will never know you as I can... as I will."

Viviane caught her breath but did not pull away. "Marie is not as evil as you think."

His fingers hovered near her unbound hair. "Close your mind to the nobility's condescending lies. Let me show you the true face of Versailles."

"I hardly know you..." Her will to resist faltered.

"You know me enough to dance with me." His voice was warm beneath the mask. Its gilded edges framed his lips. "Surely that is more frightening than a walk through the king's garden!"

She giggled in spite herself. He was right. Her fear of falling eclipsed her fear of this refined *bourgeois*. Viviane paused as thoughts buzzed in her mind like a hive of bees.

Alexandre enticed her into subservience. She didn't resent it. On the contrary she found she enjoyed the company of this man who could persuade her to do what she knew was unwise.

There will be no danger. Over five thousand people were on the palace grounds tonight. Surely if he tried to harm her, someone would hear her cries.

A spark of rebellion struck her and silenced the subtle inner voice of resistance. The queen had no need of her and she would be back within the hour. *I should not but I will.*

She tossed her head. "What kind of flowers will we see in the king's garden?"

Alexandre extended his hand and Viviane placed her small palm within his own. "When in the presence of such an intoxicating rose," he led her out of the Gallery, "all else will seem only weeds."

⚜

The crescent moon cast an ethereal glow over the *parterre* of the Orangery, giving Viviane the exhilarating impression of having slipped into another world—one in which the stifling rules of propriety no longer applied. Each step into the darkness with Alexandre pulled her further from her inhibitions. The silken *swish* of her scarlet dress reached her ears, bringing with it a sense of seductive empowerment. She was beautiful. Hadn't Alexandre said so? *An exotic beauty.*

"Tell me more about yourself." He broke the silence. Viviane, lost in a strange mix of emotions encouraged by the provocative atmosphere, told him about her mother and the reason she had come to Versailles. He listened attentively, asking questions that showed his interest was genuine.

The *parterre* was strewn with ancient trees whose primal flowers perfumed the night air.

"Over a thousand trees," Alexandre explained when she had finished, "spend the winter months inside." He gestured toward the enormous building that sprawled out before them. "With the return of spring, they reclaim their places throughout the courtyard."

Viviane breathed in the ambrosial scents. They flooded her body, kissing away her cares and banishing her reservations. She had thought that other couples would have taken advantage of the warm night, but no one was near. Rather than being frightened, she relished the thought of being alone with this masked man whose dramatic approach had already made its mark on her life.

She glanced over her shoulder. The Hall of Mirrors was far behind them, but the conflagration of torches placed throughout the palace grounds cast flickering firelight upon the solitary couple, making the entire atmosphere surreal.

Viviane cast dreamy eyes upon Alexandre, taking pleasure from the sight of the strong set of his shoulders and the thick wavy hair that fell to the nape of his neck. Her eyes wandered again to his mouth.

"This is one of my favorites," he motioned toward a tree that stood twice his height. Small white flowers projected a subtle, sweet aroma that wrapped her in its embrace.

"What is it?" Her voice was husky and low.

He picked a small blossom from the tree, waved it under her nose then tucked it neatly behind her left earlobe. "It is a white pomegranate tree from India that is over a hundred years old. It has an unusual color, but its fruit is sweet."

"The flowers make me think of a bride's veil on her wedding day." She laughed. "I will call it the Bride Tree."

Alexandre became still. "Is there a man fortunate enough to call you his own?"

Viviane bit her lip. "No." Her days had been spent taking care of smelly chickens and helping her mother scrub laundry. Romance was a fanciful dream, nothing more. Versailles was a new world that begged to be explored.

"Will you allow me to see you again, Viviane?" He took both her hands in his. "Your presence is a light that banishes the darkness of my soul."

She trembled as his words sunk into her mind. She barely knew him but the way he spoke! Such tender words that made her feel so desirable... so *powerful*. They drew her like nothing else could. No man could speak so eloquently if he were not a true gentleman.

"Yes." Her eyes lingered on his. "I think I would like that very much."

The magic of the warm night air pressed upon them and one moment melted into another with neither breaking the gaze that bound them together. Alexandre leaned closer, placing his masked face just inches from her own. Viviane's pulse spiked as she realized what he was about to do. She turned her face toward his own and closed her eyes. He moved closer and Viviane's mouth parted in anticipation.

Their lips touched.

Her entire body thrummed with the jarring pleasure of her first kiss. She lost herself in his embrace, her arms wrapping around his neck as the world spun in a flaming arc around her.

At length Alexandre pulled away, a slight smile tugging at the corners of his mouth. "You are magnificent."

Viviane looked away, her conscience wrestling with the rebellious passion that surged within her. She was slipping away from the principles that had governed her life until this moment. But she no longer cared.

"I want to see you again... soon." She breathed the words, passion turning her blood to fire.

He chuckled. "As do I, but my work will keep me busy for the next few weeks." He took her arm. "Instead of rushing the future, let us savor the moments we have together."

They ambled back to the *parterre* outside the doors of the castle as Alexandre pointed out the various plants and told their stories. Viviane listened more to the music in his voice than to his actual words.

By the time they reached the glass doors, most of the guests had departed but a few lingered to wash the last morsels of gossip down with a goblet of Bourgogne wine. Viviane turned to him.

Alexandre bowed low and kissed her extended hand. "Each moment will be an hour until I see you again." She nodded once then turned away, not trusting herself to speak.

⚜

That night she lay for a long time on her luxurious bed of silk and lace, listened to the gentle rain that fell outside, and tried to understand the feelings that Alexandre aroused. Her eyes probed the darkness as she interrogated her own soul. Her attraction to him was genuine and his words showed his interest but were they true? *Truth. What is the truth?*

Prince Philippe's words echoed in her mind. *The difference between absolute truth and a mortal lie is nothing more than one word misrepresented.*

The prince!

A sickening wave of embarrassment rose from the pit of Viviane's gut. She had promised Philippe she would return, but Alexandre had whisked her away to the Orangery. She had left the prince who had saved her life forgotten in the corner while she consorted with a *bourgeois*. The insult was unpardonable.

Sleep was slow in coming. When she did drift into fitful slumber, her dreams were hideous nightmares in which she hung chained between two pillars inside a large marble hall. Before her, a colossal red dragon opened its mouth with the obvious intent of devouring her whole.

She screamed as its hot, fetid breath scorched her face. Out of the darkness, two masked men—one dressed in white and the other clothed in black—materialized on either side of her. To her horror, instead of using their drawn swords on the dragon, they turned their blades on each other.

Viviane's screams filled the hall as the man in black lifted his blade and leapt for his white-clad opponent. Their weapons clashed together with the sound of thunder, but it was drowned out by the roar of the beast whose maw opened still wider and swallowed her whole.

She tossed on her bed and drifted back into sporadic sleep. A curious thought crossed her mind in the last seconds of consciousness. Despite the passion of their kiss, not once had either she or Alexandre removed their masks.

⚜

"I missed you last night."

It was more a question than a statement and, since it came from the queen, Viviane was compelled to answer. The lady-in-waiting fumbled with the clasp of the queen's elaborate diamond necklace. Memories of being alone with Alexandre and of the taste of his lips sparked a fresh surge of excitement that hindered her concentration.

"Well?"

"I am sorry Your Grace, I was… distracted." Viviane's fingers trembled as she removed her hands.

Marie-Antoinette had turned to face her, the demand for an explanation clearly written on every inch of her high-born face.

"I was with a man." Viviane wanted to shove the words back in her mouth seconds after they were spoken, certain Marie's licentious mind would misinterpret them.

The queen arched a finely plucked eyebrow. "Philippe? I must say that I am surprised. Rumor has it that he has never touched a woman in his life."

"No." The crimson in Viviane's cheeks could have provoked a rose to jealousy. "I am sorry, *Altesse*. I meant that I was in a man's presence."

She went out of her way to remove all ambiguity, her words tripping over themselves in a mad rush to be heard. "His name is Alexandre. A gardener who lives on the palace grounds. He is a commoner who knows the lawyer Robespierre. H-he would like to see me again."

"You've ensnared a friend of Robespierre?" Marie's eyes were riveted on her face, but the queen seemed to have entered a different world. "Well done, Viviane. Well done indeed!"

She laid a jeweled hand on her lady-in-waiting's shoulder. "This is the perfect means of achieving our goal." She began to pace, her eyes glittering like the diamonds in around her throat. "Your lover's friendship with Robespierre gives me a direct link to my enemy through you. Do you understand?"

"He's not my lover."

Marie waved a dismissive hand in the air. "It is only a matter of time." She danced across the floor and seized Viviane's arms in her firm grip. "I give you free reign to see him as you please. Stay close to him. Marry him if he asks!"

Viviane's mind whirled at the queen's implications. Marie-Antoinette wanted her to use her budding relationship with Alexandre as a means of destroying Maximilien Robespierre, the man the queen suspected of defaming her character in the ultimate bid for revenge.

"Do you genuinely care for this man?" Marie's eyes probed her servant's face.

Viviane opened her mouth. "I—" She could not finish. This strange storm of emotions was too new, too raw to be positively identified as love. Attraction? Yes. But love? She could not yet be sure.

An image of Philippe riding to her rescue on his white horse flitted through her mind. That memory collided with the thought of Alexandre's strong arms as he spun her through the air above the ballroom floor.

"I do not know, *Altesse*. I am attracted to him, but as to love..." She ended her thought with a helpless shrug.

"So much the better." Marie gave a sage nod. "It is easier to manipulate a man if you do not love him than if you do."

She turned back to the mirror. "The representatives from the Three Estates have arrived for the king's meeting. When I see Robespierre, I will know if the boy who tried to kill me has become the man who threatens my throne."

"And if it is him?" Viviane found her voice at last. "Will you have the king arrest him?"

"We would do better to slit our own wrists." Marie-Antoinette shook her head. "We are beyond that point, my dear. When my husband called for all Three Estates to meet to discuss the current financial crisis, he sent a clear message that our power is limited. Any action taken against Robespierre now will be interpreted as a petty attempt to strike back at those who seek reform."

She stepped closer. "That is why I am depending on you, my faithful *dame d'honneur,* to use your relationship with this man to our advantage. Say you will!"

Viviane tugged at a tendril of her hair. Had not Robespierre attacked and sullied the queen's name? What if God had allowed her to meet Alexandre so that she could right the wrongs Marie had endured? Hadn't Alexandre come into her life with the unexpected passion of a summer storm on a clear day? Could it be coincidence that he knew Maximilien Robespierre? Perhaps these circumstances were all signs that she should help Marie attain justice.

She pursed her lips. Alexandre was not the target of the queen's wrath and would therefore not be harmed. When this was all over, she would tell him the truth. If he did love her, as it certainly seemed he did, he would understand and forgive.

Vivian raised her chin and met her mistress's eyes. "I will."

Chapter Eight

June 1789. Hôtel de Menus, Versailles Estate

Robespierre stood outside the *Hôtel de Menus Plaisirs*. The spacious complex, situated on the grounds of the Versailles palace, would host the historic meeting of the Estates General over the course of the following months. He adjusted his gray wig while letting his eyes roll over the building.

In some respects, it reminded him of a prison in his hometown of Arras. Solemn, colorless walls formed a three-sided rectangle around the cobblestone courtyard. The roof, the color of a drab winter sky, meandered upward while hundreds of harried servants rushed about the structure like jailers in a penitentiary.

Robespierre adjusted the wig again making sure that the powdered hair concealed the patch of pink flesh on his scalp that had just begun to heal.

True, this structure was much more luxurious than the prison of Arras, but he could not escape the feeling that, if all did not go as planned, he and all of France would become prisoners.

No, he thumped his black walking stick against the stones below. *We are already prisoners.* They were the captives of an absolute monarch who had neither the ability to lead nor the will to understand the needs of his people. The next few months would determine whether the people would free themselves from the shackles cast upon them by their ancestors or lengthen their sentence interminably.

⚜

Marie-Antoinette bustled toward the *Salle de Menu*, the extensive hall where over one thousand delegates representing the Three Estates of France had gathered to present their grievances to their monarch, Louis XVI. The king and other members of his court had already been seated. They awaited only her arrival to begin the conclave.

The queen came to an abrupt stop and Viviane, who followed closely behind, shifted to one side to avoid a collision with her rigid back. Marie's eyes settled on someone at the far end of the hall, a man who also had his impassive gaze fixed on her.

He was small, with hunched shoulders and a head that seemed too large for his thin neck. His slight frame reminded her of a black bat. He was shrouded in a relatively simple dark gray waistcoat with a high-drawn collar and leaned on a black walking stick whose brass handle contrasted sharply with his otherwise somber attire.

Marie stole a quick glance over her shoulder. None of the palace guards were within hearing distance. She and Viviane were alone with this phantom who had materialized from the mists of her past.

"Is it you?" His voice was the rasp of death and the queen felt her blood run cold. He took two steps in her direction and then stopped.

"Who dares address the queen in so familiar a manner?" Viviane's voice rang out in challenge.

The black bat of a man shifted in her direction, his expression unreadable behind the tinted glasses that covered his eyes. Then his bloodless lips twisted in a disquieting blend of a sneer and a smile. He dipped his head, removed his glasses, and glared at the queen.

Those eyes! Marie's heart rose to her throat and she grabbed Viviane's arm, trying to steady her buckling knees. *I will never forget those eyes!* Twenty years melted away like wax before a burning flame. In an instant, she was again the young girl facing a maniac armed with a knife and eyes the color of a wolf.

"Robespierre?" Her voice rose in question.

"I see you have not forgotten me." He spoke softly but Marie heard every syllable as distinctly as if he shouted them in her ears.

"How could I forget?" The initial shock faded and she jerked her chin upright, determined to meet this foe as a queen and not as a woman. It was the one piece of the puzzle that had eluded her for twenty years. She had never discovered the identity of her assailant but, when the name of Robespierre became associated with rabid attacks against the monarchy, Marie's astute mind wondered if the boy whom she had spurned years ago had grown into the man who now sought to destroy her.

He bowed low again. "In the flesh, Madame, in the flesh." Then, tapping his right cheek, he took another step closer. "You see that your gentle touch has left an indelible mark."

From this distance, Marie could just discern the jagged path of a scar that ran from his lower eyelid to his jaw.

Robespierre bared his teeth. "Each time I see my reflection, I remember the queen who called my mother a whore, the pretentious female who dared revile the family of Robespierre. And now," he spread his hands wide, "your world of glass has begun to shatter. At this very moment, invisible cracks widen and spread throughout your kingdom, fracturing the very structure of France."

"That is what you seek?" Marie's eyes blazed with fury. "Revenge?" She forced a laugh. "And I thought this was all about justice!"

He wiggled his eyebrows. "Believe this lawyer when he says that justice is rarely black and white. I prefer to think of it as being multiple shades of gray."

"You will never have justice!" She stamped her foot.

Robespierre stepped back and cocked his head. "You doubt my abilities?"

"Abilities?" Marie scoffed. "You are a spoiled child seeking to punish those who defy his will."

"You mock me?" Robespierre's face darkened. "Again?"

"Believe this queen when she says that you will not prevail!" Marie advanced, fists clenched. "I have already begun to spin my web. I swear to you that whatever *cracks* now exist in France will be healed as soon as you no longer exist."

She turned to her lady-in-waiting. "Viviane? Come with me. Let us leave this *child* to his games." Marie straightened her shoulders, glared at him once more, then bustled off with Viviane in her wake.

⚜

Robespierre stared after her, his heart clenching with longing and wounded pride. Any normal woman would have already felt the ravaging hand of time—a wrinkle here, some sagging flesh there. But she had somehow learned to make time bend to her will. The years had enhanced rather than destroyed her beauty. *Such fire! Such an indomitable spirit!*

He spun on his heel and paced to his right. *The contemptuous wretch. She deserves the misery that I will rain down upon her.* He continued his pacing back and forth for several minutes as ravenous desire and cold hatred for this unreachable woman battled for control of his heart.

Then he froze mid-stride and repeated the words that Marie had shouted just before flouncing off. "I have already begun to spin my web."

His mind probed her comment, dissecting each syllable for hidden clues.

"Now what did she mean by that?" He folded his arms across his bony chest. "How could a woman like her... trap a man... like me?"

Robespierre swatted his left palm with the thick end of his walking stick as though the stinging pain would provide the answer. In the twenty years that had passed since their fateful meeting he had amassed popularity, success and moderate wealth. But in her eyes, he was still no more than a lowly beast.

His fingers tightened on the hilt of the baton. "Beasts feel pain. *Beasts* can cause pain."

Pain. That was the answer. He remembered the epiphany he had experienced in his room—a glorious release of emotional agony that could only be tasted when his body was tormented.

The lawyer's lips twisted into a grimace. She would always be his enemy. War had been declared and it could only end when all that she loved lay in ashes at his feet. Marie would feel the pain that had tortured him for two decades and then—when she had no more tears to cry, when agony became the only emotion she felt—then she would succumb to the sultry embrace of death.

He smiled as an image of her beautiful face rose before his mind's eye. She screamed, writhing in terror before a furious crowd that demanded her head.

"Amen." Robespierre pumped a black gloved fist in the air, lost in the rapture of his dark thoughts. "So be it!"

⚜

Prince Philippe de Valence strode out of the *Salle de Menus*, closed the doors firmly behind him and made for the exit that led to the courtyard near the Orangery. Four hours of hypocritical wrangling and senseless debate between the representatives of the Three Estates had produced nothing more than a social quagmire manipulated by selfish motives.

No one—not king, clergy, nobles or *bourgeois*—understood what was happening here. Philippe feared that if he did not escape the oppressive atmosphere he would lose the self-control for which he was legendary.

An attendant hurried to him and bowed while offering him a goblet of Bourgogne, but Philippe waved the man off. It would take more than wine to ease the frustration that threatened to consume him.

He crossed the threshold and breathed a sigh of relief as the sweet morning air burst upon his nostrils with refreshing candor. Philippe ambled about the garden as his mind categorized the problems that confronted him.

One: France was a tinderbox of social division that would explode given the right provocation.

Two: He stood as heir to the throne should Louis and his sons die before him. This claim, coupled with his desire for reform, made him suspect to both his cousin King Louis and the queen. His reluctance to accept both the monarchy's indifference to the suffering of the masses and the shallow nature of the court's faith certainly did not improve his position. In their eyes, he stood to benefit from the darkness that threatened France and was therefore the enemy from within.

Three: He could not get Marie's lady-in-waiting out of his mind. Her beauty was stunning. The curve of her lips, the music in her voice all made his head spin but, when he examined his heart more closely, he realized that there was more about Viviane de Lussan that drew him than physical desire.

It was an innate hunger for more than what she had. He had first sensed it when she shared the pain of her past. Something in her heart had given her the ability to see beyond the obvious loss of her father, thereby granting her the strength to hold on to her faith. This intrigued him. It showed she had a wealth of greatness that he longed to explore.

Hence the problem.

She was of a lower social status which, for most noblemen, would be an insurmountable obstacle, but for Philippe it was yet another reason to seek her out. He was drawn to impossible situations. In some ways he was almost a romantic.

A robin perched on the branch of a nearby white pomegranate tree caught his attention. It cocked its head and chirped.

"You see, *mon ami*," he drew his shoulders together in a shrug, "it is impossible."

The bird bobbed its head as though agreeing and then flitted to a higher branch.

"I barely know her and I hunger to know her more. She has so much to offer the world but could there be a relationship between us? My family would never accept it!"

Philippe spun on his heel and renewed his pacing. "And then, there is the question of love." He placed a gloved finger over his lips and squinted up at the robin. "Who says that she would love me? Really love me as a woman should love a man?"

His shoulders sagged as the memory of the ball crowded his consciousness. "She was so caught up with that rogue, she never returned."

Philippe turned away from the tree and made his way to a nearby bench. For several moments he sat in silence, contemplating the interwoven dilemmas. A kingdom that was falling to pieces. His heart that was falling for an unreachable woman. A soft breeze tousled his dark hair then moved into the distance taking his thoughts back to a day when a simple choice in England had forever altered his future.

"It all seemed so simple as a boy, but now the world has fallen into madness. I need a sign."

Philippe waited, hoping for some miraculous response. A clap of thunder or an angel with drawn sword—anything. But all he heard was the warbling of the robin and the silent cries of his heart.

⚜

Viviane teased a rebellious tendril of her hair back into place and eyed herself in the mirror.

"You are not needed here," Marie had whispered before she had entered the conclave. "Amuse yourself in my absence."

Viviane intended to do just that. "Today is the day." She tried to sound confident, but the slight tremble of her lower lip belied her attempt at courage. She intended to see Alexandre face-to-face. She would return to the Bride Tree, ask him to tell her about himself and see what would happen next.

"Right." She straightened her shoulders and lifted her chin as she had seen the queen do when challenging Robespierre. Looking at her reflection, Viviane was not sure she could consider what she was about to do amusing. It had taken a sleepless night to work her courage to the point where she decided to seek out Alexandre and she had awoken with pale cheeks accentuated by dark circles beneath her eyelids.

She had covered them up with powder—something that was taboo in Lussan—and took a deep breath. "I've made up my mind and I'm not going to change it."

Then she pivoted on her heel and disappeared through the door.

⚜

Viviane hesitated as she approached the slim, dark haired man who sat before the Bride Tree. "Alexandre?"

He rose and turned.

Her heart stood still.

Philippe just stared at her. He did not blink or move for what seemed years though it was only several moments. She wanted to run, not because she feared him, but because of the shame that filled her heart.

"Hello." He spoke at last. His simple clothing made him seem more like a commoner than a part of the royal family. The crease in his brow and his tousled hair showed the weight of burdens that preyed upon his mind.

"Hello." She looked from tree to bush to flower, not meeting his eyes. "It is good to see you again."

Is it? It was difficult to identify the whirlwind of emotions that swirled within her, but she doubted that joy at the sight of the man she had insulted was one of them.

Philippe stepped back, tipped his head and raised his voice to the sky. "My answer!" A smile broke across his face. "I see it now."

"What do you mean, Your Grace?" Viviane furrowed her brow.

Philippe came closer, cheeks flushed. "I needed some clarification about... well, something. I asked for a sign. Nothing happened but then—"

He softened his voice and let his eyes roam across her features, as though he were committing each detail to memory. "And then you came. As flawless as a perfect dawn."

She flushed under his piercing gaze. "Your Grace, I have many flaws, but you are kind to think so well of me, especially," Viviane folded her arms across her chest, "especially after the way that I have treated you."

Philippe's silence forced her to continue.

"I promised to come back." She lowered her voice as she confessed. "One dance became another and then..."

Viviane slowly raised her eyes to his. She paused, unwilling to say more and yet knowing that she would tell him everything. There was an aura of quiet command about him that no simple clothes could disguise. It gently pulled truth from reluctant hearts. Unable to stop herself, Viviane found the words pouring out, swelling up from within her.

"We walked into the Orangery, alone." Her gaze strayed to the white pomegranate tree that reached up to embrace the heavens. She swallowed hard. In his presence, what had seemed so alluring now seemed so wrong.

"I let him kiss me... here... beneath this tree."

Enticed by a world with no moral code, she had encouraged Alexandre's advances. If he had asked, she might have—

"I know." Philippe's whisper was like a rumble of thunder.

"What did you say?"

"I know." He grilled her with his eyes. "I was here although you did not see me. I saw the two of you leave the *château*. Through the window, I saw you walking toward the Orangery. When you did not return, I decided to come after you, fearing the worst."

Viviane's palms grew moist. "Then you know what happened next?"

"You called this pomegranate the 'Bride Tree' and he..." Philippe broke off. The pain in his face was so poignant that she took a step back. Anger at being thrown over for someone in a lower social bracket she could understand, but the look in his eyes was one of pure anguish. *Why?*

"I could bear it no more and left." His shoulders sagged. "It seemed to me that you were willing to partake in whatever misdeed this villain proposed."

It was his last remark that ignited a chain of explosive revelations.

One: His opinions about her actions affected her own feelings of self-worth. She had somehow hurt him. His disapproval of her actions made her disappointed in herself. Some hidden niche in her heart craved his approval.

Two: While he didn't know Alexandre's name or anything about him, Philippe had classified him a villain. Viviane's mind flew back to the moment when he had revealed the deep divisions that existed within his family. He had spoken more harshly about Alexandre than he had of the king or even the queen. The question surfaced again: *why?*

Three: Philippe had every reason to be angry with her. She had chosen to spend her evening with a commoner instead of a peer of the realm. But instead of being furious at the affront, he seemed more concerned with her welfare than his pride.

Does he... care about me in some way?

The question broke upon her like a spray of cold water, leaving her breathless and dazed. She didn't know the answer, but she did know that she had to say something to atone.

"Your Grace," Viviane dared to lay a hand on his arm. "It went no further than a kiss."

For a moment, the prince did not respond and Viviane worried that she had driven the knife in deeper.

"It is forgotten." He placed his hand over hers. "Think no more on it."

She expelled a tightly-held breath. "Thank you."

"Would you sit with me?" He gestured to the bench.

Viviane complied. Her back was rigid, and she folded her hands primly on top of her crossed knees.

"You must wonder why I called you 'my answer.'" Philippe sat beside her.

Viviane felt the warmth of his nearness and a comforting, settled peace began to gently unravel the tension in her body. She closed her eyes, inhaling the subtle scent of sandalwood that clung to his clothes.

"I admit you are the first to call me that." A hint of a smile tugged at her lips.

"It is because I believe that God sent you to me."

"*Non*. It was my cousin Gabrielle who summoned me to Versailles—not God. Besides, why would God send a bereft woman to a prince? Surely you do not think that I expect your charity."

"Perhaps it is *I* who need your charity." His dark eyes sparkled with humor.

She spread her hands. "I have nothing to give while *you* are as wealthy as the king himself!"

"My wealth is not measured in gold and diamonds but in faith and truth."

"Of course, faith is more important than gold." Viviane uncrossed her legs and turned toward him. "But faith does not bring tangible results."

Philippe's lips turned downward. "Perhaps you should alter your understanding of what faith truly is."

Viviane smoothed out her skirt, shaking her head. The man was impossible to understand. She thought to leave but the settled assurance that infused the very air he breathed drew her to him like a safe harbor draws the captain of a broken ship on a storm-tossed sea. Besides, the idea of debating philosophy with a prince was intriguing to say the least.

"Then, Your Grace, kindly tell me about your perception of faith."

For the next hour, Philippe spoke about the power of faith, weaving his memories of the itinerant preacher John Wesley into his own study of Scripture. Viviane leaned toward him, her eyes wide as he taught her that it was by faith *alone* in the ultimate sacrifice of Jesus Christ that she could be saved. She challenged his claims but he was unfazed by her direct questions, going so far as to prod her for more.

At length, the flow of his words stopped. "What do you think?" He studied her face and leaned back against the bench.

"I-I do not know what to think." Viviane could not begin to put in words the thoughts and questions that mushroomed in her mind.

"Then listen to a question that I have for you before you go." Philippe's eyes locked with hers.

Viviane nodded. She was surprised to discover that she was reluctant to leave.

"Will you meet me here again tomorrow?"

She froze. It was one thing to come across him by chance, but quite another to intentionally seek him out. Everyone at court knew that the prince did not engage in illicit affairs. If anyone, especially the queen, discovered them and assumed that they were romantically involved it would lead to consequences she dreaded to consider. But another part of her *wanted* to learn more, not just of his beliefs but also of the man himself.

"Your Grace," she glanced at her hands, "if we were discovered, it would cause quite a scandal."

Philippe responded with a question. "Which is more important, truth or perception?"

"The truth." After a brief pause, Viviane met his gaze.

Philippe took her hands in his. "In you I see a heart of courage, a heart that will pursue truth relentlessly. You must not allow the perceptions of others to prevent you from satisfying the true hunger of your heart."

Viviane toyed with the clutch that dangled from her wrist, mulling over his words. He was right. The pursuit of truth, even when it challenged her own ideas, was an intoxicating frontier that begged to be explored.

"The queen does not need me this time of day." She straightened. "So, if you are willing to teach, Your Grace, I would like to hear more of this... truth." She omitted the fact that she also wanted to learn about him.

They met each day over the course of the next three weeks and Philippe flooded her mind with illuminating light, transforming the dull rhetoric she had learned as a child into a living experience. He punctuated his animated teachings with stories of his past.

Slowly a picture of his life began to take shape in her mind. She knew that he had led a rather solitary childhood. At some point his only friendship had been cut off and he had retreated to the security of isolation and faith, rejecting his father's efforts to marry him off.

Their moments together became a sort of sanctuary. Philippe projected a peace that filled her own heart while she was with him. The web of intrigue that had dogged her steps since her arrival at Versailles faded from her mind whenever they sat together, allowing her to focus on Philippe and the thirst that his spirituality created in her own heart. He was the center of calm that held everything else at bay.

All that was about to change.

After three weeks, Philippe took a deep breath and asked a question that shattered any tranquility left in her world. "Will you allow me to see you, Viviane?"

It was the first time that he had called her by her first name and the magnitude of the moment overwhelmed her. Numbness seized her entire body and when she tried to speak, her voice was an incredulous squeak. "See me? As in... romantically?"

"If you would have it so." A strange light burned in Philippe's eyes. She could not tell if it was the light of love or insanity. Given his question, she feared the latter.

It certainly was not what she expected to hear. Religion she could have anticipated. His opinions on the political nightmare that was unfolding in the building behind them was also logical.

But nothing could have prepared her for the words that Philippe, Prince of Valence and possible successor to the throne, had just uttered.

There was only one plausible explanation—he was mocking her.

"Me?" Viviane rose to her feet, her surprise deforming into fury. "You would court a commoner?" She sucked in deep breaths. "A pauper from Lussan?"

The idea was ludicrous. It had to be some sort of twisted joke. *Close your mind to the nobility's condescending lies.* Alexandre's words exploded in her mind.

Alexandre was right. "You are toying with me, sir!" Her fingers trembled as she touched the growing crimson flush on her cheeks.

Philippe leapt to his feet. "Viviane, wait."

She rounded on him, her hands bunched into fists at her sides. "Do you think, Your Grace, that I am some object that you can use for your own pleasure?"

Her voice cracked, and Viviane felt the first trickle of tears course down her cheeks.

"Do I appear so miserable in your eyes that you feel lies such as these would bring me comfort?"

This is how he takes his revenge. The realization blotted everything else from her mind. *I insulted him that night at the ball and now he plans to mocks me before the entire court!*

The idea was incongruous with what she knew of his character but there was no other possible explanation. He had devoted the last three weeks to looping cords of trust around her heart with which he planned to drag her through the mud of public ridicule. The sheer cruelty of the scheme hurt.

Philippe reached for her hand, but she slapped it away.

"Stay where you are, Sir!"

"You do not understand." Philippe's hand remained outstretched. "I want to know you better." His voice was choked.

"To what end?" Nausea swelled within her. "Your cousin, the king, would sooner renounce his crown than permit us to marry."

Philippe hung his head. "I know."

"Then why ask?" Her eyes darkened. "What, would you use me, then discard me? Would you make me the laughing stock of the entire court?"

The words flew like bullets from a pistol, each one striking hard and true but Viviane felt as though she were the target, not him. The pain of each accusation ripped into the fabric of her soul. With this hurt came the subtle recognition that some part of her craved his love.

"I understand your confusion—"

Viviane cut him off. "You are too far above me to understand me!" She was sobbing now but she no longer cared. "What you are saying is too impossible to be true."

"I mean what I say." Philippe stepped toward her, his eyes holding her own in a vice-like grip.

Viviane's blood ran cold. *How could he?* The thought that he was sincere was preposterous. Philippe knew that, as a member of the royal family, he needed the king's permission to marry. Louis would never allow his cousin to weaken the monarchial status further by bringing a *bourgeoise* into the family. If so much as a word of this conversation reached the ears of the queen or her vindictive cousin Gabrielle—

"I bid you good day Your Grace." Viviane sniffed, wiped her eyes and blinked back tears. She absolutely refused to cry anymore in his presence. She pushed past him and stumbled to the cobblestone path that led back to the castle. "I never imagined that you, of all people, would seek to hurt me so!"

Philippe's hand reached out to the fleeing woman. He whispered her name as a gentle breeze ruffled the dark hair that hung loosely about his shoulders. "Viviane."

How can I make her understand?

The retreating figure slipped out of his sight and he turned to face the flower-laden pomegranate tree once more as the shadow of a plan grew in his mind. If she would not believe his words, perhaps she would believe his actions.

"She is my Eve." He stood, legs spread apart in a wide stance and with tightened fists at his side. "But to bring her to my paradise, I must walk through the fires of hell."

⚜

Gabrielle de Polignac let the gold-and-scarlet curtain slip free from her fingers as she eased back from the window pane through which she had watched the spirited exchange between her cousin and the prince of Valence.

The pair had first come to her attention earlier this week, when she happened to notice Viviane walking to the Orangery from her own terrace. For months, her cousin had chipped away at her own influence with Marie-Antoinette while inserting herself in the queen's favors. Gabrielle had concealed her growing frustration while waiting for Viviane to make one wrong step. Her thin lips curved in a triumphant smile. Her cousin had taken that step when she walked to her waiting prince.

She picked up her gray Turkish Angora which sported a collar of emeralds inlaid in silver. "So, my little Soumise, the prince is besotted with my cousin and the nitwit does not know it."

The cat yawned idly and opened his blue eyes.

"And what shall we do about that, hmm?" Gabrielle stroked the long hairs of his back. "Shall we let our cousin steal the attentions of both queen and prince?"

The long-haired feline yawned again, then snapped his jaws shut and licked his lips.

"That is right!" Gabrielle cackled as she rubbed her nose against that of her pet. "We keep this knowledge to ourselves and, when the time is right, we will snap our jaws around her."

She kissed the animal's pink mouth. "How clever you are Soumise."

Chapter Nine

June 1789. Tenements of Paris.

"Are you sure this is the place?" Augustin, brother of Maximilien Robespierre covered his mouth and nose with a silk handkerchief, trying in vain to ward off the stench that seemed to paint the very air of the squalid *arrondissement* around them.

"I am certain," Maximilien said in a voice that reminded his brother of death. It was a fitting image since death was what they had come to acquire.

Maximilien lifted his black brass-handled walking stick and rapped sharply on the weathered frame of a dilapidated shanty. They were surrounded by many such structures, buildings whose derelict status reflected the conditions of their inhabitants' dreams.

A wheezing, liquid cough from within the house arrested Augustin's attention. He peeked through a fist-sized hole in the paper-thin walls. Inside a woman, whose pale, haggard face showed her despair, made futile efforts to stand. Spurts of bright, red blood ringed her toothless mouth. Augustin felt nausea rise in his gut.

"She cannot rise Maximilien." His voice was muffled by the thick cloth that covered his face.

Robespierre shoved the door inward with his shoulder. It gave under the first blow and he stepped inside, framed in the dying sunlight as clouds of dust swirled about lazily on all sides.

"Wh-who comes?" The woman rasped the words, then succumbed to another fit of violent coughs. Augustin followed his brother but pressed his back against the far wall.

"Shh..." Robespierre lifted his black-gloved finger to the cotton cloth that covered his face. "It is I, Maximilien Robespierre."

A glimmer of light shone in the old woman's eye. "T-the Incorruptible comes to my door?" She fell backward on the bed, weakened from the effort of speech.

Robespierre glanced back at Augustin. "Do not be idle, brother. Bring the supplies!"

Augustin hesitated, then stumbled forward, carrying a large canvas satchel from which he pulled out another handkerchief. Bending over the old woman he wiped the blood from her face.

"Bless you child." The corners of the woman's mouth twitched as she attempted a smile. Augustin froze but his brother's nod compelled him to proceed. He cast the stained cloth into the sack, placed a fresh one over the invalid's mouth and waited.

Within seconds the coughs began again, and Augustin took care to keep her entire mouth covered by the handkerchief. When it subsided, he carefully folded the napkin with gloved fingers and placed it inside the satchel with the others.

"Take her blankets too." Robespierre pointed to the stained sheets. "We must make the outcome certain."

Augustin nodded and pulled the blankets out from under the dazed woman who was too weak to protest. He placed everything inside the sack and then hurriedly drew it shut.

Robespierre nodded toward the door. "Now wait outside." His younger brother glanced once at the woman then hurried outside and closed the door.

⚜

Robespierre eyed the decrepit carcass that lay prostrate on the rickety bedframe.

"The Incorruptible... c-come to see old Marthe." The woman's cracked lips pulled back to reveal blackened gums. "God is good."

God? He supposed the wretched fool was not too far from the truth. He did hold the power of life and death over her in his hands. Unfortunately for Marthe, today he was not in a merciful mood.

Robespierre stepped closer and knelt beside the bed.

"Shh." He smoothed back the wrinkles of her forehead.

"You are... the life... of France." Each word was gurgled rather than spoken.

A thin smile snaked across his face. Her voice was barely audible which meant that no one would hear her die.

"Life and death are intertwined." A gleaming dagger appeared in his gloved fist. "You have served your purpose, you pathetic old fool." He slit her throat. "Now die."

Shock registered on the woman's face as her blood spurted through the gash in her throat. She tried to speak but only gurgles escaped her lips.

"Don't worry." Robespierre wiped his blade upon another handkerchief from his pocket and sheathed the dagger as he watched her body jerk in the bed. "It will be over soon."

His victim convulsed twice more, then lay still, her sightless eyes staring at him in accusing silence.

Robespierre rose and, without a backward glance, left the old woman's body on the cot. Augustin waited outside. His furrowed brow and downturned lips spoke volumes to Robespierre. It was obvious that Augustin still wrestled with that annoying part of the human brain called a conscience. *Too bad for him.*

"You know what you must do?" The older lawyer glanced around to be sure the darkening street was empty. His brother nodded but Maximilien was not satisfied. "What are your orders?"

"I must take the wooden toy horse that you have purchased and rub it down with this blanket," Augustin said in crisp tones. "Then I will leave it inside this bag overnight, so the disease carried by this woman will pass on to the recipient of the gift."

"And who is the recipient?" Maximilien folded his arms across his chest. He knew that Augustin had committed the plan to memory, but his meticulous nature demanded that every detail be reviewed one final time.

"The son of Louis XVI, Louis-Joseph, *dauphin* and heir to the throne."

"Who is giver?"

"The note attached to the gift will read that it is from his loving uncle, Philippe de Valence." Augustin scratched his head.

"You have secured his seal?"

Augustin tapped his left breast pocket. "His nurse, Geneviève Poitrine, who is a member of Alexandre's Moustiques managed to infiltrate his chambers while the prince was at a session of the Estates General. She delivered it to Alexandre who had one of his men—a goldsmith I believe—make an exact replica. The original was back in the prince's *appartement* within the hour."

Robespierre's mind shifted to his dark accomplice, Alexandre. Through Salomé, Alexandre had requested a clandestine meeting attended by only himself, Robespierre, Augustin and Alexandre's personal giant named Simon. Together they had outlined the next phase of their plan, working until the gray light of dawn touched the eastern sky.

Early in the meeting, Alexandre had revealed that he was the head of a powerful organization called the Moustiques. This had been a surprise, but Robespierre always found ways to profit from surprises. In this instance, the assassin's network had been invaluable—even if their leader had proved to be a disappointment.

It had taken some persuasion on his part to convince Alexandre to participate in the plot as, for some inconceivable reason, the spineless man hesitated to take the life of a child. In the end, Robespierre had threatened to dissolve the alliance between his associates and those of Alexandre, gambling upon the man's need for his political clout. He had been right. Alexandre had grudgingly acquiesced, giving firm orders to his lieutenant to do whatever was necessary for Robespierre's diabolical plot to succeed. Now the path was set, and the outcome was sure.

Maximilien tugged at his chin. "Who will take the infected package to the dauphin?"

"The aforesaid nurse, Geneviève," came the reply. "The wrapped package will be passed to Alexandre through Salomé, who will in turn deliver it to his agent Geneviève. She will ensure that the dauphin, who has always been frail and has already demonstrated extreme vulnerability to the disease, opens the package when alone."

"Good Augustin, good!" Robespierre thumped his stick against this palm. He had come to enjoy the brief stint of pain each blow produced. It was a tantalizing *hors d'oeuvre* that reminded him of the main course soon to come. He would feast upon the queen's agony when she learned that her beloved son had succumbed to the ravaging disease known as consumption.

"But what is to prevent the prince from simply denying any involvement?" Augustin raised a valid point—one Maximilien had already considered.

"The simple fact that he will be not at Versailles." Robespierre's lips twitched in a feline smile. "Prince Philippe de Valence has left for an unannounced journey. No one knows where he has gone. When he returns, the consumption will have run its course and the child will be dead."

He drew his shoulders together in a shrug. "The queen already hates him and will believe whatever lies the nurse Geneviève feeds her." He thumped his stick again. "Besides, Philippe's seal will be on the note that *seals* the boy's fate!"

Robespierre chortled at his own twisted humor. "It is not the child's birthday so why send him a gift? With the right seed planted in her mind, Marie *will* believe that he is the culprit. After all, he can only inherit the throne if both her sons are dead."

Maximilien grabbed his brother's arm, his words spilling over each other. "The Prince will be unable to defend himself, the worthless brat will be dead, and the queen will be disconsolate. Philippe will return to find the court arrayed against him and the royal family will be irrevocably fractured; do you see what this means, Augustin?" He sucked in a deep breath.

"Yes brother." Augustin pried his brother's fingers off his arm.

"He will die a bloody death." Robespierre's shoulders shook with silent laughter. "Imagine, the little urchin coughing up fountains of blood until he drowns in his own body fluids—what a sight!"

He swerved to face the deepening shadows. "This is the beginning of her pain." His knuckles went white around the shaft of his walking stick. "The darkness of my soul will cover those beautiful eyes, driving her mad with grief until at last she sees no more."

Chapter Ten

June 1789. Outskirts of the Versailles Estate.

Salomé squinted at the narrow blade of a dagger, given to her by Alexandre, and tried to see her reflection. In a time when glass was as valuable as gold, the mirrors of the poor were made of dirty puddles or knives. Alexandre had laughed at the rusty blade she had snatched up the night of Germain's death, calling it nothing more than a toothpick. He had then handed her one of the many stilettos whose scabbards were sewn into the dark fabric of his clothes.

"Keep it," he had said. "In case one of your clients gets a little heavy-handed."

Salomé smiled now at his thoughtfulness while trying to make sure that her thick tresses, which held bright blue pansies in place over her left ear, were neatly combed. She pursed her lips and frowned as she caught sight of her pot of *rouge*. The expensive paint was meant to enhance the beauty of her lips and she reserved it for very special clients who could afford to pay for extras. But for Alexandre...

Salomé sighed and dipped her finger in the jar. Sometimes one had to make sacrifices. She glanced at her worn dress. It was the same one that she had worn every day since she met him five months ago. The blood of the hapless coach driver still darkened the hem of her skirt, defying her best efforts to remove it.

I'm sure the aristo girl has plenty to wear. Her pretty mouth curled in a snarl and Salomé pushed the thought away. This was not a time for dark thoughts. *He* would be here soon, and she must be ready to receive him.

"Hello love." She practiced her greeting in front of her reflection and grimaced. Too artificial. "Hello handsome."

Salomé groaned. That was a tired phrase, one she used with almost all her clients. Tonight, her prey was not a customer but the one man who sought to avoid her charms.

She glanced across the one-room shanty to three stumps of maple trees around which the cabin had been built. The sawed-off logs served as their table and chairs. Two wooden trenchers, placed on the middle stump, were filled with a steaming concoction—her attempt at soup. Salomé ran her moist hands over her skirt. It had taken the better part of the morning to prepare it and she hoped that it would set the stage for the part of the game that she knew best.

The sure tread of a man's feet outside the door made her pulse beat even faster. Maybe, just maybe, he would notice her today. Maybe this time, he would spend his evening wrapped in her arms instead of the chains that Viviane de Lussan had wrapped around his mind.

She squinted at her reflection once more before slipping the knife back into its sheath, then passed her hands over her skirt one more time and positioned herself by the door. It opened and Alexandre stepped inside. His gray eyes took in everything with a cursory glance.

"Welcome home, Alexandre."

Salomé smiled up at him. She was not sure when her feelings had progressed from simple admiration to love. Perhaps it had been on the night he had effortlessly disarmed her on the banks of the Seine. Maybe it was the moment he suggested infiltrating the queen's household and manipulating Viviane. Possibly it had been his thoughtful gift of the knife or a combination of all three.

She could not specify when she had fallen in love, but she did know that each night it grew harder to leave Alexandre for other men. The money given to her by Robespierre had long been spent but she never asked for more. She was no longer here because she had been bought—she was here by choice.

"Are you expecting company?" Alexandre jerked his head toward the table with his head. He dropped onto one of the stumps. Salomé's shoulders slumped but she refused to admit defeat. The evening was still young and hope still lingered.

"No." She minced over to him letting each motion accentuate the sensuality of her rolling hips. Then she knelt at his feet, offering him a full view of her creamy skin and feminine features.

"I was to meet a man this evenin' but I decided that I was too tired. I will be here instead. With you... all... night... long." She let each word work its way into his mind, hoping for some sign that he wanted her, some small indication that he cared.

She felt his eyes glide over her, but he remained silent and unmoving. *What is he thinking?* The moments passed with the speed of a snail. Surely if he was interested he would have done something by now! When the embarrassment that put twin spots of fire in her cheeks grew too obvious, Salomé shoved herself upright.

Then he spoke. "I saw her today but she did not see me."

Salomé's stomach tightened. There was no need to ask who he was talking about. She bit her tongue and clenched her fists as she fought off the urge to rip Alexandre's sightless eyes out of his skull. *Viviane?* He was thinking of the aristo while *she* offered him her love?

Rising, she moved to the opposite side of the table. "You mean Viviane." Her voice cracked as she spat out the hated name.

"Yes, of course." Alexandre's tone became animated and he straightened in his seat. "She was leaving that snake, Philippe."

"I see." Salomé focused her anger on the wooden trencher she gripped between her fingers. When he wasn't spouting plans to destroy the king, Alexandre was always griping about Viviane and Philippe. *It's as though he loves her himself.* A sickening lump rose to her throat as the thought embedded itself in her mind. *He can't see me because the aristo witch blinded him at the masquerade!*

"What is this?" He motioned to the bowl.

"Dinner."

If Alexandre noted the change in her tone, he said nothing. They had no spoons so each simply lifted the bowl to their lips. Alexandre swallowed some of the brew first and immediately began to gag. Red-faced, he leapt to his feet, his elbow inadvertently knocking the trencher and remainder of soup to the floor.

Salomé watched in mortified stupor as her entire day's work seeped into the cracks that traversed the dirt beneath their feet.

He coughed twice and pounded his fist against his chest. "Are you trying to kill me, woman?"

Salomé glanced at her own soup which still rested at the border of her lips. She touched her tongue to the brew and made a face as a sulfurous, bitter taste filled her mouth.

"Ugh!" She dropped the concoction on the table and buried her face in her hands. Like the soup, everything she touched was ruined.

Alexandre regained his breath, reached across the table and pried her hands away. A trace of a smile tugged at the corners of his soup-rimmed mouth.

"You tried," he said. "And for that I thank you."

Salomé glanced down at their intertwined fingers, her heart pounding in her chest. "I'm sorry." Heat crept again into her cheeks. "My mother never had time to teach me much of what I needed to know."

"You've never spoken of your mother." Alexandre's voice softened. "Who is she?"

Salomé pulled away and picked up the wooden bowls. "Some things are not worth mentionin'."

"Secrets run rampant in times like these, Salomé." Alexandre took hold of her elbow and turned her toward him. "You and I have them. Robespierre has them. Philippe de Valence has them. And it is this last that concerns me the most. It seems that our Prince Charming has decided to also play the part of *Cendrillon* and go missing at the midnight hour of his cousin's reign."

Salomé's eyes dropped from his face to his fingers that still touched her elbows. If only he could touch her like that forever. If only she could have been his and his alone. If only he would forget the conniving schemes that crowded his mind and see none but her. If only—

"I will discover what Philippe is planning and will rescue Viviane from his princely claws."

Salomé felt sick. If he uttered Viviane's name one more time she...

There was a knock on the door and then a pause. Alexandre cocked his head listening.

Three more knocks followed in quick succession.

"It's a friend of mine." He pulled on his boots. "I'll be back."

Salomé's spine stiffened but she said nothing. She watched in cold silence as Alexandre glanced at her once more and slipped out the door.

⚜

"Is it done?"

Simon's nod was barely visible in the moonless night, but Alexandre knew him well enough to know the unspoken answer.

He let out a pent-up breath. "He's a seven-year-old boy, Simon."

"He's the heir to the throne." There was no pity in Simon's voice. "That *boy* will one day grow up to become a man just like his father. A man who sees nothin' wrong with breaking the backs of his own people to satisfy the whims of his woman."

Alexandre tugged at his chin. "What did you say to Geneviève? She nursed him since he was an infant."

A soft *pop* reached his ears as Simon cracked his neck. "She was eager to help. A year ago, things might've been different. But it was her boy, Germain, that was killed in the streets by that drunk aristo's carriage a few months ago. She sees this as a chance to even the score—to strike back at the aristocracy."

Alexandre fell silent, contemplating this bit of information. He had not known of the connection between Salomé and Geneviève. *Why had neither woman ever mentioned the other?*

Simon's gaze drilled him. "What? You didn't know that Geneviève was your woman's mum? You're losin' your touch."

His fist shot out and grazed Alexandre's cheek. Alexandre stumbled to one side, thrown off-balance by the unforeseen blow but he did not retaliate. This was the nature of their relationship. Simon pushed him to the limits of his patience and he always took it with good grace until the opportunity arose to prove that brains, not brawn, were the ultimate masters in any fight.

"See what I mean?" Simon laid his meaty palm on Alexandre's shoulder. "Five months ago, you would've seen that comin' if you were blindfolded. Your obsession with Valence and his country wench is makin' you lose focus!"

Alexandre's good humor vanished. "My war with Valence has nothing to do with you."

Simon barked a non-committal grunt and backed away. "I've heard the prince has gone missing."

Alexandre glared at him. "Yes. I want you to send word to all our agents across the country. Tell them to keep watch for the prince who will probably be dressed as a commoner. Luc, our journalist who creates our cartoons about the queen, should have posters of Philippe prepared by now. Make sure each agent has one."

"It almost sounds as though you want to get rid of a rival." Simon folded his muscled arms across his chest. "Don't tell me you're developin' feelings for the aristo girl."

Alexandre closed his eyes, trying not to let his fading patience disappear altogether. Winning Viviane's trust had been his initial reason for infiltrating Versailles but Philippe's reaction to Viviane the night of the ball and their series of clandestine meetings near the white pomegranate had changed everything. Although he was never close enough to hear their words, Alexandre had observed the pair. He was convinced that his archenemy loved this woman.

Alexandre did not love Viviane but his enemy did. He fondled the hilt of a hidden blade. As Philippe had once separated him from Juliette, the woman he had loved, so he would come between the prince and the object of his affections. He had already obtained a kiss but that was not enough. Alexandre would pursue Viviane until, by her own will, she rejected the man who loved her and chose him instead.

"My feelings, whatever they are," he opened his eyes, "are mine alone."

Simon straightened, his jaw snapping shut with an audible *click*.

"Is that understood?" Alexandre pushed the point home, demanding a response.

"Understood." His friend stared at him through narrowed eyes then, without another word, spun on his heel and disappeared into the night.

BRIDE TREE

⚜

"The whole thing has become a veritable nightmare, your Grace." Gabrielle de Polignac flitted a lace fan in front of her face. "Think of it! All those dirty savages, eating and sleeping on the palace compound. What if they all rise at once and decide to murder us while we sleep? What if they steal all the king's gold from the *Hôtel de Menus*? Oh, I can't stand it any longer."

Marie-Antoinette stepped from her bath, dressed in a long garment that fully covered her body. Bath time for the queen was an affair to be witnessed by the women of the court. Marie, who refused to waste her time among the wrangling Estates, used the event to apprise herself of the latest news.

"I am afraid, Gabrielle, that you must bear it whether you like it or not." Marie stepped behind a large silk screen and extended her arms as her assistants helped her dress.

"My husband Jules tells me that a new, very radical faction has formed." Gabrielle's voice floated over the screen to her. "They call themselves the Club Breton and are led by the lawyer Maximilien Robespierre. He is advocating that France do away with the monarchy altogether. Can you imagine?"

Marie felt a cold chill run down her spine. So, it had come to this. Open talk of rebellion. Louis knew this, of course. He still joined the wretched meetings but, apparently, the King of France was unable to squash the scorpion of rebellion that scuttled about under his own roof.

Well, if he won't act then I will. When her maids had finished buttoning her dress, Marie stepped from behind the screen and addressed Gabrielle.

"Everything will be handled in good time, my dear friend." She smiled at Viviane's cousin and then turned to Viviane herself. "Madame de Lussan, walk with me."

⚜

Viviane followed the queen, but in her peripheral vision, she caught a glimpse of Gabrielle. Her cousin flitted her fan again, a smug expression on her face. *Something is not right.* They passed through a corridor that led to the queen's bedroom and

Viviane's thoughts flew through the litany of problems that she faced, trying to discern the source of Gabrielle's happiness.

My encounter with Alexandre? No, there was no way her cousin could know about that.

My rejection of Philippe? The thought gave her pause. She had told no one, of course, about yesterday's debacle but that did not mean that Gabrielle had not somehow unearthed the raw truth of the affair. The implications of what such a discovery would mean made her shudder.

They had reached Marie-Antoinette's bedchamber, a spacious room whose walls were covered by a bright floral pattern of intertwined roses. A large bed whose headboard was trimmed with intricately-woven golden filigrees lay in its center. The queen made a slight gesture and the remaining servants retreated. When the door closed behind them, the monarch spoke.

"Our enemy grows stronger." She bit her lip and began to pace in front of a low golden barricade at the foot of her bed, built to separate the queen from select members of court who were privileged to witness her morning ablutions or special occasions such as childbirth.

Marie's gaze settled on Viviane's face. "Have you met with your gardener, Aristotle?"

"Alexandre, *Souveraine*." Viviane curtsied as she corrected the queen. "No, not since that first night. He had said he would be busy in the weeks following the masquerade."

Marie's brow furrowed. "Then you must seek him out. Find him and do whatever it takes to convince him that you are madly in love with him." She locked eyes with her servant.

"Your Grace I—"

"*Whatever* it takes." Marie held up an imperious finger.

Viviane fell silent and the queen continued as she turned to face the far window.

"Under no circumstances must he suspect that you are part of a plot to destroy his friend. If you win a man's heart, he will not see the deceit that hides within your own. He will not perceive the net that I am spreading because you, the woman he loves, will be my messenger. When the moment is right, you will tell him that you carry a letter for Robespierre from the queen."

Viviane's voice reflected her confusion. "What more could you possibly have to say to a man as vile as Robespierre?"

Marie turned back to her, the face of the serious monarch replaced by the coquettish smile of an experienced seductress.

"I will have nothing to say to him, my dear, but you will. It will not be a message of hate." Marie flitted her lashes in mock flirtation. "It will be a message... of love."

"Love?" Viviane stared at the queen, stunned by her duplicity. Gone was the worried pacing, the nervous agitation. Within seconds, Marie had become the monarch who oozed confidence with every breath. It was as if she were certain her plan would succeed because she, the queen, had concocted it.

"I'm sorry your majesty but I do not understand what you are asking. You want me to write love letters to Robespierre?" Viviane's voice caught in her throat and a shiver slipped down her spine as she thought of the frail-looking man with unnatural eyes.

"Yes." Marie cocked her head to one side. "You will write letters on my behalf. Create them as if you were writing to this man you love, this Alexandre." Marie's voice became more animated and she made sweeping gestures with her arms. "Woo him Viviane. Win him!"

Viviane sank into one of the gold and ivory stools that lined the queen's bed. Her head ached. Marie wanted her to write letters to Robespierre in first person. Not only was this treasonous but it was a scandal that could spark the very revolution she hoped to avoid.

"To what end, my Queen?"

Marie's cheeks were flushed. "Do you not see, Viviane?"

"No, my lady, I fear I do not."

The queen dropped to her knees, alongside her servant and gripped her arm. "To win a fight you must always prey upon your adversary's weaknesses, *non?*"

Viviane thought this through, then nodded. She was distracted by the sight of the queen kneeling at her feet. It was almost as though they were... equals. The sensational thought pleased her. *Is equality so evil?*

"What *is* Robespierre's weakness, Viviane?"

Again, the queen's *dame d'honneur* thought the matter through but this time she only shrugged. "None that I can see. He has a strong following among the common people, he enjoys the support of this Bretons Club, and every decision made by the king appears to be working in his favor."

Marie tightened her grip. "*I* am his weakness. This has always been about him and me—nothing else. He has taken advantage of my husband's political mistakes to destroy *me* because I once rejected him."

"So, if you concede defeat..."

"It will mean that he has triumphed." Marie smiled up at her. "At least in part."

"In part?" Viviane nibbled on her fingernail. "What more could he want?"

The queen's smile faded. "He will still fight to limit our power. He has come too far to draw back now but perhaps, after reading my letter, Robespierre will become more tolerant. If Louis plays his hand well, in time the situation can be defused." She rocked back on her haunches, smiles once again wreathing her face. "Eventually, all will be as it once was."

Viviane's eyes locked with the queen's. "I do not think that power is all he wants."

"You are right." Marie averted her gaze. "In the end, I am the prize. That is the final piece of the puzzle." She pushed herself upright and began pacing again.

"You must be careful with the letters. Write nothing too affectionate at first. More apologetic, I think, expressing his superiority. He will like that. Men like to feel superior. But hint at desire. Tantalize, tantalize, always make him feel that I mean much while saying very little."

Viviane's eyes widened. This was the manipulative monarch at her best. Never would she have imagined that such a devious mind lay beneath the frivolous mask Marie donned each day with practiced ease.

"What is the goal, my Queen?" She bit her lip as she waited for a response. If she was to risk her reputation and possibly her life, she deserved to know why!

Marie stopped her pacing and turned to Viviane. "You will make him think that I wish to belong to him. When the time is right, you will entice him to come to a clandestine meeting with me. And then—"

"And then?"

Marie sucked in a deep breath. "Then I will finish what I began twenty-five years ago."

"You will have him assassinated?"

"I hope to do the deed myself." The icy response caused her servant to shiver.

In the silence that followed, Viviane examined her own soul. They were talking about taking a man's life! A man who belonged to the same social group as herself. *Am I betraying my own kind?*

But there was no way out. Not now. She had agreed to help Marie obtain justice but now, murder was involved, and she was trapped. Her brows knitted together in a frown.

"You find the plan impractical?" Marie sat next to her servant.

"I find it... deceitful." Viviane's hand fluttered to her neck. "And perhaps flawed."

She rounded on the queen, firing questions in an attempt to dissuade her from this dark path. "What if my letters are not sufficient to the task? How do you know that Alexandre will not read the notes that you send? What guarantee do you have that Robespierre will not suspect a plot and if so, why not publish the letters and start a riot that will destroy you?"

Marie-Antoinette sat as though frozen, her dark eyes never leaving Viviane's face.

"I will read your letters and determine if they are sufficient. As to Alexandre reading my letters," Marie laid a delicate finger on her lips, "they will all be sealed. If he does touch them, it will be evident to Robespierre that his friend has tampered with his most private of secrets."

"Pardon my insolence Your Grace." Viviane dipped her head. "Just one more question."

Marie shrugged her bare shoulders. "Ask me anything."

Viviane pulled in and slowly released a deep breath. "Would the letters not be more authentic if they were written by your own hand?"

Marie crossed over to the far window of her *boudoir*. Light streamed in from the outdoors, turning the diamond necklace and earrings into fire.

"I cannot write them," she said flatly. "I despise the man and every blot of the pen would proclaim my abhorrence more loudly than if I shouted it from the rooftops."

She shook her head. "No. If we are to have a chance at success, the letters must come from a woman who dislikes him enough to write cunningly, who fears him enough to appear his inferior."

She turned back to Viviane, her dark eyes flashing like lightning in a summer storm. "I am *not* that woman."

Viviane raised her hands in a pleading gesture. "But if you use your seal you give him leverage against you! What is to prevent him from sharing your notes with all of France, using them to prove that the rumors about you are true?"

Marie stiffened. She had seen the pamphlets that circulated among the masses, suggesting the worst of immoralities.

"I confess that I am responsible for many of the problems that I now face." The queen's face paled. "Austrian sensibilities are much less rigid than those of France. I was bored Viviane!" She flung her hands wide. "I needed parties and, yes, men to keep me entertained in this prison of a castle."

Her eyes misted. "Everything changed when my children arrived. Now, for their sake, I must strengthen the kingdom that my own vices enfeebled. I must risk everything in a pitched battle against the man who incites the people's fury: Robespierre."

"But to affix your seal incriminates you." Viviane grabbed the monarch's elbow, her concern overriding the social barriers between them.

"I must do it." Marie looked away. "Without the seal, he will not believe that the letters are from me."

"But with it he will destroy you!"

"That is a risk that I must take." Marie fingered her diamond necklace. "I must pay the price for my sins."

Silence filled the room. Then the queen spoke again.

"If I know the man at all, he will not publish anything—at least, not until he has everything he wants." Her eyes flitted to Viviane's face to be sure her maid caught her meaning. "When that night comes, he will be dead and our most hideous problem will be no more."

"And how will I find Alexandre?" Viviane knotted then unknotted her fingers. "The palace grounds are enormous; he could be anywhere at any time!"

Marie waved a dismissive hand. "Nothing could be simpler. I will tell Claude, the head gardener, that I have heard this Alexandre has a gift for tending the pomegranate trees. I wish him to tend only the trees in the Orangery until further notice. How long has it been since you have seen him?"

Viviane answered without thinking. "Thirty-one days."

Marie's eyebrows shot upward. "Such a precise number! He must be quite a man to have such an effect. Is he a stunning specimen?"

Viviane turned away, fanning her heated face with her hands. "He wore a mask at the ball. I didn't see his face."

"Hmm, such an impact without even a glimpse of the man?" Marie strolled back into Viviane's line of view. "Well, I would advise that you write and tell him that you'd like to... pick up where you left off before."

"I couldn't—"

The queen held up a finger, cutting off Viviane's scandalized protest. "You can. You want to. You must." Her lips curled in a coy smile. "At Versailles, we do not judge. We know what it is like to be free."

A timid knock on the large doors forestalled the blizzard of questions that swirled in Viviane's mind. Everything made sense, yet nothing made sense. She was being asked to give everything—her body, her heart, perhaps her very life—to protect a woman who had no conception of the appalling realities that lurked on the other side of the gilded entrance to the castle that she called home.

The image of Versailles's golden gate loomed in Viviane's mind. *On what side of that gate do I belong?* She had asked herself the question a thousand times since arriving at the opulent cage occupied by the rich. At first, the glamorous lifestyle had appeared liberating but, as the cost to her peace of mind grew ever higher, she had begun to realize that the freedom of pleasure-mad Versailles was only an illusion.

"Enter." Marie turned toward the door.

The door of ivory inlaid with swirling patterns of gold, swung open and the tousled head of Louis-Joseph, seven-year-old heir to the throne of France peeked in.

"*Maman! Mam—*" A fit of harsh, throaty coughs cut off his delighted squeal. The boy was followed by his nurse, Geneviève Poitrine.

Marie rushed over to her son. "What is wrong, *mon petit chou?*"

"I fear the worst, my Queen," Geneviève said. She was about the same age as Marie but her dark eyes concealed more emotion than they revealed. Her stocky build and pale, angular face reminded Viviane of a hawk: proud, fierce and unforgiving.

Geneviève raised fearful eyes to the queen's. "His skin has become so pale that I fear—"

"What?" Marie interrupted, her voice shrill. "What is it?"

"I fear the consumption has returned."

Silence filled the room—a silence soon broken by a renewed fit of violent coughs from the young prince's lungs. This time when he looked up at his mother, his fingers and the corners of his mouth were tinged with bright red blood.

"Maman?" His thin voice barely reached Viviane's ears.

Marie gripped her son and began to rock him in her arms. "Yes, my son?" She kissed the thin hair that dangled to his shoulders.

"Am I going to die, maman?"

A spasm wracked Marie's face. "No, my son." She kissed the top of his head again and clutched him to her breast. "*Maman* will not let you will die."

She glared at Geneviève. "How long has he been in this state?"

The woman shrugged. "A little more than a day. I would have notified you sooner, but I thought it best to wait until things were a little more certain. It began shortly after he received the gift from the Duke of Valence."

"What gift?" Marie growled the words.

Geneviève took a step back. "Why, I thought surely you knew, Majesty."

"What... gift?" The queen eyes bored holes into the servant's skull.

"Why, the wooden horse, Your Grace." Geneviève's face grew pale. "It was wrapped in a curious, dirty blanket. I thought it was to be a joke of sorts: a horse blanket for a wooden horse but I noticed that shortly after the child opened the gift, he began to show signs of a relapse. I had it burnt just in case it somehow carried the disease. Then the coughing began and—"

"Oh, my son!" Marie's shriek cut her off. "My son!"

"Send for my husband at once." Her eyes screamed for help and Viviane rushed from the room in search of the king's valet.

⚜

Marie rocked back and forth holding a semi-lucid child in her arms. She glanced at Geneviève and held out her hand, in need of some form of human comfort. The nurse squeezed hard.

"My son." Tears streamed down her face as her heart fragmented into a thousand tiny slivers of relentless pain. "I swear to you that if there is any treachery, those involved will pay with their lives!"

"I am sorry, Your Grace." Geneviève hung her head. "No matter what happens, know that you always have my full devotion."

"Thank you." The queen pressed her servant's hand to her lips. "Thank you."

⚜

Louis XVI, King of France and Navarre, cradled his son in his arms, trying to ward off the unstoppable hand of death. He had rushed into his wife's *boudoir*, followed by the court physician and several of his advisors. A small crowd of about fifteen people stood at a loss, trying to comprehend this latest assault on the House of Bourbon.

The physician's statement confirmed that the child was dying of consumption and all suspicion was cast at the door of Philippe de Valence. Heartbreaking coughs wracked Louis's frail body which was already ragged from a lifelong struggle for health.

"Papa?" The child reached up to touch his father's sagging cheek. His mouth had been covered by a silken scarf to reduce the chance of spreading the contagion, but his father pushed it to one side.

"My son?" Louis blinked away tears, determined that his son's last memory of his father be the strong ruler Louis wished he had been. *If I had crushed Valence years ago, my son would not now lay dying.*

"Forgive Phippy." *Phippy.* It was the child's pet name for his favorite uncle.

The king's voice broke. "Forgive *him*?"

How could his son ask him to pardon the man responsible for his own death? Philippe knew that the *dauphin's* health had always been frail. He had barely survived the first attack of consumption a few years earlier. To deliberately expose him to the disease was tantamount to murder.

The child gave a weak nod. "It is not his fault." He closed his eyes, his chest barely moving. A sudden motion made Louis glance upward. Marie's arms were now folded across her chest. Her head was tilted to one side and a murderous gleam burned in her eyes. She had chosen to wear all black today—a coincidence he was sure—but the somber clothing served to emphasize the darkness that was ripping out the few remaining shards of light from their lives.

"We should talk, husband." Bitterness laced each syllable.

Talk? Louis twisted his wedding band that encircled a pudgy finger. *The one thing we never do. Talk about what? The rumors of your affairs? The fact that I have failed as a king? Our son who lies dying in my arms? Talk! Whatever can we talk about now?* He nodded stiffly, rose to his feet and placed his son into Geneviève's arms. The nurse slid one hand out from under the boy to replace the handkerchief over Louis's mouth.

The king cleared his throat and glanced at the servants and courtiers that had gathered in the room.

"Would you all, please..." He struggled to put the words together. "My wife and I would... appreciate it if you would, ahem, step outside, please."

A short-lived silence followed this request, but it was soon broken by Monsieur Necker, the king's Minister of Finance.

"Your Majesty, if the *dauphin* is indeed dying then now would be the time to discuss the succession—"

"Leave us!" Marie-Antoinette stormed forward, her eyes flashing. "Your king has spoken. You may await our pleasure in the Hall of Nobles. Geneviève, return our son to his chambers."

The room began to empty.

"Madame de Lussan, you will remain with us." Marie's toe tapped a staccato rhythm as she waited. Vivian hurried to close the doors behind the courtiers then waited in silence.

Marie closed the gap between herself and her husband in choppy strides.

"You are not thinking of letting him go unpunished, Louis?"

"My dear." The king averted his eyes from his wife's protruding orbs. "You heard the boy. He wants me to forgive Phippy."

"Phippy?" Marie screeched. "He is your enemy! He is the man who has murdered our son and wants nothing more than to take that royal crown from your head and place it on his own."

Louis shifted his feet. He did not wish to dishonor his son's dying request but neither did he wish to alienate his wife. "We have no concrete proof that Philippe was behind this, Marie."

The queen held up a piece of paper. "Geneviève found *this* on the package."

He glanced at the note. His heart plummeted as he recognized Philippe's seal. Louis had always mistrusted his cousin, recognizing him as the one man who could replace his family line should a sudden misfortune befall him and his heirs. It had taken over eight years for Louis's first child to arrive, and that child had been a girl whose sex prohibited her from inheriting the throne. Three other children had followed, but only Louis-Joseph and his brother could perpetuate their father's lineage.

King Louis grimaced, a bitter taste in his mouth. He dropped onto the bed and the jowls of his cheeks trembled. "You do realize that a large portion of the population admires Philippe." He shook his head. "Many of the commoners would rather see him on the throne than myself."

Marie stamped her foot. "That is because all commoners are fools!"

Louis glanced from Viviane to his wife. "You may want to curb your tongue." Marie colored but did not apologize.

Louis heaved himself back to his feet, groaning as his weight crashed down on his knees. "If we publicly accuse Philippe of murdering our son, it is possible that the populace will seize upon our internal feuding and start a revolution."

Marie grabbed her husband's jeweled hand. "To allow a murderer to remain unpunished is to allow him to attack again. Take definitive action against him, my lord. For once, show yourself to be a man and act like a king!"

He jerked free of her touch. "What do you think I have been doing?" His shout filled the room. "What have I been doing all these years but acting out the part of a king?" He made a sweeping gesture. "Do you think I wanted any of this?"

"What would your great-grandfather, the Sun King, have done?" Marie pulled her lips back and bared her teeth. "I will tell you. He would have had his entire army combing through France, turning over every rock looking for the butcher. When found, Philippe would have his hands hacked off, his back and limbs broken then be left on the breaking wheel until it pleased God to end his miserable life!"

She jabbed her finger against his bloated chest. "But you my corpulent husband? You sit here, whimpering like a child while *Phippy* plots to exterminate your seed!" She spun away from him, arms folded across her chest.

Silence reigned in the room for a long moment. Then Louis dragged himself over to his irate wife and knelt at her feet.

"You are right." His tears ran down his red face. "I am not the man he was. I never wanted to be king. I never wanted this to happen!"

Marie turned her head and refused to look at him. "But you *are* king. And now you need to play the part. Find your enemy and bring him back in chains."

He looked up, lips trembling, and touched her hand. "I will do it. For our son, I will do it."

She looked down at him, placed her hands on his head and readjusted his curly, powdered wig. "Not only for our son's sake, but for yourself... and for me."

After her husband had left the room, Marie-Antoinette approached Viviane.

"That, my dear," her voice was cold and unemotional, "is how you deal with a man."

Viviane's mouth went dry. "Forgive me, *Altesse,* but are you saying that your actions... your words—they were all an act?"

If Marie can so completely twist her husband's emotions and bend him to her will, what else is she capable of doing? "But your voice, your anger, your tears! It all seemed so sincere!"

Her mistress smiled but no humor reached her eyes. "Believe me, my tears and anger were quite real. My son is dying. That is real. My enemies are multiplying. That is also real. If we fail to stop both Philippe and Robespierre, I will die. And that will be very, very real."

She studied Viviane, brows knit together. "It was a lesson for Louis. And for you." The queen ran trembling fingers over her black dress. "Philippe must be brought to justice. Robespierre must be destroyed. You are my only link to Robespierre, so you must convince your gardener that you love him even if everything you do is nothing more than an act."

"Majesty, I must say that I find it hard to believe that the Duke of Valence is responsible. Even with the note it seems—"

"Impossible?" Marie's nostrils flared. "Incongruous with his character?" A mutilated laugh escaped her slender throat. "Believe me I know."

She rubbed her hands together briskly as though the summer air held the chill of winter. "But you must know, Viviane, that at court, day is night and darkness is light. The cardinal rule of Versailles is that nothing is as it seems. We are all actors here."

Marie looked away. "Do it, Viviane. Do whatever it takes."

⚜

Louis-Joseph Xavier François, heir to the throne, died three days later and was buried in a private ceremony. Throughout the country, church bells pealed the news that the child-prince had been called to heaven. The announcement was received with sadness by some but with joy by others who claimed that God had stricken down the seed of the "tyrant king and his queen, Madame Deficit."

They claimed it was a clear sign that the monarchy was no longer the voice of God to France. A few days later, the political infighting that had stagnated meeting of the Estates General came to a head as the Third Estate, which now met in an abandoned indoor tennis court, swore to never disband until they had formed a new constitution for France.

Viviane, who lay sleepless in her bed, heard the mournful peals of the bells as well as the whispers that floated around Versailles. *On which side do I belong?* She could not identify with the rich who played games with human lives as though they were pawns on a chessboard, but neither could she join with those that wished ill on a family who fought to maintain their way of life.

Philippe. Alexandre. Marie. Gabrielle. Robespierre.

"In the end, we all wear a mask." Viviane whispered the words as she stared at the darkened ceiling of her room. "Perhaps we ourselves do not know what is hidden behind it until we are somehow forced to come face-to-face with who we really are."

Could she win Alexandre's trust and contrive a meeting with Robespierre to lead him into a trap that would cost his life? Her breath escaped in a deep sigh. A deadly web surrounded her. *But am I the spider or am I the prey?*

Neither prospect appealed to her. The question haunted her until, at last, she drifted into the arms of sleep.

Part Two

Chapter Eleven

June 1789. Lussan, France

Philippe de Valence slowed his chestnut Cheval de Mérens to a walk as he crested a hill and glimpsed the village of Lussan below. It had taken him the better part of a week to reach the small community that was hidden in the Languedoc-Roussillon region of southern France but, as he soaked in the sun-kissed smattering of houses that adjoined acres of fertile farmland, anticipation swelled within him. A cluster of pale houses and a gleaming church spire were surrounded by a medieval wall that separated the village from the expansive flat fields in which spring wheat already sprouted.

"Well done, boy." He patted the horse's long neck. He had left his own white stallion at Versailles. His mission would be better served if he did not draw attention to himself. *As if that were possible.*

He shook his head as he descended the hill and approached an opening in the enclave. Any stranger in this small town was sure to attract notice but Philippe had taken several steps to avoid minimize the impact he would undoubtedly cause.

He had stuffed his luxurious white cloak into his saddlebag, and instead wore a faded brown tunic and muddy leather boots. Besides his cloak, the only valuable he carried was the signet ring of the House of Valence which was buried in the money pouch that hung from his belt. He wanted to be unrecognizable. He could not understand these people as a prince, but if he became one of them...

The steady *thump* of his horse's hooves on the village's dirt streets could not expel Viviane's words from his mind. *You are too far above me to understand me!* But he wanted to understand her. He was consumed by the desire to see life as she saw it.

What is it like to have nothing? He, who had been surrounded by luxury from birth, had no idea. She knew the stark feeling of utter despair while he did not. Her words had sparked a desire to become as she was, to understand her way of thinking. Perhaps then he would be better able to win her love.

Philippe had told no one of his plan and had left without much notice. He had simply ordered his steward to pack some dried food and about three hundred *livres* while he prepared a horse, stuffed his cloak and ring into a saddlebag and changed his clothes. Louis would never have understood his motives and Viviane also would have balked at the idea. *If she would even talk to me.*

He sighed. When Viviane had left him at the tree, it was as though a part of his soul walked away from him. That moment confirmed he loved her as he would never love anyone else. The thought of an existence without her emptied his life of meaning. *But how to convince her of the truth?*

Viviane had nothing by which to gauge the sincerity of his feelings. What prince had ever married a commoner? It was the stuff of fairy tales, not the real world! She would therefore naturally conclude that he wanted to degrade her with what seemed to be an impossible relationship. The loose, wagging tongues of the court gossips would never believe that he genuinely loved this girl from a place that few people even knew existed. Whispers behind flitting fans, nods and winks would create an atmosphere of shame that she would not survive.

Armed with that understanding, Philippe had chosen to wage war on the gulf that separated them. But before he could win her heart, he needed to understand her mind. She had said that her mother was a laundress. He sniffed his armpits and wrinkled his nose. After six days in the saddle, a trip to the laundress was definitely in order.

⚜

Ariadné groaned as she straightened up from over her washtub and squinted at the sun. Noon. The time that everyone in Lussan stopped their menial chores and took their midday meal. *Everyone but me.* She would forgo lunch as she often did, squelching the pangs of hunger with a cup of water and a tightly wound belt until evening, in hopes that her meager food supply would last a little longer.

Ariadné tossed a gray, threadbare shirt against the ribs of the washboard. *Schlop.* The cloth hit the wooden frame that housed the washboard with a sickening slap. She dried her hands on the grimy apron that covered her worn body, catching sight of callouses and bloodied knuckles that gave mute testimony to her hardworking nature.

Like her hands, Ariadné had been altered by life's cruel demands. The past thirty years had transformed her from a gentle wife and mother to a calloused widow and breadwinner. The change had not come easily, but Gilbert had often remarked that she possessed the inner strength of a lioness.

A faint smile flitted across her face as she thought of her late husband. The smile faded when she glanced at the wooden shelf that rose from the frame, encasing the washboard. Ariadné had asked Maurice, the village carpenter, to build the structure when it had become apparent that both she and her daughter, Viviane, would have to find some way to survive without a man.

She could have remarried—indeed it would have been wiser—but Gilbert had been the love of her life. No other man could stand in his shadow at high noon. Even after thirty years of widowhood, the thought of being in another man's arms was like the sound made by the soaking shirt she had just tossed aside: it was sickening.

She shoved aside a cackling hen and peered into the water, catching a glimpse of her reflection. The few mirrors that their small estate once contained had been sold early in the ongoing war to keep her home as mounting taxes continued to plague the widow and her young daughter. Three decades later, water was still the only way she could keep abreast of the ravaging effects that time and hard labor had wrought upon her body.

Dark eyes, still haunted by grief, peered out from hooded lids grown thick and puffy from constant lack of sleep. Her silver-streaked hair, once a long mane of smooth chocolate Gilbert loved to wrap around his fingers, was now stuffed in a tangled bun atop her head. Ariadné dashed some water upon her face, feeling the cool liquid sinking into the wrinkles that financial pressures had carved into her skin with a relentless knife of worry.

"Madame de Lussan?"

Her sagging shoulders slumped still further at the sound of that voice. Ariadné did not need to turn around to know that Victor leCupide stood at the wooden gate at the far end of the courtyard. But then her spine stiffened. She would not allow this man to see one ounce of weakness. *Not while I'm still alive.*

Ariadné turned and faced him, a calm smile plastered on her lips.

"Ah, Monsieur *leCupide*, you're earlier than expected!" She moved toward him, fists placed squarely on each of her wide hips.

"Ahem, uh, *oui*." The tax collector rubbed the back of his neck.

What had brought the weasel to her door? Another new tax that the king had invented, no doubt. A rooster pecked at a beetle near her feet. If he pushed her too hard today, she would pick it up and throw it at him!

"Ahem, in fact, Madame, it is not I who am early but you who are late." Victor's voice came out as a squeak instead of its normal bass.

"Late?" Ariadné's heart plummeted to her stomach at the direction this conversation seemed to be taking. She feigned ignorance and arched a thick eyebrow.

Victor retreated a step for each one that she moved forward. "Yes, you are late. Again."

His chest swelled as he glanced around at the property. Her lands, which abutted his own, contained large tracts of untilled pasture. In the proper hands, they promised to deliver vast amounts of wealth to the owner. On her own, she was unable to put the land to good use. Perhaps that was why Victor stood, drooling over her property like a dog after a bone.

Was he fool enough to think that she would sell it to him? She pulled herself up straight. Not while she still had two hands and a washtub! She snuck a look at her rooster. It had moved a little closer.

"What does this mean?" Ariadné's smile was gone, replaced by a red flush that glowed in her cheeks.

Now it was Victor who smiled. "It means that you are critically in arrears and your property will be given to the crown in thirty days."

Utter silence filled the courtyard. Even the hens stopped their clucking.

Ariadné went numb. It was as though a thick fog had descended upon her mind, momentarily sheltering her emotions from an unexpected violent assault. Then, one by one, his words penetrated the shield, sinking into her mind with agonizing clarity.

"My property? Given to the crown?" She mouthed the words, speaking slowly as if giving him time to deny them. *Thirty years of fighting... wasted!*

"It is unfortunate, Madame, but—"

"Given to the crown." It was not a question but a statement. The anger that had bubbled beneath the surface of tranquility now erupted with volcanic force.

"I have slaved for *thirty* years, scrubbin' shirts with my own two hands and you mean to take it all away?" She raised her voice and held up bronzed hands that were covered with tough callouses. Her shock had evaporated, leaving a blinding rage that consumed her. Her brow furrowed and every muscle in her body was taut with fury.

Victor licked his lips. "*Du calme,* Madame." He waggled a pudgy finger in her face. "You have not met your financial obligation. How can you expect the king to protect our glorious country if every citizen does not do his duty?"

"Don't talk to me about being calm, you overstuffed cow!" Ariadné's breathing became heavy as she took a threatening step toward the heavyset tax collector. "I paid the ridiculous property tax—"

"It was late, incurring fees." Victor lifted his index finger once again.

Ariadné ignored him. "Then I paid the individual tax—"

"Late, meaning more fees."

"But they were paid! After thirty years of fightin' to keep my home do you honestly think that I am goin' to let *you* take it away?"

"Madame de Lussan." Victor struggled to reach the small button that held the two flaps of his vest together below his swelling belly. Finally succeeding, he pulled a thin, small red notebook from his inner pocket. The tax collector had a slip of paper already in place to mark the page he wanted.

"Madame de Lussan," he repeated, opening the book. "You have been consistently late in all of your taxes resulting in an enormous amount of debt."

"I—"

Victor lifted a hand, forestalling the coming protests. "In addition to being late, this year you have forgotten to pay the salt tax, the tobacco tax—required even though you do not smoke—the consumption tax and," he paused and raked his free hand through the few strands of graying hair that remained upon his balding head, "you have neglected the income tax. Five percent of all your profits from this… laundry affair you run."

Victor wrinkled his nose as if dirty laundry was offensive.

Ariadné trembled as she struggled to hold on to the last shreds of her self-control.

"Why am I about to lose my home?" She spat the words out as she ground her molars together.

Victor flashed a smile, baring yellowed teeth. "Because, as we speak, you owe the king a total of three hundred pieces of silver."

"But that's… that's impossible." She gasped. "Three hundred!"

"I assure you Madame that it is quite possible." Victor grimaced. "And, while it grieves me to say it, my books never lie."

"Your books?" Ariadné's voice broke. "You expect me to believe a *book?* I'm a human not a book!"

Her eyes widened. "Your books say what you write in them. You are not showin' what I have paid, and the crown thinks that I've not been payin' what I owe!" She pointed a finger at the man whose greasy presence she loathed.

Victor sent her a pained look. "You accuse me of dishonesty? I assure you that everything in these books is fully accurate. Besides, it makes no difference what you believe, only what I report. The Chamber of Accounts in Paris does not take into consideration the wild accusations of angry peasant women!"

"I will never leave my home." She folded her arms across her chest and planted her feet shoulder width apart.

Victor pursed his lips, then folded his red notebook and placed it back in his vest pocket. "There may be a way to save your lands." He rubbed his thumb and forefingers together.

"How?"

"Marry me." He said the words without preamble as though discussing a matter of business. "Marry me and I will settle all your debts. Your lands and mine will be joined together, which is only natural since we are neighbors, and I will even allow you to remain in your own home."

"Marry me," he said again, "and all of your problems will be solved. If you do not, your property will be confiscated by the king's agents."

Ariàdné saw black. Her last thread of self-control snapped when the final syllable slithered out of his mouth.

"You pathetic monster!" She grabbed the rooster and launched the animal at the tax collector's face.

Victor reached out to deflect the flying object but he mistimed the motion and, instead of warding it off, he caught the squawking bundle of feathers which immediately began to shred his face.

"*Aie!*" The tax collector screamed. "Get it off me!"

He jumped back and stumbled as he released the angry bird. The rooster leapt upon the man, who lay prone in the mud, and began jabbing violently at his eyes.

A wail of agony rose from the ground as the bird's three-inch spurs ripped into Victor's cheeks. "Off, off!" He shoved the bird aside and staggered to his feet, blood streaming from deep gashes in his cheeks and jawline.

"Pompous roach!" Ariàdné shrieked as she grabbed her washboard and slammed it into his expansive gut.

"Oof!" Victor reeled backward as the air was forcibly expelled from his lungs.

He stumbled as he moved his bulky form with surprising speed toward the wooden gate, his heels still under attack by the pursuing rooster. "I'll see you destroyed Ariàdné! You and your *chicken!*" He shrieked as the rooster's beak dug into his bloodied heel.

"Never, you bloated old goat!" Ariadné's screech bounced off the fleeing man's back. "And in case my *rooster* didn't tell you, the answer to your proposal is *no!*"

She glared after him until the man's gray-coated back became a speck in the distance and then sank to her knees. The rooster crowed with all his might and swaggered back to his hens. While he squawked his triumph, his mistress lay with her graying head tucked between her legs, feeling the stinging pain of defeat.

"Oh God, why?" Ariadné's voice was muffled by the grains of soil that she and Gilbert had called their own for over forty years. She would not cry. Years of hardship had long sucked the last tears from her eyes.

"Thirty years of fighting only to lose now to that crooked beast of a man?" She slammed her fist against the hard ground. "Oh Gilbert, what will happen to me? To Viviane?"

"Excuse me."

For a moment, Ariadné thought that her nemesis had returned, and her fingers twitched as they reached for her washboard. But, as she raised her head, she realized that this voice was not Victor's. It was gentler... kinder. She squinted upward. The noonday sun drew a halo around the man's head. He appeared to notice her discomfort and led his horse around her in a half-circle so that the sun was in *his* eyes and not hers.

Ariadné rose to her feet, brushing off the dusty cuffs of her faded *chemisier*. "Who are you?" She glared at him through narrowed eyes.

The stranger's bearded face appeared to suppress a grin but he bowed to her.

"I am Philippe."

"Philippe is a common name in these parts." She waited for a surname but he offered nothing more. The tense muscles in Ariadné's shoulders loosened somewhat. She tilted her head as she considered this intruder. He did not *appear* threatening. "What do you want?"

Philippe glanced over his shoulder at the stone cottage whose crumbling façade still maintained an echo of its refined elegance. Ivy was rampant in the cracks of the gray, weather-beaten stone and beyond the dilapidated fence lay fields that were overgrown with weeds.

"Well?" She looked at him expectantly.

"I would like a place to stay, Madame..."

"Ariadné."

"Ah!" Philippe's eyes twinkled again. "The legends of antiquity depict Ariadné, lover of the hero Theseus, as a strong woman. Based upon the man that I saw run screaming past me, I am persuaded that you have more in common with the Ariadné of legend than your name."

She stared at him, nonplussed. What *was* he babbling about? Legends? Antiquity? The man made no sense!

"Who are you and what do you want?" Her right foot rapped several times against the floor. "Spit it out and be done."

"Um, yes." He patted his horses' neck. "I am a traveler who plans to spend a few weeks in Lussan. In the village, I asked for the location of an inn—"

Ariadné's laugh brought him up short. "There's no inn in Lussan, I can tell you that! Most folks are tryin' to get out, not the reverse."

Philippe smiled. "That is what I was told. Someone mentioned that the only laundress in town might have some space for rent."

Her gaze sharpened. "Show me your hands." She stepped toward him. Philippe held them out for her inspection.

"Hmm..." The woman examined his palms. "Looks like you've never worked at all in your life."

Philippe inclined his head to one side. "Manual labor is not the only honest trade.

She looked him up and down with furrowed brows. "You're not a tax collector, are you?"

"No, I am not."

"Some agent of the king out to rob an honest widow blind so he can give more money to that brat of a queen?"

He shook his head. "I can pay."

Ariadné was about to speak but stopped at his words. She pressed her mouth into a thin line and mulled the idea over, torn between giving lodging to a stranger and the ongoing plague of financial worry.

Finally, she nodded. "Alright, I'll do it. Room and board for twenty *sous* a night but you'll have to stay in the barn... with the rooster." She nodded toward a rickety wooden structure whose bowed roof appeared ready to collapse at the next strong gust of wind.

"'Tisn't proper for an unmarried woman to have a strange man stay in her home, even if I am old enough to be your mother!" Her laugh was coarse and hollow.

"Do you have any children?" Philippe clucked at his horse and began leading it to the barn.

"One." Ariadné trudged along at his side. "A daughter named Viviane. She's away in Paris with her cousin." The deep crease in her brow smoothed out at the mention of her daughter's name.

"You have much confidence in her." He glanced at her sidelong.

Ariadné rounded on him. "That girl could be the queen of the world if she set her mind to it!" She gave a firm nod. "Thinks for herself, she does."

Philippe smiled. "Some traits must be hereditary."

They had reached the barn, a derelict gray structure made of rotting wood and cracked stone. "It's not much but it'll keep you dry." Ariadné cackled in wicked delight. "If it doesn't rain."

She put her hands on the twin doors and pulled hard. The groaning hinges yielded to her strength and a cloud of dancing dust motes swirled into the sunlit air. Philippe doubled over, gagging at the pungent odor of manure and rotting hay.

"Ah... home sweet home." Ariadné inhaled deeply, held her breath, then released it with a contented sigh. "Don't worry, you'll get used to the smell." She glanced down at the prone man in pity. "Definitely not a farm boy. What are you, a lawyer?"

Philippe straightened up slowly "One could say that I am a visionary... a leader of sorts." He made a choking sound in his throat.

Ariadné's eyes narrowed. "A man who talks like a king but dresses like a commoner." She shook her head. "I don't know who you are or what you're doin' and if it weren't for the fact that I'm a bit short on money, I wouldn't take you in."

She stepped closer, putting her face inches from his chin. "But let me set somethin' straight. I might be only an old widow, but I'll not be takin' any nonsense, money or no money. *Comprends-tu?*"

Philippe's eyes watered and he gasped. "Yes, I understand." Ariadné nodded once then thrust her hand forward. "Payment in advance."

Philippe's hand dropped down to his waist where his money pouch dangled. He jerked the drawstring, feeling the pressure in his chest grow greater with every passing second. He pulled out the first coin that slid between his fingers and placed it into Ariadné's hands. She froze as a silver *livre* glimmered up at her. It was the most money she had ever seen, let alone held. Her eyes flew to Philippe's purpling face.

"I-I can't accept this. It's too much!"

Philippe held up four fingers. "Four weeks." The words were barely a whisper. He spun around and rushed to where his horse waited outside, patiently flicking away flies. Ariadné heard him gulping down the clean air but she continued to stare at the coin. It would easily pay for two months of room and board at an inn of quality, but the stranger had handed it over without a moment's hesitation!

She shook her head, clearing her thoughts, and hurriedly pocketed the coin. *Never question a blessin.'*

Her crusty exterior reasserted itself and she bustled by the still-recovering Philippe. She had piles of laundry to do before dusk and could waste no more time with this strange but well-spoken man. "Dinner is at sunset. I hope you like moldy bread and water 'cause that's what's on the menu!"

⚜

Philippe straightened and laid his hand across the back of his horse. *If only Louis could see this place. This is how real people—his people—live.* He had overheard enough of the conversation with the tax collector to recognize that Ariadné was in serious financial trouble. Three hundred pieces of silver. That was the cost to redeem her fallen estate. It was a price that the villainous tax collector knew she could never pay.

Abuse, hopelessness and corruption fanned the flames of resentment that burned in the hearts of France's poor. Now, the one remaining hope of this widow was about to be snatched from her because she refused to yield to the demands of a tax collector who was more beast than man.

His eyes wandered over to where Ariadné battled with her pile of laundry. Stubby arms thumped and smacked soiled linen into obedience just as they had for three decades. His admiration for the woman's fortitude grew with each passing moment. *Three hundred pieces of silver.* The sum was nothing to him but to a woman who *had* nothing, the redemption price was unattainable.

He felt something scratching at his leg and he glanced downward. Glaring up at him with beady eyes was the rooster that had proved a critical ally in the fight against tyranny. Its red cockscomb jangled below its neck as it assessed this newcomer from different angles.

Philippe smiled at the protective bird who, apparently satisfied, meandered off to his hens. Philippe then turned back to face the barn and stepped back into the semi-dark interior. He inhaled and held his breath, imitating Ariadné, and then released it. After a few seconds, he did it again. *You are too far above me to understand me.*

This was where Viviane had lived; the barn where she had no doubt played. If this was what condescension meant, then he would gladly do it. He led his horse deep inside the shelter, sending chittering mice scurrying for cover with every step. Philippe unsaddled his horse and pulled the half-gate shut behind him. He then found some dry straw and lumped it together to form a sort of bed for himself in another stall.

"Dry if it doesn't rain?"

He repeated Ariadné's words as he threw a few handfuls of the hay to his horse then grimaced as he cast a doubtful glance at the sagging roof. There were some parts of peasant life he'd be willing to forgo.

Chapter Twelve

June 1789. Château de Versailles

Viviane draped a scarlet shawl over her hair and wrapped its length around her bare shoulders. A chill that gripped her from within made her shiver despite the warm evening air. The sun slipped below the horizon as she descended the broad staircase called the Hundred Steps and made her way toward the Orangery where Alexandre waited.

Fire rose in her cheeks as she thought about the suggestive words in the note she had penned. *I want to pick up where we left off before.* The words had been the queen's, but the passion behind it was her own.

Was this what Maman intended when she sent me here to make a better life? The question, rising like an unwelcome ghost, gave her pause. Loyalty to her mistress and her own attraction to Alexandre battled against the very essence of what she knew to be right.

No. Maman would not approve. But did she have to do what her mother wished? Did she not have a right to choose her own path? She was tired of playing the game of life by everyone else's rules. Gabrielle. Marie-Antoinette. Philippe. Even her mother. *It is my life.* The spark of rebellion, nourished by her own will, burst into an open flame.

Alexandre. He drew her with a seductive allure that appealed to the darkest corners of her imagination. She had never seen his face unmasked, but his charm eclipsed that of Philippe, making the prince appear rather plain.

Philippe. Her shoulders slumped. *My wealth is not measured in gold and diamonds but in faith and truth.* She had tried and failed to drive the phrase from her mind. While he did not have Alexandre's appeal, Philippe's words touched her spirit and illuminated her mind.

Viviane clenched her jaw. Philippe was lying—there could be no other explanation. How could any man who valued truth more than gold pretend to love her only to satisfy his wounded pride? How could a man of faith sanction the murder of an innocent child? Of his own flesh and blood?

Unless, of course, he is telling the truth. But that was impossible. She had already explored that road; it led to a dead end. Even if Philippe truly loved her, even *if* he somehow could look past the lowliness of her station, Louis would never permit his cousin to marry a *bourgeoise*. Not only would it break centuries of tradition and consign Versailles to yet another political fiasco, but the public would interpret it as a sign that the struggling monarchy was on the verge of collapse!

Philippe is a liar and a murderer. There was no other possibility. She hardened her heart against him. *Focus.*

The soft glow of the moonlight reflecting off the gushing fountain before the Bride Tree caught her eye, and all thoughts of the Duke of Valence vanished as quickly as they had come.

She hesitated. *Why am I doing this?* She smoothed the folds of her dress. *I am not going because I must.* She closed her eyes, took a deep breath and released it. *I am going because...*

The truth screamed at her and Viviane knew that to deny this reality would be to lie to herself. She was going to Alexandre because this was what *she* wanted.

Her pulse quickened. Waiting underneath that tree was a man whose touch made her mind swim and whose scent turned her blood into fire. Viviane dropped her defenses as a rush of exhilaration made her spine tingle. One evening with this man had been enough to make her long to surrender to her darkest desires. His dark charisma, his raw strength, his exhilarating abandon for propriety touched an earthy part of her spirit that every part of her body wanted to celebrate.

There! She saw him, leaning casually against the flower-laden branches of the white pomegranate. A gasp escaped her lips as she caught sight of his face for the first time. His eyes spoke of hidden mysteries, his mouth promised passion. The sight of him made every remaining inhibition melt like wax before a flame.

The chill that had surrounded her all evening disappeared as heat spread throughout her body. She slipped the shawl off her shoulders, then let it drop from her outstretched hand onto the stones. Nothing could have prepared her for this moment.

She watched his eyes roam over her body and felt a flush of pleasure as he drank in the sight of the white gown that clung to her figure. Her lips parted, her breath came in short bursts, and each step that she took forward seemed too hurried... yet not fast enough.

Three thoughts exploded simultaneously in her mind. *At Versailles, pleasure is the only rule. I will do whatever it takes. This is my life.*

"Yes." The hoarse whisper echoed the change in her thinking. No longer was she the prudish country girl who was willing to forgo pleasure for rules. She was an independent woman with the right to decide her own fate. She was drawn to the dark mystery of the man whose gaze locked on hers with an intensity she could feel even from this distance. She wanted the flames that burned within her to consume them both. She wanted *him*.

He stepped out from the overhang of branches, hand extended, and she ran the final few steps, halting an arm's length away, chest heaving. Desire made her tremble as she placed her small palm in his. At that moment, everything but him faded from her sight. The illuminated palace, the empty courtyard, time itself vanished beneath the swirling darkness that sprang from the man whose touch unhinged her world.

She parted her lips a little wider but, before she could speak, Alexandre closed the small distance between them. His mouth hovered over her own, waiting for her permission, and Viviane could resist no longer. She pressed her lips against his.

They parted, and he led her through a small door into the heart of the Orangery itself. They were alone but, even if multitudes had been present, she would have noticed only one man. It was her first time in the sumptuous indoor garden, but she had no eyes for the miniature torches that cast a sensual glow around its interior. She did not hear the music of the fountains or smell the heady scent of roses in bloom.

She could only see Alexandre who led her to a secluded divan, nestled in the embrace of a trinity of verdant bushes. His eyes locked onto her own, seeking her answer to an unspoken question.

Her heart tumbled.

Her mind reeled.

Her legs turned to water.

Viviane leaned into his arms and breathed one word. It was all she could say. It was all that she wanted to say. Once it left her lips, nothing would ever be the same.

"Yes."

⚜

Flickering candles cast long shadows against the walls of Madame L'Orage's cellar. The twisted images made Salomé think of writhing demons on a mission to snatch up human souls. Outside, the sun was now setting but here darkness held absolute sway.

Her lip curled in a snarl. Perhaps the devil had snatched her soul. Maybe that was why she could think of nothing else but her love for Alexandre and her rabid hatred for Viviane de Lussan.

Salomé switched her gaze to the rough circle of twenty women that surrounded her. They were mostly her age but a few were older. Some had holes in their mouths from sores caused by malnutrition while others exposed blackened gums when they smiled. None but her had all their teeth—food shortages had seen to that.

Salomé knew that she kept her teeth because she had chosen a lifestyle that many of these women, mostly married with children, refused to accept. These were the women who feared her more than they did consumption. These were the women who shunned her as they passed her by on the street, heckling their husbands to give her a wide berth.

In ordinary times, her presence would not be at all welcome. But these were not ordinary times. These were times of revolution; times where women broke the barriers of social divisions to unite around a cause that affected them all.

Salomé had begun spreading the word only an hour ago, going from house to house in the district where she had lived and worked. She had announced that a secret meeting for only the bravest of women would take place in the cellar of Madame L'Orage at dusk. The place was appropriate as L'Orage was an outspoken advocate of revolution. Now, twenty of the district's maidens, wives and mothers were waiting for *her*, the outcast, to speak. An unexpected thrill of anticipation shot through her.

"You called us together, my dear?" Madame L'Orage squinted at her.

Salomé thought the woman was probably the oldest of them all. She had seen the abrupt end of Louis XV's totalitarian reign and the unexpected rise to power of his grandson, Louis XVI. A few decades earlier, neither this old crone nor her friends could have predicted that the shy, indecisive Louis would have inherited the throne of his ancestors. When his father and older brother both died unexpectedly, the reluctant prince had been forced to step into the role of king.

She drew a sharp breath and collected her thoughts. The outcome of the next few moments could well determine the future of Paris. It could also determine the outcome of the unseen battle between herself and Viviane over the heart of Alexandre.

"Women of Paris." Her voice was soft. So soft that the women who sat furthest from her leaned forward on the rough cinderblocks, straining to hear. "I am Salomé, the woman who first shed blood in pursuit of justice."

Heads began to nod. Her exploits on the night of her brother's death had made her a legend. That was why they had come. They knew that, where others might talk, *she* would act.

"We all know the problem." Salomé raised her voice. "There is no hope, our loved ones are dyin' in our arms and no one is doin' anythin' about it."

Heads bobbed but their eyes remained fixed on her.

"What shall we do, Salomé?" A young woman who called herself Aimée leaned forward.

She can't be a day older than fifteen. But then Salomé considered the girl's eyes and saw the iron bitterness of cruel experience. The devil had snatched this girl's soul as well.

"We fight back!" Salomé slammed her fist into her palm.

"How?" Someone she did not recognize called out from the rear. "We're not soldiers," another voice protested. "We're women."

Salomé stood to her feet. "Yes, women who can be soldiers! Are you not already fighters? Do you not endure the pain of childbirth? The constant battle for survival? Do you not feel the agony of death when your children starve?" She brandished a fist.

"Is cowardice the legacy you wish to leave to your sons?" The protests died away and a somber silence reclaimed the group. "To your daughters?" *Easy Salomé. No need to push them too far.*

She softened her tone. "You already fight. All you must do is change your battleground."

"There is no need to convince us to act." It was Madame L'Orage who now spoke in a solemn and low voice. "The question is simply, what do we do and how do we do it?"

Salomé nodded at the old woman, grateful for her guidance. "We pull together and storm the Bastille." She let the words fall like a hammer knowing that the time of decision had come.

"T-the Bastille?" Marguerite, the doll-maker, stared open-mouthed. "The enormous fortress in the middle of Paris? The prison?"

Salomé eyed her, knowing that what she proposed would require a courage that was perhaps beyond this woman's ability.

"Marguerite, think of your daughter." Salomé's voice was soft but, in the silence that enveloped the room, she may as well have shouted the words.

The doll-maker's face crumpled as though an invisible hand squeezed it together. "Don't!"

Salomé ignored her plea. "She was hired by a wealthy family but was dismissed after she was found to be pregnant."

Marguerite's head jerked upward. "Please, don't!" Strands of saliva stretched between the gaps in her teeth.

Compassion swelled in Salomé's heart but she forged ahead. "She was raped. We all knew who the father was, and the family did too."

The older woman's shoulders quivered. "He was their eldest son."

Salomé nodded. "Despite the rapist's guilt, the rich chose to blame your daughter whose only crime was to do her job in the kitchens."

She leaned forward. "But did they apologize? No!" Her gaze swept over the other women. "They ridiculed her until one day, Marguerite's husband found their only child swingin' from a beam in her bedroom! To be sure she wouldn't survive, the girl slit her wrists before hangin' herself."

A wail erupted from Marguerite. She sank to the floor and tore at her hair.

Salomé let her anguished sobs die down before she spoke again.

"So you see, there is no turnin' back." She pointed to the shuddering figure. "We must avenge our own. We start by takin' the Bastille."

Alexandre's words from last night came to the forefront of her mind. *I need you to recruit a weapon neither the king nor his soldiers will expect—the women of the city. I know you can do it. I've seen you in action.*

It was his smile more than his words that had compelled her to act.

"We will not be alone." She hurried to put their fears to rest. They were listening and that was good. "A friend of mine is convincin' the men to join us, but we must show the king that we are *all* united in this."

They began to mutter, looking at each other as though the answer to all their problems lay hidden in each other's faces.

"It's brilliant!" Aimée's enthusiastic outburst silenced them all. "Don't you see?" She stood next to Salomé, eyes bright. "The Bastille is the ultimate symbol of the king's power in the city. You know that it only holds prisoners he feels are especially dangerous. If we destroy the Bastille, we send a message to Louis that his days as tyrant are over!"

"But there are guards, men and cannons!" Clementine, the aged wood seller struggled to her feet. "How do we get past them?"

Aimée deferred to Salomé who smiled at her and then turned to the crowd. "By makin' sure that enough of Paris marches with *us*!"

She moved around the circle, making eye contact with each woman. "The time for games is over. This is war! Tell your husbands, your sons, your daughters—tell everyone you know that they must march on the Bastille. The Estates meetin' at Versailles won't help us and the king will just ignore us unless *we* show him that we all stand *together*!"

Energy pulsed through Salomé's being. "If we don't strike now, then when? In another twenty years, after you've buried more children?"

The message was getting through. Understanding lightened their eyes—they had no other choice. Starvation, disease, and hopelessness were the currencies of the day. The only product for sale... was death.

Slowly one head began to nod, then two, then five, fifteen... Salomé stopped counting, knowing that she had won. These twenty would convince a hundred and the hundred would convince a thousand. Elation flooded her heart, but even as she lifted her fists in triumph, a stab of jealousy marred her joy. Alexandre had left for the palace grounds tonight. The look in his eyes told her that he was going to meet Viviane.

She slammed her eyelids shut. If he was meeting her at this hour, it could be for only one reason. *No, it can't be.* She thrust the thought aside as complex emotions threatened to swallow her whole.

Salomé hated the society that forced her to sell her body to stay alive. She raged against the nobility who had stolen her brother and set an unforgivable wedge between herself and her mother. She envied Viviane, the woman who had so much while she had nothing. This same woman now stood between herself and the first man she had ever truly loved.

Patience, Salomé. She pushed back the gloom. *She may have escaped your knife but she will die.*

"When do we strike?" The voice of L'Orage brought her back to the moment. Alexandre had wanted to take advantage of the fear that had spread from Paris to the farthest provinces of

France but needed time to organize what promised to be the greatest rebellion against tyranny in modern times.

"The fourteenth of July." Her eyes glittered. "It gives us enough time to convince your men to join the fight. Enough time to sharpen your cookin' knives and sickles. It is your wombs that carry the future of France. I ask you now, daughters of the revolution, will the future be as dismal as the past?"

Her face, beautiful in its anger, turned from one woman to another, compelling them to action. "I say no!"

"*Non!*" Aimée shouted. The young woman had been first to join Salomé on the floor but she was quickly followed by a swarm of listeners whose fury overcame their fear.

"*Non!*" Another voice chimed in from the back.

"No, no!" The shouts came faster now as the women rose to their feet and joined her in the center of the cellar.

"No!" That was Marguerite's voice. Salomé glanced to her right only to see the bereaved mother moving toward her, tears still streaming down her haggard cheeks. After Marguerite came Clementine, the wood seller, fist pumping the air. "*Non!*"

I've done it. Salomé pulled out a small blue, white and red triangle that unfurled in her hand. It was the tri-colored flag that the revolutionaries had adopted for their own.

"Spread the word, sisters. *Liberté, égalité, fraternité!* Liberty, equality, brotherhood!" Salomé raised her right arm high and the women reached up with her, straining to touch the cloth that represented the most cherished of their hopes.

They echoed her words, a resounding shout that was muted by the damp earth of the cellar's walls. "Tonight, we cry out in secret." Salomé's voice was as sharp as the dagger Alexandre had given her. "But tomorrow we will raise a cry at the Bastille that the whole world will hear. Are you with me?"

Their answering shouts made her ears ring and some part of her mind wondered if Louis and his court could hear the upraised voices of the women of the city. *I am comin' for you Viviane, but this time I'm not comin' alone.*

Alexandre rose and dressed quickly. Viviane reached for him but he pulled away.

"No," he said. "Not until you are truly mine... and *only* mine."

She shook her head, dazed. Now that it was over, a strange mix of longing and shame tumbled about in her heart. *What have I done?*

"What do you mean?" Her mind whirled as she pulled on her clothes. "After this, how can you doubt me?"

Alexandre looked at her, his arms now hanging limp at his sides. "You cannot have the two of us, Viviane." His eyes, normally dark pools of mystery, were now hard stones. "It is him or me. You must choose."

She flushed and looked at her feet. His words conjured up memories of a prince rising to greet her. Philippe seated on the bench outside, telling her of his faith in God. Philippe begging her to allow him to show her his love.

Lies. All of it!

Pain swelled in her chest until she could hardly breathe.

"Even now you struggle to keep him out of your mind." His voice was a sinuous whisper laced with fury.

"Alexandre... please." Viviane pulled away. His words were were knives that diced her heart into bloody chunks. "Please don't do this! I don't know who I am anymore." She covered her hands with her eyes for a moment then gestured to the palace. "Where do I belong? With them?"

"You belong with me... with us!"

"Then take me with you." The words astounded even her. "I mean it." She gestured toward the divan. "Every bridge is burned behind me now. There's no going back!"

Alexandre stepped within inches of her heaving chest, gripped her chin in his strong fingers and turned it upward. Viviane's eyes watered but she held his gaze.

"You have what I want," she whispered. "No one else."

"This isn't just about your body, Viviane." His voice was distant. Cold. "This is about your soul. Only when that is mine can we truly be one."

He released her and turned away. "You are not yet ready."

Viviane stared at his shoulders and felt a tear roll down her cheek. As he moved away, Marie's words echoed in her mind. *Whatever it takes.*

"You think I love Philippe de Valence?" She grabbed his arm.

Alexandre's spine stiffened. He whirled toward her, eyes blazing with black fire. "Don't speak his name in my presence!"

Viviane's lip trembled. The fate of a kingdom as well as her own destiny depended upon this moment. "You think I love him?" She forced the words out in a rush. "Well, I don't."

Liar!

"What did you say?" Alexandre came closer, ears perked.

Viviane felt nausea swirling within her, but she lifted her chin and said the words she knew he wanted to hear. "I... do not... love him!"

"Say it again!" He fondled her neck and pulled her to him as he inhaled the scent of the roses she had woven into her hair. Roses whose petals now lay scattered on the divan behind them.

Viviane shifted her feet and swallowed hard. "I do not love him."

"But you love me?" Again, the soft whisper that was more serpentine than human.

"Yes." She tilted her head, eyes probing his face. *Does he believe me?* His fingers lightly caressed her shoulders, sending fresh tendrils of excitement throughout her body. She had nothing left to offer any man, not anymore. If he rejected her...

"Yes, I love you, Alexandre. Haven't I just shown that to you?"

He gripped her shoulders. "Then leave with me."

"Leave?" She had proposed the idea but to hear the words come out of his mouth startled her. He wanted her to run away with him but had said nothing of marriage.

Does it really matter? What was marriage more than a piece of paper? Who needed marriage when they had love?

"Will you come with me?"

Her eyes widened. This was a test of her loyalty. To hesitate would be to fail and to fail was to condemn herself to a lifetime of shame.

Viviane made up her mind. "Yes."

"You will?" Now it was Alexandre who drew back.

She nodded, lips tight. "Yes."

"Then get ready. We will leave on the thirteenth of July."

"Only a month to prepare?" Viviane could not control the quaver in her voice. "Why so soon? Why the thirteenth?"

He tilted his head to one side. "You know that the people of Paris are afraid?"

She nodded. "They are calling it *la Grande Peur*, the Great Fear."

"Do you know why they are afraid?"

She hesitated. The queen had explained it all in detail but would not approve of her sharing her knowledge.

"No, I do not." Viviane looked away as she lied.

Alexandre continued. "The Third Estate has become more radical. They have defied the king's authority by forming their own government called the National Assembly. King Louis has responded by calling twenty thousand soldiers, many of them foreigners, into Paris. Riots have exploded across the country." The corners of his mouth turned upward. "Some very well organized, in fact."

"What does that have to do with us?" She turned back to him, laying her fingers on his chest.

He took a deep breath and then released it before answering. "Things will soon be different around Paris and, if we are to have a chance at escaping whatever is coming, we should leave very soon."

"What shall I say to the queen?"

Alexandre shrugged. "Tell her that you have finally found your place among your own people. The days when we bowed and scraped to the nobility are over. Revolution is springing up around us. The sooner they realize that, the better for us all."

She laid her head on his chest, considering. He was right. She would have to decide one way or another whose side she was on. And since she had renounced Philippe and given herself to Alexandre, her choice was clear. Perhaps she could convince him to move back with her to Lussan. She ignored the subtle voice inside her heart that questioned the sincerity of his love. *If he loves me, why hasn't he mentioned marriage?* She shook her head and focused on her desire to be with him. *We love each other. That is enough.*

The thought nudged her memory. "Will you do something for me, Alexandre?"

He smiled down at her, the corners of his smoke-gray eyes crinkling. "Anything for the woman who has made me her prisoner."

Viviane picked up the clutch that she had dropped near the divan. "I have a letter that I would like you to give to your friend—to Robespierre."

"Robespierre?" His gaze sharpened. "What has he said to you? Has he harmed you?"

She was touched by his concern. "No, no, it's nothing like that." She smiled at him and tucked a stray tendril of her hair back in place. "But I thank you for your concern."

She pulled the note free and laid it in his open hand. "It is a letter from the queen."

"She knew we were going to meet tonight?" His voice was mildly curious.

"Who do you think ordered the change in your workload?"

He considered the implications of her words. "Then she knows about us."

Viviane nodded. "She knows."

"And she approves?"

"Whether she approves or not makes no difference to me, my love." She tugged at the high-rise collar of his coat and kissed him. This time he did not pull away. "But she can't be seen sending a letter to a man who champions revolution, now can she?"

Alexandre considered this. "So, she asked you—"

"To give it to the man I love, in hopes that he would give it to his friend." She handed him the note.

Alexandre frowned. "If the queen knows that I am a friend of Robespierre then why does she allow me to continue my employment here?"

"Because you are the man I love and a queen's *dame d'honneur* can be very persuasive." It was not true, but Viviane had gained too much to lose it all now.

"Will you deliver the letter?" She batted her eyelids as Marie had done.

"I will."

Viviane laced her fingers with his own. "Thank you. Will I see you again soon?"

"Yes. Soon."

She smiled and turned to leave but he caught her arm and pulled her to him. "Remember who you love." His voice hardened. "Remember."

Her eyes locked with his. "I will. I swear it."

⚜

Alexandre threw himself onto the stump that served as his chair, wincing as his backside connected with the rough wood. Sometimes he wondered if it would be better to forget the stump and sit on the floor. But the mice who also called the shanty home were as comfortable on the floor as he was and would be a distraction. And in times when he needed to think, Alexandre could afford no distractions.

His heart thrummed with victory. She was fallen. When Philippe knew what his precious love had done...

He gently eased his legs onto the uneven edge of the table and angled his body into a sort of V-shape, putting the note that Viviane had given him into his pocket. The coarse wood bit into his ankles but the discomfort helped keep his mind on the real challenge before him.

Viviane. He did not love her but Philippe did. His enemy's unreasonable love for the deluded girl made Alexandre desperate to possess both her soul and body. It was the ultimate form of revenge.

He smirked. When Philippe realized that the love of his life had freely given herself to his archenemy, the pain would crush him. As to the girl herself, well, she was just a casualty of the unseen war.

"I have won!" But just as quickly he frowned. Her body might belong to him, but what about her soul?

Despite Viviane's passion and her outright denial of the prince, there was something about her that still reeked of Philippe.

Alexandre's mouth twisted in a cynical sneer. "What a pathetic, Protestant-loving swine!" He spat, wishing that the globs of saliva had landed on Philippe's face instead of the dirt floor. Why would a man, almost as rich as the king himself, want to see the common people of France strong when their gain would make him weak?

Alexandre rubbed the rough growth on his chin. *It makes no sense.* Philippe was undoubtedly trying to curry favor with the people, biding his time until Louis was overthrown by the dissatisfied masses. Then they would remember his kindness and would hail him as the savior of their world. Philippe would step in as the legitimate heir and become as much a tyrant as his predecessor. It was a clever plot.

Despite her best efforts to convince him she didn't care, Alexandre had seen the hurt in Viviane's eyes when he had mentioned Philippe's name. Something had happened between them that rankled her emotions. This could only mean that she still cared about him.

He had not expected her to agree to his invitation to run away with him. It had been an unplanned test and her reaction had created another problem: where would she stay? Alexandre slammed the table with his palm. He was not thinking clearly.

Salomé would slit the girl's throat the instant she laid eyes on her and Viviane was no use to him dead. He would have to find a solution, or he would have to leave. The thought of abandoning Salomé brought an unexpected twinge to his heart. *Now what does that mean?*

His mind rolled back to the night when she had knelt at his feet. The resemblance to Juliette was even stronger in the full light. Her face, her build, even her voice were haunting reminders of the woman that he had loved and lost.

Alexandre groaned and forked his fingers through his hair. He recognized Salomé's attempts at seduction but refused to sully his memories of Juliette by allowing himself to develop feelings for another woman. He would never share the painful secret of his past and had shut Salomé out of every part of his life that was not part of their mission to dethrone the Bourbons. Still, he had to admit that sharing a home with a woman of her beauty for the better part of a year had weakened his resolve.

Alexandre sighed again and lifted his legs off the table. Simon had been right. His hunger for revenge had somehow impaired his ability to carry out his mission. Times like these demanded a harsh method of bringing himself back to the right path. It was only in the stinging torment of self-inflicted pain that he could find the necessary insight to navigate difficult challenges.

He walked to the one trunk he possessed, a black box with leather edges. He opened the case, and reverently touched each of the items inside. A glittering rapier whose black pommel had been anointed with holy oil by Cardinal Rezzonico, five of six deadly throwing knives and, most precious of all, a black-handled whip whose five leather thongs were tipped with lead balls. He withdrew the whip and closed the box.

"I will mortify my flesh," Alexandre unbuttoned his black shirt, "and in my pain, I will hear the voice of God." He knelt, chest bare except for the rosary that dangled from his neck, alongside his straw bed and firmly gripped the whip.

"Hail Mary, full of grace..." *Sssthunk*. The weighted balls crashed against his muscled back with a meaty thump. Alexandre stiffened but did not cry out. *Sssthunk*.

As pain mushroomed in his mind, he realized that taking Viviane from Paris was not an option. He would be needed at the attack on the Bastille. But where to send her? *Sssthunk*. *Robespierre. I will ask him to shelter her until the attack is over.* Yes, why hadn't he thought of that before?

Sssthunk! He was momentarily dazed but this was good. It meant that he was leaving the realms of physical limitations and would soon be in a spiritual atmosphere of enlightenment.

Salomé. What to do about Salomé's feelings for him? And of his own growing attraction to her? Whereas his mind was caught up with obtaining Viviane's complete devotion and his heart belonged to Juliette, his body had become intoxicated by Salomé's nearness.

Sssthunk!

"...pray for us sinners."

A thought struck him. It was not just Salomé's beauty that troubled him but the miniscule shred of doubt that appeared whenever those gray eyes flashed at him with concern. Compassion was a sentiment that he had never known. Despite his intention to keep his emotions locked away in the icy chambers of his heart, her efforts to please him were moving.

"Hail Mary, full of—"

Alexandre suddenly became aware of two things. One: his thoughts of Salomé had made him lose focus on his prayer. Two: he was no longer alone. *She* had joined him, escaping the realm of his thoughts and materializing into alluring flesh and blood.

"You did this to yourself?" Salomé's voice was soft. It was the first time that she had seen him without a shirt and he had no doubt that the sight made her shudder. A mass of fresh discolorations spread across his back, joining older scars below them.

"Yes."

"Why?" She laid a finger on a bruise that had already begun to swell.

Alexandre jerked away, rising to his feet in one fluid motion. "Do not touch!"

"I'm only tryin' to help you!" Spots of color rose in her cheeks. "Why would you *beat* yourself? Isn't there enough pain in the world already?"

Alexandre paused, at loss for a moment. "It... it helps me think."

Her hands flew to her hips. "I'd hate to know what you were thinkin' about!"

"Nothing at all to do with you." He reached for his shirt. "Leave me be."

"I will not!" Salomé grabbed it from his hands.

Alexandre clenched his jaw. "I said," his gray eyes turned to daggers of steel, "leave... me... be."

"Maybe you whipped your ears as well as your back," Salomé tossed the shirt out of reach, "but *I* said, 'I will not'. You are goin' to lie down on the bed and let me rub oil into those bruises."

He gaped at her, momentarily robbed of speech. Salomé was always spirited. She was a woman whose temper sported a penchant for violence that he secretly liked, but this was unusual even for her. Her experience with the women that evening must have aroused a sense of aggressive liberation that had brought her inner tigress to fever pitch.

"Watch yourself, woman." He raised a warning finger and backed away.

❖

Salomé glared at Alexandre and bit back a stinging reply. He wasn't going to let her rule him—that much was clear. Truth be told, she would think less of him if he did. She had admired his rugged masculinity from the first night he had responded to her knife at his throat by pressing his own blade against her stomach on the banks of the River Seine. Something had churned within her, whispering to her mind that she had at last met her match.

During the months in which they had shared the one-room shanty, her admiration had matured to a possessive love that longed to express itself to this man who seemed so alone in the world. A part of her ached to comfort him, to soothe his wounds and urge him to follow a better path than the one he now walked. But his mind was so entangled with Viviane that he could not see the value of what she offered. Her heart clenched. He had just met with her rival.

Did anythin' happen between them? Salomé sucked in a breath and pushed the unwelcome thought from her mind. Only one path lay open to her. If she could not tell him of her love, then she would show him.

"Alexandre," she laid her hand on the leather whip that he clutched between his fingers, "please let me help you." She fingered the black lead balls that had ravaged his skin. He did not move and she took the opportunity to pull the whip from his grasp.

"I need no one's help." Alexandre folded his arms across his taut chest. "This is standard practice for me. My childhood training was worse. Much worse."

Salomé's curiosity was piqued. "I do not doubt it." She tossed the whip aside. "But I have not had such trainin'. It bothers me to know you are hurtin' and not do somethin' about it."

She took his hand and gently pushed him to a sitting position on the bed then turned to her own corner of the room in which she kept a few oils and herbs.

"You've seen suffering all your life." She could feel his eyes on her, following her every movement. "Your own brother was killed, and you didn't even shed a tear. Why is it different with me?"

"Because—" Salomé bit back the words that sprang to her lips.

I can't tell him that I love him. As far as Alexandre could tell, everything she did was a clumsy attempt to seduce him. She was a prostitute—seduction was in her nature. He had not realized that she craved something more, a relationship that could set her free from the life that she despised and give her a new beginning.

Salomé decided to try another angle, one that was often used by her sex for the simple reason that it worked. "Are you afraid of me, Alexandre?"

Whatever training he had received had formed him into an efficient leader, but she was willing to gamble that he lacked enough experience with women to recognize that she was toying with him, appealing to his masculine pride to bend him to her will.

"Afraid?" He barked out a laugh. "I spent years in the sewers of Paris, fighting for my life. I fear nothing."

"Then why not let me touch you?" She turned back toward him, jar of oil in her right palm. "Surely you wouldn't tremble at the touch of a woman?"

Alexandre pressed his lips into a firm line. "Be quick."

He stretched out facedown upon his bed. Salomé hid a smile of victory and poured a small amount of the precious liquid into her hands, warming it between her palms before gently massaging it into the swelling welts on his back.

She was silent, but questions swarmed in her mind like a hive of angry bees. *Training? What sort of training? The sewers?* Was it possible that his life had been more miserable than her own? She pushed past her curiosity, swallowing her questions back down her throat. It had taken the man five months to divulge one sentence about his past. She wasn't willing to risk what little ground she had gained.

After months of subtle attacks, the first crack in the impregnable fortress of his heart had finally appeared. The corners of her mouth tilted upward. Let him dream of tearing apart the Bastille. She would be content with ripping down the walls that remained between them.

⚜

Alexandre lay still for several long moments, letting her skillful hands woo away the pain and tension that knotted his muscles. *A man could easily get used to this kind of thing.* An image of Salomé in a sunlit home filled with three or four children flooded his mind. He scowled at the traitorous thought. Where was his loyalty to Juliette? To the Church?

It was time to get to the business at hand. He turned his head to one side. "When were you going to tell me about your mother?"

Salomé's hands froze mid-spiral at the unexpected question. He didn't need to see her face to know that it had gone pale.

"What about my mother?" Salomé tried to make her voice sound as nonchalant as possible. She resumed her massage but, lithe as a python, Alexandre rolled over and assumed a sitting position, elbows balanced lightly on his knees and his fingertips joined in front of his face.

"Geneviève Poitrine is your mother."

Salomé's face was a rigid mask of tightly held emotions. "How do you know this?"

"That does not matter."

"Tell me." She wiped her hands on her skirt.

He looked at her carefully, weighing the value of the information she could supply against the cost of divulging his secrets. *Time to strike a bargain.*

"All right." He stood up and rubbed his chin. "Tell me about your mother and I—"

"You will tell me who you are."

"Who I am also doesn't matter." Alexandre frowned as a sinking feeling rose in his gut.

"Then my mother's story doesn't matter either."

He felt the back of his neck grow hot. *Must the woman be so obstinate?*

Salomé had the upper hand and she knew it. He could not afford to run an organization as covert as the Moustiques without knowing the names, background and family associates of each member. If anyone affiliated with the clandestine group of agitators was ever arrested and questioned, the threat against a member of their family might be the undoing of all.

For this reason, he had personally identified all immediate family members of each constituent of the Moustiques in France. How Geneviève had managed to hide the fact that she had two children in Paris, he could not fathom. Why she would do so was another fact that sat ill with him. His frown deepened as he realized that his attempt at negotiation was already doomed.

Salomé did not know about the Moustiques but that was about to change. Simon's implication that Alexandre was losing control of his own organization may have been friendly, but it was a friendly warning that could not be ignored. The fact that Alexandre had not known of the relationship between a highly-placed agent such as Geneviève Poitrine and Salomé was unacceptable. He had to come to terms with Salomé. After all, a bad agreement was better than no agreement.

"Fine." He made an exaggerated bow. *Maybe I can get her to tell me first and then—*

"I will tell you what you need to know about me if you give me the information that I want."

Salomé arched an eyebrow. "Gentlemen first."

Alexandre sighed and raked his fingers through his shaggy dark hair. There was no winning with this woman!

"Sit down." He gestured toward the wooden stumps and pulled on his shirt. He would tell her just enough and then he would say no more. He waited until she sat, back straight and hands folded in her lap, then began his tale.

"I lead a group of revolutionaries, called Moustiques, whose main goal is the destruction of the French monarchy. Like the mosquito, we are small but, when we sting, the impact is felt."

Salomé caught her breath. "That is why you were so eager to meet Robespierre!"

Alexandre nodded. "For years, I have been building an invisible army across France, ready to wreak havoc at a moment's notice." A note of pride rang out in his voice as he continued. "As we speak, my agents are spread out across the country, planting thoughts in the minds of the people. These thoughts will fester, ultimately guiding them to take the actions that are already determined."

"How?" Salomé frowned. "How can one man control the thoughts of tens of thousands of people?"

Alexandre shrugged. "Human nature is predictable. We create dissent and dissatisfaction with life in its present form. We point out flaws in others and incite the weak-minded to violence. We spread lies and distort the truth while keeping our eyes on the goal: the destruction of the Bourbon line."

Salomé absorbed this information in silence.

"You mentioned Geneviève." She turned her eyes to meet his own. Alexandre noticed that she did not refer to the woman as *mother*.

"Geneviève Poitrine." He tapped the tips of his fingers together. "She is one of the few agents that has access to the royal household. I need to know everything about her. It is she who exposed the late prince, Louis-Joseph, to consumption." He looked at the floor.

Salomé's gaze shifted to his chest. "You said you were trained. Trained by who? For what?"

"There are some things that you cannot know," he said. Not even Juliette had known the full truth of his mission.

She took a deep breath. "When I was a child my father, who was a baker on *Rue de Bac* in Paris, was ordered to appear before the magistrate for a crime that he did not commit."

"What was the crime?" Alexandre settled onto the stump beside her.

"The attempted murder of a nobleman." A bitter laugh escaped her lips. "My mother's lover."

With those words, the source of the rift between Geneviève and her daughter became apparent.

"There was no evidence," she said. "The aristo never even came to the trial. He claimed he had to stay in bed due to his injuries."

"And your mother?" Alexandre leaned forward. "Did she defend your father?"

"Defend him?" Anger flashed in Salomé's eyes. "She told the judge that my father was an insanely jealous man who beat her and often threatened to kill any man she looked at twice."

Salomé threw her head back with a snort. "The swine saw a chance to get a better life and took it. My father never touched that man. I know because I was helpin' him bake bread when he supposedly committed the crime!"

"What happened to your father?" Alexandre knew the answer before she spoke. In times like these, there was only one penalty for such a crime.

Salomé's chin trembled. "They hung him on the gallows." Tears misted the corners of her gray eyes. "I can still see him twistin' in the wind, hands reachin' out to me as though he wanted to comfort me—to wipe the tears from the eyes of his little girl one more time!"

She buried her face in her palms. "I was the only one who stood by him while he died." Her voice was muffled but nothing could disguise her pain. "She never even came to her own husband's murder!"

Alexandre reached over, picked up a stained cloth from the table and handed it to her. He waited until she had wiped her eyes, then asked, "What happened to Geneviève after?"

"She gave birth to Germain, who had been fathered by the man she thought would change her life forever." *So, the boy was not her full brother.* Alexandre now understood why she had been so detached at the scene of his death.

She dabbed at her eyes again. "The aristo kept her until he was tired of a baker's wife but, because of the child he had fathered, Geneviève pressured him into gettin' her a worthy position in court."

She shrugged. "Apparently, this gent had some sort of influence. One day she was charged with helpin' the other servants clean up after the king's brats. Over time she gained the queen's trust, and was made one of the official nurses to the late *dauphin.*"

Alexandre tapped his finger against his temple. "In a sense she did get a new life."

"If you can call that livin'." Salomé glared at Alexandre, silently daring him to contradict her. "To me, it's a livin' death!" Her gaze softened. "Geneviève sent Germain to me. She was too ashamed to have a mute cripple at court, especially as she couldn't produce a husband who could've fathered him. From the day she turned her back on us till now, I've had nothin' to do with her."

"So, that is why you hate the aristocrats." Alexandre rose as he spoke. "Your father's murder began it all."

"But now I know that he will be avenged. With you, I can finally see a way out." Salomé sprang to her feet, electrified by the thought. "Twenty women agreed to convince their husbands to join the fight."

"You've done well." Alexandre missed the glow his praise brought to Salomé's eyes. "Twenty will soon become hundreds."

He walked back to the table and drummed his fingers on the wood. "The Bastille is considered impregnable." He barked out a laugh. "I will change that. It holds few prisoners, but it does contain the gunpowder that we will need to attack the king's men in force."

"May fortune ever favor the bold." Salomé gripped his arm, eyes bright with excitement.

Alexandre returned her smile. "Amen!"

Chapter Thirteen

June 1789. Lussan, France

Philippe rammed the last wooden post into the waiting hole in the ground and stepped back from the fence to admire the results of his work. He was no craftsman, but whatever skill he lacked was replaced by enthusiasm.

As an adolescent, woodwork had been his passion. His love for carpentry was coupled with talent. Unfortunately, the responsibilities of a prince did not include building tables. Coming to Lussan had reawakened his old interests and developed his understanding. Life among France's poor had convinced him of his responsibility to right the wrongs that plagued the country.

"I'd offer a penny for your thoughts but I don't have one." Ariadné's sardonic humor brought a wry smile to his lips.

"My!" The older woman took in the sight of the repaired fence. "Who would've thought that rich boy here could put up such a straight fence?" She rapped the sturdy slabs of wood with her knuckles. "I ought to be payin' you for this."

Philippe waggled his hands in front of her face. "Look, callouses!" He smiled at his palms.

Ariadné's shoulders quivered. "Congratulations, young man. I am quite impressed!"

Would her daughter be equally impressed if she could see me now? Philippe fell silent.

Ariadné threw a thoughtful look in his direction then turned to face the house. "I hardly recognize the place." She squinted in the sudden glare of the setting sun. "You've cleaned out the overgrowth and cut down the wild weeds. It looks almost as good as it did when my husband was alive."

"You are too kind, Madame." Philippe walked next to her as they went to supper. "Although I think the most critical of reparations was the upper level of the storehouse."

Her brow crinkled. "You mean the barn?"

He nodded.

"We don't say storehouse, just *barn* around here."

"Oh." He made a mental note of her correction. "I see."

"Well, after all the rain we've had I can see why you were in a hurry to get that done!" Ariadné dropped two cracked wooden troughs onto the small table. They were followed by two hard-baked clay cups.

Philippe's stomach rumbled.

"Ah, the working man is a hungry man." She disappeared for a few moments into an alcove that ran alongside the house, then reappeared, carrying a wicker basket in one hand and a bucket in the next. "Lucky for you I'm in a nicer mood than when you arrived."

"Does that mean...?" Philippe hardly dared to hope. He could have gone to town and purchased whatever supplies were available but he had not wanted to offend her.

"Yes sir!" The widow's careworn face split with a bright grin. "Things are on the mend."

His eyes widened. "Is that right?"

After three weeks of moldy bread and water, Philippe was beginning to wonder if hay might be a tastier option. The woman had never discarded a loaf of bread in her life, he was sure of it.

He had hoped the money he paid might improve the farm fare but, as nothing had changed, he could only conclude that Ariadné was storing up the coins to secure a future elsewhere. That or try to pay off her debt.

"Forgive my impatience, Madame but—"

Ariadné's gleeful voice cut him off. "Yes sir, no moldy bread and water tonight, young man." She pointed to the bucket. "It's moldy bread and milk for you!"

❦

Victor scowled as the long shadow of a stranger blocked the light by which he counted the silver coins that were scheduled to go to the king's coffers in Paris tomorrow.

"Do you mind?" The rotund tax collector winced as he spoke. The wounds he had received during his ill-fated visit to Ariadné's house had not fully healed and the pain increased his irritability. "Idiot. You are blocking the light!"

The shadow did not move and Victor, incensed, glared up at him. A glimmer of sunlight peered over the man's shoulder and glinted into his still-sensitive eyes.

"Ah!" He covered his face with a pudgy hand. "Who are you? What do you want?" Victor peeked out through the slits between his fingers.

The stranger was heavily muscled and sported the plumed hat of a *cavalier*. Dark hair fell loosely about his shoulders and a long scar traversed a nose that had obviously been broken more than once. He answered neither question but tossed a thin sheet of paper onto the table.

"My brothers and I are looking for this man." His voice was the growl of a stalking bear. "Have you seen him?"

"No, no." Victor's words came out in a tumble. He didn't bother to look at the paper. "I haven't seen anyone."

The stranger spat on the floor and sighed. Then, in a blur of motion, his left fist shot out, catching the tax collector square on the upper level of his double chin. For a moment, Victor's body was airborne, lifted from the ground by the raw power of his assailant's fist. Then he crashed heavily against a wooden bookshelf. The jarring impact of his ponderous weight knocked several books off the shelves and they slid in rapid succession upon his balding head.

He groaned and slumped downward. Striding over to the prone man, the unwelcome guest slapped his face twice and jerked him to his feet. Consciousness swiftly returned, helped along by the cold bite of a dagger against his bobbing Adam's apple.

"I don't like repeating myself." The stranger put some pressure on the blade. "Especially when I've had a long day in the saddle with nothing to show for it." He released his grip on the tax collector's collar and reached over to the table. Thrusting the crumpled mass before Victor's bulging eyes, "Let's try this again. Does he look familiar?"

This time the tax collector stared at the portrayal for a full minute. Then he made a barely discernable motion with his head. "N-no sir."

The tall man stared him down, then snorted and spat again—a long stream of brown tobacco that splattered on Victor's new shoes. He pulled back on the knife, twirled it once, and thrust it into a sheath on his belt. "Any new faces in town recently?"

The tax collector had slumped back against the wall, wiping the sudden stream of perspiration from his flushed brow when the stranger's words registered in his mind.

"O-one. I've heard talk of a man who is staying at the widow's house." His face darkened at the thought of Ariadné.

"Huh." The other man's grunt sent a shiver down Victor's spine. "When did he arrive?"

Victor did some quick mental calculations. The whole town had been discussing the mysterious stranger who rode a horse like a gentleman but dressed like a peasant.

"About three weeks ago, sir." He passed a thick finger tentatively over his bruised throat and timidly raised it to his eyes. *No blood!*

"Huh." Another grunt. Clearly, conversation was not this brute's forté. But perhaps this violent assault could be turned to his own financial benefit.

"Ahem." Victor tugged at his waistcoat. "Is there anything specific you wish to know, Monsieur?" He forced a slight smile. It was a long-standing practice of his to smile whenever he hoped to conclude a deal. It made the other person feel like they had come off with the upper hand.

"Where does this widow live?"

Victor hesitated. If he revealed this tidbit of information he would lose out on the possibility of a reward. "Surely this information is worth a little, Monsieur? Perhaps...fifty *livres*?"

"How much do you value your life?"

Victor's throat suddenly felt tight. "Very much, Sir. Very much indeed."

"You have until my spit reaches your shirt to tell me where she lives. Where my dribble goes, my dagger follows. *Tu comprends?*" Light glinted off the edge of the wicked-looking blade as he slid it again from his belt.

The words exploded out of Victor's mouth before the stranger could even hawk up another stream of brown saliva. When he had finished, the intruder stepped back and nodded at the dark stain that blossomed on his victim's white shirt. "Looks better. A man shouldn't wear white. Means he doesn't do any dirty work."

He thumped his plumed hat onto his obtuse head. "I'll head out there at first light tomorrow. If you think of anything else, my brothers and I will be at the tavern. Ask for Roland."

Victor bobbed his head up and down, then sank to his knees when the door slammed shut. Between this uncultured ruffian and Ariadné's mad chicken, he was done for!

⚜

"Do you believe in God, Madame Ariadné?" Philippe sat on the bare earth, cradling a wooden cup of warmed milk in his hands.

Ariadné looked across the small fire that blazed between them then nodded once. "Ah yes, son, I do. There's too much of his handiwork in the world around us to doubt he exists." Her silver eyebrow furrowed in concentration. "Seems to me though that 'tis we humans who make things hard."

"Such as?"

She picked up a gnarled branch and prodded the dying flames, sending sparks shooting upward. "Religion. Killin'." Ariadné shrugged. "I see God's face when I look at the sunset. I see his hand when I do my laundry or milk my cow."

Philippe squared an ankle over his knee. "You mean that he is your provider who is always with you."

"That's it. Well said, young man!" The widow twisted her calloused hands around the branch. She had grown to appreciate her guest's company and not just for his money. She didn't understand many of his well-chosen words or why such an affluent man was in Lussan, but she did see that he was a man of honor.

"It is not only in church that I see God. If you have him on the inside, you can see him on the outside. I see him everywhere I look, except..." Her voice trailed off as she slipped into her own private world.

"Except?" Philippe tilted his head to one side.

"Except in us." Ariadné stared into the fire. "We can be so cruel to each other while claimin' to have God's love in our hearts."

Their conversation stilled for a few moments then Philippe broke the silence. "Who was the man I saw leaving the day I arrived?"

Ariadné rubbed a hand over her brow. "The closest thing to an archenemy that I have." She thumped the fire with the stick again. "When my husband Gilbert was killed in the great stampede of Paris—you're old enough to remember that—I swore I'd hold this farm in honor of the life we had built together."

"You must have loved him very much," Philippe said in a soft voice.

"Gilbert used to say 'no one has ever loved like us before and no one will ever love like us again.'" She blinked several times to clear her wet eyes. "Victor, my neighbor who is also a schemin' tax collector, seems to feel that now is the time to do me in."

"Does this injustice cause you to feel that God has abandoned you?"

"Never!" Ariadné's response was fierce. "God will make a way. My eyes are dim and I cannot see very far ahead but he knows each step that I must take."

Philippe nodded. "You inspire me." He rose and drained the cup. "I am certain that your faith will be rewarded." He bowed his head to her. "Goodnight Madame."

"Philippe?" Ariadné's voice rose over the flames. This man, Philippe, was the kind of husband she wished Viviane would marry.

"Yes?" He turned back to her.

Her crooked teeth gleamed in the firelight as she smiled. "I see God in you."

Philippe lay awake in the pile of straw, mulling over Ariadné's predicament. Moonlight streamed in from the makeshift skylight he had put in the recently repaired roof of the barn, illuminating the interior with an unearthly glow. For once, he found the chittering of the mice easy to ignore. Compared to the decision that pressed on his shoulders, the hyperactive rodents were nothing more than a slight inconvenience.

He could not let this woman lose her estate, not while he had the means of her deliverance in his hands! But paying Ariadné's debt would drain all his available resources. He would literally have the wealth of a beggar for a full week of hard travel until he returned to his home at Versailles.

"But how can I not pay the price?" He looked toward the heavens as he spoke. "This is not some ploy to win Viviane's hand—this is the duty I owe to a wronged woman."

He searched his soul. "Is there any other way?"

But that was just it. There *was* no other way. There was no time to ride back to Paris and return with an authorization for Victor's arrest. Even if he could somehow make the journey in time, the crooked tax collector had written proof of the woman's debt. Admittedly, the proof was written by his own hand but it was still enough to present a strong defense in a court of law that was set to work *against* France's poor not for them.

Then there was the fact that the people were seeking any excuse to revile the monarchy. Victor had been appointed by a palace official. Arresting and exposing him as a corrupt tax collector could ignite a rebellion against Louis.

No. If anything could be done to help Ariadné, it would have to be done by him while he was in Lussan. Unless he stepped in the gap, an innocent woman would be robbed of the home and lands that she had fought gallantly to maintain. Furthermore, he would have to devise a means of setting her free from Victor's grasping hands once and for all.

Philippe rose, decisive now. The beginnings of a plan bloomed in his mind. He crossed the narrow, straw-littered aisle to the stall in which his horse was kept. The animal greeted him with a soft nicker as he opened the gate and led it out into the moonlight.

"Easy." Philippe patted the horse's muscular shoulder as he slipped a bridle over its head. "Our work will be best done at night." He slipped the saddle onto its back and tightened the cinch. Then, rummaging through his bag, he pulled out the rumpled white cloak he had last worn in the palace and slipped on his royal signet. He had not anticipated using either but now he was grateful that, in his hurry, he had stuffed them both into his sack.

He straightened his shoulders and led his horse to the gate. Then he pushed the doors open and stepped out into the moonlit summer night.

⚜

A relentless pounding in his head ripped Victor from deep slumber.

Whoomp whoomp, whoomp! Whoomp, whoomp, whoomp!

He blinked rapidly several times then placed his hands over his head, trying to silence the interminable drubbing. His fingers touched the cotton edge of his stocking cap. It was then that he realized the hammering inside his head was actually someone banging on the door of his home.

"Monsieur Victor. Monsieur Victor!" The panicked hiss of his servant, Grimault, reached him through the oak door of his bedroom.

"Come in Grimault." Victor heaved his bulk from his bed as the excitable servant burst into the room, clutching a lit candle between trembling fingers.

"Oh Monsieur!" The candle jerked about in Grimault's trembling hands. "There is a man at the door."

"Yes, I can hear that you idiot. The question is: who is he and why is he trying to tear the roof off my house?"

"It is... it is—"

A renewed set of thumps drowned out the servant's voice. *The man's fist must be made of lead!* Victor winced as he touched his chin, remembering the blow that he had received earlier that afternoon.

"Who, Grimault, who?" He gripped the man's shoulder.

"Open the door in the name of the King of France!" The voice was muffled but the words were heard distinctly enough.

Grimault's eyes rolled wildly in his sockets. "It's him. It's—" He clutched at the collar of his nightgown then slumped to the floor in a dead faint.

Victor stared at him in mute disbelief then, realizing that the candle burned perilously close to his linen bedsheets, he dropped to his knees and grabbed it just in time.

"Grimault!" He forced himself upright and kicked the older man savagely in the side. There was no response. Terror had made the servant collapse like a woman, leaving him to face the wrathful intruder alone. Victor's own hands began to tremble. What if it was Roland, the ruffian who had accosted him earlier, returned to finish the job?

"Open immediately in the name of the king!"

Victor's heart beat wildly in his chest. Could he defy a servant of the king? The very thought was absurd. Images of his body twitching from a scaffold flashed through his mind, and his shaking hands grew damp. He had to open that door. He had no choice.

His feet dragged over the floor, as though the ground itself was unwilling to let him go to his death. Victor pulled open his bedroom door and peeked out.

Whoomp, whoomp, whoomp! It was the roar of a lion, ready to devour him.

He inched forward, dreading the thought of what lurked on the other side. What awaited him? Torches? Soldiers?

He peeked out of a small window near the door. A groan escaped his dry lips. A giant, swathed in a blazing cloak of white armor sat mounted on a snorting, pawing stallion! Moonlight flashed around the warrior, casting an ethereal glow around his garments. The man's eyes blazed as he waited impatiently for his summons to be answered.

Victor's knees began to shake. "Why me?" Had his crooked dealings been somehow discovered by the king's chamber of accounts? *That's it!* His blood ran cold in his veins. *I am done for. Ruined!*

The stallion neighed and pawed again at the ground. One blow from those hooves and his door would splinter like kindling. *So would my head.* Victor gulped and shoved the image from his mind. There was no point avoiding the inevitable. He forced back the latch with hands made of ice... and opened the door.

⚜

Philippe's first thought was that he should pity the man who peeked around the door's edge with bulging eyes. But then he remembered the reason he was here and fury replaced any thought of pity.

"You are the man called Victor, tax collector of Lussan?" His voice split the night air like the keen edge of a sword.

Victor trembled visibly as he looked up at the man who glowered down at him. "Y-yes?"

He sounded as though he was uncertain.

Philippe edged his horse forward, making his already great height even more imposing. "I am Philippe, Prince of the House of Valence, cousin to Louis XVI, sovereign King of France and of Navarre by the grace of God. Bow before your lord!"

Victor let the candle clatter onto the stones below and prostrated himself before Philippe. "I am your servant, Your Grace."

"You stand accused of abusing the power of your office in a contemptible attempt at augmenting your own wealth. Your corruption sullies the good name of the king! What do you say to this?"

Victor did not dare lift his head from the ground.

"Speak, swine!" Fury gathered in an explosive ball in Philippe's chest. He tightened his grip on the reins and edged the horse even closer. Its hooves dug into the ground inches from the kneeling thief.

"Y-yes!" Victor's wail rose up from the ground. "Yes, I did, I confess!"

"And now you wish to add to your crimes by forcing the widow, Ariadné de Lussan, to marry you or see her lands confiscated!" His voice thundered with the force of an exploding cannonball.

Victor sucked in air. The voice roared out once more and he covered his ears, burying his face in the dirt.

"If she marries you, her property will become yours under the law. Do you deny it?"

"N-no my lord, no!"

"You could turn her out any time you choose, is this true?"

"No, my lord. I mean, yes my lord."

"You deserve to die."

"No!" Victor struggled to his feet. His pale face shone in the moonlight. "Please, spare me, please." He fell to his knees again and grabbed at the snorting horse's bridle. "Spare me, I beg you. I will make it right."

Philippe paused for a long moment as though considering the matter.

"I beg you my Prince, my lord, exalted example of righteousness, most noble of—"

"Enough!" Philippe stared the man down. Instant silence followed his command as Victor pressed his face to the earth again.

"You deserve death—"

Victor's shriek of terror ripped through the night.

"But I will spare you if you do exactly as I command."

Victor leapt to his feet clasping both hands before him. "Anything my lord, anything, I swear it on my honor."

Philippe descended from his horse, his long cape flowing out behind him. "You have no honor, reprobate, but I will accept your word against your life." He tossed the reigns of his horse over the tie post. Even on foot he towered over the tax collector.

"True, my lord, I-I have no honor, just as you say." Victor edged toward his door. "What must I do?"

Philippe gestured to the man's home. "Enter."

Victor skulked inside.

The prince's eyes probed the darkened hallway. "Where do you keep your records?"

"I-in here my lord." Victor pointed to an adjoining room.

"Inside. Now!"

The tax collector hurried to obey.

"Find Madame de Lussan's account."

"My lord she—"

"I have spoken!" The veins throbbed in Philippe's throat.

"Yes, my lord, at once." Victor picked up the book that he had tossed on his desk and flipped it open to where the bookmark still rested.

"Here you are, Your Grace." He offered the book to Philippe who scanned it, frowning.

"Her debts have only increased over the past two years." He glared at the tax collector. "Why is that? Has she not made payment?"

"Yes, she has, Your Grace." Victor retreated a step with each word. "The fact is—"

"The fact is that you have fraudulently manipulated official records of the king!" Philippe snapped the book shut. "A crime that carries a heavy penalty."

"Mercy." Victor shrank under Philippe's look of fury. "Mercy, please!"

Philippe tossed the book aside, reached under his cloak and pulled out a swollen money bag. The sight made the tax collector's bulging eyes widen further. At the sound of clinking coins, he licked his lips.

"Her debt totals three hundred silver coins." He dropped the sack on the table with a heavy *thud*. "Today, I pay the price that she cannot."

Philippe glowered at him, ripped the page out of the book, and held it over the glittering candle.

"My lord—" Victor fell silent when Philippe thrust a finger in his face.

"These records are not true and therefore will be cast out of both your memory and mine. Is that understood?"

The trembling man nodded and watched with wide eyes as the edges of the paper containing his accusations against Ariadné began to curl upward. Tendrils of smoke rose from the document then the flame began to spread.

"Say it!" Philippe held the blazing document just underneath the man's nose.

"Y-yes Your Grace!"

The prince walked to the fireplace, tossed the documents within, and watched until the last shred of the record against Ariadné was destroyed.

He stalked back to Victor and shoved his face only inches from that of the profusely sweating tax collector.

"You will not harass this woman any further on pain of immediate arrest, trial and—upon conviction—your death. Should she but send word to me that you have violated her peace, I swear to you that within a week, you will die. Do you understand?"

Victor grimaced. "Yes, my lord."

"In addition, you will immediately issue a written record that her debt is paid in full."

The tax collector ogled the prince.

"Write!"

Victor grabbed a plumed pen, dipped it in a pot of ink, and scratched out a receipt of payment for Ariadné's past debt. When he had finished, Philippe examined the letter carefully and then motioned for Victor to give him the pen.

This document has been signed in the presence of Philippe Joseph Duke of Montpensier, Chartres and Valence, First Royal Prince of the Blood.

"Give me sealing wax."

Victor handed over a cube of scarlet wax and Philippe held it over the flame for a few moments until it dripped like red blood upon the document that testified of Ariadné's freedom. Then he sealed it with his ring.

Philippe folded the document and placed it in his pocket, returning his iron gaze to the frozen statue before him.

"All future taxes are to be charged to the House of Valence. Upon my return to Paris, I will instruct the Chamber of Accounts to make the adjustment. She will pay nothing ever again. Is that understood?"

The man swallowed as he nodded.

"Then there is nothing further to say." With an imperious swirl of his cloak, Philippe stepped through the door, leapt onto his snorting horse and disappeared into the night.

Victor sank into his chair and mopped his brow, contemplating this strange turn of events. His deceitful handling of public funds had been discovered and used against him. If he had time to consider, an opportunity to face a court of sympathetic *financiers* he might be able to concoct a reasonable reply. But he had been dragged from his bed in the middle of the night and almost burnt to death by his cowardly steward only to be accused by this Prince of Valence!

A prince? His thoughts, so confused at first, began to sort themselves out. How had Ariadné convinced the Duke of Valence to intervene? For that matter, why would a prince be interested in a bankrupt widow?

Now that the immediate danger was gone, doubt began to gnaw at the corner of his mind. *Did I really see the prince?* Impossible. Where were his guards? His royal entourage? No prince would travel alone at… whatever time it was. No prince would stoop so low! True, he had the seal, money and cloak but perhaps he had only stolen them.

Victor shrugged, trying to find ways to justify his growing belief that the man was only an imposter. He rose to go upstairs, determined to knock sense into Grimault and, as he stood up, his eye fell upon the poster that Roland, the abusive bounty hunter, had left upon his desk. A wave of shock paralyzed him, making his breath come in short gasps. There, on his desk, was the face of the man who had beaten down his door, dragged him from his bed and threatened him with death.

"I was right!" Victor slammed his fist on the desk then sucked on his stinging fingers. "He's nothing more than a criminal."

He grabbed the paper and lurched toward the door. "The tavern. Roland is staying at the tavern!"

Chapter Fourteen

June 1789. Third Precinct, Paris.

Maximilien Robespierre reclined against the brown, high-backed leather chair that was the only luxury his austere office contained. The dark walls of mottled green were devoid of any paintings; the hickory desk at which he worked boasted no medals or ornaments. Despite its many compartments, a plumed pen, a box of private papers and an unopened note were the only items visible on the writing table. One might find the stark atmosphere oppressive but Robespierre preferred it this way. It was the elimination of unnecessary frivolities that allowed him to concentrate on the essential. At this moment, the essential was a small note that lay sealed on the dark wood before him.

Robespierre stood, straightened the long, high-necked blue waistcoat that covered his cream *gilet,* and stalked to the window while wiping sweat from his palms onto his cotton breeches. *How can a note unnerve me?* But he knew the answer. This was no ordinary note. This was a note from *her.*

A knot formed in his gut as he edged back to the desk. Salomé had delivered the note a few moments before. Robespierre shuddered as he thought of the prostitute's hands touching such a treasure.

His eyes roamed again over the seal. Red wax featured an embossed image of a queen seated on a throne under the shining rays of the sun. At her feet two children held a shield which sported the emblems of the two kingdoms ruled by the queen. *Marie par la grace de Dieu, Reine de France et de Navarre 1725,* Marie by the Grace of God, Queen of France and Navarre. The words boldly proclaimed that this was indeed a note from his mortal enemy, a message from the woman he still loved.

A cacophony of sound rose from Rue de Saintonge, the street just outside his home, but Robespierre was oblivious to the hawking of the vendors and to the cries of the starving. Neither the preachers who condemned the licentious queen nor the activists who vilified her husband caught his ear.

Not today.

Not now.

He touched the paper with reverent trepidation, mustered his courage and, with a sigh, he broke the seal.

⚜

"Any word?" Alexandre sat across from Simon in an inconspicuous corner of *L'Ivrogne*, a squalid tavern whose murky atmosphere resurrected dark memories of his years in the sewers. A boisterous crowd had just rushed in, eager to spend what meagre pennies they possessed on enough liquor to make them forget their misery. With the beer came the women, tavern girls whose painted faces hid the despair that crushed them all.

"Nothin'." Simon threw back his head and guzzled down his sour beer. Some of the amber liquid sloshed over his bearded face and he stretched his tongue out of the corner of his mouth to catch the falling droplets.

"Ah, that was good!" He slammed the empty tankard down on the table, and smacked his lips together. "I don't know how you do it, *amico mio.*" He gestured to Alexandre's cup which contained only water. "No beer? No wine? No women? Not ever?"

His acid breath made the master assassin's nostrils twitch. "That kind of life isn't healthy for an Italian." Simon wiggled his eyebrows at Alexandre.

Alexandre shrugged. "Alcohol affects a man's judgment, Simon. I cannot afford bad judgement—not ever."

Simon grunted. "There are other things than beer that can cloud a man's judgment."

Alexandre pinned him with warning glare.

"But no," Simon yawned and scratched his armpit, "I've heard no report from the men you ordered to Lussan or from any of the agents."

Alexandre thoughtfully tapped his wooden cup against the table.

"Why did you order Roland to go to Lussan of all places?" Simon leaned forward. "Granted, it's in his assigned territory but *Lussan?* Never even heard of the place!"

"Just a hunch." Alexandre flicked a piece of lint off his sleeve. "Someone Philippe loves grew up there."

Simon was quiet for a long moment and Alexandre knew that his friend understood. Despite his bulk and coarse manners, Simon was no fool. His instinct for strategy and insight into human nature had played a key role in the development of their organization.

"I see." At length the giant slanted him a speculative nod. "So, this is your way of gettin' revenge? A private struggle with the Duke of Valence over a woman's heart?"

Alexandre shot him another warning glare. "Drop it, Simon."

"Alright, alright." Simon lifted both hands in the air. "I'm just tryin' to save your neck."

"The agents know what to do if they find him?" Alexandre's voice was hushed. Many in this part of Paris supported Philippe and he had no intention of dying in a tavern—especially not *this* tavern.

Simon nodded. "They kill on sight. Shoot first. Ask questions later. That's the best way, if you ask me."

"Good." Alexandre eased back into his chair. "And the Bastille. Are we ready?"

His friend grimaced as he tilted his cup and realized the tankard was now empty. "Almost. The prison is also a weapons storehouse and we're goin' to need all the powder and arms it holds." He squinted at Alexandre. "You got a plan for getting' us inside?"

Alexandre nodded. "When the time comes, you'll see."

Simon snorted. "Well, until that time, this ol' boy needs some more beer." He turned toward the door.

"Waiter!" His shout rang out over the raucous noise of the crowd. "More beer!"

⚜

Augustin Robespierre entered his brother's study with a growing sense of trepidation. For days, a sense of pending evil had soured his mood. At first, he had attributed it to the murder Robespierre had committed. Surely a just God would avenge the old woman's death. But after several weeks without a lightning bolt blasting either himself or Robespierre to oblivion, Augustin's conscience lost sight of its immediate remorse. This fact intensified his perturbation. *Now I find murder acceptable?*

"What do you want brother?"

Augustin started as he heard a voice without seeing a body. Frankly, he had not seen anything because the room was immersed in total darkness. His groping fingers struck the base of a candle. "Maximilien?" After several failed attempts, the flickering light illuminated the room with a steady glow.

"I am seated at my desk, Augustin. Now what is it you want? Speak quickly for I am terribly busy."

Augustin held up the candle and, by its radiant flame, he made out the form of his brother who clutched a thin piece of paper between trembling fingers.

"Maximilien, what are you doing?" He loved his elder brother dearly but there were times when he questioned Robespierre's sanity. Now was one of those times.

"Well what does it look like I am doing, brother?" Maximilien thrust the letter forward. "I am *reading*."

"Reading? In the dark?" Augustin deposited the candle on Maximilien's desk. "It is the middle of the night and you hope to read a letter with no candle?"

"Is it truly night?" Robespierre glanced at the darkened window. "I had not noticed." He tapped the paper. "You see, I received this note around noon today and have been reading it ever since."

"What?" Augustin's eyebrows flew upward. "You have spent ten hours reading the same letter—and in the dark?"

"Yes... well... one does not need to see what one has memorized." His elder brother drummed his fingers on the desk.

"I think you had better let me see that letter." Augustin held out his hand.

When the seal caught his eye, Augustin almost dropped the page. "It is from the queen!"

"Mmm... yes." Robespierre pursed his lips together and tapped them with his index finger. "From the queen."

Augustin flung his hands wide. "Would you kindly explain *why* the Queen of France is sending you personal notes?"

Maximilian shrugged. "Why don't you read it yourself?"

Augustin blinked twice. The brother he knew would never allow him to read a note from the woman he both idolized and abhorred. *Something is wrong.* The presentiment of danger deepened. He took a deep breath, opened the folded page and began to read.

Most noble enemy.

I should greet you, but any salutations on my part would be nothing more than a sham for you are undoubtedly the most detestable man ever created by God. I will therefore dispense with such formalities and proceed to the heart of the matter.

I find myself in an impossible circumstance. Your incessant attacks against both my good name and my family's security have led to a time of difficulty between myself and my husband. Furthermore, I fear that new danger still threatens and therefore recognize that it is perhaps time for my enemy to become my savior.

It is with this mindset that I concede defeat. I appeal to your sense of honor and ask that you help me rebuild a peaceful life for myself and the children that remain to me. You have won. To you, the victor, the spoils must be given. It is my hope that our future correspondence will offer a mutually satisfying conclusion.

In hopes of a peaceful future.
Marie-Antoinette.

Augustin put the paper down with trembling hands. "Is she saying...?" He could not bring himself to finish his thought. "The Austrian whore!" He raked a hand through his hair.

"Yes..." Robespierre nodded. "A whore."

"How can you just sit there?" Augustin slammed the paper onto the desk and began pacing. "She is offering herself to you on the condition that you take the children and herself to safety!"

He pointed a trembling finger. "T-that note incriminates her. It shows her true face. She is a woman who would forsake her husband, her crown and her country to secure her own future!"

"You are correct, Augustin."

Augustin opened his mouth to speak, then closed it and drew a ragged breath. "You should show this to the people of France. Let them see how low Madame Deficit has truly sunk."

"That is not a good idea." Robespierre steepled his fingers and eyed his pacing brother.

"And why not?" Augustin rounded on him. "Do you wish to keep your little love life a secret? Do you hope that she will actually go through with this little scheme of hers?" He drew back his upper lip in a sneer. "I, for one, will not—"

"The queen did not write the letter." Robespierre's voice was hollow.

Augustin froze mid-step, his flow of words cut off as cleanly as if they had been severed from his lips by a headsman's axe.

"*What?*" He spun back to meet his brother's unblinking stare. A nervous tic in Maximilien's right cheek told Augustin that Maximilien was battling very powerful emotions.

"The letter was not written by the queen."

"But that is impossible!" Augustin spoke through clenched teeth. "Tell me brother, how can such a thing be possible?"

"It is quite simple Augustin. The queen has asked someone to correspond on her behalf, giving this individual her personal seal."

"But how can you know?" Augustin grabbed the letter again and scanned it quickly. "Nothing here sounds less imperious than our spiteful monarch herself would say."

Robespierre sighed and rubbed his temples. "That is because Marie read the letter and, undoubtedly, corrected all mistakes that she noticed."

"Then what about this letter makes you feel that it is a forgery?"

Robespierre leaned back in his chair. "Point one: in the last line of the second paragraph," he quoted from memory, "'...*it is perhaps time for my enemy to become my savior.*' Marie would never ask that I become her savior nor would she accept my services should I deign to offer them. She would sooner turn to the devil himself."

He laid his index finger on his pursed lips. "Point two: Marie insinuates that there is trouble in her relationship with the king. This is no secret. All of France knows that they have their differences, so why bring it up at all?"

"Because she wants you to take his place in her bed!" Augustin dropped into the chair across from Robespierre. "That much is obvious."

"Yes, Augustin, but think of this as if it were a case of law. You and I both know that the cleverest of felons rely on the most obvious forms of evidence to confuse the authorities. Simply put, they plant evidence where it is most likely to be found."

Robespierre sniffed. "The queen is no fool. She knows that I, like all of France, am aware of her marriage troubles. Why state the obvious unless she *wants* me to notice it?"

He rose to his feet, a lawyer now and no longer just a wounded man. "She has refused me from the first time we met. Nothing has changed except that we both have become more set in our ways."

He began to pace, becoming more animated with each step. "No, Marie does not want a new lover, not at all. She wants to plant a seed—evidence if you will—in my mind to prepare me for something else. Something yet to come."

Augustin stared at his brother, whose deductive reasoning had led to such an abstract but sensible conclusion.

"Point three," Robespierre continued. "There is an obvious blunder that the queen herself overlooked."

"What is it?"

"Her name is signed 'Marie-Antoinette.'" Robespierre met his brother's gaze. "European royalty always sign official documents with only their first name. If this letter had been written by the hand of the queen, she would have simply signed it "Marie," just as the king signs his documents, "Louis.""

Augustin's mind flashed to the handful of personal notes from the king to his clients that he had perused in his practice as a lawyer. *Maximilien is right.* It was impossible that a hand used to signing documents such as letters and notes would forget an established protocol that had been in place for centuries. It was an easy enough mistake to *overlook* but not an easy one to make.

"So, you think that this is… a trap?" Augustin leaned forward in his chair.

"Undoubtedly." Robespierre's lips parted in a twisted grin. "This is her counterattack to *our* assault and I must say that her cunning inspires me!" His voice became quiet. "What a wife she would have made."

It was no secret that his brother never intended to marry. He had courted the daughter of his landlord but the matter had never become concrete. Augustin suspected that the girl had been a distraction, a futile attempt to keep his mind from the woman who still haunted his soul. "What will you do? Assuming you are right of course."

Robespierre smiled again. This time it was an ugly grimace that reeked of evil.

"Respond." He tapped his cheek. "I want to see how far she intends to carry our little game."

Augustin shuddered. "Such games are dangerous. Lately, I have had this horrible sense of foreboding, as though something bad is about to happen to us."

"Something evil *will* happen to us." His brother yawned and stretched. "We will all die."

Augustin just stared at him and Maximilien continued. "We will probably all die horrible deaths and then our souls will be condemned to hell for eternity."

"And you are… *happy* about this?"

Robespierre evaded the question. "The real issue, brother, is not death but life. What will we do in the brief moments left to us?"

"For you, it seems clearly a matter of revenge."

"No, Augustin." Robespierre, the famed lawyer, sat at his desk and picked up his plumed pen. He dipped it in the inkwell and then selected one of his finest sheets of paper. "Never revenge. Only justice… always justice."

Chapter Fifteen

July 1789. Lussan, France

Roland, *mousquetaire* in charge of field operations in the Languedoc-Roussillon region of France, put a plug of chewing tobacco in his mouth and patted the neck of his horse.

"Easy there, girl." He chewed the wad with gusto. "Just another daybreak ride." Even at dawn the air was hot and humid, a fact that promised to make a miserable day in the saddle.

Roland cracked each of his fingers with a loud *pop*, then twisted the upper half of his body to see if his four comrades were ready to move out. There were normally only two of the clandestine group in each region of France, but Alexandre had ordered the rangers from the adjoining region to coordinate with Roland and his partner, Claude, as they searched the area around Lussan for the missing prince. Roland had not expected to find Philippe in so remote a place as Lussan, but Alexandre had always been an able leader. It seemed that, once again, his instincts had proven correct.

"Ready?" His guttural voice broke the early morning quiet. Three heads nodded in unison and Roland prepared to spur the sides of his mount but stopped, a frown appearing on his unshaven face.

"Claude!" He swung around in the saddle. "Bring the babbler. We may need him."

Claude leapt from the saddle and thumped on the door. It opened with surprising swiftness and a bleary-eyed Victor stumbled out.

"You. Tax collector!" Roland thrust a thick finger in his direction. "You ride with us."

Victor groaned but did not protest.

"Mount up!" Roland spat to one side. It was high time to finish this unpleasant business. While Victor staggered off to saddle his horse, Roland paced his mount in a half-circle to face his men.

"Remember, we shoot on sight. As soon as I identify the prince—kill him. The master wants him out of the way. Clear?"

He sighed in frustration. "How long does it take a man to saddle a horse?"

As if in response, the sound of drumming hooves caught his ear. His first thought was that the bloated tax collector was finally ready to leave, but then Roland realized that the sound was coming from the main road behind him. Wheeling his mount around, he laid a hand on the hilt of his sword. Seeing the motion, the others immediately spread out on either side of him, forming a loose defensive perimeter.

The rumble of hooves grew closer and a large cloud of dust rose from the base of the hill leading up to Victor's property. *Whoever is coming is not alone.*

"Prepare yourselves." Roland shouted the command. He drew his sword and heard the rough scrape of sliding metal as the others did likewise.

The main road was a muddy track with sprigs of grass growing wildly in the middle. It capped a hill and passed just in front of the commons area of Victor's yard. This was a challenge for Roland for it meant that he would not see the newcomers until they were literally right in front of his face.

"C'mon, show yourself." He muttered the words through gritted teeth. "Come to Roland!"

⚜

Captain François Jacourt, leader of the royal mounted cavalry unit called the *Condé-Dragoons,* spotted the men with drawn swords as soon as he crested the hill. Behind him rode twenty elite soldiers dispatched by the Minister of Finance, Monsieur Necker, to ensure that the taxes from Languedoc-Roussillon did not fall into the hands of the smugglers and thieves that plagued France's rural areas.

Seeing the men in front of him, Jacourt was [cut] brought so many troops. His own sword flew out o[cut] and, instead of drawing his horse to a halt, he spurred onward.

"Split ranks!" He bellowed the order, his voice rising above the thunder that rose with the dust from the below the horses' hooves. His men reacted with smooth precision. The division split into two columns, each riding in a different direction with blades extended toward the small group before him. Within moments, the small squadron of men found themselves surrounded.

"Identify yourselves." Captain Jacourt drew hard on his stallion's reins.

The four men uneasy glances.

"Well?" Jacourt pressed his way through the circle of soldiers and stopped his horse directly in front of an ugly brute who carried himself like a leader. "Answer me or surrender your weapons."

"We are rangers, sir—"

"Rangers?" Jacourt threw his head back with a contemptuous laugh. "You mean smugglers! The king has no rangers. You will surrender your weapons now or die." He spat on the ground. "You smugglers have been a scourge on the kingdom. No doubt the king would reward me for bringing back your heads. Your name?"

"Roland." The man grimaced but extended his arm and released his grip on his sword. The weapon clattered to the ground where it was soon joined by those of the other three who rode with him.

"Pistols also!" Jacourt gestured for a soldier to relieve the men of their firearms and collect the blades on the ground.

"You're making a mistake." Roland sighed while extending his pistol, butt first.

"Yes, I am letting you live." Jacourt rested the tip of his sword against Roland's chest. "Don't tempt me. If you behave, I will conduct you to Paris as my prisoner along with the king's taxes where you will receive a fair trial."

Jacourt shoved the supposed ranger out of his way as a solitary horse and rider approached from behind the tax collector's house.

Roland twisted in the saddle and then spun back to Jacourt. "This is all a misunderstanding. There is a man recently come to Lussan who has murdered the prince of Valence. He threatened the tax collector," Roland gestured at Victor, "and my friends and I were about to bring him to justice."

Jacourt started at the mention of the prince's name. Before his departure from Paris, the entire king's army had been informed by their commanding officers that a massive manhunt was on for the king's cousin, the Duke of Valence. He stood up in his stirrups.

"A killer, you say?" He scratched his chin. "Bring the *percepteur* here!"

A space materialized in the circle of troops and Victor rode toward the impatient captain.

"Victor the tax collector." Jacourt casually slung a hand over the pommel of his saddle. "We had come to collect the king's revenue, but it seems that we may have a bigger prize at hand."

"*Oui, mon capitaine.*" Victor dropped to his knees then held up his hands in a pleading gesture. "He dragged me from bed, claiming to be the Duke of Valence. And in the middle of the night!"

Jacourt's eyebrows slid together as he frowned down at the man. It appeared that no word of the *dauphin's* murder had reached the isolated town of Lussan. As such, they believed that there was an imposter who had killed the real Philippe while he was almost certain that the man the tax collector described was indeed the Duke of Valence. In any case, his duty was clear.

"You will take us to this man and *we* will arrest him." He spoke to Victor but his words reached Roland.

"My lord, it is better that my men and I resolve the situation." Roland edged his horse closer. His face had gone pale beneath its ruddy tan. "Why trouble yourself with such an insignificant matter"

The captain ignored his question. "I have spoken. If it is as you say, I will release you once the villain is in our hands. Are my orders clear?"

Roland released a long, brown stream of spittle. "Clear as mud."

Jacourt refused to belittle himself by acknowledging the man's disrespect.

"Fall in!" He jerked hard on the reins and cantered down the hill. The soldiers immediately broke the circle and formed two streaming lines of clanking metal and squeaking harness. They kept Roland and his men at their center. Victor rode at the head of the contingent, leading the way to Ariadné's farm.

⚜

Captain François Jacourt gnawed at his lower lip as he surveyed the property of Madame Ariadné, the laundress of Lussan who had the singular misfortune of being neighbor to a tax collector. The next few moments would define the length of his career and, quite possibly, his life. If the true Prince of the Blood, Philippe, Duke of Valence, *was* within those weather-beaten walls, Jacourt was obligated by oath to arrest him.

The very thought of arresting so great a man made him wrinkle his nose in disgust for, while Jacourt was an officer of King Louis's *Condé Dragoons*, he was also quite sympathetic to the revolutionary winds that were blowing across Paris. Because Philippe had been able to overcome the prejudices ingrained in him from birth and openly support the rights of the common man, he commanded a great deal of Jacourt's respect. To arrest the prince would be an act of treason against his conscience. To let him go free would be an act of treason against his country.

"Permission to proceed, sir?" It was the voice of his second-in-command, Henri.

The young officer pulled off his hat. "Sir?"

Jacourt sighed, knowing that he had no choice. His eyes shifted to the twenty men-at-arms who rode with him then to Henri. *They will testify that I let the murderer of the king's son walk free.* He would hang as surely as the sun hung in the eastern sky.

At least this way I'll be sure he makes it back to Paris alive. The murderous look in Roland's eye had not escaped him. He had the distinct impression that if he had not stumbled upon the group of self-styled rangers, Philippe de Valence would already lie stiff and cold upon the ground.

"Permission granted. But no harm comes to the prince."

Henri nodded and then waved his fist in a slow circle. Quietly the men began to close in with a cluster of six remaining behind to guard Roland and his compatriots.

"Forgive me." Jacourt crossed himself and then raised his eyes to heaven. "Forgive me."

⚜

Ariadné's hand flew to her mouth as she stared at the paper Philippe waved in front of her face. She had struggled to piece the words together but, when she at last understood what the document was saying, she had dropped into the single chair that remained in her home.

"A prince?" She stared at Philippe as though he were an angel from God, then tore her gaze from him and devoured the paper again with her eyes. *An heir to the throne?* Even Ariadné, as far removed from politics as she was, knew that the man who stood so meekly before her was one of the most powerful men in France.

She slipped out of the chair and staggered toward him, mouth opening and closing in a futile attempt to express the inexpressible. How could she say what was in her heart? Ariadné slumped to her knees and, for the first time in thirty years, tears collected in the corners of her eyes and dripped into the canyons of her cheeks.

"Why?" She tried to rationalize the goodness of this stranger, this prince who owed her nothing. "Who am I that you should show such kindness... to me?"

Philippe knelt with her, cupping her own hands in his own. "This is why I came. Our Father, yours and mine, desires that we his own great plan of redemption. You were enslaved by the fraudulent deceit of the tax collector and it was within my power to set you free." He shrugged. "How could I do anything else?"

She stared at him, waves of gratitude washing over her. "Thank you." She reached out to touch his face.

Philippe smiled at the widow and lifted her to her feet. "I came to better understand your daughter, Viviane, but I soon realized that there was a higher purpose: your freedom!"

"You know my daughter?" Ariadné's mind reeled with this second revelation. "How—"

"I will tell you all tonight." Philippe's eyes twinkled. "Like you she is—"

A fist pounded on the door and cut off his words. "Open in the name of the king!"

Ariadné glanced at him, the fingers of one hand touching her lips. "Did you bring your family along with you?" She wiped tears from her cheeks.

"I divulged my plans to no one." Philippe stepped to the door. "But if it is indeed a servant of my cousin the king, we have nothing to fear." He opened the door and stepped back, shading his eyes from the sudden glare.

"Philippe de Valence, *Prince du Sang*?" The young officer's Adam's apple bounced as he pronounced the title.

"Yes, it is I." Philippe inclined his head. "How may I be of service?"

Again, the nervous swallow.

"Do not fear, good man." The prince laid one hand on the frame of the door. "Say what you must, but please, do it quickly."

The soldier took a sharp breath and squared his shoulders. "I am Henri Touché, second-in-command of His Majesty's *Condé Dragoons*. I regret to say, Your Grace, that you are, as of this moment, my prisoner and must return at once to the *Château de Versailles*. You stand accused of the murder of His Majesty Louis XVI's son and heir, Louis-Joseph of the House of Bourbon."

⚜

For a moment, Philippe just stared at him. Then his hand flew out and he gripped the man's shoulder with tight fingers. "My nephew is dead?" He shook Henri forcefully. "Are you telling me that my beloved nephew is dead?"

"Y-yes Your Grace." Henri cleared his throat. "He was murdered four weeks ago... by your hand."

"By my—?" Philippe released the man and drew back as though he were diseased. "Louis believes that I—"

"I am ordered to bring you back to Versailles where you will answer to the king's justice." The soldier laid his hand on the hilt of his sword. "Will you come peacefully, Your Grace?"

Philippe turned his back, closing his eyes to the pain that ravaged his soul. His own family despised him so much that they were willing to believe that he had murdered the nephew that he loved as he would his own son!

"Your Grace?" The sounds of stomping boots and snorting horses reached Philippe's ears and he knew that a full division of soldiers awaited him. *How did they find me? Why the ruthless show of force?*

The questions burning in his heart left him dazed and confused. Pain scorched his soul, blotting out all conscious thought. Philippe clenched his fists, lost to the world, and wailed in agony. *How could Louis believe this?* He screamed until his throat burned, ravaged by the grief that flooded his soul.

Then he felt a cool, aged hand pry apart his gritted fingers.

"Ariadné." His voice was a hollow croak. "Am I so dangerous that, even in their grief, they must murder me with their slander?"

Ariadné turned him around, a mother's pain etched in her face. "I don't know who's sayin' what, son." She touched his face again. "But I do know that you're innocent."

"Innocent." Philippe could barely speak past the lump in his throat. "My own cousin believes that I murdered his son!"

"But you didn't." The widow raised her voice. "And you're going to go back to that palace and prove to that fat old king that you did nothin' of the sort!"

She clutched his shirt between her fists. "You're too good a man to have done that. Right now, he and his queen are hurtin' and they're looking for someone to blame. Who better to falsely accuse than you, a man with a pure heart?"

She smiled, and he drew strength from her confidence. He remained where he was for a moment, then walked over to the desk, picked up the letter that cancelled Ariadné's debt and turned to Henri.

"Take me to your commander."

The soldier bowed again and led Philippe outside to where his captain waited.

Victor, astride his bowlegged dappled gray mare, jeered at the royal prisoner. "A prince, eh?" He sneered. "How the mighty have fallen!"

"Silence, you fool!" Captain Jacourt slammed his gloved fist into the obese tax collector's side, sending him tumbling from the horse. "Do you not recognize Prince Philippe of Valence? Bow before a peer of the realm!"

Jacourt slid from the saddle and knelt before his sovereign.

"Forgive me this task, Your Grace." He bowed his head. "But I am charged to bring you back to Versailles."

Philippe lifted his chin high. "Rise captain. The guilt is not yours but the one who has slandered my name. His is the greater sin."

He narrowed his eyes. "I do, however, desire that you render me one service."

"Speak, my lord. Anything!"

"Deliver this letter to Monsieur Necker, the official Minister of Finance." Philippe placed the letter in his hand then raised his voice so that Victor, who still groveled in the dirt, could hear clearly. "It states I have paid this woman's obligations and all future taxes are to be charged to the House of Valence. Is that understood?"

Jacourt dipped his head. "As you command, my liege." He clapped his hands twice, commanding Henri's attention.

"Saddle the prince's horse. We ride for Versailles!"

⚜

Viviane watched with narrowed eyes as Marie-Antoinette yawned and stretched, twisting on her side to reach over the stern of the wide-bottomed canoe and dabble her fingers into the sparkling emerald water that slid smoothly beneath her. Her canoe was one of several which dotted the large lake that lay at the center of the private retreat known as *le Petit Trianon*. The small castle and the two hundred acres that made up the Trianon had been a gift from the king and Marie had spared no expense in making the property uniquely hers.

Over the past decade, her architects had created a colonnaded limestone temple dedicated to the fabled god of love, Eros, a reception hall and series of sumptuously-decorated cottages in which she hosted exclusive late-night parties—most of which took place when her husband could not attend. To make her bucolic world even more appealing, Marie had installed a complete Norman-style peasant village and working farm where she and her serving women could dress as milkmaids and tend cattle for the day.

The verdant embrace of summer reigned with the power of an absolute monarch in this corner of Versailles. The fruits of summer's rule were evident in the lush greenery and the English-style rose gardens, whose fragrance wafted across the limpid pool to the queen and her friends—all women apart from Count Axel von Fersen.

It was the count who now rowed across the lake to the dairy, where the queen, Viviane and the rest of her inner circle would milk cows and feed lambs that sported pink bows. Marie had informed Viviane that she intended to return to the Belvedere, a small domed structure, whose uncluttered design made it the perfect open-air living room, just before the afternoon sun disturbed her hair.

"Axel." Marie sat upright as she called over Viviane's shoulder to the count. "Do you think it is right for me to enjoy myself again so soon after my son's burial?"

Viviane, who sat between the pair with her back to the Count, frowned. The growing affection that the queen showered upon von Fersen disturbed her.

"What you do is your affair, my Queen." Though Swedish by birth, von Fersen had become a colonel of the French army and had recently returned from helping the Americans win their war of independence. His military career kept his physique in top form—a stark contrast to the king's fleshy body.

"I say," the count pulled on the oars again, "that you should indulge in whatever pleases you."

Marie cast a sweet smile in his direction. Viviane began to feel sick. She understood the power of passion—God knew that Alexandre's magnetism could make a nun faint—but her liaison with the gardener had awakened a sensibility to Marie's flirtations that she could no longer ignore. The memory of her own actions in the Orangery brought fresh spots of red to her cheeks. *At least I am not married. Marie has a husband!*

"Viviane." Marie laid a white-gloved hand upon the simple dress that Viviane wore. "My dear friend, the count, is correct. One must never allow the judgements of others to obscure the pursuit of one's own pleasure."

She shifted her gaze to von Fersen. "I know the people believe that I have built this place for my own folly, but in truth Axel, this is the only place where I feel truly liberated. Here *I* reign with unquestioned authority."

"Will not the king miss your presence, Your Grace?" Viviane scrambled for a subtle way to remind Marie that she was a married woman.

"Oh, the king!" Marie rolled her eyes as she flicked droplets of lake water from her hands. "My husband is so preoccupied with affairs of state that he will not even notice my absence. My son is dead, true, but I am alive."

Her voice floated around Viviane to the man whose powerful shoulders made the little boat skim over the water. "I must take advantage of every opportunity to enjoy what fleeting pleasures life can offer."

Viviane noticed that Von Fersen, to his credit, did not react to the queen's thinly-veiled insinuation. For her part, she knew that Marie's flirtation was genuine for the simple reason that there was no reason for pretense. Her disgust grew stronger. Although he failed as a leader, King Louis was a good man who merited his wife's fidelity.

Von Fersen changed the topic. "I have news. One of the men under my command returned from the field with his report just moments before we left the palace. Prince Philippe has been apprehended."

The news silenced the two women, but Viviane felt an unexpected jolt rip through her heart. *Philippe... arrested?*

Marie gazed off into the distance, her voice as flat as the water beneath them. "Where was the murderer found?"

"That is the curious thing." Von Fersen's lips thinned. "He had gone to a remote town called Lussan."

Marie's head swiveled with the speed of a viper. "Lussan?" Her eyes locked on Viviane's face.

"Yes," the Count continued. "Apparently, he paid off the debt of a certain widow, a laundress, I believe, and issued a signed statement that was delivered to Monsieur Necker only this morning. All future taxes owed by this woman are to be charged to his own estate."

"Is that so?" Marie bit off the words.

Von Fersen shrugged. "Philippe always was a bit odd, but this is strange even for him." The oars rose, dripping water. "In any case, the captain of the *Condé Dragoons* will bring him to face the king's justice by the end of the week. He has asked for reinforcements. Philippe is quite popular in some parts of the city and, if word reaches the rabble that their hero has been arrested, there may be violence."

Viviane felt positively sick. The revelation that Philippe had gone to the speck in the mud she called home and eliminated her mother's debt was enough to tangle her stomach into knots!

Why?

Could it be true that Philippe *did* love her? But that was impossible. It was far easier to believe that he had tried to distance himself from the scene of the crime and had decided to perfect his ridiculous pretense of loving her by paying off her mother's debt. She grabbed at this straw of probability, desperate to make logical sense of what appeared to be a web of madness.

"Lussan, Viviane?" All color had left the queen's face.

Viviane's brow crinkled. Why was she so upset? Granted it was an odd place for a prince to take vacation but—

The answer flooded her mind. She gripped the edges of the rocking boat, her knuckles white. Because Philippe had gone to her home, Marie wrongfully suspected her of collaborating with one of her archenemies.

God help me.

"I had no knowledge of it, Your Grace." Viviane leaned forward hoping that the rhythmic *swish* of the oars cutting through the water would prevent the Count from hearing her words.

The queen's eyes drilled holes into her skull. "He went to Lussan! He went to your home and paid off your mother's debt. Do you honestly expect me to believe that you knew *nothing?*"

"Is something amiss, my dear?" Von Fersen's voice rang out from behind Viviane. In an instant, Marie's face lost its fierce glare.

"Nothing at all, Axel." She waggled her fingers playfully at the boatman. "I only rejoice at the fact that the murderer has been found."

"Do you think Louis will pursue the full extent of the law? As a nobleman myself, I believe that his views about the common people are a positive betrayal of his bloodline. Now, with the murder of the *dauphin*, Philippe has shown how callous he has become."

"My husband..." Marie's voice trailed off as she slipped her left hand into the water but not before Viviane noticed that she had removed her wedding band. "My husband will give me whatever I want."

She laughed and clasped her hands together. "But enough talk of death, justice and husbands! Tonight, after spending the afternoon in the Belvedere, we shall return to my *théâtre* in the Trianon where I shall perform a special piece just for you. I have been practicing my part in it for weeks."

"You spoil me, my queen." Axel's voice bounced off the shimmering water. "Might I be permitted to know the name of the performance?"

Marie leaned forward, giving Axel a generous view of her neckline. "It is something special that my writers at court have adapted from the English poet John Milton. I play the part of Eve," she laid a finger between her parted lips and winked at him, "in *Le Paradis perdu...* Paradise Lost."

⚜

Alexandre slumped on the earthen floor and hung his head between his hands. "My men failed to kill him." He massaged his temples with the balls of his thumbs, ignoring Salomé who slammed a pair of wooden plates onto the table and whirled toward him. "Philippe will keep coming after her unless he dies."

A sickening grin twisted his mouth. "But when he learns that I had my way with her first…"

Salomé grabbed an unwashed trencher and launched it at his head. "You wretched excuse of a man!" Before it could make contact, Alexandre pushed himself upright and plucked it from mid-air.

"What—"

Anticipating his quick reflexes, Salomé had cleverly followed the trencher with a blow from her iron skillet. Alexandre sunk to his knees, blood trickling from a small cut near his temple.

"You are obsessed with this aristo witch!" She swung her hand toward his cheek but Alexandre saw the blow coming and grabbed her wrist, pulling her into his lap.

Salomé spat in his face and pummeled his taut chest, her long fingernails ripping through his shirt.

"You touched her?" Her voice was shrill, more a shriek of rage than a question. "You actually *lay* with her?"

He pinned her arms to her sides. "I don't love her Salomé, if that's what you're thinking."

"Really?" She writhed in his arms. "Do I look like a fool? We've been livin' here for over six months and you've never even *looked* at me twice, but you run after her like a stupid old goat!"

Alexandre pushed her away and rolled to his feet. "I don't know what you're talking about."

"How do you think that makes me feel?" Salomé shoved her face against his own. "To hear the man I live with moanin' for a spoiled brat of a woman when he won't even see what's starin' him in the face!"

Alexandre stepped back, casting a wary eye on the skillet that she gripped between clenched fingers. "You knew from the beginning that our relationship was not a romantic one. Why this sudden change?"

"Sudden?" Salomé screamed as she lurched toward him and swung the skillet. He grabbed it, ripped it out of her hand and tossed it to one side.

Smack! Her right hand connected with his cheek. "Haven't you seen anythin' I've been doin'?" She shoved him backward, choked by her surging emotions. The pain of the knowing that he had loved her hated rival forced the words out of her mouth.

"What's the matter with you?" Alexandre rubbed his face.

"With me?" A bitter laugh escaped her lips. "Six months, here with you when the money you got for me was long gone."

He shrugged. "You're here because you care about the revolution not because of Robespierre's money."

"No, Alexandre!" She buried her face in her hands. He would never understand, not unless she told him. He was a skilled warrior and a brilliant strategist but, when it came to understanding a woman's heart, he was as thick as a stone wall.

She lifted her flushed face and met his gaze. "Six months of turnin' down all my clients. Six months of tryin' to cook decent meals." Her voice softened. "I'm not here because I care about the revolution. I'm here because I care about *you*."

⚜

Alexandre clutched his rosary and gaped at her as the meaning of her words sunk into his mind. "What a fool I've been!" What he had mistaken for lust was her way of expressing genuine affection.

She slung her arms across her chest. "I'm glad to hear you admittin' it!" Her black hair fanned out in wild tendrils around her shoulders as she jerked her head to one side and, in that moment, Alexandre felt his heart stop.

Juliette. Twelve years were ripped away in an instant. He stood with trembling fingers outstretched toward the woman who screamed his name as her tyrannical father dragged her away. Her gray eyes had been dim with unshed tears just as Salomé's were now.

Juliette. Her hair, a fountain of ebony, had cascaded around her shoulders just as Salomé's hair did at this very moment.

"I—" Alexandre stumbled over his words, for once unsure of himself. Before his whirling mind could find its center, she threw herself into his arms and pressed her lips against his own.

Alexandre held her for a long moment then broke free from the spell.

"No!" He pushed her away, breathing hard. *I cannot let any woman replace Juliette.*

Salomé stiffened. "You would touch the aristo but not me?"

"Some things are better left unsaid." Alexandre turned his back.

Salomé was quiet for several moments then slid around him, one arm lightly resting on his waist. "What is it you want Alexandre?" She touched his face. "Behind this iron mask there is a man who is cryin' out for somethin'." She traced a slow spiral on his lips with her finger. "What is it?"

The strength of his resolve began to crumble. Salomé's gentle touch, her words and her beauty unearthed caches of powerful emotions that he had thought were irrevocably buried. A tidal wave of memories washed over him, rousing an intense pain that unhinged the foundations of his world.

Salomé kissed him again but this time he did not pull away, tasting in her lips the lost sweetness of Juliette's embrace.

"What is it, Alexandre?" Her voice was a hoarse whisper. "Tell me what you want…"

He closed his eyes, hearing her voice but seeing the face of another woman. *Juliette.*

Emotion swelled in his heart, a burgeoning need that threatened everything he sought to achieve. "I want…"

"Yes?" Her whispered plea wrapped itself around his soul.

He slowly opened his eyes. "I want to fulfil our dream."

"What dream?"

"I want to be—" He hesitated, embarrassed by his own humanity.

"Tell me, my love."

Her gray eyes sucked him into their stormy depths. His wounded mind blurred the line between the present and the past, momentarily transforming Salomé into the woman he had loved and lost.

"I want to be a father."

There. He had said them. Six words that expressed his deepest desire. He wanted to be the father that he had never known, raising children in a France far different from the one that now existed. This was the dream that he had shared with

Juliette. But Philippe's betrayal had thrust the cold knife of reality through the heart of their fantasy.

Philippe. He gritted his teeth together as the hallucination yielded to cold reality. It was Salomé who stood before him, not Juliette!

"Now you know." His gaze dropped to the floor. "It can never happen, you know that."

Salomé put her hand in his and gently pulled him toward the pile of dirty straw that served as her bed. "Let go of the past, Alexandre."

Let go. Alexandre's pulse surged as he followed her lead.

A maelstrom of feelings—longing for Juliette, regret for what could have been, grief at the lost dreams they had shared—intertwined in an inescapable net around his soul.

"Let go." Salomé pressed his body against her own. Her uncanny similarities to his first love sang to him like a siren's song, drawing him away from the present and into the past. "Love me, Alexandre. Love me always."

His eyes were closed and, with his sight now unable to contradict what his ears declared to be Juliette's voice, the last shreds of his resistance faded away.

Juliette. Memories swirled through his mind with overwhelming force, snapping the bonds of time like desiccated twigs. She was here, now, in his arms, where she had always belonged. The illusion swept him away like fallen leaves before a hurricane. Lost in the turmoil of his emotions... Alexandre surrendered.

Chapter Sixteen

July 1789. Outskirts of Paris.

The afternoon sun had just begun its descent when Captain Jacourt pulled his snorting horse to an abrupt halt on the peak of a hill and twisted in his saddle while raising his gloved fist. The serpentine belt of sixty armed soldiers behind him ground to a halt then fanned out.

Jacourt pulled a handkerchief from his pocket and dabbed beads of perspiration from his brow, admitting to himself that it was not only the day's ride that made him sweat. It was the thought that between this hill and the palace of Versailles were five hundred thousand desperate people who saw the man that he held prisoner as a hero. Five hundred thousand citizens who would gladly rip any man guilty of abusing Philippe de Valence into pieces and spit upon the shredded remains.

He had treated Philippe more like a guest than a prisoner, not only because of his rank but because the prince commanded his respect in a way that Louis never could.

Jacourt had known from the moment he left Lussan that rumors of Philippe's arrest would outrun his horses. As suspected, at each town they crossed on their return to Versailles, his men encountered increasing hostility from the locals. At Rheims, where he had reconnoitered with the reinforcements from Paris, his men had been forced to beat their way through a furious mob who demanded Philippe's release.

The captain sighed and motioned for Philippe to ride up next to him. Truth be told, he was pleased with the popular support for the prince. He had never heard of a member of the royal family being executed, but Jacourt feared that the queen's wrath would cause her husband to kill the one man who could possibly save France from anarchy.

"There it is, Your Grace." Jacourt nodded toward the sprawling city below. "Paris. Twelve miles north-east of Versailles."

Smoke rose in thick plumes from thirty thousand tenements which scraped at the clouds. It was as though the buildings themselves sought to escape the squalor surrounding them.

Jacourt gestured toward the charred ruins of a large section of the buildings. "Someone's home has burned down."

Philippe grimaced. "A lifetime of work destroyed in only a few hours."

Jacourt twisted in his saddle, eyes probing the prince's face. "With respect, Your Grace, what does it matter? The poor live only to be bled dry and then, when they can give no more, they die." He dipped his head. "I beg your pardon for speaking so freely."

"Granted." Philippe's eyes drifted toward the Bastille. The prison dominated the horizon like an enormous vulture ready to swoop down on the carcasses of those who lay in its shadow.

The soldier followed his gaze. "That will be your home for the next few years. Assuming, of course, that the king does not have you killed." He swatted at a horsefly that hovered near his eyes. "They've already determined your guilt, you know. There will be no fair trial."

"I know." Philippe continued to scan the horizon. "My time in Lussan has taught me much, Captain. I now understand what it is like to live with nothing. The sheer enormity of the injustice that enslaves this kingdom is inexcusable." He sighed. "I chastise myself for wasting so many years when I could have already taken decisive action."

Philippe pulled on his mount's reins, making the spirited animal gnaw at the bit in protest. "Jacourt, as God knows my heart, I swear that, if I survive the days ahead, I will no longer sit idly by while the people of France sweat drops of blood to survive!"

The captain slanted him a glance as the shadow of a plan began to take shape in his mind. It was radically foolish. Perhaps even suicidal. But these were desperate times. *If I die, it will be with honor.*

"I know you mean that, Your Grace." Jacourt noted that Philippe's face had become tan from weeks of labor in the fields. The change in his appearance would further alienate him from his peers. Bronzed skin meant that the wearer was forced to work outdoors for a living. There could be no greater shame.

"My time has come." Philippe straightened in his saddle. "Are you with me?"

Jacourt made up his mind. "Men!" He wheeled his mount around and let his gaze flicker from one face then to another. They were good men—scarred, battle-hardened and loyal.

"We are about to enter Paris which, I do not need to remind you, is hostile to the present king." Silence answered him and Jacourt waited a moment, letting them ruminate about his use of the word *present*.

"I am therefore ordering a change in plans. We will escort the Duke of Valence to Versailles, not as a prisoner but as a hero!"

The silence was broken only by the stomp of a stallion's hoof or the whinny of a mare.

"Your duty." Jacourt thrust an arm in Philippe's direction. "Your duty is to be the honor guard to the prince who is truly a man of the people: Philippe de Valence! Give him a triumphal entry for he alone can bind the wounds that divide us."

There. He had made his stand. There was no going back now. In defending a man wanted by the crown Jacourt had defied the will of both king and queen.

He drew his sword, a thirty-seven-inch blade with a hilt of iron and brass that glittered brilliantly in the morning light. "*Vive la France!*"

His voice ripped through the air with the force of a cannon. It was a war cry. It was a shout of defiance. It was an invitation for his men to follow him into treason as they had always followed him into battle.

"*Vive la France!*" Now the silence was shattered, broken by the throats of sixty men who understood that, with those words, they had crossed the line between loyal soldier and rebel.

"*Vive la France!*" Their shouts spilled out across the rolling hills, crashing against the walls of the city they would soon enter. "*Vive la France!*"

Jacourt turned back to Philippe, his face set in a grim smile. "There is your answer, Your Grace. We are with you." He inclined his head. "Lead us into Paris."

⚜

Alexandre crouched behind a series of abandoned wagons that formed a sort of rough barricade on the eastern side of the Bastille near the Porte Saint-Antoine, and assessed the scene before him. At first glance, the Bastille seemed oddly out of place. It was a mammoth fortress whose colossal walls jutted upward at least a hundred feet and whose outer perimeter was encompassed by cluttered tenements. A closer inspection revealed that the threatening structure was separated from the adjoining neighborhoods by a large stone courtyard.

A moat that could only be crossed by two drawbridges, separated the actual prison from the courtyard. Both bridges had been raised by the military governor of the Bastille, Bernard de Launay. Fears of an uprising by the mob had caused the governor to transfer over two hundred kegs of gunpowder from the less-secure royal arsenal of Paris to the Bastille stronghold.

Alexandre clenched his fingers into a fist. He needed that powder. By committing it all to the Bastille, De Launay had forced his hand. The Bastille had to fall.

Simon glared up at the offensive prison. Behind him, thirty Moustiquaires stood intermingled with over a thousand of Paris's citizens. They carried whatever weapons or tools they had at their disposal, muttering imprecations and waiting with seething impatience for the shot that would signal the dawn of a new era.

"Repeat your orders." Alexandre spoke without taking his eyes from the towering turrets that teemed with French soldiers and Swiss mercenaries.

Simon scratched his head and yawned. "We bloody 'em a bit, knock off a few of the idiots, then pull back for the main event."

"Which is?"

"The royal arsenal where we get to kill everyone and grab whatever weapons we find."

"Show no mercy." Alexandre spit on the cobblestone streets. "We'll need the weapons for the main attack on the Bastille tomorrow."

"Mercy?" Simon barked out a laugh. "Leave mercy to God." He grinned and rolled his neck. "Leave death to me."

Alexandre frowned, unsure whether he should be pleased or offended by Simon's flippant remark. He decided that now was not the time to quibble. "My horse is ready?"

Simon jerked his head to his left. "Waitin' behind the bridge with one of our men."

Alexandre didn't reply but pulled a pair of black, hand-carved Lazarino pistols from his waist. Only Simon would ever know that the first shot of the French Revolution was fired by a son of Italy, using an Italian weapon.

Alexandre leapt to his feet, animated by the realization that twenty years of intricate planning and political maneuvering were about to end. What words could form the spark that would ignite this powder keg of mutinous citizens and make them explode into action?

His eyes fell on the blue, white and red cockades that dotted the crowd. Salomé had pinned one on his black shirt this morning before leaving their shanty to walk the eight miles to her district where she would work to win more recruits for tomorrow's assault on the Bastille. She had whispered three words in his ear. Three words that embodied the soul of the revolution.

Alexandre spun back toward the Bastille, inspired by the memory. "Liberté!" He aimed the first of his guns at a random face that peered over the turret. He gently squeezed the trigger. The man's scream as he tumbled backward was lost in the roaring echo that swelled up from a thousand throats behind him.

"Liberté!"

"Fraternité!" Simon's musket roared to life as the mob bellowed their cry for brotherhood.

"Égalité!" Alexandre emptied the contents of his second pistol in tandem with those in the crowd behind him. A few more holes appeared in the line of soldiers who stared down at them in absolute horror.

A bestial cry erupted from the mob. Alexandre stepped aside to let Paris's masses vent the first wave of their fury upon those who glared at them from on high, superior in both their elevation and in the pride that filled their stony hearts.

"The mighty will fall!" Alexandre clapped Simon on the shoulder. "I leave this in your hands." He had to shout to make himself heard among the crackling of guns around him.

"Take cover." Alexandre pointed at the tower. "They'll soon return fire."

Simon pulled the trigger of his weapon and laughed as another defender fell backward. "I was born for this!"

Alexandre released an enthusiastic howl. "We both were, Simon!"

Pride swelled his chest as he watched his Moustiquaires urge on the crowd that had sworn to break the chains that bound them. He shoved his pistols into his belt, then sprinted for the horse that pawed the ground as gunfire from both sides filled the air.

This was a day of beginnings. Today marked the beginning of the Bourbon's demise. Today marked the beginning of his own retaliation. Today marked the beginning of the rise of Rome.

He leaped into the saddle and dug his heels into the horse's sides, pointing it south toward Versailles where Viviane waited. Today marked the beginning of the end.

⚜

At first it was an amazed whisper that escaped the lips of a bedraggled boy.

"*Maman.*" He tugged at his mother's frayed skirts. "It's him!"

The woman turned, following her son's outstretched arm with her eyes and saw the noble who preached a message of love to the poor, riding down a hill into the fifteenth *arrondissement* of Paris. The despair that lingered in her tired eyes evaporated and the bitter scowl that twisted her face faded into an excited expression of hope.

"It's him!" She dropped the bucket of well water that she had gripped moments before. Her voice bounced off the tenement walls as she called to her neighbors. "Come see! Isn't that Philippe, the Friend of the People?"

Within seconds the whisper became a shout that rebounded off the stone walls. A trickle of observers quickly swelled into a stream of exuberant spectators. Cries of, "Philippe, Friend of the People!" were interspersed with cheers and even calls for "the new King of France!"

A hundred voices had become a thousand by the time Captain Jacourt and his men reached the end of the narrow street. The throng followed them, screaming with joy at the sight of the prince who had returned to right the wrong against him and lead them all into freedom.

Jacourt and his men rode slowly, two abreast in a rectangular formation that gave the masses full view of the prince of the House of Valence. Some in the crowd stripped off what ragged garments they wore and threw them in the way of his horse, screaming "Hail Philippe! Hail the Savior of France!"

Jacourt's men added to the clamor, telling whoever could hear that Philippe had given up his wealth to save an impoverished widow. The news—when it could finally be heard—created such a surge in enthusiasm that the soldiers had to pull more closely together to resist the press of the crowd as hands strained to touch even the border of the prince's travel-stained cloak.

Philippe rode with relaxed confidence, acknowledging the crowd with a dignified smile.

"Steady men." Jacourt admonished those nearest him. "Keep a sharp lookout, now. Not everyone in this crowd is friendly." He pointed to a group of men that stood slightly apart from the throng, the corners of their mouths turned down.

One of them dropped to one knee and scooped up a rock. "Who is this Philippe? No friend to us. He's just another bloodsucking aristo!" He pulled his arm backward and prepared to let fly.

"*Attention!*" Jacourt grabbed at Philippe's arm, but the prince had already seen the man. Philippe pulled his horse to a sudden stop and leaped down from the animal, landing directly in front of his adversary. A hush fell over those nearest to the pair then spread like a wave to the furthest end of the street where thousands craned their necks for one glimpse of the celebrated prince.

"What do you want most, my friend?" Philippe's voice was gentle but unyielding as he stared down his attacker.

The man gawked at him, stunned by this unexpected reaction. "I-I d-dunno." Then he glanced back to his friends who shrugged and shook their heads. "Bread... some food... a new life?"

"That is exactly what I bring to the people of France. A new life, totally different from everything that you have ever known."

A low murmur swept through those close enough to hear and they spreading the word to others.

"What did he say?" An old vagrant jabbed a bystander with his cane.

"He's goin' to give us a new life."

The wizened beggar jabbed his neighbor again. "He's gettin' a new wife?"

"No, *vieillard*," came the exasperated reply. "Life. He's givin' us a new *life!*"

Philippe plucked the rock from the slack fingers of his opponent, tucked it in the crease of his elbow and swung easily into the saddle.

"Why do you let them say such things about you?" The erstwhile attacker indicated the crowd with a wide sweep of his arms. "Will you indeed become our king?"

Say it. Jacourt mentally shouted the words. *Give them what they want. You have them in the palm of your hand!*

Philippe smiled as he held up the stone. "People of Paris." His voice rang like a trumpet to the furthest reach of the throng. "Your suffering is proclaimed on every stone of our city!"

Just say the word and they'll tear Louis apart. Jacourt's hands were clammy as he waited for the signal.

"The very rocks of Paris cry out for justice and I swear to you that I will no longer stay in a gilded palace while my people have no hope for tomorrow!"

"*Vive la France!*" His words were swallowed up by the scream of the ecstatic multitudes. Tricolor flags burst into view. Hands passed them about as the mob hailed the prince who rode through their midst.

Hundreds marched alongside him, singing songs of revolution, while others shimmied up on lampposts for a better view of a moment they would never forget. Still others hung precariously from fragile banisters in tenements four stories up, gladly risking their lives for a glimpse of Philippe, the one man who could heal their fragmented country.

Jacourt smiled. For the first time in over three hundred years, Paris had hope.

⚜

Viviane bowed in a deep curtsy before her mistress. She held the subservient position until Marie's voice reached her.

"You may rise."

Viviane obeyed but kept her eyes downcast. She wanted the monarch to have no doubt of her devotion but, even as the thought crossed her mind, resentment gnawed at her heart. *What right does she have to doubt my loyalty?*

"So, we each have a question that must be answered." Marie sighed as she broke the silence and flopped onto the floral-patterned divan that sat underneath a gilded wall-length mirror. She flung her small feet up onto the divan, propped up her head on the matching bolster and crooked her finger at Viviane.

"You want to know what happened between Axel and me last night after I ordered you to leave us in the Trianon's grotto." Marie drilled Viviane with her eyes. "I want to know if I can trust a woman who denies knowing that my nemesis has gone out of his way to settle her mother's debts."

Viviane had no interest in whatever had transpired between Count von Fersen and the queen. Frankly, Marie's allusion to their relationship was enough to make her want to stuff her ears with wax. It was the queen's second remark held her interest. *Trust.*

"Majesty I—"

"What did you give Philippe that made him *so* generous, Viviane? You have no money and no political influence, so your options are limited. Either you sold him my secrets or..." Marie laced her hands beneath the pillow that propped up her head and waggled her toes, "you sold him your body."

"I assure you Majesty that I—"

"Oh, spare me the two-faced fluff, Viviane! In a sense, I am glad to see you loosening up a bit. Your prudish nature was beginning to make me feel rather uncomfortable."

Viviane could stand it no longer. A few months ago, she would have tolerated this kind of sultry wordplay, perhaps even enjoyed it. But the *dauphin's* death and her own weakness had shown her how much was at stake in this unending game of truth and lies. A queen who did not reveal her true nature. A king who was dishonored by his wife. A politician who incited the masses to revolt so he could avenge his wounded pride. When did it end? She would no longer sacrifice her honor on the altar of hypocrisy.

She stalked over to the queen, face pinched and muscles taut. "Forgive me Your Grace, but you are wrong. I did *not* give myself to Philippe de Valence nor did I know that he would show such kindness to my mother."

Marie pushed herself upright. "The question is *why*, Viviane." She jabbed Viviane's stomach. "Why *you*? What does Philippe hope to gain?"

Viviane felt the back of her neck begin to burn. "I do not know." It was true. She thought she had driven Philippe away at their last meeting, certain that his words of love were only a cruel attempt to drag her through the mud of court gossip.

Marie perused her for a long moment then dropped onto one of the seven fringed benches that bordered the golden banister around her bed. She motioned for Viviane to sit next to her.

"Very well. I will put this matter behind me." She wrinkled her nose. "It seems that I have no choice but to trust you—even if you are a *bourgoise*."

At the insult, a cold feeling spread throughout Viviane's chest but she refused to show any emotion.

"You have the second letter for Robespierre?" Marie extended an upturned hand.

"*Oui, Altesse.*" She reached into her pocket and withdrew the short note but hesitated before handing it to the queen.

"Give it to me, quickly!" Marie snatched the letter and unfolded it, her glittering eyes devouring its contents. "Good, good. It is passionate, just as I wanted."

She folded the note again and strode to her desk where her seal rested. "You were born to write Viviane," she said while pressing the seal against the melted wax. "Your talents are genuine."

She blew gently on the sealed letter, dropped it on her desk, then reclaimed her seat.

"Thank you, Majesty." Viviane lowered her eyes.

"The king has informed me that Prince Philippe has arrived."

Viviane looked up but her face remained the very picture of calm. Marie, by contrast, began to tug at the fringes that dangled along the side of her stool.

"He brought a virtual army with him!" She tugged too hard and pulled the fringe off the floral cushion. Marie stared briefly at the object and then tossed it in the corner.

She stood, wrapped her arms around her chest and stepped to the large double-doors that opened to the white veranda that overlooked the estate's massive Apollo fountain.

"They are still out there somewhere." Marie shook her head, making her pearl earrings bob wildly. "Chanting his name and failing to see him for the murderous villain he truly is."

Pity laid its soothing hand upon Viviane's heart and she felt the tide of her anger begin to ebb. *Her son was just murdered. Does she not have reason to suspect everyone?* She walked over to her queen and gently squeezed her hand.

"Things are not always as they seem." She tried to comfort the monarch.

Marie's head snapped toward her. "That is exactly my fear, Madame de Lussan." She licked her lips twice. "In any case, his trial will be held in the *Salon Apollo* within the hour."

She examined Viviane's face. "I want you to be there."

The younger woman's heart sank like a rock. Philippe's trial would be a farce. If he were tried, he would be condemned. She did not want to witness such a spectacle.

"This troubles you." Marie's voice was the soft hiss of a serpent. "Why?"

Viviane did not respond but turned her gaze outside. The Orangery caught her attention. *Alexandre. I am supposed to meet him in two hours!*

"You have feelings for him." In Marie's mouth the words seemed like a crime. "You... love him."

"No, Your Grace." Viviane shook her head. *I don't love him, I don't.* She wrestled with the persistent voice in her skull that called her a liar.

"Then why not attend the trial?"

"Because," Viviane's mind groped madly for an excuse, "b-because I am to meet Alexandre in the Orangery. As Your Grace commanded," Viviane added.

"Oh. I see." Marie averted her eyes. "Well, tonight I have need of you. Attend the trial, hear the outcome then return to my chambers. Your gardener can wait until tomorrow evening."

A wave of nausea swelled within Viviane. Then she realized that this was an elaborate test to determine the extent of her loyalty. If she was present at the trial and showed visible support for the crown's position, Marie would have less reason to suspect her devotion.

If I don't attend...

The silence had become pregnant. Viviane curtsied and lowered her gaze to hide the anger that glittered in her eyes. "As you command, my Queen."

⚜

Fear. It was an animal, relentlessly shredding her insides with vicious claws. Its scent—a bitter, iron-laced stench—assaulted Viviane's nostrils as she pressed her way through the heavily congested War Room, stepped underneath the green marble entrance and wedged herself into a corner of the *Salon Apollo*. Some of the courtiers recognized her as the queen's *dame d'honneur* and reluctantly let her pass. Viviane nodded her thanks but she would have given anything to escape the luxurious prison she had just entered.

Scarlet, satin-covered walls, embellished with elaborate designs, closed in on her on all sides. Her eyes wandered to the ceiling on which a series of frescos, showing scenes of the cloud-filled heavens, were imprisoned in the golden cages of their frames. Semi-nude angels pressed against the borders of the paintings as though to prevent the flight of the characters depicted within. The austere face of Apollo himself stared at the drama unfolding in the world of mortals below. His lips, curled back in a snarl, reminded Viviane that there was no escape.

Calm down, Viviane. Breathe. But her silent commands did nothing to slow her racing pulse as her eyes scanned the room, seeking the face of the prince who was now on trial for his life. They all were prisoners of fear here. They were slaves who masqueraded at freedom while they spent their days scurrying around like rats in an elaborate golden cage.

Louis—whose fingers tapped a staccato rhythm on his knees as he slouched in his seat—feared losing a kingdom that was slipping from his grasp. Marie—who sat stiffly next to her husband on a silver throne before a blue and gold tapestry—shrank from losing her remaining children and her dissolute way of life. The nobles—whose clamoring surrendered to an eerie hush as Philippe stepped forward—dreaded the retaliatory wrath of the poor.

And Viviane? She trembled at the thought of Philippe's death.

Why?

She struggled to understand the complex emotions that threatened to choke her. *I don't love him. Whether he lives or dies has nothing to do with me.*

She tried to reason away the terror that grew with each step Philippe took, but nothing could change the fact that his death *did* matter. Questions burned in her mind like the candles that blazed in the six massive candelabras near the thrones. Why had Philippe gone to her home? Why had he helped her mother?

The prince turned toward the crowd. *Is he looking for me?* Viviane shrank back, hoping that the crowd would conceal her from his searching gaze. The moment his eyes turned toward her corner, the man in front of her shifted and their eyes locked for what felt like ten lifetimes but was only as many heartbeats.

Viviane stared at him, lost in wonder at the changes to his appearance. His dark hair fell about his shoulders, wild from weeks of blowing free in the wind. His face was bronzed from the southeastern sun and contrasted sharply with the pale, powdered appearance of those around him. It was ironic, but he who had the most to fear seemed to fear the least. *Out of all of us, he alone is guiltless.*

"Philippe de Valence, *Prince du Sang* and peer of the realm." The voice of Gaston du Poitier, the king's chancellor, sounded like the rusty squeal of a closing prison gate. "You stand accused of the murder of the *dauphin,* Prince Louis-Joseph, heir to the throne of France. What do you say in your defense?"

A silence so complete filled the room that Viviane swore Philippe could hear the pounding of her heart.

"Your Grace? Are you innocent or guilty?"

The Chancellor repeated the question but again, Philippe did not answer. He simply stared at Louis, his expression one of unspeakable sorrow.

"I am afraid, Your Grace, that you *must* answer the question." Du Poitier gestured helplessly then looked at the king.

Philippe said nothing and Louis, after a prolonged silence, rose to his feet. "Cousin Philippe, I command you to speak. If you are a loyal subject, then you *will* answer the charge. Are you or are you not guilty of the murder of my son?"

Philippe made them wait a moment longer then opened his mouth. "I am a loyal subject. A loyal subject to truth and justice, none of which appear in this court!"

Shock at the stern rebuff numbed Viviane and she leaned against the frame of the ceiling-high glass door for support.

Louis took a step back. "What do you mean?" He clasped his jeweled hands together. "Explain yourself!"

Philippe did not hold back. "The people starve, helpless and abused, while you inebriate yourself with riches and ungodly pleasures." The prince's eyes flashed to Marie with these last words. She lifted her chin in silent defiance.

"You, Louis, have the power to right the wrongs and heal the wounds of France but you choose instead to vilify my name, believing false accusations because of your own hatred for the truth!"

"And what is the truth?"

It was Marie who had spoken and every head in the room swung toward her. The queen leapt from her throne and thrust herself between her husband and Philippe. The diamonds in her hair were dull when compared to the fury that glittered in her eyes.

"The truth is that you murdered my son." She pointed an accusing finger at his face. "You thought that your note would be destroyed by his nurse when the package was opened!" The queen raised her strident voice in triumph as she held out her hand. Geneviève rushed forward and bowed while giving her the incriminating evidence.

"But you were wrong, you deceiver of men. You were so wrong! God bore witness to the evil of your perfidious heart. This good woman kept the evidence that will condemn you."

Marie held the small piece of paper inches from Philippe's face. "The crimson seal of the Duke of Valence. Red with the blood of an innocent child."

"I did not write that note nor send any gift to the prince," Philippe said.

"Oh, pitiful liar!" Marie screamed sending flecks of spittle from her mouth. "Perjurer!" She slapped Philippe's cheek, ignoring the scandalized whispers that flew about the room.

Viviane caught a glimpse of Marie's incensed eyes and saw in them only calculating cunning. A chill swept through her as she realized, in that moment, that the goal of the royal actress was not to avenge her son's death but to destroy her hated enemy.

The swine!

Marie *knew* Philippe was innocent. This was not a pull for justice; it was a cynical manipulation of a tragedy with the goal of ending Philippe's life.

A sudden motion to her left made Viviane glance over her shoulder. Through the gold-encrusted glass panels, the figure of a man steadily leading a horse toward the Orangery grabbed her attention. He turned his face toward the château as a beam of light illuminated his features. *Alexandre.*

Her heart convulsed. The queen had ordered her to stay, but she had seen the cost of Marie's duplicity and it was too high a price to pay. She was *bourgeoise* and she belonged with Alexandre not with this murderous group of wealthy hypocrites.

"My God, don't let them kill him." She whispered the prayer as she glanced over her shoulder again. Her poignant concern for

Philippe warred against her desire to flee the madness of this purgatory with Alexandre. Viviane knew she could not change the outcome of the trial but, if Philippe was going to be condemned, she would not be part of the mob that sanctioned his murder.

"My lord the king." Marie's voice jerked Viviane's attention back to the throne. The queen fell to her knees, eyes filling with tears as she beat her heaving breasts in the very picture of sorrow.

Deceiver.

"This man," she cast an arm wildly behind her, "has been proven guilty of the most despicable of crimes. By accusing you, the King of France, of injustice he has condemned himself with his own mouth."

The corners of Viviane's mouth turned downward. *Vixen.* The manipulative queen had seized upon Phillippe's words to force her husband into action. No king could tolerate such an insinuation by a possible rival and let him live.

Louis laced his fingers together over his rotund stomach and twiddled his thumbs. "What would you have me do? You will recall our son's final words."

"There is only one punishment fit for such a creature, my lord." Marie raised herself to her full height. "An eye for an eye, a tooth for a tooth, a life for a life." She thrust a finger at Philippe's face. "He must die!"

Louis's eyes darted between his wife and the murmuring crowd of courtiers. Viviane felt a surge of sympathy for the embattled monarch. His wife's conduct had been disgraceful. She had commandeered control of a trial that Louis should have directed. The people already suspected that she ruled France and, after news of today's debacle spread, there would be no doubt as to who was the true head of the kingdom.

Viviane began to tremble, every fiber of her being screaming in protest at the queen's decree. *I can't stand this any longer.* Her sweaty hand gripped the golden handle of the door behind her. She pressed down and felt the door swing outward. She had to leave before Louis pronounced the dreadful sentence. All eyes were focused on the king. *Now!*

She slipped outside and closed the door, then filled her lungs with the warm July air. She would need to gather a few essentials before meeting Alexandre. Viviane made her way along the side the building, glancing occasionally over her shoulder.

No one followed. Slipping into the side entrance that granted access to the Hall of Mirrors, she ran the remaining distance to her room.

☘

Alexandre led his horse around the corner of the massive ornamental lake known as *la Pièce d'Eau des Suisses*, trying to avoid notice as he approached the Orangery. Trees lined the path like an army of sentinels, momentarily sheltering him from view. No guards had challenged his entry due to the dissipating masses who had apparently followed Philippe de Valence as he returned to Versailles. The soldiers on duty had been too occupied with the cheering, brash throngs to notice the stealthy movements of a trained assassin.

Alexandre snorted and scuffed the gravel below his feet as he passed a pair of citrus palm trees. The fools did not realize that Philippe was the true enemy. He was even more of a threat than the king they detested. But they did not know the prince as he knew him. They did not know that he was a traitorous liar who preyed upon the emotions of the weak to satisfy his own need for praise.

He had been fighting far from the scene of Philippe's triumphant entry into Paris and had missed the entire spectacle. A scowl darkened Alexandre's brow as he passed another large circular pool whose tranquility was broken by a spurting fountain. If he had only been near the scene of Philippe's triumphant entry, his bullet would have brought the nobleman down from his high horse.

No. The last rays of sunshine lingered over the pool's water, turning it to blood. *Death is not enough.* His eyes shifted beyond the red waters to the flowering branches of the white pomegranate tree. *He must know the pain of rejection.*

Alexandre crossed himself and prayed that Viviane would not be late. He cast a furtive glance over his shoulder. It was only a matter of time before his presence was discovered. He ran his hands over his chest, instinctively feeling for the throwing knives and pistols that were concealed beneath his clothes. *Come, little aristo. Come.*

✤

"Not immediate death?" Marie gaped at her husband. "No beheading?"

The king's face flushed crimson at his wife's outburst. He fingered the scepter that lay across his lap and thrust himself out of his throne. "The king has spoken!"

Louis shot an irate glance at his high-strung wife, willing her not to publicly undermine his judgement.

"General Lafayette?"

Lafayette, general of the king's guard, stepped forward and saluted.

"The Duke of Valence has been found guilty of murder." The king frowned as he thumped his scepter against the fleshy palm of his other hand. "It is my decision that he be given one hour to collect his necessary belongings. The prisoner shall then be transferred under heavy guard to the Bastille where he shall remain until *I,*" Louis stressed the personal pronoun as he glared at his wife, "see fit to execute the prescribed sentence of death by hanging."

The king scowled at Marie, enjoying watching her squirm. *Let the little minx remember who rules the kingdom.*

A murmur swept through the crowd. Although Philippe counted few of his peers as friends, the thought of one royal house exterminating another sat ill with many of the nobles. If, God forbid, Louis's one remaining son should die before assuming the throne and producing an heir, France could slide into anarchy.

Du Poitier, the chancellor, stepped forward and stamped the base of his long rod against the floor, commanding silence. "Does Prince Philippe, a peer of the realm, have any final words?"

Philippe's head had been lowered as the king's decree was pronounced but he now looked up with blazing eyes.

"You call me a prince, but this is not my kingdom." He spun to the crowd and flung both of his arms wide. "I will no longer be privileged while my people are bound in chains, slaves to fear and tyranny."

"The French are enslaved to no man!" Louis hurled the words through gritted teeth, furious with both his wife and his cousin.

Philippe moved to a corner of the room so that both monarchs and the audience fell within the range of his eyes. He unbuttoned the diamond brooch that secured the voluminous white cloak around his shoulders and cast it on the ground in front of Louis's throne.

"What are you doing?" Louis's beady eyes were round with horror.

"This day I relinquish my name and my title." Philippe's shout rang out across the crowd.

Then he pulled off the signet ring that identified him as a part of the royal family and threw it on top of the robe. "Let my sacrifice inspire you all to do as I have done."

"What are you saying?" Marie recoiled. "You are condemned! You want us to die with you?"

"I will die." He shrugged off the gold and white waistcoat that dangled to his calves. "But when I do it will be as one of them and not as a prince of Valence!" With his bronzed skin and simple clothing, he could have passed for any of the thousands of commoners who had milled about him earlier that afternoon.

"I am no longer a prince. From now until my death, I will take on a new name. A name that will show all of France that I am one of the people."

Silence gripped the assembled nobles. Even Marie gaped at him, speechless. To renounce his name and his title was to renounce whatever fragments of honor that would outlive him. Such a thing had never happened before.

"W-what will you call yourself?" Louis found his voice first.

"Philippe... Égalité."

Philippe's announcement unleashed a roar of protest. The word, which meant *equality*, was commonly spouted by the

Third Estate. To take that word as a name was tantamount to heresy in the eyes of the privileged.

"Equality?" A single voice rose above the others. "Scandalous!"

"He's lost his mind," another bellowed. "Take him away!"

Pandemonium swallowed the crowd and Philippe had to shout to make himself heard.

"If I can lay aside my wealth and power, you can also lay aside your greed. Follow my example and save France!"

"Traitor!" The shouts became still more heated.

"Take him to the Bastille!"

"Execute him! Now!"

The crowd shoved him forward, hurling insults upon his head. General Lafayette snapped his fingers. In response, ten officers pressed their way through the mob of nobles and clapped a pair of shackles upon Philippe's hands.

"Order!" The chancellor's bellow was lost in the riotous clamor. "Order!"

Lafayette's men hurriedly formed a perimeter around Philippe and made their way through the gauntlet of enraged gentry who lashed out with gilded canes and walking sticks, landing a few blows upon the prisoner's head and shoulders.

"Get out of here!"

"Traitorous dog! Kill him!"

"Order!" Du Poitier stamped his foot against the floor. "Order please!"

But no one was listening.

Marie-Antoinette rose, trembling with fury. With huff and furious swirl of her skirts, she left the debacle behind her. Louis shouted for a servant as he rushed to his apartment. He fled from his own court—a court that had fallen into madness.

⚜

Philippe Égalité, erstwhile Duke of Valence, Prince of France and possible heir to the throne, rubbed his chin with his thumb as he stared down at the empty courtyard from the balcony of his appartement. He had received one hour to prepare himself for the last days of his life but he needed nothing. Now only thirty minutes remained. *It was considerate of Louis to give me the time.* Or perhaps the small gesture was his cousin's attempt at washing his hands of his guilt.

"Ahem." A voice intruded on his thoughts. Philippe turned to see Captain Jacourt standing in the doorway, a worshipful expression on his face.

"Your Grace—"

"Just Philippe, Jacourt." Philippe held out an upturned palm. "I am no longer a prince, remember?"

A wide smile split the captain's face. "Philippe. I have never..." Jacourt spread his hands apart, at a loss for words. "You..." The older man finally gave up and clasped the erstwhile prince in his arms.

At first Philippe held himself aloof, startled by this unexpected display of emotion. Then he remembered that Jacourt was now his equal and returned the embrace.

"It is an honor to know you." Tears shone in the soldier's eyes. "To take such a life would be a crime against France!"

Philippe shook his head and turned to stare at the vast estates of Versailles. His greatest regret was that Viviane had not been there when he had announced that he would become one of the people.

It was true that he had renounced his title hoping to be an example of service, but he wanted to die knowing that she believed in his love for her. He now understood why she could never accept the love of a prince, but he had hoped that she would believe in the love of a pauper. They could never be together, but the knowledge that she believed him would be consolation enough. But Viviane had left.

"My life is worthless Jacourt unless the people learn to love as God loves." He shrugged. "Love is the foundation of every just society."

Motion among the trees near the Orangery caught his attention. Philippe squinted, his sharp eyes making out a man, a horse and a woman. A man and a woman near the Orangery at evening? He frowned. *The woman. I know her.*

Realization flooded his mind.

"Captain, I must ask you one favor." He spun to Jacourt, his heart thudding.

"Anything for you Philippe. Anything."

"I need to get out of my apartment."

The silver-haired soldier frowned. "You are planning an escape?"

"No, but there is someone I must see before I am taken."

Jacourt hesitated. "I have the unfortunate duty of conducting you to the Bastille with a hundred of General Lafayette's men." He stroked his chin. "Lafayette himself is treading on dangerous ground by letting me live after I supported you this afternoon. He is a man of honor and must therefore obey the king's command but, in his heart, I believe he supports the revolutionaries. In truth, about four-fifths of the army wish for change but..."

Jacourt's words fell on deaf ears as Philippe rushed back to the balcony. At this moment, he could care less about the revolution or Lafayette's political opinions. Viviane was down there and he had to see her! Madness born of a desperation seized him.

He peered over the edge of the balcony, mentally calculating the distance to the ground. Thirty feet. Philippe rushed to his bed, jerked off the silken sheets that covered it, picked up a dagger from his dresser and began to stab madly at the fabric.

The soldier gaped at him.

"Help me!" Philippe gestured toward the window. "There's no other way I can get down. There will be soldiers blocking all exits of the palace. If I leave they will think I am trying to escape."

"And you are sure you are not?" Jacourt began to knot the ends of the shredded sheets.

"No." Philippe's hands worked with feverish ardor. "You can bring your men to the Orangery and arrest me there. I swear that I will not resist."

Jacourt nodded. "I am staking my reputation and my life upon your word but, after what I have seen tonight, I believe the odds are in my favor."

"Done!" Philippe ran to the balcony and hurriedly knotted one end of the makeshift rope around the stone railing of the balcony. Then he tossed the other end over the edge, glanced down to be sure that no one was below, and leapt off the edge of the terrace.

"Alexandre?"

Viviane's low voice brought the spy to his feet. She cast troubled eyes upon him and clutched a small bag in her hand. The dying light of the sun cast a red glow around his face and shoulders, giving him the look of a man covered in blood. The darkness of his hair contrasted sharply with the white flowers of the Bride Tree.

"You came." Alexandre's voice, gentle and alluring, once would have sent her pulse racing, but Viviane was surprised to realize that the surge of passion she had once felt was gone. Now, the sight of him triggered only a sense of shame.

"As promised." The words were stilted. Forced. She licked her lips and glanced at the Orangery, the memory of their encounter making her feel sick. *God, how I regret it!*

"What is the matter, my love?" Alexandre stepped closer and traced her chin with his thumb.

She cringed at his touch. "It's... it's nothing."

Viviane bit her lip, her unspoken emotions balling up within her. How could she admit that she regretted giving in to her passions? How could she confess that knowing Philippe would die filled her with grief?

There was no option but to finish what she had started. To stay at the palace would make her a spectator to Philippe's murder, but to leave was to abandon the man who had kept her mother from losing everything. Guilt hung like a millstone around her shoulders, rooting her to the ground.

"Then, if nothing is the matter, we must go." Alexandre reached for her hand but Viviane drew back. In abandoning Philippe to his fate she felt as though she were about to commit yet another sin. This man had saved her mother! How could she leave without thanking him?

"Let's go," he said between clenched teeth.

"Viviane!"

Alexandre's entire body went stiff at the unexpected voice.

"Viviane!"

She turned and saw him rushing toward her, hair streaming and eyes sparkling with joy.

"Philippe!" The guilt that plagued her evaporated. She began to run to him but Alexandre's feral growl pulled her up short.

"Philippe? You call this dog by his name?"

Philippe slowed to a walk.

"Alexandre?" His brow crinkled as his gaze shifted from Viviane's smiling face to the man who stood with clenched fists and legs spread apart behind her.

"Philippe." On Alexandre's lips, the word sounded like a curse.

Viviane's smile faded as her eyes darted from one to the other. She realized that the two men were connected by some hostile bond of which she was ignorant.

"Does this remind you of something, Philippe?" Alexandre's fingers twitched as he angled forward, shoving Viviane to one side.

"Alexandre—" She grabbed at his arm.

"*Chut!*" He lifted two black-gloved fingers to his lips. The sun had set but the courtyard was illuminated by firelight, cast by rows of torches lining the château and the two grand staircases.

"It was raining that night, do you remember?" Another threatening step forward.

Philippe held his ground.

"Even the heavens wept at your betrayal, you Judas!" Alexandre began to circle his nemesis. He flung a shock of hair out of his eyes.

"My intent was to save Juliette from a life of misery, Alexandre, not to tear you apart." Philippe's eyes followed his every move.

"To *save* her? What a hero!" Alexandre's cynical laugh mocked him. "Saving her from what? My love?"

A cold tremor ran down Viviane's spine as his words unveiled a critical element of truth.

Alexandre has loved another woman?

"You were *stealing* her from her father." Philippe thrust a finger in Alexandre's face. "You would have ruined her life!"

"No!" Alexandre rammed his fist into Philippe's gut, sending him reeling backward. "I trusted you! I told you that we were going to run away and you," a downward chop of his hand against Philippe's neck drove him to his knees on the cobblestones, "you ran, squealing like the pig you are, to your father."

"You did not love her." Philippe pushed himself upright. "What kind of love poisons a girl's mind and turns her against her own family? She died cursing her father's name. You ruined her relationship with parents who adored her. You call that love?"

"Stop!" Alexandre pressed his hands against his eyes. "We loved each other! We shared the same mind, the same heart."

"Yes, Juliette wanted a revolution, but you did not love her any more than you love Viviane!"

Alexandre howled as he slid a dagger from inside his vest. The flickering firelight cast demonic silhouettes upon his face as he launched himself forward.

"Let the past go, Alexandre!" Philippe caught his downswing and shoved Alexandre back. "Your hate will not bring her back."

"Maybe not," fury twisted his face, "but it will get rid of you!" He lifted his hand to send the dagger into Philippe's heart but pulled up short as the sound of tramping boots reached their ears.

Alexandre made a choking sound in his throat. He slammed the dagger back into its sheathe and swung up in the saddle of his stomping horse. "Viviane," he extended a hand, "we must go. Now!"

She hesitated, torn between her burgeoning desire to understand Philippe and the certainty that she did not belong in his world. Alexandre had secrets she didn't know about, and that knowledge made her hesitate.

"Viviane, don't trust him." Philippe rushed forward. "Leave him now!"

"Come quickly!" Alexandre shouted at the same time. "I'll explain everything."

"Viviane, he's a liar!" Philippe reached for her.

"Come with me, Viviane," Alexandre leaned over the neck of his stallion. "I'll explain everything, I swear it. You belong with us, not this aristo whose idea of truth is nothing but twisted lies."

Hot tears blurred Viviane's vision. She needed answers, but her decision had to be made now.

"You're right." A tremor ran through her body. She had to go with Alexandre. Not only had he been her lover but, with Philippe condemned to die, she knew that she could never call Versailles her home. Heartsick, she put her hand into Alexandre's and swung up in the saddle behind him.

"Philippe." Viviane's voice broke as she called his name.

There was so much she wanted to say. She wanted to thank him, to ask him to forgive her but time itself had become her enemy. If she did not leave now with Alexandre, he could be arrested and, when Marie discovered that she had disobeyed her orders, she would share his fate.

Philippe ran toward her again, trying to grab the bridle of the pawing horse but Alexandre dug his heels into the animal's sides and trotted just out of reach.

"How does it feel to be separated from the woman you love, Philippe?" He taunted his nemesis as he urged his mount toward the gates. "Did you know that Viviane was my lover?"

Philippe blanched. "It's not true." His eyes flew to Viviane's face. "Tell me it's not true!"

She covered her burning face with her palms as a ragged sob ripped out of her throat.

"She came to me of her own free will," Alexandre crowed. "In the Orangery while you were busy playing the hero for her dear old *maman*." He rode closer. "You know what part I enjoyed best?" Strident laughter spilled out from his chest.

"While she was gasping with pleasure, I could only imagine this moment." He bent low over the animal's neck and spat on Philippe's stricken face. "My only thought was how you would feel when you learned that the woman you saved from death— the woman you love—gave herself to me first!"

The stallion snorted as Alexandre pulled sharply on the reins. "You once called me a pauper who could not provide for a woman. Well this woman chose me, a pauper, instead of you—a prince."

He threw back his head with a maniacal laugh then kicked the horse's sides. "Think on that while you die. Hyah!"

The horse leapt down the main path, sprinting past the *Pièce d'Eau des Suisses* as the first line of Lafayette's men came into view. They clapped heavy iron shackles around Philippe's wrists and feet, then led him through the growing darkness to the Bastille.

Chapter Seventeen

July 1789. Third Precinct, Paris.

A steady rain, born of the summer's fetid heat, plastered Viviane's long hair to her scalp and soaked through her clothes. She rode behind Alexandre, hearing in her mind the echoes of Philippe's cry. *Tell me it's not true!* She screwed her face into a tight ball. *If only I could undo it.*

The streets of Paris swarmed with unruly crowds who targeted anyone riding in a carriage or had the misfortune of being known as a friend to those in power. The lambs had become lions and, like lions, they were on the hunt. The screams of their victims rose from darkened corners of the city as the rage that had been suppressed for three hundred years spilled over in a violent excess of blood.

Viviane shuddered as Alexandre's horse splashed past the burned-out hull of a shattered buggy. The overturned wheels spun listlessly through the air, propelled by the rain that fell like heaven's tears.

Across the street, a drunk revolutionary staggered about in the rain singing, "*Ça ira, ça ira.* Things will get better, my beauty!" His mouth cracked in a lustful grin as she rode past.

She jerked her eyes away, and focused on the carriage. Murky splotches of blood, made visible by the sputtering lampposts lining the streets, dripped from the door onto the dark cobblestones below. In the smashed remnants of its window, someone had jabbed the blue, white and red flag that embodied the resistance. The thought of the revolution jerked Philippe's stunning accusation back into sharp mental focus.

"Who was she?" She forced her eyes away from the violent scene and loosened her grip on Alexandre's waist. The horse's bouncing gait forced her to hold onto him, but she needed some straight answers before she would touch him any more than was necessary.

"*She* was Juliette." Alexandre's back was as unyielding as an iron gate. "The woman I loved."

So, it was true! Viviane felt the breath leave her lungs, as though his words were fists that pummeled her gut. She reached up to brush a soaking clump of hair out of her eyes.

"Philippe betrayed us the night we planned to run away. We were separated." Alexandre ignored the falling showers. "Juliette was married off and died while giving her beast of a husband his first child."

The coldness in his voice numbed her.

"I'm sorry." Viviane touched his shoulder.

Alexandre did not reply.

Viviane hesitated to ask the question that burned in her mind but couldn't resist.

"Why didn't you tell me?"

"There was no need."

"No need?" Her reply was more an incredulous shriek than an echo of his words. "You loved another woman and didn't feel it necessary to tell *me?*" She fell silent. "Don't you love me?"

Silence.

Panic seized her heart. "Alexandre?" She grabbed his elbow. "Don't you love me?" She was desperate now for his assurance but none was forthcoming.

Pounding rain filled the silence and, in that silence, she *felt* Alexandre's answer. The sudden stiffness of his spine, the rigid set of his jaw all shouted—

"No."

He carefully stepped the horse around the rain-spattered, mangled remnants of a woman's corpse.

That was it.

No.

One word that condemned her tattered feelings to an emotional firing squad. Viviane's throat tightened. She had said "yes" to the most intimate of questions, convinced that he loved her. She had said "yes" to his litany of promises. She had abandoned everything to follow him. Now, when she asked the most important question of all, he responded with one word that was powerful enough to rip the heart out of her chest.

No.

"If you don't love me," she forced the words past the lump in her throat, "then why—"

He cut off her question. "Can't you tell?"

Realization sliced into her mind with the cutting edge of a dagger.

"Revenge?" She could barely breathe. "You seduced me for revenge!" Viviane raked wet fingers through her stringy hair, sucking in small gulps of air as her mind sprinted through the series of events that had led to this moment.

Alexandre's sudden appearance when she had first been attracted to Philippe. Alexandre's seductive voice, luring her down a dark path from which there was no return. Alexandre's promises of true freedom, of a blissful life with people who understood her. She was a piece in the game—nothing more than his pawn when she had believed that she was his queen.

That was why he had boasted about their night in the Orangery. His pretense at love was nothing more than a vindictive attempt to woo her away from his enemy. *How does it feel to be separated from the woman you love, Philippe?* The words echoed in her mind, bringing with them a startling revelation. If Alexandre would go to such lengths to drive them apart, it meant that Philippe's love was real!

A wave of self-loathing mingled with hate threatened to choke her. She despised herself for the decisions she had made. She hated Alexandre for the part that he had played in her downfall.

"God help me." Her hand flew to her hair again, but this time, she grabbed a fistful and tugged hard while screaming at him. "You used me!"

"Didn't you do the same?" His rebuke shocked her into silence. "Or did you really believe that I was stupid enough to fall for your little charade in the garden?"

"That was genuine, Alexandre!" Viviane pulled as far away from him as she could without falling from the horse.

"Really? It wasn't a ploy to get me to deliver a letter for your little queen?"

"I needed your help but I truly I loved you."

"Then why was your heart still tied to his?" Alexandre's head whipped around. Fury and scorn played across his face. "Even as your breath was hot on my lips, your eyes told me that he was on your mind!"

She could stand it no longer. Viviane swung her leg over the side of the horse and dropped to the ground, banging her shin on the rough cobblestones. She glared up at him as she pushed herself to her feet.

"What are you doing?" Alexandre pulled hard on the reins.

Tears mingled with the rain that slid down her face. Viviane shook her head. The darkly seductive angel of light had disappeared, revealing the true evil that lurked within.

"I'm not going anywhere with you!" She stood, legs spread apart and hands curled into fists. "You're a beast—a cynical monster!"

Alexandre spat and edged the horse closer but she held her ground.

"Fine! Then stay here and enjoy the company of the hungry men of Paris." He pointed over her shoulder and, instinctively, her eyes followed his finger.

As soon as her attention was diverted, Alexandre clucked his tongue against the side of his cheek and the horse leapt forward. He leaned over and caught her around the side of the waist, his arm of iron lifting her over the prow of his saddle in an effortless motion.

"Let me go!" She writhed in his grasp screaming as her head dangled wildly by the animal's sweaty foreleg.

"Would you rather this *beast* left you for the mob?" Alexandre spurred the horse to a slow canter. The world flew by in an inverted series of blurred motions, made worse by the occasional spray of water in her face when the horse plowed through a puddle.

"Put me down." Viviane swung her right elbow into his side but Alexandre's mocking laughter rang in her ear.

"With a dress as fancy as the one you're wearing, you'd be lucky to survive an hour."

She grew still, mind reeling as the blood rushing to her head was sloshed around by the horse's uneven gait. He was right.

There would be no mercy. The mob would gorge on whatever victims it could find, not bothering to ask any questions.

"Stop!" Her voice was hoarse and her head dizzy.

"You'll behave?" He did not slow down at all. Viviane gritted her teeth but knew she had no choice.

"Hyah!" Alexandre spurred the horse to a brisk trot. The abrupt change in motion made her head slam into a wall of solid muscle underneath horseflesh. Spurts of sticky blood gushed out of her nose.

"Yes!" She spit long, wet hairs from between her teeth. "Yes!"

The horse came to a shuddering stop and Alexandre jerked her upright. Viviane made a dizzy swing at his head which he easily dodged.

"Bad girl." He waggled a finger in her face. "Good thing for you, we're there."

He jumped down from the horse and tugged at the lining of his black vest. Leaving her to make her own way down from the snorting mount, he rapped twice on the door.

Viviane moaned and slid limply off the back of the horse.

"Where are we?" She ripped off a piece of the fabric of her dress and pressed it against her nose, trying to gauge her location while staunching the flow of blood. She had never returned to Paris after the fateful night when Salomé had murdered her carriage driver. To be here again with another insane revolutionary was to return to a living nightmare.

Her gaze wandered to the series of high-rise apartments that enclosed them. She blinked rapidly as raindrops splashed into her eyes. *Another prison. Worse than the one I just left.*

"At a friend's house." Alexandre rapped again on the dark door.

"If you come with me, Salomé will kill you within three heartbeats and I won't be able to stop her. Here you'll survive—at least until dawn."

He grinned and turned to rap on the door again.

Viviane hung her head. Her lover had become her jailer. What could be worse than that?

⚜

Robespierre massaged his temples and scowled at his brother.

"We should join them, Maximilien!" Augustin pounded his fist into his left palm. He had been beating the same dead horse for the past twenty minutes and Robespierre felt his patience wearing thin.

"Yes, Augustin, join them and get killed within five minutes. I'll give you a hero's funeral!" Robespierre pushed himself to his feet and took his brother's elbow. "Men like us direct the winds of war that blow others to the frontlines. We never go there ourselves."

"Brother—"

An exasperated wave of Maximilien's hand interrupted Augustin's flow of words. "Enough said. You and I are too important to the future republic of France to risk our necks in a senseless fight over a stupid pile of rocks!"

Maximilien paced to his desk, leaving his little brother to sulk alone. He had far greater concerns than the battle which would be waged in a few hours. His battle was one of the mind. It was a fight far deadlier than the kind waged by Alexandre and the ridiculous gangs of Parisian thugs. His attention shifted to his response to the queen's letter which lay open on his desk.

Dear degraded Queen of France.

I should refer to you as "my queen" but the circumstances of our first acquaintance have forever disqualified you from that position. No woman who insults my birth and demeans my family name could ever hope to be considered a queen in my eyes.

I am aware that your present circumstances are difficult. It gives me great satisfaction to know of your failed attempt at marriage. I relish the thought of your family's imminent obliteration. Know that on the day your soul leaves the magnificent temple in which it is enshrined, France will celebrate its deliverance. I, Maximilien Robespierre, will be foremost in the revelry.

In hope of your swift annihilation,

Maximilien Robespierre.

"What exactly is your plan brother? To woo her or make her die of fright?"

Robespierre started at the sound of Augustin's voice. Engrossed in the message that had taken at least six hours to write, he had failed to notice that Augustin was reading over his shoulder.

"Hmm... yes. It is beautiful, *non?*" Robespierre smiled wolfishly. "Such profound violence and naked hatred. *C'est parfait!*"

Augustin snorted. "Perfect if you want to scare her off."

"What do you mean?" Robespierre frowned, surprised at this assertive behavior.

"Do you or do you not want the queen to continue to write to you?" Augustin crossed his arms as he observed Robespierre.

"Well... yes." His brother tapped his fingertips together. "I will ensnare her with her own devices."

Augustin shook his head. "Maximilien, you are an excellent politician, but you have no head for romance. The queen will read your letter, realize that you have detected her scheme and never communicate with you again. Subtlety, brother. Subtlety is needed here."

"Well then, illustrious Romeo," Robespierre bowed and made a sweeping gesture to his desk. "Be my muse and write her a sonnet in my name!"

Augustin grunted and seated himself at his brother's desk, dipping his pen into the inkwell. "What exactly do you intend?" He scratched a few lines onto a fresh sheet of paper. "Surely her first letter was enough to show the world the sort of woman she is. Have it printed in the paper and she will be deposed or dead within the week!"

Robespierre rubbed his chin. "It is not enough, Augustin. She knows that it is not enough—not for me." He chuckled deep in his throat. "Clever vixen. She baits the trap by placing in my hands the power to destroy her, knowing that I will not do so until I have obtained what I want. She knows that I am not content to dethrone her, not until..."

"Spare me the sordid details." Augustin grimaced and glanced up at his brother.

Maximilien grabbed a mouse-brown cushion that Augustin had tossed onto the floor and crushed it against his chest.

"She is tantalizing me with the ultimate battle of minds! One night in which the fate of France will be decided." He pressed the fringe of the cushion against his lips. "She wants to lure me into a trap to arrest or murder me, and I," he licked his lips, "I only want one taste of—"

"Maximilien." Augustin raised his voice. "Please! I am *trying* to write."

Robespierre caught his breath as he glanced at his brother. He had forgotten Augustin was in the room.

"I must find another means of getting my notes to her." The amorous lawyer sniffed and spoke over the sound of the scraping quill. "I won't have that prostitute, Salomé's hands on my letters."

A fist pounded on the door below and he darted to the window. Augustin looked up, but Robespierre motioned for him to continue writing. He stood to one side of the glass and drew the curtain back an inch. The dim light of a streetlamp illuminated a face that he did not want to see.

Robespierre groaned then moved to the door.

"Who is it?" Augustin scratched a few more lines on the paper and then threw the plume on the desk.

"The devil's own brother." Robespierre tossed the pillow onto a chair. "Standing in the rain instead of in hell's fires where he belongs." Then his eyes drifted to the cream paper that Augustin gripped in his right hand.

"You answer it." Maximilien licked his lips again. "I will read what you have written."

"You are obsessed with her brother." The corners of Augustin's mouth turned upward. "Obsessed, do you hear me?"

The angry fist below drowned out his words.

"Go!" Maximilien snatched the paper and shoved his brother toward the door. His thin, bloodless lips moved wordlessly as his eyes devoured the paper that he clutched between trembling fingers.

Augustin shook his head and hurried down the narrow staircase to the door to let the "devil's own brother" come inside.

Marie-Antoinette stared at her reflection for a long moment. Night had blanketed Versailles and she waited for Viviane to help her undress. In the queen's hand was a cream, pearl-encrusted mirror that was markedly like the one she had smashed against Maximilien Robespierre's cheek twenty years earlier.

"If I had known how much grief the wretch would cause me, I would have turned Rheims inside out to have him killed." She idly watched the moisture in her breath fog the mirror's expensive glass. But she had not had Robespierre killed. The fourteen-year-old princess had been so incensed to learn that a peasant dared touch her that she had not bothered to learn his name.

The boy had become a man—a man who not only coveted her body but also her crown. She was prepared to sacrifice the former if, in so doing, she would save the latter. Other men had replaced her husband before. The touch of an enemy was a small price to pay if it brought Robespierre close enough to sink a dagger into his stubby neck or wolfish eyes. His death would atone for the murder of Louis-Joseph and would also protect her remaining son.

She closed her eyes, imagining that Robespierre lay on the bed next to her and that in her hand was not the mirror but a pearl-handled dagger.

"I know you did it, filthy peasant scum." Marie's mouth twisted. "You, not Philippe, murdered my son." Oh, how she would relish sinking a knife into the lawyer's coal-black heart. Her eyes flew open.

Despite her claims to the contrary, the queen knew that Philippe had not been behind the death of her son. Not only had he always loved the boy but he did not possess the cunning to concoct such a devious plot. This was the work of a much darker mind. Only one man had the Machiavellian intelligence and the motive to exterminate her seed in such a barbarous way. That man was Maximilien Robespierre.

Marie shrugged and pouted at her reflection. "But why not get two for the price of one?"

Eliminating a rival as powerful as Philippe was no small feat. But to tarnish his name in the process? That was a stroke of sheer genius.

She sighed and threw herself against the mountain of cushions that had been carefully arranged on her bed. If only Viviane could be trusted—

Marie frowned, propped herself onto one elbow and threw the mirror onto the dresser. "Where is my *dame d'honneur*?"

"I am afraid, Your Grace, that your lady-in-waiting will not be coming this evening."

The queen whirled around at the unexpected voice that spoke from behind her.

"Gabrielle!" She stood to her feet and held out her arms. Gabrielle de Polignac glided forward, elegant and poised as ever.

"Why have you not visited me these past months?" Marie pouted again. "I only see you at public sessions of court or some other such nonsense. It is nothing like the old times!"

Gabrielle glanced at her benefactor's feet, sadness working its way across her beautiful face. "I am afraid, Your Grace, that the fault is mine."

"Whatever do you mean?" Marie drew back and pressed a hand to her chest, fingers splayed. "You tire of your queen's presence?"

"Never, my lady." Gabrielle fell to one knee, the skirt of her azure-blue dress billowing around her ankles in a cloud of silk and lace. "But the fault is mine because it is I who invited my cousin, Viviane de Lussan, to Versailles and urged Your Majesty to place in her hands a position of trust."

"Oh, do get up Gabrielle and speak plainly!"

Gabrielle rose, her face and eyes the picture of contrite sorrow. "I fear that the trust that I urged Your Grace to bestow upon my cousin was... misplaced."

"Misplaced?" Marie arched an eyebrow. "How so? Where is Viviane?"

"Gone, my Queen."

Marie-Antoinette's blood turned to ice. A chill that started at the pit of her stomach spread throughout her body, numbing her mind. "Gone?"

Gabrielle nodded, a strange gleam in her eyes. "She sleeps in one of the rooms that Your Grace so kindly assigned to me. I was looking for her and noticed that she was nowhere to be found. Her maid stated that Viviane had hastily packed a bag during the trial. She then left in the direction of the Orangery."

The Orangery! Marie sank into the bed. Her mind began to slowly thaw, probing at the implications of Viviane's decision to disobey her direct command. Not only had the traitor abandoned her position but she carried the queen's most trusted secret to those who could do her the most harm. One enemy had been eliminated but, like the fabled hydra, would countless others spring up in Philippe's place?

"Gabrielle." She raised a trembling hand. "I've been such a fool. Such a complete, utter fool!"

"*Mais non, Altesse.*" Gabrielle rushed to her side. "She deceived us all. A few weeks ago, I discovered that she and the Duke of Valence were romantically involved and—"

"What?" Marie felt faint.

Gabrielle spoke again. "I tried to obtain an audience with you to warn you, but my cousin would let me nowhere in your presence alone."

The pieces began to fall into place. Viviane had manipulated both the Duke of Valence and the gardener, unsure of whether she truly belonged at Versailles or among those of her own class. At some point during the trial, she had realized that she could no longer count on Philippe's love, so she had traded him for her gardener, Alexandre, disobeying the queen's command.

You clever, clever girl.

"I have misplaced my trust, dear Gabrielle." Marie clapped a sweaty palm to her powdered forehead. "If she could deceive me, who can I trust?"

"*Altesse.*" Gabrielle dipped her head. "Rest assured that I will never leave your side."

Marie patted her hand, her mind still entangled in the web of intrigue that she had created. Robespierre had murdered her son, but she had successfully used the situation to eliminate a dangerous rival, Philippe of Valence. Viviane had fled the palace in the company of Alexandre, a *bourgeois*, who was a friend of her archenemy Robespierre. If Viviane shared Marie's intention to woo Robespierre into a trap with Alexandre, it would effectively destroy her plans before she could strike.

"I need her back." The queen bit down on her lower lip.

Gabrielle gasped. "But would it not be better to let her run wild with the peasant savages? Who needs her when you have loyal servants, like myself, at your call?"

"You don't understand." Marie rose and slid over to her window. Gone was the flush of self-assured victory. If Viviane betrayed her, everything was lost. She remained motionless by the window, idly noting the *pitter-patter* of falling rain as she considered her options.

Louis would never agree to a manhunt for a *bourgeoise* who had fled her service. If such knowledge became public, it would be touted by every newspaper in France. She needed to send the second letter to Robespierre before Viviane could warn him. But with Viviane gone, who could she trust?

She glanced back at Gabrielle's pale face. Something the woman had said tugged at her memory. *Loyal.* That was it. Someone had recently sworn absolute fealty when her son lay dying—

"Send for Geneviève, the late *dauphin's* nurse." She locked eyes with her friend.

Gabrielle swayed as she rose. "His nurse? Of course, my queen. Do you wish me to return with her?"

Marie's lips thinned in a tight smile. "No, my dear Gabrielle. I will send for you when I need you."

"As you wish, *Altesse*."

⚜

Ten minutes later Marie was joined by Geneviève. As soon as the doors closed behind the nurse, Marie rushed forward and clasped her hands in her own.

"Thank you for coming." She motioned for Geneviève to sit beside her on the divan.

"But of course." Geneviève dipped her head, then slid into the chair. "When my queen commands, I come."

A spark of renewed hope struck Marie's heart. "It is exactly such loyalty that I need at this moment."

She stepped to her desk and slipped a silver key into the drawer. Withdrawing the letter that Viviane had given her earlier, the queen turned back to the nurse.

"You are familiar with Paris, Madame Geneviève?" She tapped the letter against her left palm.

Geneviève nodded. "No one knows Paris better than I, Your Grace."

"Then you will know where to find the infamous rogue Maximilien Robespierre?"

Marie's words brought a pause, but Geneviève quickly recovered. "I know the area in which he's reported to live, Your Grace."

"I would like you to deliver this message to the infidel tonight. It is a letter in which I denounce him as a ridiculous tyrant who will surely feel the wrath of God."

The letter contained nothing of the sort but, while Marie was grateful for Geneviève's past service, she couldn't bring herself to trust the servant with the message's true contents—not with Viviane's betrayal so fresh in her mind.

"As you wish." Geneviève took the letter from Marie's outstretched hand and tucked it into the bosom of her dress. She hesitated. "The night is dark and the lawyer lives in the heart of the city."

"That is why I have also asked General Lafayette to join us." Marie tapped her foot. "He should be here at any moment."

A knock sounded at the door.

"Enter!" The queen spun toward the door.

General Lafayette strode into the room. "My queen requested my presence?" He bowed low. "How may I serve?"

Marie suppressed a small smile. This was why she loved Lafayette. No matter how grim the situation he had an uncanny ability to make her feel that all was well.

Unlike my husband.

She spoke quickly. "The good Geneviève will be travelling to Paris on a mission of utmost importance. Can you secure a horse and carriage?"

Lafayette straightened. "For you, my queen, I can secure the moon itself!"

He pursed his lips. "A horse is wise however I would not suggest the use of a carriage, particularly one marked with the royal emblem."

He turned to Geneviève. "My men have reported rioting in the streets and, if you travel on anything other than a horse or your own two feet," the general crinkled his brow, "you had better wear a brace of pistols."

"Can you send men with her?" Marie wrung her hands together. *I must get to Robespierre before Viviane reveals what she knows!*

"No, Majesty." Geneviève stood. "It would be better if I went alone. The king's men would only attract unwanted attention."

"Hmm..." Lafayette nodded his agreement. "Exactly what I was about to propose."

He faced Marie and shrugged his shoulders. "Unfortunately, radiant Star of France, the best solution would be for your servant to enter Paris on horseback with no more protection than a gun that I will lend her." He smiled. "Assuming of course, that the good nurse can shoot."

"Can you ride and shoot?" Marie searched the servant's eyes.

"I am *bourgeoise*." Geneviève lifted her chin.

Marie hesitated, unsure of how to respond, then moved to the general and rested her palms on Lafayette's decorated chest. "I know I can count on your discretion *my* general?"

Lafayette cleared his throat but did not withdraw. "Madame, you hold my heart between your hands." He smiled at his own humor then bowed low and, with a quick nod at Geneviève, he left the room.

"Will there be anything else, Your Grace?" Geneviève folded her hands in her lap.

"Nothing more than the assurance of your discretion, Madame." Marie pulled a small purse of coins from her left pocket. "While the king will understand my need to express my anger at such an instrument of evil, there may be those who would try to misrepresent the fact that I have written to such a man. Do you understand?"

"Of course, Your Grace." Geneviève held the queen's gaze as she pocketed the pouch. "You never can trust the rabble, ma'am."

I've heard that they've got spies and agents all over just lookin' for an opportunity to do a good woman like yourself some harm."

Marie squeezed her hand again. This time, her gratitude was sincere. "Thank you, Geneviève. Your devotion means more than I could ever say."

"You can always trust me, Your Grace." Geneviève curtsied and left the room.

Marie watched as the doors closed behind the servant, then paced to the veranda and stared out of the dark, rain-spattered window. Out there, lurking somewhere in the dark, Robespierre dreamed of destroying everything she loved. Her kingdom, her life, her children were all at risk.

"You will not prevail, you devil." She spoke the words aloud as she dug her nails into the flesh of her palm. "I will do whatever it takes to win. Whatever it takes."

Chapter Eighteen

July 1789. Bastille Fortress, Paris.

Philippe gazed at the walls of his cell with unseeing eyes. It was the last room that he would ever occupy in this life. *No matter.* He was dead already. Alexandre's triumphant declaration had killed him as effectively as a blade to the heart. This cavern of dark stone was only a premature tomb.

The thought of escape had entered his mind, but Philippe discarded the idea. No one escaped from the Bastille. Even if he succeeded, what would be the point? Viviane had made her choice, recklessly giving herself to a monster instead of a man who loved her. *How could she?*

He felt his way through the gloom until his outstretched flingers scraped the rough stone wall. The shackles around his wrists clinked as he turned and dropped into the rancid straw that littered the ground. The guilt on her face had shouted more clearly than words that Alexandre, for once, spoke the truth. She had traded a man who loved her more than life, for his enemy—a man who offered a handsome face and a web of enticing lies. Now he waited in the dark, alone and bitter, for his life to end.

How did this happen?

Philippe's body was bound but his mind was free to contemplate the strange twists of fate that had brought him to this moment.

First, he stood accused of murdering the heir to the throne.

Second, he was condemned to die by hanging, a fate so ignoble that he shuddered to think of it.

Third, he loved a *bourgeoise* whose fickle nature had broken his heart.

Fourth, the man he had once called friend had sabotaged his relationship in retaliation for his own actions years before.

"I warned him not to pursue Juliette." Philippe groaned as he drew his knees to his chest. At the time, Alexandre had no plans beyond running away with the girl. He would have ripped the woman away from a family who loved her, leading her to a life of misery and regret.

He rattled the chains, voicing the thoughts that consumed his mind. "How could I stand by and watch them sneak away to a nightmare of their own making?" When Alexandre had refused to see sense, Philippe had been left with only one option—to expose his plans.

Years later, his friend-turned-enemy had evened the score. As he had come between Alexandre and the woman he loved, so Alexandre had stepped between himself and Viviane. It was bad enough to die for a crime he had not committed. But to die knowing that Alexandre had seduced the woman for whom he had sacrificed everything? To leave this world knowing she had spurned his love and chosen his enemy? That was sheer agony.

Even now, Philippe's concern for Viviane's welfare drove him to the point of madness. If Alexandre truly loved her, Philippe would have resigned himself to the fact that he had fought and lost. But to see her ride away with that brute, unaware of the evil that lurked in his heart...

"God, why?" He pounded his fist against the unyielding stone. "What have I done to deserve this?" His body shook with sobs. Imprisoned and condemned though he had done no wrong. God had forsaken him.

"Why?" He screamed his throat raw. "Why have you left me?"

He wept for himself. He wept for Viviane who rode toward a life of regret. Philippe knew that, as surely as he was imprisoned in the Bastille, Alexandre was locked inside a prison of hatred.

"She needs to know the truth!" He pushed himself up and began to pace the small confines of the cell. Fear for Viviane's life merged with bitter anger at the choices she had made.

Why would God want him to love a woman who seemed determined to break his heart? It made no sense.

"I've done everything I could." His groan echoed around the small cell. "I went to her home. I gave up my old life and still it wasn't enough."

This woman chose me—a pauper—instead of you, a prince! Alexandre's parting words ripped into his soul like the merciless fangs of a beast.

Philippe gripped the chains between clenched fists. "Why did she do it?" He clenched his eyelids, walling out the darkness and wishing that he could shut out the pain of her rejection.

The darkness found a voice that slid into the numbed corners of his mind.

FOOL! EVERYTHING YOU HAVE DONE HAS BEEN IN VAIN.

It was true. Nothing between himself and Viviane had changed despite his efforts. But he still loved her. He was more a prisoner of his love than of the Bastille. It was his love that brought a pain he could not escape.

Even now the feeling that he was *supposed* to love her surged within him.

"I don't want this! God, take this pain away from me." He slumped to his knees, broken by the weight of his own humanity. Minutes swelled into hours as time itself was swallowed by the darkness. Still he remained prostrate on the ground.

Love seeks not her own. The words came from within, ringing in his ears like a whisper in the night.

Philippe ground his fists against the stones below. "When has this ever been about me?"

Love bears all things.

"Not this." He spat the words through clenched teeth. "It can't bear this!"

Love rejoices in the truth.

That gave him pause. The truth?

What is the truth? Marie had asked the question before the court.

Philippe slowly shoved himself upright, heedless of the hay that clung to the stubble on his chin. The truth was that he still loved Viviane. The truth was that, now that his revenge was complete, Alexandre would either cast her aside or destroy her.

He rocked back on his heels. *She is the victim of his cunning.* She had only been a pawn in his grand scheme, a means of making him die in torment. A glimmer of understanding peeked through the bitterness that filled his mind. Viviane had been deceived into thinking Alexandre loved her; her choices were therefore based upon lies and *not* truth.

Philippe sucked in a sharp breath. If he died hating Viviane then Alexandre would triumph. If, however, he could look beyond his own pain, her own needs came into focus. Only then could he die in peace.

Love never fails. This final phrase crystallized his understanding.

"Never... fails." He mouthed the words, eyes wide as he peered into the gloom.

The random pieces of their encounters fused into a clear picture in his mind. Her callous rejection at the Bride Tree, her frailty before Alexandre's diabolical charms, her foolish choices—none of it was stronger than the understanding that he loved her. That he would always love her.

On the heels of that thought came another, equally powerful. Alexandre had intended to break him by driving an impossible wedge between himself and Viviane. Alexandre wanted to grind him into the dust with the knowledge of their night in the Orangery. There was only one way to defeat his enemy. He had to forgive her. He would die, holding in his mind the realization that Viviane's actions were the result of deception and not clear-headed thinking.

Philippe pushed himself upward, chest heaving as he wrestled with his emotions. The pain in his heart was still there—God knew it tore his soul to shreds—but, the understanding that she was a victim of his enemy's wiles opened the door just enough for forgiveness to slip to the forefront of his heart.

"The truest form of devotion," he stepped back, tipped his head and raised his voice to the sky, "is to keep on loving when love itself is spurned." The thought awed him, bringing with it a tendril of peace.

She needs me. The realization filled his mind. He could not allow Alexandre to prevail. The conflict between them was not over, not yet.

Philippe clamped his jaw shut. He had to survive, if not for his sake then for hers! Then reality broke into his thoughts. He was a prisoner in the Bastille. For those who entered the Bastille, the only way out was death itself.

Robespierre stared in stunned silence at the woman before him. Water streamed from her arms and legs, but it was not her disheveled appearance that held his attention nor the fact that Alexandre stood beside her. He stood rooted to the ground because this was none other than Marie-Antoinette's lady-in-waiting. He had seen her standing near the queen on the opening day Estates General meeting at Versailles.

What was her name? Viviane. Yes, Marie had called her Viviane. Rumor had it that she was originally a member of the Third Estate with a distant connection to nobility. Wheels began spinning in Robespierre's mind, his thoughts working like the cogs of a well-oiled clock.

No one else was as privy to the intimate details of a queen's life as her chief lady-in-waiting. Not even her own husband could hope to be as informed as the woman before him. Could *this* be the author of the incriminating note that consumed his thoughts?

But she was here, not at her post in Versailles. This could mean one of two things. Either Marie had sent her or she had committed the ultimate crime of abandoning her post and joining the revolutionaries. Robespierre cleared his throat.

"Welcome Madame Viviane." He bowed. "Forgive my surprise but it is not every day that the queen's *dame d'honneur* graces my home. It is an honor." His eyes slid back to her face, probing its emotions. He caught the imprint of fear.

"I don't consider it an honor." Viviane jerked her chin upright and stepped away from Alexandre, glaring at him. "An innocent man stands accused of murdering the *dauphin* and I suspect that you are behind it."

Robespierre bared his teeth in a smile. "Let us put these wild accusations to one side for the moment, and address the real question before us." He shrugged. "Why are you here?"

"She has recognized that her place is with her own people." Alexandre stepped forward. "She has joined the revolution."

"Well, life *is* full of surprises." Robespierre clucked his tongue. "To think that the queen's very own *dame d'honneur* would join our cause!"

He stepped back, eyes wide. "But you are all wet, Madame! We cannot have you dying of pneumonia when you have at last begun to live."

Robespierre exchanged a glance with his brother. "Augustin, go upstairs and ask our landlord's daughter, Charlotte, if she would be kind enough to share some of her clothes with a sister of the revolution."

Augustin dipped his head and hurried from the room.

"I still do not understand why you have brought the lovely lady here." Robespierre looked to Alexandre.

"She needs a place to stay, out of sight for a while, and my thoughts turned to you," Alexandre's eyes met his. "I didn't have the time to make... other arrangements."

"Really?" Robespierre pursed his lips. "The leader of France's most clandestine group of assassins asks me to shelter the queen's erstwhile lady-in-waiting. Now what am I to make of that?"

"Assassin?" Viviane's hand flew to her mouth. "A leader of murderers?"

Alexandre shot a cold look at Robespierre.

"What is it, dear Alexandre?" A cat-like smile slid across the lawyer's face. "Didn't you tell her?"

"There wasn't time." Steel crept into the Italian's voice. "I've been busy preparing for an attack on the Bastille at dawn, if you recall."

Robespierre pretended not to notice his ally's growing irritation. For her part, Viviane clapped her hand to her forehead and slumped, groaning, against the wall.

"I wish you good fortune tomorrow." Robespierre shoved his hands into his pockets.

"You won't be joining us?"

"Regrettably, no. There are those of us who fight by using our heads and those of us whose intellectual ability only allows us to bash in the heads of others."

Robespierre's mouth twisted in a smile. "I am the former while you, my violent friend, are clearly the latter." He smirked. "No offense."

"I'm fully aware of the extent of your bravery, Robespierre." Alexandre's nostrils flared. "A little boy is now cold in his grave because of it."

The smile faded from Robespierre's face. He stepped toward the assassin and raised a threatening finger. "Never forget, *Moustiquaire,* that my pen is much mightier than your sword. It is my pen that brings down my adversaries—whoever they might be."

Robespierre observed Alexandre through narrowed eyes. No doubt the assassin was wrestling with the overpowering urge to slit him from belly to nose. Robespierre knew that Alexandre could have his weapons in hand and do the deed before he drew his next breath. But he also knew that Alexandre needed him to be the public face of the revolution. Alexandre would do no violence until the king, queen and Philippe were all wiped from the earth. At that point, Robespierre would strike first.

Alexandre sucked in a deep breath, held it, and then released it slowly. "Understood." He jerked his head in Viviane's direction. "Can she stay?"

Robespierre blinked twice, his large eyes gliding from his unwanted ally to the woman who now trembled with cold. That there was more to their relationship than Alexandre let on was obvious to the man who sifted truth from lies for a living. Furthermore, this woman had once been the very gateway to Marie-Antoinette herself. She would know the queen's mind as few others did. He could not let such a trove of information slip through his fingers.

"But of course." Robespierre stepped back and spread his arms wide. "My home is hers."

At this moment Augustin pulled open the door. He was followed by Charlotte, the landlord's daughter. The motherly brunette took one look at Viviane and launched into a tirade of ceaseless babble.

"For shame Monsieur Augustin." She waggled a finger at him. "You should have called for me sooner. Look at the poor dear; she's trembling with cold!"

"I did—" Augustin's protest was forestalled by a blizzard of motion punctuated by Charlotte's loud criticisms about his insensitivity.

"She is coming with me," the young woman said flatly.

"She will sleep in our guest room, Madame Charlotte." Robespierre spoke when the woman finally paused to draw breath. "Please send her back when you have finished."

She glared at him and, with a firm grasp on Viviane's arm, led her self-appointed charge from the room.

⚜

Maximilien sat alone in his study, curled into a fetal position on his leather chair while contemplating the meaning of Viviane's arrival. There was always more to a situation than what one saw at the surface. His analytical mind dissected the facts as he knew them, probing and discarding possibilities with the thoroughness of a gold digger.

"Why her?" He whispered to the thin air above. It might be thought that he was praying, but Robespierre had long stopped believing that God was anything more than a useful tool to control the masses. "Why here? Why now?"

It was to the god of reason that he appealed—the intellectual power that existed in every man on the planet. He closed his eyes in an effort to concentrate but the sudden clopping of hooves outside his window intruded on his meditation. Robespierre waited for the horse to move on, but the ostentatious animal stopped outside his apartment, pawing and snorting as if it were about to keel over and die from hyperventilation.

Sighing, he waited for the inevitable. As expected, within a few moments, a hand tapped lightly on the door.

⚜

Geneviève Poitrine stared into the face of Maximilien Robespierre, the revolution's celebrated hero. Other than a passing glimpse of the man during his stay on the palace grounds, it was the first time she had ever seen The Incorruptible.

"May a daughter of the revolution enter?" The showers had stopped but her clothes were still damp from the miles that she had ridden in the rain. "I bring news from the queen."

"The queen?" Robespierre gawked at her for a moment. He caught himself and peered hurriedly over her shoulder into the darkness. The street was empty, and he motioned for her to enter.

Geneviève opened her mouth, but Robespierre pressed his fingers against his lips.

"In my study." He motioned with his arm. She followed him up the stairs and down a narrow corridor that was illuminated by wax candles tucked into tapered alcoves.

He opened the door and allowed Geneviève to enter first. Robespierre strode across the room to the fireplace, stirred up the dying flame and wiped beads of perspiration from his forehead.

Then he motioned for his guest to sit. "Now," he cleared his throat, "speak freely. Who are you and what do you want?"

⚜

Viviane made her way down the corridor toward Robespierre's study after having slipped out of the room when Charlotte's back was turned. She appreciated the woman's company but needed space to think. She had been certain that things could not get any worse when she had stood outside with Alexandre but, when she caught sight of the man whose yellow eyes drilled into her soul, she had realized how wrong she had been. Maximilien Robespierre had frightened her when in the relative security of Versailles. In his own lair, he petrified her.

Why am I afraid? The thought gave her pause and, in that moment of mental stillness, she heard the whisper of a memory. *I see in you a heart of courage, a heart that pursues truth relentlessly.* Philippe had said that. Strange that his words should comfort her when the man himself was condemned to die. But they shoved aside the stone of fear and paved the way for another powerful emotion: undiluted rage.

With rage came a decision. She would leave at first light. The pain of Alexandre's betrayal was gone and all she felt was a burning anger mixed with shame. The shift in her emotions made her wonder if she had ever loved him at all.

Can hatred replace love so quickly? She contrasted Alexandre and Philippe. The former had used her to obtain a cruel revenge while the latter had sacrificed everything to save someone she loved. Memories of her meetings with Philippe rolled across her mind. His words had been a lifeline to her—a slim tendril of hope in a world of uncertainty. *You hunger for truth,* he had told her.

What was the truth? His confession of love? The stirrings in her heart each time she thought of him? He was condemned to die but, were he not, could truth have overcome the differences in their social status?

Viviane rubbed her eyes wearily. She regretted leaving Philippe because of the pain that she had heard in his voice, not because she believed that staying would have changed their destiny.

"My destiny is my own to make." She traced her finger along the wall. She would spend the night here then slip out at dawn. She would escape the madness of Paris and try to evade her grief at Philippe's death. She would find a way back to her mother in Lussan and there, surrounded by acres of peaceful farmland, she would start her life over.

She had reached Robespierre's study and was about to enter when a woman's voice slipped through a small space between the partially-closed door and into her ears. *Odd.*

"I am Geneviève Poitrine," the woman said. "I bring a letter to you from Marie-Antoinette, the Queen of France."

Geneviève? Viviane froze, her every sense tuned into the scene that was playing out on the other side of the door. *What is the late dauphin's nurse doing here?*

For a long moment, the only sound she heard was the thunder in her own chest.

Letter? The sound of scraping wood told her that Robespierre had risen from his chair, presumably to take the note. It could be nothing other than the one she had written on the queen's behalf.

"Give me a few moments to read this."

His footsteps moved further away, telling Viviane that he had turned his back to Geneviève for privacy. Heat rose in the eavesdropper's cheeks as she thought of the note's contents. The words were seared into her memory.

> My dearest enemy,
>
> You and I share a bond of ardent loathing, one that can only be dissolved when both of us are dead. I say both for, as long as one of us walks this earth, the other will be consumed by a loving hatred for the deceased. But enough talk of death! Let us postpone that inevitable fate by focusing on the desire that has ripped us apart only to reunite us after twenty years of separation.
>
> Never have I been pursued by a man such as you—a man who prays for my death yet longs to possess me. I admit that your obsession has a dark quality that I find compelling.
>
> Here is my proposal. Meet me in the Belvedere tomorrow at sunset if you dare. One of us... both of us... or neither of us will leave the grounds alive.
>
> The die is cast, and my challenge must be answered.
>
> Marie-Antoinette.

One long moment of silence stretched into another as Robespierre undoubtedly read and reread the short note. Finally, she heard the squeak of his chair as his weight fell into it.

"Geneviève Poitrine, you say?" He switched topics in a voice that had the emotional depth of a stone. "It is an honor to meet the woman responsible for the death of the *dauphin*. Were it not for you, my plan to kill the boy and tear the royal family apart would have failed."

Viviane's mouth went dry, as though someone had stuffed a wad of cotton down her throat. Geneviève was an accomplice of Robespierre and the true murderer of the *dauphin!*

Geneviève snorted. "It was justice." She was silent for a moment. Then, "You heard of the boy killed by an aristo carriage a few months ago?"

"Who did not?" Robespierre barked out a dry laugh. "The newspapers dubbed the boy the 'martyr of Paris.'"

"I knew him by a different name." Geneviève's voice was hollow. "I called him '*son*.'"

Silence.

Viviane felt her knees grow weak. She fell back against the wall, groping for support. Her flailing elbow banged into a candle that clattered to the wooden floor. She dropped to her knees and grabbed the sputtering flame. *Had they heard her?*

The silence gave way to footsteps that approached the door. They were coming! She glanced around, her throat tight. There was no place to hide. Within seconds, the door would open, and Robespierre would learn that she had discovered his deepest secrets.

Incorruptible or not, Viviane had little doubt what would happen if Robespierre knew what she had overheard. The doorknob rattled. *I see in you a heart of courage, a heart that pursues truth relentlessly.* Viviane took a deep breath and turned to face the door. There was only one way to handle this.

⚜

Robespierre stumbled out of the way as the door swung open and Viviane entered the room. His hand had been upon the knob when the woman pushed it open.

"Geneviève?" Viviane, dressed in a simple woolen skirt, cream blouse and dark leather shoes, stepped toward the queen's nurse.

Geneviève scrambled to her feet at the sight of the queen's *dame d'honneur*. "Madame de Lussan!" Her eyes were wide.

"Whatever are you doing here, Geneviève?" Viviane feigned innocence, arching an eyebrow.

"I-I had a message to deliver for the queen." The nurse took a step backward. "And you?"

Inspiration struck Viviane. She glanced at Robespierre who had come to stand between both women. She opened her mouth, but Robespierre spoke first.

"The queen's lady-in-waiting has at last seen the light that is spreading throughout France."

He faced Geneviève directly. Viviane felt the nurse's eyes on her and she shook her head so that only the woman would notice.

No. This is not what it seems.
Geneviève's face was expressionless but she jerked her sharp chin downward in a slow nod.

"Isn't that so, Madame de Lussan?" Robespierre turned back to her.

Viviane folded her arms across her chest. "I have seen where my true loyalties lie."

The words were true, but she knew that Robespierre would interpret them to mean that she had joined the side of the revolution while she hoped that Geneviève would tell the queen that Viviane was still trustworthy. What Marie would make of it all, she had no idea. She only wanted Marie to know that she had *not* betrayed her trust.

For her part, Viviane was through with the intrigue and lies that tarnished both sides of the revolution. An innocent child was dead, her life was ruined, and the one man whom she could possibly love was about to be killed because of the mutual hatred that festered like a boil. Her loyalties were to Philippe, herself and her mother. Nothing else mattered now.

"Well!" Geneviève's crisp voice pulled her back to the moment. "I will share with the queen what I have both *seen* and heard tonight." Her slight emphasis on the word *seen* assured Viviane that the shrewd nurse had indeed understood her subtle action.

Geneviève rubbed her hands and made her way to the door.

"Before you leave," Robespierre's voice made her pause. "It so happens that I too have a message for Madame Deficit." He bustled over to his desk and picked up a sealed letter.

"Tell your queen that my final message will be delivered in person. She will understand."

Geneviève curtsied, glanced again at Viviane, and left the room.

"No one will sleep tonight." Robespierre moved to the window and watched Geneviève depart. "Not the poor nurse, not Alexandre... nor I."

His steady gaze fell on Viviane. She returned his stare, refusing to cower in front of a man who used murder and slander as his principal weapons.

"I can assure you that I will be one of those who do." She turned away. "The guest room you mentioned?"

Minutes later, Viviane locked the door behind her and sank into an exhausted pile on the stiff mattress. Despite her boast, she knew that dawn would find her wide-awake.

Chapter Nineteen

July 14, 1789. The Bastille, Paris.

Salomé wove her way forward in a crouch, moving around discarded barrels, overturned carriages and other signs of the rage that had gripped the Parisian mob during the night. In her right hand, she held a short-barreled pistol that Madame L'Orage had pressed into her palm, while in her left she clutched the dagger given to her by Alexandre. Her lips thinned in a tight smile. Her most powerful weapon was neither the knife nor pistol. It was the relentless hate that had driven her to rouse the women of Paris in a struggle that would forever alter their lives.

Salomé waved her army forward. Her heart swelled as she caught sight of three thousand women, prowling through the mist like ravenous wolves who had caught the scent of blood. They were ready for the kill.

She glanced to her right, squinting in the hazy morning fog. Her eyes picked out Alexandre who sat astride a red warhorse that Simon had commandeered for today's fight. One arm rested on the hilt of his black sword, like a valiant knight about to charge a fierce dragon of stone and fire. Salomé waved and, catching sight of the motion, he lifted his other hand in salute. Fear for his safety rippled through her heart but she crushed the emotion. Her knight might be going to battle but his princess would fight alongside him. *Whatever happens to him will happen to me. I won't outlive him.*

"Are you ready?" Aimée, the teenage girl who had been the first of the women to support her plan to storm the Bastille, spoke up at her side. It was fitting that the girl stood with her.

Salomé glanced up at the overcast sky. A cool morning breeze blew among the crowd, bringing with it the acrid scent of used gunpowder. "Paris is ready." She straightened and stood as a soldier, back straight, shoulders back and chest thrust out. "We are ready."

Alexandre's sharp voice commanded her attention. He and a small cohort of fifteen men had separated themselves from the uncountable thousands that followed. Among the ridged turrets of the Bastille that soared above his head, she could just make out the grim face of a man dressed in the royal blue overcoat that identified him as the garrison commander.

"Governor de Launay." Alexandre's clear voice rang out like a trumpet, eating up the distance between them. Behind de Launay, several members of the Swiss Guard trained their muskets on the revolutionaries, but the governor shook his head. "Stand down!" He turned back to Alexandre. "What is it you want, sir?"

"Freedom!" Alexandre thrust his fist in the air. A thunderous roar of approval from the thousands milling about him shook the pebbles on the ground near Salomé's feet.

De Launay waited until the raucous crowd had quieted. "I am afraid that is beyond my power to grant. Ask me for something reasonable." He raised both arms, palms turned outward. "There is no need for French blood to be spilled today."

"Alright." Alexandre grinned. The spirited stallion trotted in a circle on the cobblestones of the Bastille's courtyard, whinnying in anticipation of the coming fight. "If you want to avoid having your head impaled on a pike..." Again, a boisterous cheer swelled, punctuated with cries of "String 'im up!" and "Kill 'em all!"

Alexandre let the crowd have their fun and, when their cries died away, he continued. "If you want to live, surrender the Bastille and release its prisoners."

The rigid white curls of de Launay's wig trembled as he shook his head. "I cannot do that! But if you disperse now, I swear that no harm will come to you. Only abandon this suicidal mission, I beg you." He gestured to the cannons that menaced the crowd. "My canons are unloaded as proof of my goodwill."

Alexandre spun his horse in a half-circle and caught Simon's eye. If the canons were unloaded...

He nodded once and the burly giant sprang into action.

"Men!" Simon swung his beefy fist in a tight circle. "To me!"

A small detachment of about twenty revolutionaries ran after him.

"Get the first drawbridge lowered!" Simon shoved a long dagger between his teeth, threw himself at the outer wall of the courtyard and began to pull himself upward.

Alexandre wheeled his horse around again. Salomé noted his head moving from his men to the moat to the defenders of the Bastille. She could imagine the thoughts that flew through his mind.

His army was stationed in the Bastille's courtyard which was separated from the actual prison by an eighty-foot moat that could only be crossed by two drawbridges, both of which were raised. To further protect the fortress against invasion, tall walls had been built on either side of the first drawbridge.

She followed his gaze as it flitted to Simon and his detachment. They were now scaling the outer wall on the right. From his perch on the turret, de Launay was oblivious to the threat rising to meet him but it appeared that Alexandre would not gamble with success. Simon needed a diversion to cover his advance.

Salomé sucked in a breath as Alexandre raised his arm high then swung it downward in a chopping motion. "Fire at will!"

Thousands of thunderous guns barked out their response. Billows of smoke poured from the long-barreled muskets while those who were unarmed among the crowd threw themselves at the walls in a frenzy, pummeling the stones as though they would rip them apart with their bleeding hands. The attack of the Bastille had begun.

⚜

The guns were out of range but de Launay was so focused upon the futile attack that neither he nor his men noticed Simon's bulky form until it was too late. The first defender took a wild swing at Simon's head, but the giant caught his arm mid-punch and, grinning, snapped it backward, breaking the bone.

The man fell, screaming, to his knees.

Simon spit the dagger from between his teeth and into his palm. "Shh. It's alright." He hushed him as he would a baby, then with a wild cackle, he buried the blade in the man's heart. He sprang to the drawbridge and began hacking away at the ropes that held the bridge suspended while those who followed dealt with the second guard.

Crash!

After a few decisive blows, the entire structure slammed downward, making the long poles that supported the base splash loudly into the water below.

"Again!" Simon grabbed the shoulder of the man nearest him and pointed to the next drawbridge. A small crowd of revolutionaries followed their mad race forward, dodging the sporadic musket fire that bit off shards of wood around them.

Simon pressed forward, hearing the rumble of the mob behind him as they surged forward across the bridge.

Got to open the gate!

He launched himself onto the wall, wedged his fingers in the creases between the stones and used the bulging muscles of his forearms to pull himself upward. Five feet became ten, then twenty.

De Launay, now fully aware of the small attack force, ordered his Swiss Guard to fire at the revolutionary climbers. The air around Simon's head was split by flying musket balls. Screams filled the air, telling him that those who followed his savage ascent were being cut down. After a few maddening moments, he no longer heard the hoarse grunts of fellow climbers. He was the only one still alive. A bullet bit into the wall near his hand and Simon scrabbled wildly at the wall.

C'mon Alexandre, amico mio! He needed return fire to draw away the attention of those who shot at him from the towers.

An explosive roar filled the air and he chanced a glance under his shoulder. Salomé and her army of women were reloading their firearms and taking cover behind wheelbarrows as the soldiers on the roof peppered the courtyard floor with bullets.

Simon shook his head. "*Che donna!* What a woman."

He vaulted over the wall and landed on the balls of his feet, only to find himself surrounded by three Swiss mercenaries with guns trained on him.

Salomé ducked as a musket ball smacked the cart that formed a sort of shield for herself and the nearby women. The surging throng pushed along a string of such makeshift defenses while others returned fire with antiquated muskets. They were still too far out of range to use the pikes that they clutched between sweaty fingers. Those would come into play when they reached the inside of the Bastille. *If we get inside.*

"Is this what battle is like?" Aimée's eyes gleamed as she strained to shove the heavy cart forward.

"No wonder men like it so much." Salomé grinned at her. "I've only felt so alive when in my lover's arms!" She pushed the distracting thought of Alexandre to the back of her mind. *Not the time to think about his arms, Salomé.*

"Where is Alexandre?" She glanced around the courtyard. Her heart raced as she pushed the cart forward. *God, don't let him be hit, please don't—*

"Forward!"

She followed the sound of his commanding voice and saw him at the forefront of the fight, urging on the masses. He was a prime target, more visible than the rest because of the red horse on which he rode.

"The idiot!" Salomé thrust the handles of her cart into Aimée's hands. "Hold this!"

She gathered her skirts and was about to run to Alexandre when a scream from behind pulled her up short. Aimée stared at the fallen body of Marguerite, the doll-maker's wife. Her twisted form lay on the cobblestones and her vacant eyes stared up at the sky. A spot of red bloomed ominously across the cream of her worn blouse and Salomé knew without a second glance that Marguerite was dead.

"Leave her." She grabbed Aimée's arm. The sudden death of her friend had snuffed the light out of the girl's eyes.

"She's with her daughter now." Salomé shoved the cart's handles into the girl's trembling hands, noting the wet tearstains on her arms. "Keep movin'. Stay alive!"

Then she rushed forward on cobblestones that were now slick with blood toward Alexandre's red demon of a horse. Bodies lay scattered around her like scraps of meat, blown to pieces by merciless bullets. Salomé could see that the revolutionaries were taking the worst of the fight.

"Forward!" Her voice rose loud and shrill in the storm of noise that raged around her. A blazing side outpost billowed black smoke, blocking her view of Alexandre. She flung her hands in front of her eyes, bent low and gasped for breath as she crawled forward to where she had last seen him.

If he dies...

A horse reared in front of her and Salomé jumped back as Alexandre, eyes blazing with battle-rage, caught sight of her.

"You need to get off the horse!" She waved her pistol toward the soldiers on the tower. "You'll get killed!"

He ignored her warning. "Get on!" He held out his hand.

Salomé didn't hesitate. *Smack! Smack!* Bullets plowed into the ground around her as she leapt into the saddle and wrapped her arms around his waist. She cocked the hammer on her pistol. He spun the horse around and together they thundered toward the end of the first drawbridge.

"Alexandre, the second drawbridge is still up!" She squeezed him tight again. "There's nowhere to go."

"I know," he said. She glanced behind and saw the mob that hurtled forward. If they tried to go back, they would be crushed under the feet of their own people. If they stayed where they were they would be cut to pieces by the blistering gunfire from the towers. If the second drawbridge didn't fall now, they would be shoved by the surging crowd into the deep moat below.

The edge of the bridge was about thirty feet away. Twenty. Ten. Salomé's heart rose to her throat. They were about to ride off the edge!

"Alexandre?"

She glanced down at the brackish water that chugged below her, already feeling its watery depths closing over her head. Unless the second drawbridge fell within the next ten seconds, they would both die.

"Simon won't let me down." His words did little to reassure her.

Ten feet became five and Alexandre urged his horse to move still faster. Behind them, the surging crowd turned in on itself.

Those in front tried uselessly to resist the crush of those that followed. Gunfire from the royalist soldiers in the towers above mowed dozens down at a time. Screams filled the air, punctuated by the staccato echo of gunfire.

Salomé closed her eyes and gripped Alexandre's waist with a strength born of desperation. They were both going to die. She could feel the muscles of his stallion clenching into balls of steel between her legs as it prepared for one last jump.

"I love you!" She shouted the words one final time.

And then she heard it. It was the grinding cry of a dragon whose soft underbelly had been pierced by the knight's conquering lance. She opened her eyes as the horse's feet left the ground.

Time slowed to a crawl as the couple flew through the air. She could feel the wild crashing of her heart, but its rhythm was drowned in a tidal wave of love for the man to whom she clung. Then the horse's iron shod hooves smashed onto the wooden plank of the drawbridge as it descended the last few feet before dovetailing with the first segment.

"Hyah!" Alexandre did not pause but spurred his horse through the gate and into the Bastille. He flew by Simon who stood, panting and bruised, among three very dead soldiers.

"Took you so long to kill just three?" Alexandre called over his shoulder.

"Yeah, yeah, *prego*. You're welcome, my friend!" Simon knitted his brow and doubled over, panting.

Alexandre launched himself from his still-moving horse in a juggler's tumble and came up with two daggers in his hands. Salomé dropped form the horse and began jabbing away at the men closest to her.

Alexandre grunted and rolled his neck. It was time to do what an assassin did best.

⚜

Robespierre examined the knot of his cravat in a mirror he had commandeered from his brother Augustin. As a rule, he detested mirrors, believing them to be too closely linked to the vanity of the nobility. Augustin, ever the lover, did not share his compunctions and today Maximilien was glad that his still-slumbering brother owned one of the devices.

He could hear the clamor outside as the mob attacked the Bastille but the storm of emotions that raged in his own heart held his undivided attention. In sixteen hours and thirty-three minutes, he would participate in the ultimate battle. This time his opponent was not some petty lawyer but the Queen of France. At stake were not a few measly silver *livres*, but a kingdom for her and his life, for him. If she killed him tonight the revolution might grind to a halt. This was undoubtedly her plan. Wisdom urged him to avoid Marie's evident trap, but wisdom bowed to the iron will of desire.

His thoughts turned to his unexpected guest. "And where is the good Madame de Lussan?"

Robespierre arched a bushy eyebrow and then put down the mirror. Striding to his door, he flung it open and walked to the guest room. He rapped twice on the door then, without waiting on a response, flung it open.

"Gone!" His fist clenched as he slammed the door and spun on his heel. "Augustin! Augustin!"

A series of thumps followed by a loud *crash* told Robespierre that his brother had been jolted from sleep and was making his way to the door.

Augustin flung open his bedroom door. "What is it brother?" The lines of sleep were still printed on his face.

"The tender dove has flown the coop, you slugabed." Robespierre scowled.

Augustin stared at him with unfocused eyes for several seconds and Maximilien sighed.

"She is gone, idiot. Viviane de Lussan slipped out of the house while you were dreaming about daisies!"

Augustin gave his head a slight shake and his eyes cleared. "You want her back?"

"Of course, I want her back." His brother jerked the cravat off his neck. "Tonight, I am to engage in the ultimate form of combat. I want every piece of information she can provide! How many curls are in the queen's hair? How many times does she bat her eyes when flirting? Does she snore when she's truly asleep—*whatever* the woman knows, I must know!"

It was Augustin's turn to sigh as he rubbed the back of his neck. "I will take a quick look Maximilien but there is a battle going on and it will be difficult to find her." He shrugged. "She might even be dead."

Robespierre's face turned purple. "I don't care if you have to walk to hell's gates itself to get her, just bring her back!"

⚜

Marie-Antoinette pursed her lips as she examined the Belvedere's *salon*. She was unaware of the battle that raged only a few miles from her private world but, if she had known, she would have concluded that the dirty rebels were only getting their just deserts.

She was focused on winning the war on a different front— one in which a man and a woman competed for supremacy. A virtual army of servants had worked through the night to transport parts of her private theatre away from her husband's prying eyes and into the part of Versailles where she alone reigned as absolute monarch.

She fingered the last letter she had received from Robespierre through Geneviève this morning. It was short but rather conciliatory, a fact which she hoped meant that he would come to their battle with his guard lowered.

"You are sure that Viviane is not colluding with the lawyer?" Her eyes probed Geneviève's features. The woman looked as though she were about to collapse from fatigue, but Marie was not ready to let her rest. Not yet.

"It did not appear that way, Your Grace." Geneviève's eyelids drooped. "She seems to want nothing more to do with either side."

Marie tapped the letter against her palm. Either way, Viviane's involvement at this point was superficial. The time for pretense was over. The die had been cast and the gods would decide who lived... and who died.

"You are prepared for this evening?"

"Yes, Your Grace."

The queen thrust a rigid finger beneath her nose. "You will not intervene no matter what you see or hear. Madame Gabrielle de Polignac has the same orders. Is that understood?"

"Yes, Your Grace."

"Then go now and rest, dear Geneviève. Your queen will not forget your loyalty."

Marie watched her depart then closed her eyes and sighed, mentally rehearsing her part in the greatest performance of her life. It was the first time she would fight her own battle without hiding behind Louis's crown or her own wealth. This was not about queen versus commoner or rich against poor. She and Robespierre had pushed past the barriers of class to settle an old hatred on common ground. Tonight, they both competed for survival and, one way or another, tonight, she would finally be free.

♣

I've made a terrible mistake. At first Viviane's escape from Robespierre's apartment in the pre-dawn hours had seemed relatively simple. She had walked barefoot to the door, unhinged the latch and slipped outside. It was a long walk of at least eight days to Lussan but, as she had no other prospects, she gritted her teeth and prepared for the journey home. She was not familiar with Paris' winding streets but had decided her first step was simply to get across the Seine and onto the other side of the city.

Then the mob had appeared.

It was as though they had been born of the mist itself. The dark clothes, typical of the lower class, blended in with the fog and overcast sky. Viviane found herself caught in a wave of sweaty bodies. Each cried out for the destruction of the Bastille and swore to send every aristocrat back to the darkest corners of the hell from which they had escaped.

"À la Bastille!"

Fists pumped into the sky; voices screamed themselves hoarse; the very air seemed to crackle with the violent energy released by this crowd of revolutionaries who carried streaming blue, red and white flags, muskets and pikes. Soldiers were among the throng, she noticed with surprise. They were the king's men who had seen enough oppression of their own people to change sides.

At first, panic threatened to crush Viviane. Her father had been trampled to death in a crowd much like this. She forced herself to go against her instincts and stopped resisting the press. It was far better to get pushed along then to fall and never rise again.

"Our brothers and sisters are dying." A woman next to Viviane grabbed her shoulder and stared at her with frantic eyes. "We must avenge them. Rise up, Paris, rise up!" She slipped a rusty pistol into Viviane's hand. "Take this, sister of the revolution."

Then she forged ahead screaming for the death of the king. Viviane stared at the weapon for several long seconds. She had only seen her father fire a gun once when a wolf had tried to kill some of his sheep. It felt cold and impersonal. She tucked the pistol into her belt.

The domineering towers of the Bastille jutted above her and the noise around her threatened to make her eardrums explode. Everywhere, the screams of the wounded and dying echoed off the blood-soaked stones but the constant roar of gunfire drowned out their cries. Black smoke curled around the two drawbridges. Broken, twisted corpses—most of them revolutionaries—littered the ground ahead of her. Instead of discouraging the reinforcements, the sights and sounds only further enraged the crowd who shoved her forward.

Viviane felt sick. She didn't want to be here. She might die today when all she wanted was to get away from the madness of Paris. But there was no other option. She crouched low and let the tide push her toward the Bastille.

⚜

A quick glance around the perimeter told Alexandre that they were losing. Badly. On all sides the ground was covered by men, women and children who wore the revolutionary cockade while only a few royalist soldiers lay on the stones. They had the manpower but they needed more firepower. They needed cannons.

"*Préparez les canons!*" De Launay's voice sent a chill through Alexandre's veins. He thrust his sword through the belly of another attacker, used the heel of his boot to rip the body off the blade and then looked up at the tower where the governor stood.

"God help us." He crossed himself. De Launay had armed his cannons and was now aiming them at the masses of Parisians who still streamed across the drawbridge.

"*Présentez les armes!*" The loaded guns swung toward the second drawbridge. Alexandre cast wild eyes around the courtyard.

Salomé. Where is Salomé? Then he saw her. The fight had pushed her back in the direction of the bridge. She stood in direct line with the guns, oblivious to the baptism of fire that was about to fall.

"*En joue!*"

Alexandre's body was in motion before he realized it. He rammed his way through the crowd, butting aside royalist and revolutionary alike, his mind reeling with the possibility of losing her.

"Salomé!" He had only seconds to reach her, milliseconds now before the command to fire was given.

"*Feu!*"

He collided with her, knocking her to the stones below. He lay over her prone form, propping himself up on his elbows and using his body as a shield to protect her from the inferno that erupted around them. A massive *whoomp*, caused by the impact of the missiles, made the ground tremble. Splinters of stone flew by his head, slicing into his face and neck.

Alexandre had slipped his hands underneath Salomé's head, protecting it as they fell, and now he felt the stinging prickles of his bruised knuckles. He chanced a glimpse over his shoulder. At least a hundred revolutionaries had been flattened in the blast caused by three cannon balls exploding at once. Mangled arms, legs and unidentifiable body parts were strewn wildly across the sagging bridge.

He felt Salomé's fingers on his face and turned back to her. "Are you hurt?"

"You saved me." She brushed the backs of her fingers down his cheek "You *do* love me."

Alexandre was silent. He didn't understand what had driven him to save the woman. He assumed that it was an instinctive reaction sparked by a memory of losing Juliette. *But what if it was something more?*

"No time for this. There's a battle on." He lurched to his feet, helped her up then pulled her away from the bridge.

"We've got to pull back." Alexandre ground his teeth in frustration. "Without cannons we'll be slaughtered!"

"*Présentez les armes!*"

Alexandre's heart sank. *So soon?* Then he realized that the cry had not come from above but from his right.

"*En joue!*"

A group of soldiers wearing the uniforms of the king's dragoons stood on the bridge. Relief ripped through his heart. Their cannons were aimed at the Bastille! He had known that many of the king's army, especially those stationed in Paris, were sympathetic to the rebel cause but he had not expected outright mutiny.

"*Feu!*"

The thunder of ten booming guns, aimed at De Launay and his men, shook the bridge. Alexandre tilted his head back and whooped. Holes began to appear in the massive fortress as the former soldiers of the king intensified their assault on the Bastille. They had switched sides and were prepared to prove their newfound loyalties.

"*Feu!*" Again, the cannons sounded, and with a bestial roar, the masses surged forward.

"*En avant!* Forward!" Alexandre snatched up his sword. But there was no need to urge them on. Total defeat had been reversed by the appearance of these trained reinforcements and he knew, beyond a shadow of doubt, that victory was theirs.

Chapter Twenty

July 14, 1789. The Bastille, Paris.

Augustin found himself on the fringe of the screaming mob that made their way toward the burning Bastille. Smoke curled upward in thick billows, making his lungs burn even at this distance. Coughing, he followed the crowd, having no better plan than to catch what little of the battle he could and report to Robespierre that he had been unable to find Viviane. His brother was a fool to think that he could find one woman in a city that was consumed by violence.

The sight that met his eyes as he descended the hill leading to the fortress almost made him miss his footing. Billows of flame licked at the stones. Heedless of the blazing debris, Parisian citizens danced, waved the *tricolore* and chanted their slogans of *liberté*, *égalité* and *fraternité*! He made his way closer, pressing through the exuberant crowd. Children, who had joined in the fight, jeered at De Launay who stood with his head bowed before a triumphant Alexandre.

Augustin pressed in closer. He had missed the fight but he would not miss this historic moment! His pulse raced as he strained to catch the words Alexandre spoke to the defeated governor. Finally close enough to hear, Augustin's eyes moved toward Alexandre and it was then, as his eyes flickered over the crowd, that he saw her.

⚜

"On behalf of the people of Paris, I accept your surrender!" Alexandre shouted the words as a thunderous cheer exploded on all sides. To his right stood Salomé and on his left, Simon cracked his knuckles, no doubt already envisioning the governor's head on a pike.

De Launay bowed his head then drew his sword and extended it, hilt-first to Alexandre but pressed his elbow against the side of his overcoat.

"How many prisoners do you have in the Bastille?" Alexandre gestured for Simon to take the proffered weapons.

"Eight." De Launay's shoulders drooped. "They will be brought out in a moment."

"Eight?" Alexandre frowned. The latest intelligence provided by his spies was that seven prisoners were locked away in the hated fortress.

"We received one more last night." The fingers of De Launay's right hand twitched.

Alexandre's interrogation was interrupted when Captain Jacourt, leader of the mutinous dragoons, pushed his way forward.

"May I congratulate you." He extended a hand to Alexandre. "It was a victory for all of Paris!" Cheers again resounded in the Bastille's courtyard.

Alexandre gripped Jacourt's arm. "Were it not for your heroism, Captain we would be mourning instead of celebrating!"

Salomé grabbed Alexandre, spun him around, and planted her lips on his mouth. The crowd hooted as she twined thick tendrils of his black hair around her blood-stained fingers and pulled him deeper into her embrace.

Alexandre lost sight of all else. He wrapped his broad hands behind her neck, not caring about the red smears on her cheeks or fingers.

She pulled away, panting.

"You did it." Her eyes gleamed, then she kissed him again. "Against all odds, you won."

"*We* did it." Alexandre caressed her cheekbone with the ball of his thumb. "It is *our* victory."

Pough! A searing wave of pain exploded in his brain as a bullet ripped into his right shoulder. Alexandre lurched to one side and fell against Simon.

"No!" Salomé stood frozen for one second. Then she jerked the gun from her belt, leveled it against De Launay's pale, throbbing temple and, with another cry, she pulled the trigger.

The governor's body jerked twice then collapsed, but the incensed crowd grabbed the corpse. Within minutes the mob had severed the head from its trunk and, hooting with glee, paraded it around on a pike.

Simon gently probed the wound on Alexandre's shoulder. "De Launay must've had it hidden under his coat."

Salomé dropped to her knees. "Will he live?" She grabbed Simon's arm. "Please tell me he'll live!"

Simon caught her eye. "Bullet missed his lungs. It's buried deep in his shoulder. He'll live."

"Oh, thank God!" She pressed her lips against Alexandre's mouth but pulled back when he groaned.

"I'm sorry my love." She ripped a length of fabric from her already torn and bloody skirt and gave it to Simon who pressed it against the wound.

"Help me up." Alexandre grasped Simon's arm as he attempted to stand. "Must see the prisoners."

Simon exchanged a glace with Salomé whose lips were pressed in a thin line. She shook her head but Simon flashed a quick grin. "You try stoppin' him." He pulled his friend to his feet then let her take him.

A row of emaciated prisoners made their way down the cobblestone steps, encouraged by the cheering mob. To those present, each liberated captive represented another deathblow to the *ancien régime,* or Old Order, as Louis's reign was now commonly called. One by one they came down the line.

"*Cinq, six, sept.*" Simon counted them off. "Thought de Launay said there were eight?" Alexandre said nothing, unable to ignore the growing premonition that swallowed his heart.

Then he saw him.

"*Huit,*" Simon said, then also fell silent.

"Philippe de Valence?" The name was passed from one mouth to another, growing in intensity and volume as the crowd recognized the face of their hero. "Philippe!" The cry swelled to an earthshaking chant.

"Philippe!" This last cry came from Captain Jacourt who pushed his way through the throng and grabbed his friend's forearms. Philippe jumped up on top of a cart which served as a makeshift platform.

"How?" Alexandre's face reddened. "How is he here?" He had known Philippe would be condemned at the mock trial but had expected him to be either immediately executed or held on the palace compound, not transferred twelve miles to the Bastille by night!

The irony of his situation struck him more forcefully than De Launay's bullet. He had participated in Robespierre's plan to destroy Philippe, intending to rid himself of his adversary. But by reducing the Bastille to rubble, he had inadvertently set his enemy free and made him a hero in the eyes of the people.

How can it be? His mind reeled with the sudden turn of events.

"I'll kill him here and now." He thrust his way forward.

Simon grabbed his shoulder, ignoring his mangled cry of pain. "You can't touch him. Not now. You hurt one hair on that man's head and this mob will forget everythin' you've just done for them. They'll rip you to shreds just like they did to governor-boy, De Launay."

He squeezed Alexandre's shoulder, using the pain to break through the fog of his anger.

"I know you want revenge but now's not the time, *amico*. He's been in the Bastille. He's been imprisoned by the king himself. That makes him a saint in their eyes."

"Citizens of Paris!" Philippe stilled the unruly masses with an outstretched hand. "Today you have bought my freedom with the price of your blood. For that I am eternally grateful."

Alexandre clenched his teeth, shutting the door to the storm of hate that assaulted his soul. Simon was right. For the moment, Philippe was untouchable.

A resounding shout split the air. Philippe's eyes played over the crowd. His glance lingered on one face and then another, making each person feel as though they were a special part of him. "For centuries you have been oppressed, living as slaves to injustice. Today we rewrite the history of France and—"

He broke off and Alexandre followed Philippe's gaze to the smooth, upturned face of a woman who stared at him. *Viviane*.

"Simon." Alexandre motioned and his friend bent down. "Take seven of our Moustiquaires and capture that woman." He gestured with his chin. "Philippe might be untouchable, but *she* is not."

"Today," Philippe found his voice again but his eyes were still locked with Viviane's. "I tell you that I have relinquished my title and family name." A murmur rippled through the crowd.

Alexandre felt his heart clench. *Cunning as a snake.* His bruised knuckles went white as he gripped Salomé's shoulder.

"From now until the day of my death, I shall be called Philippe Égalité. I have left it all because I love you!"

The words were spoken to the crowd but they were meant for Viviane alone.

Alexandre could see that they had their intended effect. Her reaction was lost in the explosive chant that shook the loose pebbles on the courtyard floor. Thousands screamed out the name, *Égalité,* finding in his selfless act the final proof that this man was France's only hope.

Some screamed, "Make him king!" while others cried out, "Égalité forever!" They hoisted him onto their shoulders, chanting his name as they marched from the courtyard, leaving the Bastille burning behind them.

"Isn't that the aristo whore?" Salomé's voice cut into Alexandre's thoughts. She pointed to Viviane.

"Yes." Alexandre grimaced as a wave of pain shot through him. "Simon is about to take her."

"Good." Salomé positioned herself before him, blocking Viviane from his line of sight. "I will die before I let her sink those claws into *my* man again."

Her voiced dropped as she locked eyes with her lover. "Simon will capture her. Then, I will kill her."

⚜

Philippe's eyes never left Viviane's face. From his height above the crowd he caught sight of a group of men making their way toward her from the right while a single man closed in on her from across the square.

I can't lose her again. His pulse hammered in his veins. *Not now!*

"Jacourt!" His shout was barely audible above the chanting of the throng. The captain caught his gaze and saw him pointing to a woman.

"Protect her." Philippe gesticulated wildly. "Protect the woman!"

Jacourt snapped to attention. "Dragoons, to me!" At his order, twenty-four soldiers closed in around their leader and pressed with him through the mass.

⚜

Viviane saw Augustin first. She shrank back, hoping that he would not notice her in the tumult but his eyes were locked on her face. She had no choice but to run. She spun around, eyes darting wildly about as she sought an escape. To her left, a smaller group of about five men made their way toward her while Augustin pressed in from in front.

She spotted a gap in the crowd and dashed toward it, slipping with lithe grace through the throng while making her way back up the hill, in the direction of Paris's suburbs. *I can lose them in the streets.* She glanced over her shoulder and saw that Augustin, oblivious to the other group of pursuers, now moved at a light jog. His eyes clung to her face.

The second group had seen Augustin and were now following him to get to her.

Think Viviane, think!

She battled her way through the melee, her pulse hammering in her throat. Annoyed cries from those she shoved out of her way rose on all sides, but there was no time to apologize. Just ahead lay a dimly lit alley. She rushed past it, knowing that Augustin would expect her to turn off into the first road she came to, and sprinted down the next lane. A bakery stood on the corner with a green overhang covering the entrance.

A sign marked *Fermé* dangled awkwardly from the door handle. She pressed down on it, praying that, by some miracle, the owner had left it open.

Locked.

The echo of footsteps and she pressed herself against the wall. Apparently, Augustin had not fallen for her little trick. She shifted her position, trying to make herself unnoticeable beneath the overhang and, as she did so, her fingertips brushed against the butt of the pistol that protruded from her waist. She pulled the gun out and held it between loose fingers.

Augustin's pale, wigged face peeked around the corner. He took two steps forward and stopped. Her breathing slowed to a crawl. He hadn't noticed her yet, but he soon would. She couldn't allow that to happen. Not if she was going to leave Paris.

He took one more step and paused, squinting.

Viviane exploded into action. She stepped out from the overhang with her arm pulled back. As expected, Augustin pivoted in her direction, providing her with the perfect angle. She slammed the butt of the gun against his temple and then threw herself back out of reach of his flailing arms.

Augustin reeled from the blow.

She stepped forward, gun extended. "Back away or I will kill you." It was all a bluff. She didn't even know if the gun was loaded. But that did not matter if Augustin believed her.

He touched his temple which sported the beginnings of a nasty bruise. "You wouldn't dare shoot the brother of Maximilien Robespierre." He jutted his chin and stepped toward her.

"Wouldn't I?" She hoped he didn't notice the tremble in her voice. "You tell your brother that I have seen both sides of this war and I am sick of it! Tell him I don't care what he does to the queen or to Paris as long as he leaves me alone. Now get back!"

"And if I don't?" He came closer stopping only when she pulled back the hammer on the gun as she had seen her father do years before. She couldn't miss at this range, not if the gun was loaded.

"Then you will die." Viviane clenched her teeth. "It's your choice."

She stepped forward and Augustin froze. "You can tell your brother I died at the Bastille or that you couldn't find me. Tell him whatever you want but I will not be used again. Not by him. Not by the queen. Not by anyone."

Augustin licked his lips, eyes darting from the pistol, to her face, and to the gun again. At last, he nodded and backed away, hands in the air. "Very well. You died at the Bastille. I saw your body near the gates of Saint-Antoine but couldn't bring it back."

Relief coursed through Viviane, but she did not lower her guard or her weapon... not yet. "Your brother will believe you?"

Augustin nodded. "I have never lied to Maximilien before. He will believe me." He touched his brow in a small salute and paused. "You are right, Madame. No one should have the right to take advantage of you." He inclined his head in a slight bow. "I apologize on my brother's behalf." Then, he turned on his heel and disappeared.

Viviane sighed, tears of relief pricking at her eyes as she released the hammer and tucked the gun back into her belt. *I'm free!* But Philippe was alive and free as well. She couldn't leave without thanking him, without apologizing for—

The sound of running feet filled her with a renewed sense of dread. She looked up to see a line of seven men approaching her, led by the same giant who had stood next to Alexandre before he had been shot in the Bastille's courtyard. Some of his assassins, no doubt.

"Viviane de Lussan, you will hand over your weapon and come with us." The burly leader thrust out an upturned hand.

Viviane glanced around. The alley opened onto another street on the far end, but she could not hope to reach it.

"Alexandre would not want you to hurt me." She played for time as her racing mind scrambled to produce a plausible escape.

"Alexandre has ordered us to bring you back. Now come!"

"No." Viviane drew the weapon again and aimed it at the leader. "Whoever takes one step forward will die."

Simon sighed and rolled his eyes. "Woman, I have no time for these tricks."

And then he was gone.

Viviane gasped. The space that had occupied only seconds before was now only empty! He rolled toward her in a blur of motion. She jerked the trigger, heard the gun's booming report, and then he was behind her, jerking the weapon from her grasp and pinning her arms to her back.

"That might work on a soft lawyer, *donna mia,* but not on Simon."

Viviane writhed in his arms.

"Now, you will come with us." He pushed her ahead of him. "And no—"

He choked back his words as a line of soldiers spilled into the other end of the alley. Viviane did not know who the men were or how they had found her, but they had guns and those guns were pointed at the man who held her prisoner.

"Prepare to fire at will!" Their leader drew his sword and stepped forward. "I fought with you a few hours ago, lad. You know what my men can do." He pointed the blade at the giant. "Now let her go."

The alley crackled with tension as the two gangs trained their guns on each other, ready to paint the road crimson with a fresh coat of blood.

"Viviane!" Philippe's voice reached her only seconds before the man himself pressed through the group of soldiers.

Simon's hold on her had slackened and Viviane wrestled free. She flew toward Philippe and he grabbed her hands. Their eyes met in an intangible embrace.

"Ahem." Jacourt cleared his throat and the couple jerked apart, conscious once more of the two opposing bands of men that stood, primed for battle.

Philippe took charge. "You!" He pointed at the giant. "Tell Alexandre that Viviane de Lussan is forever free of him. Whatever score he has against me can be settled at the time and place of his choosing."

"Alexandre decides who is free and who is not." The assassin bared his teeth.

Philippe stepped forward. "Then tell him to face me instead. This is between us. Now, if you want to live, take your men and leave!"

"Stand down men!" Simon growled out the order.

A solitary voice protested the command. "We can take 'em sir."

"Silence *idiota!*" He spun on his heel. "If we so much as touch a hair of his head, the mob will hunt us down like dogs."

His men lowered their weapons.

"This is not over." Simon glowered at Philippe then retreated. "I swear it!"

When the last of the small band had disappeared around the bend, Jacourt's men lowered their own arms.

"Defensive shield!" The dragoon leader and his men formed a tight square around Philippe and Viviane.

"Where were you headed?" Philippe started to reach for her but let his hands fall back to his sides.

Viviane avoided his gaze, confused by the storm of emotions that swirled within her. "I-I was going back to Lussan."

"Then I will come with you. Two are better than one on the long road south."

"Would you like a military escort, sir?" The captain stood at attention and looked at Philippe.

"No, thank you, Captain. Just two horses and whatever rations you can spare."

He turned back to Viviane. "That is... if you would not mind my company?"

The sincerity behind his question was touching. A slow smile tugged at her lips. "No. I do not mind."

He clasped his hands behind his back and slanted a cautious smile in her direction. "Then to Lussan we shall go."

Chapter Twenty-One

July 14 1789. Château de Versailles

Robespierre's horse snorted and breathed out a nervous whinny. Robespierre urged his horse on, annoyed by the animal's reluctance to move forward. It shuffled through the brown tufts of grass whose sharp edges pointed accusing fingers at those who walked among the land of the living. *The world of the dead is waiting,* they silently prophesied, waving in unison as they were pushed by the unseen hand of a hot summer breeze.

Last night's rain had been unable to reverse the fatal caress of death that overwhelmed the country, and the lawyer found that the entire estate was surprisingly devoid of life. The sun's dying rays shrouded the turrets of Versailles, staining the glittering gold with a layer of crimson.

"Halt and dismount!" The challenge came from one of only two guards who waited in lazy indifference by the gate.

He clambered off his horse. "I am expected." He cleared his throat. "The queen—"

A sharp female voice spoke up from behind the guards. "I have been sent to escort Monsieur Thomas Hobbes into the presence of the queen. Now stand aside!"

The red-cloaked soldiers turned to see Geneviève striding toward them. The nurse was known to be a new favorite of Marie-Antoinette and they saluted her.

"You know this gentleman?" One of them eyed Robespierre askance. "Hobbes, is it?"

"Doesn't look like much of an Englishman to me." The other rubbed his chin. "More like a revolutionary."

Geneviève stepped between them, hands clapped onto her hips. "What you think doesn't matter, *imbéciles!* You believe the queen would invite a Jacobin to court?"

She threw back her head with a snort. "With soldiers like you to protect us, it is a wonder we are not all dead already!"

She spun to Robespierre, arm outstretched. "Monsieur Hobbes, please accept my apologies. Her Majesty has been wanting to discuss the plans for her new English-style garden in the Petit Trianon with you for some time."

Robespierre bowed, glared at the two soldiers then led his horse through the gates.

⚜

The lap of water, as it yielded to the rhythmic thrust of dripping oars, was the only sound that the lawyer's ears could detect. Robespierre, now abandoned by Geneviève, stared at the eyes of a black-hooded figure. It was a woman he guessed, based upon her slender wrists. She had coins painted over the translucent gauze that covered her face.

The allusion was not lost on him. The ancients believed that the dead were transported by Charon the boatman into the underworld. He was now being rowed across the lake to meet the queen in the Belvedere, a private villa in which she held full control. Through her boatswain, Marie-Antoinette sent a clear message that he was going to his death.

Overhead a crow cawed a raucous warning and Robespierre suppressed a shiver. Were even the crows her slaves or was it indeed an omen?

"Your mistress feels secure in her little fortress, I imagine." He leaned forward, trying to draw the sadistic rower into conversation.

Silence.

He attempted to provoke a response. "You are a servant. You should revolt against this oppression and join me."

Nothing. *Information. I need information.* Augustin's failure to procure the missing lady-in-waiting had left him with an acute sense of vulnerability. He despised that feeling.

A shift in the summer air that promised a soon-coming storm attracted his attention. *It will rain again.* Robespierre leaned back and mopped his brow but, at that moment, the rowboat glided onto the sandy beach that marked the beginning of a winding path that led upward to the Belvedere.

His conductor laid the oars in the bottom of the boat, rose, and beckoned for him to follow. The sun had almost completely slipped behind the horizon. Gathering storm clouds obscured the light of the stars. Gusts of wind blew off the water, whipping his clothes around his thin body. He followed his guide up a long dirt path that was illuminated by the curling flames of garish candles entombed in the gaping mouths of human skulls. The skulls, impaled on shoulder-height wooden pikes, were placed about every ten feet apart. Robespierre, impressed by the queen's intimidation tactics, was about to speak again when his guide whirled toward him.

The last flickering torch cast its glow upon her painted eyes, making the coins seem to glow with a fire of their own. Behind her sloped shoulder, Robespierre could clearly make out the soaring entrance of the Belvedere. He had arrived.

"Welcome," his guide said, her voice as cold as death itself. "Welcome to hell."

⚜

Simon paced back and forth in Alexandre and Salomé's cabin, fury written in every line of his muscular body.

"I swear to you Alexandre that we'll get her. I'll send men out and—"

"No." Alexandre gritted his teeth as he sat up and leaned against Salomé's chest. "Let them go."

"Let them go?" Simon glared at him. "You're givin' up? A week ago, I would have agreed but today rich boy came between me and my prey. That changes everythin'."

"That is why I lead, Simon and not you." Alexandre grimaced as he looked at the fresh bandages Salomé had wrapped around the wound. She had almost killed him when digging out the bullet. "There is more than one way to trap a fox. Now they are alert. Let time ease their watchfulness. At the right moment, I will lay a trap for Viviane that she will not be able to resist."

"How?" Simon narrowed his eyes. "You don't even know where they are."

"They've gone back to Lussan." Alexandre sighed. "Where else would she go? In time, she will come to me and dull, predictable Philippe will come trotting after her in a heroic attempt to save the love of his life. Then I will kill him."

"But the people love him." A muscle jerked in Simon's cheek.

"Humans are fickle creatures, Simon. They love Philippe today, but they will hate him tomorrow."

His lieutenant blinked several times. "Why will they—"

"Because we will make them hate him!" Alexandre cut him off, his voice raised.

"How?"

"There is one thing that Philippe cannot deny." The assassin's eyes bored into Simon's skull. "His blood. He can renounce his name but he can never deny the power of his blood. It is the blood of the aristocracy!"

Alexandre shifted. "Our victory at the Bastille is only the beginning. We will fan the flames of resistance by making every noble in France a target of the people. Within two, maybe three years, I will have the people of Paris baying like hounds for the death of the man they claim to love. Within a year after that, every man in France will want him dead."

"That's a long time." Simon's shoulders slumped. "A simple bullet will do the trick much more quickly."

"It's not enough to just kill him, Simon. We need to destroy his reputation and that takes time. I've waited fifteen years already. I can wait a few more." Alexandre winced. "Send a message to our rangers in the Languedoc-Roussillon region. I want their every move observed. They must inform us immediately of any changes."

His lieutenant turned to go but paused at the door. "Did that crazy lawyer tell you that he was to meet the queen tonight?"

A frown shadowed Alexandre's face. "No."

"Geneviève reports that the queen has a trap set at the Belvedere." Simon snorted. "She plans to kill the rat."

"I hate the man, but we need him alive." Alexandre ran his fingers through his hair. "Take five men and go after him. Night has fallen so there should be no trouble getting past the guards. You know your way to the Belvedere?"

"I've snuck in there many times to spy on the queen." Simon smirked. "Not all of what we publish is idle speculation." Then he slammed the door and disappeared into the moonless night.

⚜

Robespierre heard the sharp echo of his shoes on the stone floor of the Belvedere. Darkness, so thick it could almost be touched, surrounded him on all sides.

"Hiding in the shadows?" His voice reached the far corners of the vast expanse. "Not much like the arrogant sot I once knew!"

An explosion of blinding light at the far end of the *salon* made him cover his eyes. He stared through interlaced fingers, as from the center of the luminosity, *she* stepped forward. A sheer, white gown swirled around her ankles and, beneath a glistening silver crown, her golden hair tumbled around her bare shoulders. A diamond-studded belt crossed her plunging neckline, holding a quiver of arrows loosely in place across her heaving bosom. In one hand, Marie gripped a silver bow and, in the other, she held a matching arrow.

"Venus hides from no one, foolish god of war!" Without warning she lifted the bow, slid the arrow onto the string, and let the shaft fly.

Robespierre threw himself to one side as the arrow sped past his head and buried itself with a solid *thunk* into the wall behind him.

Venus? Her beauty could be compared to nothing less than the promiscuous fabled goddess of love. Her reference to Mars, the god of war, was yet another allusion to ancient myths. In legend, Mars—Venus's lover—was trapped and ridiculed while in her bed. Some argued that the myth showed the ultimate triumph of woman over man. Apparently, the queen also subscribed to such foolishness.

"Did you invite me here to prove who is master or to play with silly toys?" Robespierre stepped toward her, still squinting in the brightness of the light but then, with a clap of thunder that roared from outside, the light disappeared, taking the queen with it.

He was engulfed in total darkness once again. His calculating mind began to approximate her position based on her height. He shifted to his left, his senses on high alert. Although he could not see her, he could sense her nearness, hear the gentle *swish* of—

Robespierre's hand shot out and he roughly gripped her wrist. "No more games." He pulled her toward him. Lightening flickered outside the glass windows that lined the Belvedere and, in the flashing light, he saw Marie's dreamlike face upturned to his own. Her rosebud lips trembled under the impact of delicious fear.

Maximilien crushed her mouth with his own, expecting her to resist. She surprised him by pressing forward and biting down on his lips. Robespierre tasted blood—his blood—on the back of his tongue.

He finally swallowed and broke free, gasping for breath. "You..." He swayed under the impact of her kiss. He could not think! Only one word sprang to his mind. "Again!"

"Give me more!" His head swirled with the intoxicating feeling of obtaining his obsession and desire drove him to near madness.

"Only if you find me." Her voice made his palms sweat. "There is your challenge. Find me before I kill you." Then she drove the tip of an arrow into the heel of his palm and wrenched free of his grasp. Robespierre roared with pain, clutching at his bleeding hand and Marie retreated into the shadows.

⚜

She hugged the wall and spat out all remaining fluid, then peeled off the false lips that she had worn and wiped her mouth on a lace handkerchief. Her heart pounded as loudly as the crashing thunder above, not from fear, but from sheer exhilaration. *I have won!* Robespierre would soon feel the numbing effects of the fast-moving opium that she had released into his mouth at her kiss. Instead of prolonging the fight, she had decided to cripple him at their first encounter, then strike the final blow after the drug had done its work.

"Where are you?" Robespierre's voice reached her. A light flashed in a corner opposite her and he staggered toward it. Theatrical smoke began to fill the room, giving Marie the cover she needed to constantly remain just out of his reach. Flickering candles spurted into flame, transforming the smoky air into a swirling mass of red.

"Let the hunter become the prey." She flitted to one side and made her way in the direction of the massive bed that lay in the far corner of the hall. He followed the sound of her voice, and lurched toward her. Strategically placed reversing mirrors cast her reflection around the room and then flipped to a somber brown that made them virtually invisible in the smoke.

"Vixen!" Maximilien screamed as he grabbed first one image of the queen and then another, only to discover he held nothing more than an illusion in his hands. His bloodshot eyes jerked around the room as he slammed them aside, smashing glass in senseless rage.

"What's the matter, Maximilien?" Marie taunted him. "Are you angry because a woman has outwitted you?"

His face was flushed and sweat poured from his brow.

She drove the knife still deeper. "Or is it that you are outwitted by an *aristocratic* woman?"

"Stay where you are!" Robespierre shook his head.

"Remain where I am?" Her mocking laughter rebounded off the walls. "And make it easy for you?"

Marie slithered toward the gilded bed that lay just beyond them. This was the moment of sacrifice. This was the hour where she would do the unthinkable to obtain a lasting peace. She danced just out of reach of his flailing arms, whirling close and then pulling back, knowing that the musky scent of her perfume would draw him to her.

Robespierre lunged forward. She pretended to flee but he caught her easily. "Mine!" He seized her arms, pinned them behind her back and heralded his triumph with a savage howl. "I have won."

Sacrifice!

"You have won." She ground out the words through clenched teeth. "I cannot escape you." Her chest heaved as she tried to prepare her mind for what lay ahead. "The god of war has proven himself mightier than the goddess of love."

I will win, whatever it takes. She screamed as he threw her onto the bed, taking pleasure in the tortured cries that escaped her gritted teeth. *Whatever—*

Deafening claps of thunder and crackling sparks of lightening waged a furious battle in the heavens above. But their conflict could not smother the feral cries that escaped Maximilien Robespierre's lips as his lifelong obsession drove him beyond the realm of sanity and into a world where his darkest dreams became reality.

⚜

Marie rolled to the side of the bed, knowing without looking that the lower part of her dress was matted in sticky blood. She glanced down at her handiwork, the slow flush of victory stealing over her bruised and battered body. Robespierre lay on his back, his eyes wide with shock and his mouth gaping. From his side protruded the hilt of a dagger she had concealed underneath her pillow. After raping her, he had collapsed on the bed, dead to the world. It was then that Marie had played her final hand.

"Do you want us to remove the body?" Geneviève and Gabrielle de Polignac stood at her side, staring down at the man she had killed. Gabrielle, who had thrown back the hooded mask of the boatman, had cold steel in her eyes but Marie knew that she could not put her friend through more than she had already endured.

"Throw it outside Geneviève, like the trash it is." Marie sagged against the wall. "I will have the servants clean up this place in the morning."

The woman nodded and dragged the corpse out of the side door.

"You did it." Gabrielle turned her lavender eyes upon the queen.

"Yes. It is what I should have done a long time ago."

Marie swayed and Gabrielle caught her arm.

"It is not just his blood on your skirt." Her tone was gentle as she led the queen out of the room. "He hurt you badly. I will bring your cosmetics up to you so the king will not notice your bruises."

"Blood must be shed for sin to be purged." Marie dipped her hands in a bowl and watched as the water turned pink. "God knows that I have many to atone for. May the blood that I have spilled tonight wash away some of the stains that linger on my soul."

⚜

"He's over here. Come quickly!" Geneviève beckoned to the men who stole like wraiths to the top of the hill. "Why did you take so long? It might be too late!"

Simon knelt beside the body and pressed his bare fingers against the man's throat. "Barely a pulse." He grimaced. "Let's get him back to his home." Without another word, they lifted the lawyer onto their shoulders and began the long march back to Paris.

Chapter Twenty-Two

July 1789. Forêt de Fontainebleu, France.

The stifling embrace of a sweltering summer night enveloped the countryside when Philippe and Viviane crossed the Seine and entered the Fontainebleau Forest. Philippe had spent the night here on his first trip to Lussan and knew that they could find shelter in a natural stone outcropping that lay a few paces off the main trail. A spring, which drained into a shallow pool, lay just north of the cave, providing both drinking water and a place to bathe.

Philippe cleared his throat. "I will... give you some time to yourself while I get some leaves for your bed and mine."

"Thank you." She gave him a small smile, then lowered her gaze. Philippe frowned as he turned to tie their horses to nearby trees. Viviane's initial joy at seeing him again had been replaced by an awkwardness that seemed to grow with each mile they traveled. Neither of them could find the right way to voice the unspoken issues that crowded both of their minds.

He built a small fire and left, frustration building within him. A clap of thunder roared overhead as he filled his arms with fallen leaves.

Philippe sighed as he tilted his head toward the sky. Viviane needed to know that his love had not died when she chose to jump on Alexandre's horse. But where could he start? She was physically closer to him now than she had ever been at Versailles but what did that matter if her heart was still miles away?

⚜

Viviane slipped into the clear pool and gasped as its refreshing chill permeated her skin. Ripples began to spread out in slow, lazy circles. Instinctively, she began to compare her life to the pool. The invitation from Gabrielle had been the first disruption that had birthed an endless flow of ripples.

Life in Lussan had been hard and dull but she saw now that, when compared with the deceit of Versailles, it was heaven on earth. She had left home, dreaming of a better future. The glamour of court life had blinded her to the price she would have to pay to obtain it. She had been burned before realizing that she had been playing with fire.

Now she was running back to the one refuge she had ever known, hoping that the madness spreading through France would somehow pass her by. But how could it if she brought Philippe back to Lussan with her?

Viviane frowned as this question spawned others. Why had Philippe offered to come with her? Why had she agreed? Would he leave once they reached Lussan? The thought of a life without him bothered her more than she wanted to admit.

Of course, he will leave. Why would he stay? He couldn't possibly love her. Not after what she had done.

She took a deep breath and slipped completely under the water's surface, hidden from view. *If only I could hide from my feelings as easily.*

Submerged in a forest pool, Viviane examined her soul. *What are my feelings for Philippe?*

Something stirred within her each time she heard his voice. It wasn't the raw, sensual passion that Alexandre had ignited but something deeper. It was an insatiable thirst to know his mind. It was a hunger to become one with him in a more intimate way than she had ever known with Alexandre.

Viviane swam deeper into this internal pool of self-reflection. She remembered the inexplicable burst of joy she had felt when he walked out of the Bastille. Philippe had looked more like a risen conqueror than a rescued prisoner. He had given up his title. *Why?* When he had called her name on the streets of Paris she had *run* to his outstretched arms.

Why Viviane? It had not been fear that gave wings to her feet. *Then what was it?* When fear had held her prisoner in Robespierre's study, a memory of his words had liberated her.

Why does his opinion matter? Could it be that I... love him?

Her eyes shot open and she jerked upright in the pool, gasping as her head broke the surface. The thought had been so utterly unexpected that she sat, a frozen statue, unable to deny the numbing revelation that had just ripped through her defenses and exposed the secret longings of her soul.

"I... love him." She wiped water from her eyes as she tasted the words. Exhilaration made her belly quiver and a smile of wonder touched her lips. *Philippe.* His steadiness, his selflessness; he was a man who embodied all that was good in the world.

"I love him." She breathed the words freely now, imbibing on their sweet elixir. She had mistaken lust for love and that mistake had cost her dear. But *this!* This was something so rich, so pure that it defied explanation. Alexandre could never have given her *this.*

Alexandre. Remorse, as violent as the thunder that ripped the evening sky above, stabbed through the joy that had filled her heart seconds before. Hadn't she repaid Philippe's kindness with evil?

Guilt crashed down on her shoulders like a ton of stone and she slipped back under the pool's surface, trying to escape the mountain of shame whose crushing weight pressed her further into the mud. She wasn't worthy of his love. She never could be. Not anymore.

Scenes from her past flitted before her closed eyelids, each one a deafening accuser ready to hurl a recriminating stone at her trembling spirit.

Philippe, risking his life to save me from Salomé's clutches.

AND THEN YOU FORGOT HIS NAME. A dark voice slid through the blackness that surrounded her, hissing as it crawled into her skull.

Her heart clenched. It was true!

Philippe, braving public scorn to share his idea of truth.

BUT YOU FAILED TO LISTEN, WRETCH! HE WASTED HIS TIME AND NOW HE KNOWS IT.

Viviane's lungs began to burn but she ignored it, feeling the pain in her heart more acutely than anything else.

Philippe, confessing he loved me at the Bride Tree.

AND WHAT DID YOU DO? YOU CALLED HIM A LIAR!

She couldn't take it anymore. Every time he had tried to show her the depth of his love she had rebuffed him but, like a true soldier he came back, called to the front lines by a passion she could not understand.

Philippe, saving my mother's estate and then making a way to see me after his trial.

AND YOU DENIED HIM! The voice was a vicious growl inside her mind.

Shame made her throat tight. *My folly with Alexandre.*

YOU'VE GIVEN THE BEST OF YOURSELF TO ANOTHER MAN. HE WILL NEVER LOVE YOU NOW.

No! She was desperate to confirm a love whose existence she had once denied. *He promised he'd love me forever.*

HOW COULD HE AFTER WHAT YOU'VE DONE?

It made sense. Philippe had spent a whole night in the Bastille with nothing to do but think. He must have realized that there was no turning back, not for her. What man would want to purchase damaged goods?

But he renounced his title for me.

THAT WAS BEFORE HE KNEW WHAT YOU HAD DONE.

She thought of their awkward ride from Paris. Philippe certainly didn't behave like a man in love. He seemed more like a man saddled with an unpleasant task. *Why did he come?*

PITY NOT LOVE.

At that moment, she realized there was no hope. Whatever love he had once felt was gone, that much was clear. As for her, she could not hold her head up in his presence. They could never be together—her recklessness had seen to that. And what was life without Philippe?

The burning in her lungs forced its way to the front of her consciousness but she refused to break the surface.

LET GO.

Surely it was better to die here, to drown in the depths of her own folly, than to face him again!

YES, the voice purred. It was so soft now, so... inviting. HE WILL NEVER FORGIVE YOU. NEVER TRULY LOVE YOU.

She found herself agreeing. If Philippe still loved her, he would have found a way to draw her out. He would have told her how he felt.

I've hurt him too many times.

COME TO THE ABYSS. COME TO ME.

Spots of light began to dance before her eyes and Viviane felt her jaws slackening. Her sluggish mind could no longer reason. Instinct had seized control. Her mouth opened mechanically, preparing to suck in a lungful of water.

I will always love you!

Philippe's words echoed faintly in the back of her dazed mind. She stretched out her hand in a daze, imagining his face just above hers.

Forgive me, my love. Forgive me.

Consciousness ebbed but, as her mind stubbornly clung to the edge of rational thought, she felt strong arms reach down and lift her body up from the pool's miry depths.

Her mouth opened. She sucked in a shallow breath then heaved water from her tortured lungs.

Someone flipped her naked body onto its side. Violent coughs racked her frame. She sucked in air, then vomited again. Moaning, she curled into a fetal ball and everything went black.

⚜

The sound of rain and violent winds jolted her back to consciousness. Viviane opened her eyes to see Philippe squatting across a small fire, his back against a stone wall and his warm, brown eyes filled with concern. Her head *ached*. She sat up slowly and pulled at a horse blanket that he had thrown over her. Realization flooded her mind.

"You saved me." The words came out as a strangled croak but apparently, Philippe understood. He nodded once, his dark eyes somber.

"I'll let you dress." He pointed to her clothes that lay neatly folded at her side. He walked into the forest, returning only when he heard her rasp his name.

"When I came back you still had not returned." He spoke without preamble, his voice thick with emotion. "I waited a little longer and then became worried." She shivered and he prodded the fire. Viviane picked up the discarded blanket, threw it around her shoulders, and slid closer to the flames.

"I saw your clothes by the bank but there was no sign of you. Then I screamed out your name and," he averted his eyes, "said something else."

His sudden bashfulness touched her. *What had he said?* Her throat felt raw, as though it had been pummeled from the inside. It hurt to talk but she needed to ask the unvoiced questions, to discover if, by some miracle, he still loved her as much as she realized she loved him.

"I was pacing the bank of the pool," Philippe continued, "and then I saw your hand."

Viviane's brow crinkled. "My hand?"

The words spilled from Philippe's mouth. "Your hand was outstretched. It had just broken the surface of the pond. I saw it and pulled you out."

"Why?" Viviane rasped. She had to know. Now.

Philippe stared at her for a long moment. "Why what?"

"Why help my mother?" She swallowed gingerly. "Why give up your title?" The accusing memories from the pond rose fresh in her mind.

Tears welled up in the corners of her eyes and spilled over her cheeks, but she ignored them. "You must despise me now, so why rescue me from Alexandre's men? Why save my life in the pond?"

Philippe lowered his head and for a panic-filled moment she wondered if he regretted his decision. Either way she *had* to know the truth, no matter how terrible it was. Thunder crashed above, its fury matched by a fork of white lightening that blazed from heaven to earth.

Viviane pressed further, her heart throbbing with pain. "You've always been there, no matter how wrong I was. Always forgiving me." A sob escaped her throat. "A-always willing to listen, no matter what I said. Why, Philippe? Tell me why!"

He raised his head and she choked as she saw that his own face was wet with tears. Water dripped from his eyes and trickled down his beard.

"Viviane." He moaned and covered his face with his hands. "Do you truly not know?"

"Tell me!" Her voice was shrill.

He removed his hands and gazed at the ridged ceiling of their cave on which light and shadow danced in a deadly duel. "All I have done has been to show you the truth: I do and always will love you."

Viviane stared at him, wanting to cast aside her disbelief. But a love like this was inconceivable.

"How can you love me? I betrayed you!" Her voice cracked. "I-I lay with your enemy. If anything, you should despise me!" Anguish pulsed through her and she glanced away, wiping her nose with the corner of the blanket.

"In the pond, I tried to end it all." Viviane lowered her voice as she confessed. "I couldn't live with the shame of... what I had done."

She wrapped her arms around her body. "If I could undo it, I would, but I can't! I can't, Philippe, I..." Her shoulders heaved as she rocked back and forth and cried.

Philippe waited for a few moments in silence then slid closer to her. "Believe me, I was hurt." His hand covered hers. "At first, I wanted nothing more to do with you."

He sighed. "But I have learned that the greatest expression of love is to love the most when we are hurt the worst."

"I don't understand." She shook her head, numbed by his words. "How can you look beyond what I've done?"

"Because you are a part of me." Philippe slipped closer and wrapped his strong arm around her trembling shoulder. "You and I were destined to be together. Nothing—not rulers nor liars or even our own faults can ever change that."

His words reached down to the secret parts of her soul and unlocked the gates of her doubts.

"You mean it?" She hesitated. Alexandre also had promised that he loved her. "Despite everything?"

"Yes." Philippe clasped her hand in his. "Can't you believe me?" His probing gaze searched her own. "I could never hesitate to die for you."

It was true. The agony on his face was too real, the burning passion in his eyes too sincere.

A tremor worked its way from the base of her spine to her neck. "Forgive me." Viviane clutched the blanket to her neck. "I-I was so wrong." She bit her bottom lip and dropped her gaze.

Philippe was silent for a long moment. Then he said the words that she needed to hear. "It is forgotten." He placed a finger under her chin and tipped her head to look in her eyes. "Forgotten."

He paused, then spoke in a voice so quiet she barely heard him. "Do you... feel the same about me?"

Viviane leaned into his shoulder, somehow comforted by knowing that he needed her assurance as much as she needed his. "I do. I want to be with you until the last breath leaves my body."

She settled against his chest as another rumble filled the air. Her heartbeat created a thunder of its own.

Philippe pulled away, then slid to his knees and took Viviane's hand in his own. "Viviane, I need you more than I need life itself."

Her hand flew to her mouth. But he was not finished.

"Will you let me support you when your world falls apart? Will you allow me to fight your battles and carry your cross?" He squeezed her hand. "Will let me bear your pain and stand by your side when everyone else abandons you? Will you be my wife?"

Viviane tenderly replaced a stray tendril of his dark hair, lost in her admiration for the prince who thought her heart was worth more than a throne; the man who had conquered prejudice and betrayal to win her heart; the lover who wanted to be *her* soldier.

"Yes." She smiled though the tears that blurred her vision. "Yes, I will!"

⚜

They were married a week later in a simple ceremony at the village church with a beaming Ariadné as their only witness. Viviane, dressed in her mother's white wedding gown, stepped lightly toward her bridegroom, who waited at the altar.

"I, Philippe of Valence, surnamed Égalité, take Viviane de Lussan as my wife. I will honor her and love her with my substance and my body."

"I, Viviane de Lussan, take Philippe of Valence, surnamed Égalité as my husband. I will reverence him, obey him, and love him with every breath that I take."

The priest intoned the words that bound them together and pronounced them man and wife.

"You are exquisite." Philippe threw back her veil and let his eyes roam over her face.

He kissed her forehead and inhaled the scent of her skin. "I will never leave you." His lips drifted to her nose. "You are the reason I exist."

She trembled, her lips parted in anticipation. Finally, the moment came. Philippe gently pressed his mouth to hers. Viviane responded, feeling the shame of her mistakes roll away in this bond that united their souls.

She clung to him for long moments after their kiss had ended, her forehead pressed against his and her arms locked around his waist.

"You mean more to me than my life." Philippe traced the curve of her chin with his thumb. "Do you believe that?"

Viviane pulled tighter to him, savoring the power of this miraculous moment. "I do."

It was true. At last, the walls of her doubts had crumbled before a love that defied imagination. The gates of her prison had been shattered by its relentless strength and, finally, she was free.

Part Three

Four Years Later

Chapter Twenty-Three

April 1793. Apostolic Palace, Vatican City, Italy

Cardinal Rezzonico genuflected as he entered the presence of Pope Pius VI.

"Ah, Rezzonico." The aged pontiff's voice put the cardinal in mind of a croaking frog.

He kissed the ring on the pope's wrinkled hand. "I came immediately Holy Father, as you commanded."

"Yes, thank you." Pius smoothed out a fold of his long, satin robe then spoke without preamble. "The situation in France grows more desperate by the hour. I am aware that my predecessor, Clement, dreamed of weakening the Bourbon dynasty."

"Yes, Your Holiness." Rezzonico straightened as he spoke. "The vision was to place a man of his choosing on the throne of Louis XVI."

"And who was this man?"

Rezzonico chose his words carefully. If Pius had been a captain instead of a pontiff, he would be the kind of seaman who would rather see his ship strike rocks and sink than alter his course.

"While it was never official of course, the late Bishop of Rome indicated that ... *I* would serve as regent of France."

Pius regarded him for a long moment.

"I see." A momentary pause filled the room.

"I also see, dear Cardinal," the pope managed to push himself out of his chair, "that, while your agent has destroyed the power of the king, his success has resulted in an unanticipated situation. France has formed a new government—the National Assembly—which is led by an outright heathen."

"Maximilien Robespierre." Rezzonico nodded.

The pontiff's expression darkened. "He is a devil. He might as well call his government the Antichrist Assembly!"

Pius shook a liver-spotted fist. "This Robespierre seizes the Church's wealth in France to create his own currency, confiscates ecclesiastical lands and demands that the clergy answer to his government instead of Rome."

"Your Holiness," Rezzonico clasped his hands together, "do not Robespierre's actions prove that we must act without delay? His outrageous decisions targeting the Church have turned many of the Faithful in France *against* the revolution. There are those who see through his web of lies and long for the Church to reassert itself."

He fell to his knees. "Proclaim me Regent and I will make France the foremost jewel in the Church's crown."

Again, Pius eyed him for a long moment. "No, Cardinal," he said at length. "The situation has changed in a way that Clement could not have foreseen. My predecessor's meddling has created a monster in France. Now the creation seeks to destroy the creator."

He sighed. "I agree that Robespierre's rise to power demands a strong response but one that patience alone can provide."

"My lord?" Rezzonico's heart sank.

"Prudence dictates that we take no direct action." Pius tapped his fingertips together. "You say there are many in France who no longer support the revolution, but how many exactly? Enough to destroy both those still loyal to the Bourbons *and* those who answer to Robespierre?"

Pius frowned. "The papal armies are not strong enough to invade France."

"But surely—"

The pope lifted a hand, silencing the crestfallen cardinal. "Fires may rage, Rezzonico, but they always eventually burn out. We will wait until the tide turns against this fanatic while building alliances with other European powers. When the time comes, our coalition will strike."

"And should another fanatic rise from Robespierre's ashes?" Rezzonico pushed himself upright. He had waited in the shadows for over twenty years. If he wasn't given his reward now, he might never live to see his dream of power materialized. Frustration colored his voice.

"Will Rome sit and watch idly as the world slips from her grasp?" He clenched his fists. "I alone can guarantee that France will submit to the will of the Holy See."

The pontiff lifted his chin. "We may sit. We may watch." His eyes blazed and his hand, which had seemed so frail only moments before, clamped around Rezzonico's chin in a vice-like grip. The cardinal made a choking sound in his throat as he struggled to breathe.

Pius's voice turned to steel. "But believe me, Cardinal, when I say that Rome is never, *ever* idle."

⚜

The separate dining room at the rear of the Café Procope was empty, a fact which pleased Alexandre. He sat at a small, round table, across from Simon. His friend fidgeted uncomfortably—no doubt he preferred squalid brothels to the café's intellectual atmosphere—but Alexandre knew that the Procope was the ideal place to learn what lurked in the hearts of Paris's citizens. Because of its reputation as a marketplace of free thought, individuals from all niches of society came to the Procope to express their sociopolitical views. It was a microcosm of the city itself and was therefore the place that he needed to be.

They were tucked into a corner of the small room. Its wide double-doors hung open, allowing them to see and hear what transpired in the main hall. Alexandre let his keen eyes roam, absorbing both the obvious and more obscure representations of Parisian thought.

The yellow walls of the larger hall across from their table were heavily decorated, but he recalled that a portrait of King Louis XVI had been on prominent display underneath a rectangular mirror on his last visit about a year ago. The painting had been replaced by a rendition of the king and queen. The couple were depicted as a four-legged animal with a male and female head—one Louis and the other Marie-Antoinette. Underneath the drawing, the artist had scrawled the words, *"les deux ne font qu'un"*. *The two only make one.*

Alexandre's lips curled in a tight smile but then he glanced down at the table next to him and noticed a leaflet that someone had tossed next to an empty wine cup. He reached over, and caught sight of a bawdy drawing, caricaturing the queen and her lovers. He flipped the paper over and reached for his own cup of water.

A cartoon—on which the king was stretched out beneath the wooden planks of a new, supposedly humane, method of execution called the *guillotine*—caught his eye. Louis's neck was invitingly bared, and the executioner was about to pull the cord that would release the blade.

"Look at this." He handed the paper to Simon.

His friend glanced at the drawing. "About time." He slid it back across the table.

Alexandre shook his head. "You've missed the point. It is obvious that Paris wants the king dead but did you notice the bodies dangling from the lampposts *behind* the king?"

Simon reached for the paper again and took a closer look. He pointed to the smaller figures of a man and woman suspended in mid-air from lampposts abutting the tenements. "The queen?"

Alexandre sighed. "Yes, the queen, but next to her..." He lowered his voice. "Next to Marie hangs our friend, Philippe de Valence."

Simon squinted at the paper, then traced the words *Philippe Égalité* that peeked out from between the man's twitching legs. "Yeah, you're right." He flipped the paper over, looking for the artist's name.

"Georges Clément," Alexandre offered, taking another sip. "Not one of our men on a propaganda mission, but someone who believes that Philippe is indeed a threat to France."

He steepled his hands and leaned back in his chair. "Over the past four years we've worked hard to tarnish Philippe's name. We've printed false accusations, maligned his every good deed and had our agents speak against him in the streets."

"Obviously, we've done our work well." Simon folded his hands behind his head. "The Third Estate has crushed the power of the king and formed their own government, the National Assembly." He shrugged. "Robespierre's the man of the hour.

The government centers on him while the king is nothin' more than a figurehead." His lips twisted in a crooked grin. "A lot of us want Louis to be a figure without a head!"

Alexandre ignored his jibe and gestured to the article. "The National Assembly knows that if King Louis were to ever gain military support from his cousin, King Charles of Spain or even England, their dream of a French republic is over. The nobles would tear this country apart looking for rebels."

He frowned. "The people are afraid of what will happen if we don't eliminate the king *and* every noble in France. They want Louis and everyone connected to him dead—a fact which makes all of Paris hostile to Philippe. All hereditary titles have been abolished by the National Assembly, so no one considers Philippe's renunciation of his title a sacrifice anymore. And his blood still links him to the throne."

Simon gulped down some water then rocked the cup back and forth. "Anythin' stronger in this place?"

"You'll live." Alexandre shook his head. "I'm still not convinced. When the Bastille fell, I saw my archenemy walk out a free man. I was powerless to stop it."

He crumpled the paper. "That won't happen again. I need to know that he has become a man that no one in Paris will lift a finger to rescue. The next time he arrives, the only ones to celebrate will be the grave diggers!"

"Roland, our agent in Languedoc-Roussillon region has been keepin' an eye on them as ordered," Simon said. "He reports that Égalité and his wife are still livin' on her mother's farm."

Alexandre snorted. He would never have believed that Philippe would still marry the girl. His enemy's magnanimity only intensified the assassin's loathing. "Children?"

"Rumor is that she's expectin'." Simon leaned forward. "But none born... yet."

"A pity." Alexandre clucked his tongue. "Paternal love is the quickest way to break an enemy."

"Spoken like a man with experience." Simon eyed him for several moments. "Are you and Salomé—"

Alexandre cut him off with a glare. "Some things are better left unsaid."

A raucous cheer in the outer hall made their heads swing in unison toward the door. Voices shouted over the applause that filled the room.

"Here he comes!"

"The man of the hour himself."

"France's true savior: The Incorruptible!"

Simon and Alexandre exchanged a wary look. Only one man in France carried such a title.

"Citizen Robespierre." Ornan, the owner of the Procope, bustled forward.

Robespierre, shadowed by Augustin, stepped into the café. His pale face was pinched into a permanent frown. Alexandre had lost contact with Robespierre after his men had rescued him from the queen's clutches but, although it had been four years, he saw at a glance that the man had changed. A reptilian stare, punctuated by soulless eyes that glared out from a face of stone, announced that whatever good Robespierre contained had been snuffed out the night he almost lost his life.

Simon had ensured that Maximilien knew the Moustiquaires had saved him, but it appeared that nothing could bridge the widening gap between Maximilien's followers—known as Jacobins—and Alexandre's men. The two leaders were bent on a collision course.

Robespierre's vociferous attacks on the Church in France had been partly responsible for driving the National Assembly to oppress monks and nuns. Alexandre took this as the final proof that the politician was a dangerous heretic who had to be eliminated.

The tension between the two leaders was coming to a head and, while Robespierre had been recuperating from the queen's near-fatal blow, Alexandre had focused on strengthening the efficiency of his clandestine band. Tonight, they would begin the final play that would bring the weakened Louis and his harlot-queen to a prison in Paris.

"Please, allow me to serve you at a table in our *salon privé*, next to these worthy gentlemen." Ornan led the way toward Alexandre and Simon.

Robespierre, swathed entirely in black, eyed the pair.

"Do we really have to be near that snake?" Simon muttered under his breath.

"Never underestimate a snake's power." Alexandre's hand fondled the hilt of a concealed dagger. "What comes out of its mouth can kill."

Simon grunted. "Point taken."

"Right this way." Ornan personally arranged the chairs for Maximilien and Augustin. "This will give you a bit of privacy from your admirers."

Robespierre sat, back straight and shoulders set. His amber eyes bored into Alexandre.

"Um, is there anything I can get for you?" Ornan clapped his hands together. "On the house."

Augustin placed a small order. When Ornan had hustled away, Robespierre spoke. "I thought I detected a foul odor the moment I stepped through the door." He gave a disdainful sniff. "Little did I realize that I would be forced to endure the stench of your presence up close."

He shifted in his seat. "How go things in the king's garden? Still playing games with your little whore, are you?"

Alexandre's nostrils flared. "I no longer serve the king. Viviane has fled and there is no longer a need for pretense. *Salomé* and I still live in a cabin outside the palace grounds."

Robespierre did not miss his emphasis of Salomé's name. "I see." He traced his black-gloved fingers along the edge of the table. "So, you've become attached to the girl. Heed my warning, Alexandre, and never trust the fairer sex. 'Beauty is deceitful' to quote the wise King Solomon."

"Apparently, you learned that lesson first-hand." Alexandre enjoyed seeing a flush creep across Robespierre's face. "I wonder, was it the queen's beauty or the memory of your failure to kill her as a boy that drew you into such an obvious trap?"

Robespierre leapt to his feet, sending his chair clattering to the ground. "I won't listen to this! Come Augustin. We are leaving at once."

"By this time tomorrow," Alexandre stood, "your lover-queen will be a prisoner."

Robespierre froze. His head slowly swung back toward his nemesis. "A prisoner?"

"Sit. Down. Now." The spymaster tightened his lips into a thin smile.

With a grunt, the lawyer complied. "What nonsense is this?"

Alexandre glanced around to be sure that they were alone. "Simon, the door."

He gestured then reclaimed his seat. His lieutenant went to guard the door and Alexandre lowered his voice. "As you know, the king and queen have become virtual prisoners of the people."

"My National Guard, France's new militia, holds the deviants under close watch." Robespierre flicked invisible lint from his sleeve.

Alexandre arched an eyebrow. The Guard, largely directed by Robespierre and his cronies, had been formed after the fall of the Bastille. Officially, the soldiers policed Paris's streets, but he suspected Robespierre had created the body to form a militia that could rival Alexandre's shadow network.

"I have received information that will soon shift the focus of the revolution. The growing radicalism in France, such as your attacks on the Church, has so appalled the king that he, his wife, Duke Jules and Duchess Gabrielle de Polignac intend to flee tonight to Montmédy, a fortress near the German border."

He paused to let Robespierre absorb this information, then continued. "Royalist troops are garrisoned at Montmédy. Louis presumably intends to have them conduct his family to safety while gaining time to forge an alliance with Sweden or Spain that will restore him to power."

"I see." Robespierre rubbed his chin. "What do you intend to do?"

"I intend to let them escape. My men will watch the route and will arrest them at Varennes, about thirty miles from Montmédy. We will need the help of your National Guard to return them to Paris, especially if the king's soldiers stationed nearby attempt a rescue."

"Arrest them?" Robespierre sniggered. "You should kill them all and be done with it!"

"You would have us kill them without a trial?" Alexandre folded his arms across his chest and leaned back in his chair. A nervous tic pulsed in Robespierre's cheek.

"She is the root of all that is evil in France. He is just as guilty." He glared at Alexandre. "The devil himself is more innocent than Marie-Antoinette!"

"And the children?" Alexandre pressed. *How deeply does he hate her?*

"You cannot hope to get good fruit from a corrupt tree." The lawyer slammed his fist onto the table, sending a cup clattering to the floor. "If you want France to be free then you must eradicate every trace of that Jezebel. Husband. Children. The witch herself."

"Maximilien," Augustin laid a hand on his brother's arm. "Alexandre is right. Those who support the monarchy would tout their deaths as murder. Even the moderates of our own party would protest. We need to bring them to trial first."

Maximilien's eyes burned like a pair of living coals. "Very well." He glowered, first at his brother then at Alexandre. "The Guard will go after them once their escape is confirmed. Bring them back to Paris and we *will* put them on trial."

He shivered. "But I swear to you that death is the only absolution they will receive. France must be purged; it can only be cleansed by blood."

"Whose blood?" Alexandre leaned forward, and propped his chin on his fist. "The king's?"

A humorless smile slithered across Maximilien's cold face. "The blood of every noble, their families and their associates. Anyone suspected of collaborating with France's enemies must pay the ultimate price."

Alexandre straightened and nodded. It was as he suspected. After his deadly encounter with the queen, Maximilien's mind had slid into a pit of pure evil. The bloodbath that would soon engulf France would make the people realize they had traded one tyrant for another. *No matter.*

His mission was to prepare the way for a theocracy. The chaos that Robespierre was about to unleash would provide the perfect bedding ground for Rome's rule to flourish. From the ashes of civil strife and anarchy, a phoenix of spiritual enlightenment would arise.

The day after both king and queen are dead, Alexandre narrowed his eyes as he made the mental promise, *this man will join them.*

"Where will they be kept until their execution?"

Maximilien stood. "The garrison of the National Guard at Temple Prison offers maximum security."

"I will need you to arrange lodging there for myself and Salomé." Alexandre rose as well. "Are we agreed?"

Robespierre tilted his head to one side. "He that is not with me is against me." He extended his arm. "Are you with me, Alexandre?"

Alexandre stared into the yellow eyes of his enemy and gripped his hand without hesitating. "To the death."

⚜

Marie-Antoinette clutched Geneviève's hand as the two women stole across the courtyard to the six-horse carriage whose dark frame was barely visible in the night. Her mind raced as quickly as her pulse, denying the reality that she—a Princess of Austria and Queen of France and Navarre—was about to flee from her own subjects.

Two months after her encounter with Robespierre, Gabrielle had brought word that the lawyer had somehow survived the assassination attempt and was recovering. He had publicly disseminated her letters, concocting a story of how the queen sought to seduce "The Incorruptible."

All Marie could do after receiving the news was wrap her arms around her body and weep. She had endured the bestial touch of the creature by focusing on the knowledge that he would die at her hand. Even now she shuddered at the memory of his groping claws and hot, fetid breath. And it had all been for nothing! He had triumphed in the end.

Reports, detailing the fury of the people had filtered into Versailles, with the king himself seeking her out in the Trianon. She had burned Robespierre's letters and denied all knowledge, claiming that her erstwhile maid, Viviane had written the letters and forged her signature. The *bourgeoise* had collaborated with

Robespierre in an elaborate scheme to tarnish her reputation, vanishing after completing her vicious mission.

But the damage done to her tattered reputation had been irreparable. So, after four years of increasing hostility and virtual imprisonment, she had turned to the one man she knew would not disappoint her: her confidant and lover, Count Axel von Fersen.

Fersen had determined that the royal family needed to flee Paris. After much deliberation, her slug of a husband had finally agreed. As she approached the carriage, Marie could not escape the feeling that tonight's events would determine their fate.

The queen glanced at Geneviève, the faithful nurse who remained at her side, going so far as to smuggle the scullery maid's outfit that Marie now wore as a disguise.

"I cannot thank you enough Geneviève." Marie squeezed the servant's hand again. "You have been so good to me—a true friend."

Geneviève's smile was hidden in the moonless night. "I have done nothing that was not deserved, Your Grace." She curtsied. "If it please God we shall meet again. Soon."

"May it please God!" Marie crossed herself.

Louis, dressed as a servant, waved from the carriage window. "Quickly, wife we must go at once!"

Marie clambered aboard, and a whip cracked over the six horses. The buggy lurched forward.

Geneviève waited only until she was sure it had passed beyond the palace gates before spinning on her heel and rushing to find the commander of the National Guard.

⚜

Alexandre had just laid one last, lingering kiss on Salomé's lips when someone knocked on the door. "I must leave."

"Hmm, you don't sound eager to go," Salomé teased. "Could it be that the mighty Alexandre, leader of assassins and slayer of kings finds his woman more appealing than his duty?" She smiled, liking the idea of toying with him.

Alexandre returned her smile which surprised her. She had half-expected him to rail about how wrong it was to make light of the revolution. But something had changed in him after the attack on the Bastille. A few days ago, she had awakened to find several wildflowers waiting in a wooden cup by her eyes... and last night! She sighed dreamily as she remembered last night.

But he had never said that he loved her and, although four years had passed since Viviane's escape, uncertainty as to Alexandre's feelings still lingered. She needed certainty. Especially now. Questions hummed through her mind. Was she the queen of his heart or did the aristo still enslave some remote part of him? If he loved her, why not tell her? Why not marry her?

A worried frown crossing her face. "You will be careful?"

"If I live, I will come back to you." Alexandre smoothed her furrowed brow with the balls of his thumbs. "If I die, I will become a saint. I have the word of His Holiness. Either way—I win."

Salomé wrapped her arms around his neck. "I don't need a saint." She kissed him again, breathing the words. "I need a man. I need you."

Alexandre held her close. Then, as the knock sounded again, he untangled himself and slipped off into the shadows.

Salomé stared at the closed door for several long seconds and then made her way back to the bed. She glanced down at the cup of pink and blue wildflowers that he had given her and folded her hands protectively across her stomach. Then, after a minute, she picked up the flowers and began separating the pink from the blue.

Pink or blue? It was as she had said. She did not need a saint, but she did need him. Salomé hummed softly to herself, wondering just how Alexandre would respond when he learned that, within just a few more months, someone else would need him too.

⚜

Alexandre pressed his lean body against the damp earth, listening for the telltale rumble of hoofbeats. Around him, scattered in the tall grass that lined the upward slope of the main road to Varennes, waited Simon, six of his Moustiquaires, forty soldiers of the National Guard who had ridden ahead, and Geneviève. Another sixty men from the Paris militia were making their way toward Varennes to provide military support should the royalists attempt a rescue.

His mind leaped over the miles to the rundown shanty in which Salomé waited. There was something different about her... something he could not quite identify. Her caresses were softer and her look more tender. As for himself, Alexandre still refused to admit that he loved Salomé but the mere thought of leaving her side was enough to make his heart ache. *Is it possible to serve the Church and love a woman?*

The soft rumble of thunder broke into his thoughts and he filed the intriguing idea away for future reflection. Once again, Geneviève's information had proven to be good as gold. The king's carriage broke into view, lathered horses straining to pull the heavy coach up the crest of the hill. As predicted, the driver stopped near the local postmaster's office to change the team.

It was now almost one hour before midnight, but Jean-Baptiste Drouet, the postmaster and Moustiquaire in charge of this region, heard the noise and stepped outside. He was fully dressed and carried a lit torch. "Who goes there?"

Alexandre watched from the shadows as the man stepped forward and thrust the torch into the tired eyes of the driver, then flung open the doors and examined each of the passengers. He paused and fished in his pocket for a coin on which Alexandre knew the image of King Louis was engraved.

For a long moment, a tense silence held the small group prisoner.

"You are the king!" Drouet shoved the coin back into his pocket. "You are the King of France!"

He wrenched the door open, ignoring the screams of the women and children. Drouet jerked a shadowy figure from the interior and threw it onto the dirt road. The driver sprang down with a snarl on his lips and Count Axel drew his sword. At that moment, Alexandre and his men separated themselves from the darkness and formed a tight circle around the king.

"Stay where you are!" Simon's sword flickered to the count's throat.

"Louis, King of France and Navarre, you and your family are under arrest by will of the people of France!" Drouet's words were echoed by the captain of the National Guard.

"We are betrayed, Marie!" Louis called as his arms were tied behind his back. "Someone has found us out!"

Inside the coach, Gabrielle de Polignac gripped the queen's hand. "How could this have happened?"

Her husband, Jules, wailed as soldiers of the Guard closed in.

The queen's pale, frightened face appeared in the entrance of the coach. "Who could have done this? I told no one except—" Her eyes widened as a woman stepped from behind Alexandre. "Geneviève?"

"In the flesh, Madame Deficit!" Geneviève jerked off the hood that covered her face. She had asked for special permission to join Alexandre's forces. He did not refuse her, knowing that tonight would bring the justice she had sought for so long.

A hush fell over the group and, in the quiet, the queen's whisper was easily heard. "How could you, of all people, betray me?"

"Ask your lover, the count!" Geneviève's chin jutted upward. "Ask him why he abandoned me after persuading me to leave my husband and daughter. Ask him why he promised me a better life only to leave me when I birthed his crippled brat!" She glared at Von Fersen whose stricken face was clearly visible in the firelight.

"Geneviève, I—"

The woman's angry scream cut him off. "I committed an unforgiveable crime when I left my husband, but did you care?" A bitter laugh escaped her throat. "Once your seed began to grow in me, all you could think about was your own reputation. But that's what you *aristos* do best. You call yourselves Christians! You bleed us dry and, when you've had your fun, you cast us aside."

She stormed toward von Fersen and spat in his face. "Our child was crushed underneath a carriage wheel in Paris while you were lying in her bed!"

She whirled back toward Marie-Antoinette. "That is why I brought the infected blanket to your son. That is why I found a way to save Robespierre's life." Geneviève lifted a triumphant fist, ignoring Marie's mewling cries. "An eye for an eye. A life for a life. A son for a son!"

Alexandre's sharp ears caught the sound of horses' hooves behind him. "Soldiers!" He rushed toward Von Fersen, his pistol pointed at the man's temple. "Your weapons, Sir!"

The count hesitated.

"Now!"

Reluctantly, Von Fersen handed over his sword as a guard secured his hands behind his back.

The rest of the National Guard formed a rough defensive line around the king as the first wave of royalists pounded down the hill.

"Save your king!" Louis shouted. "Save us from the rebels!"

Alexandre knew that he was outnumbered. He had to stall the newcomers until the reinforcements from Paris could join them.

"Simon!" Alexandre pulled his sword free and leaped onto his horse. "Get Louis inside the carriage. Surround it and put all guns on him."

Streaking forward, he pulled the snorting animal up short ten paces before the leader of the royalist army. "Halt!" He gestured toward the carriage with his sword. "Any closer and the king is a dead man."

The royalist captain's eyes widened, and he lifted his fist. "*Arrêtez-vous!*"

The lines of soldiers behind him rolled to a slow stop and Alexandre grinned. "If anyone attacks, the king dies first."

He twisted in the saddle and shouted to Simon. "Let's go!"

Simon grabbed the carriage reins and kicked the driver over the side. "Move, *idiota!*" He slapped the reins and pulled the buggy around in a tight circle. Harness creaked and leather groaned as the horses responded to his rough handling. "Hyah!"

"Go!" Alexandre wheeled his horse around and followed with the remaining Moustiquaires, the Guard and Geneviève. The royalist troops shouted in frustration but remained in position as the carriage began the long journey back to Paris.

Louis tried to calm his frightened children while avoiding all contact with his wife. He had been lost in a stupor as the truth of his wife's infidelity and his son's murder smashed into his mind. The hope of rescue had galvanized him into action but even that hope had been denied him. His dream of returning to Paris as its absolute sovereign had disintegrated into ashes.

Life is deceitful. A friend who betrayed his trust by seducing his wife. A child who was murdered by his nurse. A king who had become a prisoner. Nothing was as it seemed. Nothing was as it should be.

"God." Louis's hoarse whisper filled the confines of the carriage. "Help us!"

Chapter Twenty-Four

April 1793. Temple Prison, Paris.

Alexandre knelt alone before the bed that he shared with Salomé. Her news had rocked the foundations on which his world was built. Stripped to the waist, he eyed the open black box that held his whip. If ever there was a time that he needed direction, it was now.

"A father."

Fear, awe and wonder filled his voice. Raising a family in a France free from oppression was the dream he had shared with Juliette. That dream had died with her. Now it appeared that God had granted him a second chance.

Or is this a trap of Satan? His mind wrestled with the emotions that pulsed in his heart. He refused to shirk this new responsibility. No child of his would be condemned to the same emptiness of a fatherless childhood that he had endured. *But my mission!* The will of Rome was a cornerstone of his life. How could he forsake the Church now?

Behind his inner turmoil was Salomé, the enigmatic wonder whose passion had penetrated the defenses he had erected around his own soul. He had persuaded himself that no one would ever replace Juliette but now...

Alexandre reached for the whip. He paused as a memory of Salomé soothing his tortured back rippled through his mind. His hand trembled, hovering over the black handled instrument of self-inflicted torture.

Salomé. She hated his whip and everything it represented. He hesitated, realizing that the hour of decision had come. Serve the Church or serve his heart? To choose one was to abandon the other.

"I can't." He groaned and his fingers clenched the empty air. "God forgive me, I can't."

He covered his contorted face with rigid fingers. None of his training had prepared him for this!

Who will you choose? The question hammered at his skull, clanging over and over in his mind like a bell at the hour of sacrament.

Alexandre reached for the whip a second time but again, her look of disapproval floated before his mind's eye. He shrank back. *What hold does this woman have over me?*

He had saved her life the day they attacked the Bastille. *Why?* This overwhelming urge to protect Salomé, to see her happy—could it be what the poets called... love?

Who will you choose?

He slowly lifted his face, tears streaming from his reddened eyes. He took the whip between his hands. For a long moment he gazed at the leather hilt and leaden balls. Then, he pressed down with all the strength he possessed.

Crack!

The black handle split into jagged edges. He stared at the pieces. Surely God would punish his decision! Surely, he would be cursed for what he had just done. *But have I ever had a choice?*

Choice. That was the element that had eluded him throughout his entire life. He had not chosen the path of an assassin; it had been delegated to him by his masters. It was not choice that had led him to Paris—it was the possibility of earning a place in heaven after completing the will of those who reigned on earth.

My... choice. For the first time in his life, he had seized control of his own destiny. Salomé was his choice.

Alexandre wavered between fear and the unfamiliar, exhilarating sensation of freedom. He rose slowly, tossed the broken pieces into a small fire that glowed in the hearth, and watched until the whip was no more than ashes.

He drew a deep breath, inhaling the pungent scent of burning pine and leather. *Choice.* His children were his choice. He would be there for them, nurturing them as a father should.

Alexandre opened the door and slowly walked to Salomé who waited outside. *Choice.*

⚜

She watched him stride toward her. A tremor ran through her body. Whatever came out of his mouth now would determine the course of her life.

Alexandre halted a few feet away. "Marry me." Alexandre gripped her arms. "Today. Now. There is a chaplain visiting the condemned. He can perform the ceremony."

She started. "What?"

"Become my wife. You are my choice."

She stood speechless, eyes bright with unshed tears.

"Do you love me?" Her voice choked with emotion. She needed to hear the words.

"I—" Alexandre released her arms and stepped back. A momentary silence walled up between them. "I-I will not let you bring our child into the world without the seal of marriage to tie us together."

She waited, searching his eyes. He had broken the tie binding him to the Church, but something still held him back. *Viviane* held him back.

The silence became uncomfortable. "I care for you," he mumbled the words, "...deeply."

Salomé glanced down. "That'll do. For now."

Alexandre came closer and wrapped his arms around her. "France will be no place for our child."

His hand hovered over her stomach for a moment, then he tenderly rubbed it. "Once Louis and his wife are dead, Robespierre will turn this place into a graveyard. Even if I kill him, his government won't rest until everyone opposed to their rule is dead. I cannot risk your safety."

He pulled back, locking eyes with her. "We have no choice but to leave the country."

"Leave?" Salomé gasped.

"Just until things calm down."

She knew he was right. They had no future in France, not now. "Where will we go?"

Alexandre gazed up at the sky. "Somewhere far from Rome's reach. Somewhere like... America."

"America?" She arched an eyebrow. "Can you survive in a Protestant country?"

Alexandre frowned but he squeezed her hand. "I will do anything to protect you and our child."

Salomé brushed his cheek with the backs of her fingers. *He is a good man.* "When will we leave?"

"As soon as Philippe is dead."

She pulled away, her eyes hardening. "Just Philippe? Not his woman?"

Alexandre hesitated. "She is with child, Salomé. How can I sanction taking the life of an unborn infant?"

Her face darkened. *Was he protecting his conscience or was he protecting Viviane?*

"It's *his* child, Alexandre." She spoke through gritted teeth. If he would not kill Viviane for her, then perhaps he would do it for himself. "Philippe's seed is growin' within her. Your *enemy's* seed."

She cupped the back of his neck with her hand and pulled him closer. "If Philippe dies but the child lives, he may one day seek to avenge his father's death. You just said you'd do anythin' to protect us both."

Alexandre mulled over her words.

"Hate isn't limited by time or by space." She paused, letting her words sink into his mind. "If we are to live in peace, Philippe and *everyone* connected to him must die."

He slammed his eyelids shut. "The Church would never favor the murder of an unborn."

"Does that matter now?" She reached for his hand and linked their fingers together. "You can believe in God, Alexandre, but be sensible about it." Her voice gentled and she leaned against his chest. "The future is ours to make. Nothin' is more important than that."

His eyes flew open. "I don't know, Salomé. Life is sacred."

She pulled back, face twisting with remorse. "You can't tell me that you loved me but it's *your* child I'm carryin'. You *owe* me somethin'."

He avoided her gaze. "I do."

"I want the aristo's life." Salomé's lips pulled back in a snarl.

Alexandre was not a woman. He would never understand the humiliation of knowing that her bitter rival had been first in his bed. He could never grasp the sense of insecurity that gnawed at her day and night.

Did Viviane linger in his thoughts? When he held her in his arms, was it Viviane's face he saw? As long as the aristo lived, Salomé feared that, in his heart, *she* would always be second-place. If he killed Viviane she would know that his heart belonged to her alone.

"I want to see her head impaled on a spike." She clutched his arm.

His eyes met hers. "You're asking for my conscience on a platter."

"If that's what it takes." She placed his hand upon her belly. "Keep us safe Alexandre. Rid both of us of this demon from our past."

Alexandre swallowed hard. "So be it."

She eyed him, mollified but still uncertain, then angled her body against his. "You wanted to become a saint. You're willin' to let that go?"

"You don't need a saint." Alexandre wrapped his arms around her then pulled her close. "You just need me."

⚜

Gabrielle de Polignac fumed as she climbed an interminable staircase that led into the cold interior of a medieval fortress called the Temple. The revolutionaries had transformed the building into a prison that was policed by several regiments of the National Guard. She had been separated from the rest and herded into the building's dank interior as if she were nothing more than a wretched cow!

She stood in a turret of the prison, led by a guard who grasped a lit torch. A narrow door swung open, yawning like the dark maw of some prehistoric beast. Gabrielle shrank back and the soldier shoved her forward.

"Go on then." He leered at her, placing his bearded face inches from her own. The light of lust gleamed in his eyes. "Unless you'd like me to sweep you off your feet!"

Gabrielle threw him a disgusted glare and edged into the room. The door behind her slammed shut.

Thunk! A heavy bolt slid into place. Gabrielle made her way toward a wooden table on which a sputtering candle rested. She groaned as she slumped into a rickety chair, her mind reeling under the impact of sudden change. How could this have happened? Only two weeks ago, her biggest problem was finding a shoe that perfectly matched her newest gown. Now the world had keeled over on its axis like a drunken sot!

The bolt squeaked. She stiffened and cast anxious eyes at the door. It flew open with a loud crash. Two men, wearing faces that would frighten the devil himself, stepped in.

"I am Alexandre," the first one said. "And I have a proposition to make."

Chapter Twenty-Five

August 1793. Lussan, France.

Viviane cracked her eyelids open as streams of daylight danced upon her face. Still groggy, she moaned and reached with groping hands for Philippe. As expected, he was not there. The man held a firm habit of rising just before dawn to pray. Daybreak always found him in the fields or in his beloved woodshop, hard at work. *You would think he was born a bourgeois.* Thankfully, he had the consideration to hold his meditations downstairs, giving her an hour or two more of sleep.

What about you? Viviane squinted as she listened to the chiding voice of her conscience. She blinked sleep from her eyes and sat up. *I should be more...*

More what? The word *religious* came to mind, but religion wasn't her husband's way. He believed in a heartfelt spiritual experience instead of mundane rituals. She had accepted this as his opinion, but the idea of having God as a gracious friend still seemed rather foreign. For the moment, she was content to put such matters to one side and simply bask in the reality of their love.

Viviane nuzzled his pillow as she inhaled his scent and remembered his passionate kisses. Who would have thought that Philippe, the man who had shunned women, could be such an ardent lover? Her eyes drifted to the slight bulge in her abdomen and a slow smile slid across her face. The pregnancy had taken so long that she had begun to worry, but now she knew that, within a few months, she would place the expression of their love into his arms.

Anticipation made her spine tingle. *I have to see him!* She slid out of bed and pulled on her clothes. As she performed her morning ablutions, her eyes fell upon a dark leather-bound book.

Philippe had bought the volume upon their return to Lussan. He began writing in it just after their marriage. He would not tell her what it contained only that she would know, "when the time was right." More than once, the temptation to sneak a look had seized her, but the thought of disappointing him was enough to staunch her curiosity.

She rammed her feet into her worn, leather boots and slipped down the stairs. Her mother, Ariadné, hummed in the kitchen as she slapped dough into a kneading trough.

Viviane opened the door and made for the west pasture where her husband harvested the few acres of summer wheat that he had planted. Her eyes drank in the changes that he had brought to her mother's estate as her feet flew over the ground.

The dilapidated farm had been literally changed from the inside out. Room by room, Philippe had ripped out rotting wood and broken beams, remaking things to suit the vision that burned in his mind. But the biggest change was unseen. Philippe had transformed despair into hope for a better future.

After officially presenting the repaired home to an astounded Ariadné, he had moved on to the barn and fields. Although unable to farm the whole property singlehandedly, he had managed to sow a few acres and was counting on the proceeds from this year's harvest to hire help for next season.

There!

Her eyes gleamed as she saw his powerful arms swinging a scythe. His worn shirt lay discarded on the ground. A strip of black leather bunched his shoulder-length hair together at the nape of his neck. Viviane stood, lost in admiration, as he effortlessly swung the blade through the standing wheat. Two years of lean food and hard labor had added about fifteen pounds of muscle to his already solid frame.

Philippe paused, mid-swing, catching sight of her. An inviting smile wreathed its way across his tanned face. She ran to him and he held her close.

"Each time I hold you in my arms, I count myself king of the world." His kisses robbed her of breath.

Viviane pulled back, holding him at arm's length. "Do you remember what today is?"

"How can you expect me to think when your beauty blinds me?" He reached for her again.

She clasped her hands to her mouth in mock horror. "You forgot?"

"Forget that today, four years ago, I became the happiest man alive?" He nuzzled her neck. "I could sooner forget my own name."

She laughed as his kisses sparked tickles along her neck, but then grew thoughtful. In a sense, he had forgotten his name—or rather renounced it. Philippe never complained about the change in his fortunes, but she knew that it could not have come easily.

"Are you truly happy here?" She put both palms on his chest and searched his eyes. "Living like a peasant?"

Philippe's arms encircled her rounded waist. "I am richer now than I ever was in Paris. You are my treasure. Never think that I could ever regret my choice."

He buried his nose in her hair and inhaled. "You give me a reason to live."

Viviane leaned her head against his chest and listened to the steady reassurance of his heart.

"Is our little prince happy this morning?"

"Prince?" She arched an eyebrow. "And if it's a princess I'm carrying, will you be less pleased?"

He looked deep into her eyes. "No part of our love could ever displease me."

"Well... if you must know, I think you're right. I think it is a prince." She threw her arms around his neck. He swung her off her feet and gently laid her on the ground.

"Philippe?" Her eyes widened as the implications of his actions sank in. "My mother—"

"Is busy in the house very far away," her husband finished.

"But if she..." He smothered her protests with his kisses and she surrendered to the sweetness of his embrace.

⚜

"Had a nice start to your mornin'?" Ariadné smirked as she slanted a glance at her daughter.

"Hmm, yes." Viviane bit off a hot chunk of crusty baguette and butter.

Ariadné sighed and shook her head. "Nothin' like hay to get the blood fired up!"

Her daughter froze mid-chew.

"At least that was your father's excuse." Ariadné winked but Viviane crinkled her nose. There were somethings she just didn't want to know!

Heat flared in her cheeks. "Um, could you excuse me?" Without waiting for an answer, she stuffed the rest of the baguette into her mouth and escaped through the door.

"Mother 'is busy in the house very far away' is she?" She stormed out of the house ready to tell Philippe just how *busy* her mother had been!

Viviane had just passed the gate when a rising cloud of dust caught her eye. She shaded her eyes with her palm and squinted.

A rider, wearing a dark cloak and the plumed hat of a cavalier sped down the lane on a lathered horse. Viviane clutched at the gate, sensing the long shadow of evil. She threw a hurried glance over her shoulder but Philippe was not in sight.

The stranger drew up at the gate, barely restraining the snorting, stomping horse. A jagged scar creased his face. "Viviane Égalité?"

She froze. *How does he know my married name?* Although the church registry recorded the marriage of Philippe de Valence, he never used the surname Égalité.

"Never mind." He removed his hat and shook out his long, dark hair. "I know who ye are even if ye don't admit it." He groped in a pouch at his waist and dug out a grubby letter.

"You've got mail!" He spat a dirty stream of tobacco at her feet. "A love letter from your cousin in Paris."

Gabrielle? Viviane's blood turned to ice. "Who are you?"

"Who I am ain't important. What counts is your response to that note. The Boss says that you have one week to be back in Paris."

"What?" Viviane hesitated, then reached the letter. "Who is the Boss?" But he had already wheeled his horse around, his back obscured by a heavy cloud of dust.

She ripped the letter open and immediately recognized Gabrielle's handwriting.

> Viviane, you have every reason to hate me, but I beg you to put aside our past differences and save my life! I have been held captive in Temple Prison of Paris for the past five months. My jailor is a fiend whose name you know. He says that he has a message for you that must be delivered in person. If you do not come, he swears that he will kill me... and the child you carry.

Below, a distinctly male hand had written,

> Viviane, my love, you left without saying goodbye. How could you?
>
> I swear, by all the saints, that if you do not come to Paris alone, first your cousin, then her husband, then your child will die. Their blood will be on your head. If you come at once, I also swear that no harm will befall you. Think of your cousin—or if not—think of your child. Remember, come alone or everyone dies.
>
> I look forward to our reunion.
> Alexandre.

Her arms fell limply to her side as her mind struggled to absorb this new threat. She had to go, that much was obvious. Not only did Alexandre know where to find her, but he also knew she was expecting. His network of spies had her in their sights.

She folded her arms across her stomach, a knot of dread growing within her. *What do I tell Philippe?*

Her husband would never believe the promise of safe conduct. He would insist on coming with her, an act which would violate Alexandre's terms. He would see this as some extreme attempt at revenge. *Which is probably exactly what it is.*

But could she leave Gabrielle to die without even trying to save her life? No matter what her cousin had done, she was still family.

And our child! This final thought obliterated all lingering doubts.

She had to go. Now.

Viviane tapped the letter against the post. "Alone. He insists that I come alone."

She would leave without telling Philippe or her mother. It was the only way. She turned, her eyes again scanning the horizon for her husband.

Nothing. Viviane bit her lip as she hurried to the house. The exhilarating joy she had felt only a few moments ago was gone, crushed by a mountain of despair. She had been a fool to think that she could escape her past. Alexandre would always be her shadow, tormenting her mind whenever she was most vulnerable.

She flew to her room, hurriedly stuffing clothes and a few essentials into a sack. Once again, the devil called. Once again, she would answer his summons. *This time, I have no choice.*

Viviane paused near Philippe's book, tugged free a corner of the precious paper and hastily scribbled a few lines. The tears she had held back escaped, splashing onto the jagged edges.

> Never doubt my love for you, my darling. I must do this. For my conscience and for our child. I will return to you. With all my love.
>
> Viviane.

She laid Alexandre's note next to her own. Philippe would make the connection and understand that he could not follow her. At least, that was her hope.

She flew downstairs. Ariadné had begun her daily washing, giving Viviane access to the pantry. When she had taken enough provisions for the journey she dropped the bag into a corner and went in search of her mother.

Ariadné was bent over the washboard, still humming when her daughter's arms flew around her.

"And what's this?" Ariadné laughed as she straightened. "Everythin' alright my love?"

"I just wanted to thank you for being the best of mothers." Viviane wiped the corners of her eyes and forced a smile. "I will always love you."

Ariadné held her at arm's length and cocked her head. "Well, 'tis true that carryin' a child affects a woman's moods. I was furious with your father every other hour when you were in my belly!"

Viviane held Ariadné for a moment, her throat burning but then stepped back. Her heart lurched as she thought about Philippe. To say anything more would alert her mother that all was not well. Philippe could not know that she was gone until this evening when he returned from the fields. By then she would be miles away.

"Well if there's nothin' else," Ariadné's lips turned upward, "this pile of laundry won't wash itself."

Viviane nodded and walked toward the house but, once out of her mother's line of sight, she doubled back and made her way to the barn. She saddled one of the two horses that she and Philippe had brought from Paris, led the animal beyond the front gate, and loaded her sack of provisions onto its back. Then, with a slight groan she heaved herself into the saddle, praying that no harm would come to the child she carried. Once more she looked toward the field where Philippe labored.

"God." She breathed the prayer, her heart fragmenting. "Make him understand. Make him forgive me. Just once more."

Then, with a ragged sob, she pressed her knees into the animal's sides and began the long journey back to Paris.

⚜

The sun had just dipped below the horizon when Philippe heard Ariadné shouting his name. *Something is wrong.* He dropped his scythe and empty lunch basket, threw on his shirt and rushed toward the house.

Ariadné met him halfway, her eyes wide with panic. Fear gripped Philippe's heart. Ariadné *never* panicked.

"She's gone." She grabbed Philippe's collar. "Viviane is gone!"

"What?" Philippe held her at arm's length and shook his head. "What do you mean?"

Ariadné swung a wild arm toward the house. "She's not here. She had planned to make cheese in the cellar today. I left off the laundry to help her with supper and she is nowhere to be found."

Philippe was in motion before she finished speaking. "Viviane!" Dread coursed through his veins. "Viviane?"

But she did not answer. She always met him each evening at the edge of the field to walk with him to dinner, but tonight there was no trace of his wife. *Where is she?*

A diabolical whisper, so improbable that, at first, he ignored it, began to chant at the back of his skull. *Alexandre... revenge.* The thought grew to a hammering roar as he slammed through first one room and then another. *Revenge.*

Philippe jerked open the door to their bedroom. Empty. He leapt inside. Clothes lay strewn across the floor. Viviane never left a mess behind her.

Abducted? Murdered?

Then he saw her note.

⚜

Ariadné heard his roar of pain from outside the house. Moments later he staggered out the door, clutching a sheet of paper in his hands.

"What is it? What's happened?" She gripped his arm.

"Paris, she's gone to Paris!" He shoved the paper into her hands and ran for the barn. A few minutes later he reappeared with the second horse.

Ariadné glanced up, her face white. "You're goin' after her." It was a statement, not a question and the fury that blazed in his eyes was answer enough.

"Wait here." She ran inside, gathered some provisions and placed them in a cloth sack while Philippe stormed into his bedroom. He returned moments later with his weapons and his leather-bound volume.

His stallion pawed anxiously at the gate. Ariadné looked up at him, tears streaming down her wrinkled cheeks. The evening sun cast a halo of blood around his head. She trembled, fearing what lay ahead. "Do not be angry with her Philippe. She meant well."

A muscle twitched in his jaw. "Her intentions do not justify her actions." He grabbed the bag and strapped it to the horse with his other affairs. "I understand her reasons but she should have talked to me, not just walked out!"

"If she had asked, would you have let her go?" The woman's voice was gentle.

"No." He averted his eyes and heaved a deep sigh. "Alexandre knew what he was doing." His hands tightened on the hilt of his sword. "One way or another, this will end when I get to Paris."

"She will be safe." He leaned over and embraced his mother-in-law. "I swear it on my life."

"Go with God, my son," she whispered. "Go with God."

⚜

Victor leCupide cackled as he watched Philippe's horse thunder down the dirt road. Not only did the welcome sight mean that he was free to leave the uncomfortable tree from which he had been forced to keep watch; it also meant that Roland, the brutal ranger, would finally carry out his threat to burn down Ariadné's property.

He clambered down the tree and waddled up the lane to his home where the ranger lay sprawled on the grass.

"He's gone! They're both gone." He danced about at the ranger's feet. "Everyone's gone!"

Victor froze and swallowed as the ranger's eyes swept over him. He wanted nothing more than to be rid of this violent man whose look alone made him wish he were invisible.

The ranger's languid posture vanished as he rose to his feet. "Let's go."

"Me too?" Victor felt the blood drain from his face. "I thought that you wouldn't need me anymore."

"You're right." The ranger stroked his chin. "I don't need you." Before Victor could blink, a pair of guns had appeared in his hands.

"You know I hate tax collectors?" A sneer crossed Roland's face. "Kill 'em every chance I get."

Victor felt his eyes bulge from their sockets. He must've somehow misheard. "Y-you k-kill—?"

"I'll give you a sporting chance." The ranger gestured with a gun. "Run."

"R-run?" Victor's legs failed to respond.

Roland leaned forward and nodded once. "Run."

Victor spun on his heel, pulse hammering in his throat. He stumbled. Fear kept him prostrate. He pushed himself up, moving as fast as his legs could carry him.

Roland waited until the man was fifty yards away, then closed his left eye and gently squeezed the trigger.

"N—" Victor's shriek was cut short as the bullet smashed into the base of his skull.

"One shot." The ranger chuckled. "Not bad at all."

He stalked over and spat on the tax collector's body. "Now let's go take care of dear old *maman*."

⚜

The acrid scent of smoke reached Ariadné's nostrils as she knelt by her bed and prayed. She stood up slowly and shuffled to a cupboard where her husband's ancient pistol lay in the drawer. She shoved a cartridge in the chamber and made her way down the hall.

The door groaned as it opened, revealing a roaring inferno that engulfed the barn, the wheat fields and the outlying buildings of her farm. Now the flames licked hungrily at her home itself but, although the scorching heat already beat down upon her skin, she felt no fear.

"This is what happens to all royal-lovin' traitors." A hoarse voice called from her side.

Ariadné slipped the gun behind her back and pivoted to her left, squinting as a tall stranger strode toward her.

"If you mean my son-in-law, Philippe, then yes," Ariadné's finger coiled around the pistol's trigger, "I do love him."

A cruel grin snaked over the man's mouth. His eyes blazed with ferocious determination.

"Then wait for him in hell!" He jerked the gun upward and pulled the trigger.

Pough! Pough!
The two weapons exploded simultaneously. Ariadné grunted with satisfaction as she saw the arsonist's jaw hang slack. He gaped, first at the hole in his chest, then at the old woman who had shot him.

"What—"An intelligible groan ended his words. He slumped to his knees, then crashed, face-down on the scorched earth.

Ariadné felt a wave of pain explode in her skull. She slumped against her washtub as spurts of blood gushed out from a hole below her lungs. A weary smile crossed her face, her breath coming in ragged bursts.

She was dying.

The realization did not bring fear, only a settled peace for which she was infinitely grateful.

I am coming, my love. The whisper, a voice she had not heard for thirty years, cut through her fading consciousness.

"Gilbert?" Ariadné lifted a trembling, wrinkled hand. "My love?"

Here, my beauty. I am here for you, my dearest Ariadné.

Darkness crowded the corners of her vision but, through the shadowy veil, she clearly saw her smiling husband, swathed in light, as he strode confidently toward her with arm outstretched.

"I-I did it, Gilbert." She gasped as her life oozed into the dirt below. "They never took... our home. I... k-kept... our home... I—"

Chapter Twenty-Six

August 1793. Temple Prison, Paris.

Viviane's horse limped to a stop outside the ominous gates of Temple prison. She slid off, muttering another prayer for her child's safety. The journey had taken six days with little time for proper rest. She sucked in deep breaths, rested protective hands over her belly, then glanced up with trepidation at the enormous turrets that soared above her. In ordinary times, the medieval castle might appear like something from a fairy tale. But these were not ordinary times.

"Identify yourself!"

She pressed closer to the horse as a patrol, carrying bayonetted muskets and wearing blue and red waistcoats and white breeches approached.

Weariness sapped her strength, but she forced herself upright. "I am Viviane Égalité. I am expected."

"Égalité?" The platoon leader raised an eyebrow. "Not a common last name. Relative of the swine Philippe Égalité, no doubt!" He spat on the ground.

Rage flooded Viviane's veins, blacking out her better judgement. "How dare you insult him? He gave up everything for you—for France!"

"I think you will find, dear Viviane, that the people of Paris have changed since you've been away. They have... seen the light." The dark, seductive voice cut through the fog of her anger. She pivoted to see Alexandre leaning casually against a stone balustrade. To his right stood a heavily pregnant Salomé.

"We meet again, love," she crooned, sidling closer to Alexandre. "I hardly recognize you. In those tattered clothes, you almost look human." She hooked her arm into his elbow. "But you'll never be one of us."

"What is it you want?" Viviane directed the question at Alexandre. "Why can't you simply leave us in peace?"

"Peace?" Alexandre disentangled himself from Salomé's embrace. "While Égalité walks the earth? The people of Paris have finally seen him for the charlatan he is. They will kill him when he arrives."

She shook her head, stunned by his words. "I've come alone. Philippe is with my mother."

"Your mother is dead. Philippe is riding here as we speak. Riding to his death to save his beloved bride." His laughter mocked her.

A low groan burst through Viviane's lips. "Dead?"

"Quite dead, love." Salomé sneered. "And that's just the beginnin'."

"After you both left, your mother's life and property were destroyed... on my orders." Alexandre stepped closer. "I must thank you for being so cooperative."

Fear stabbed at her heart. "What do you mean?"

He thrust a finger in her face. "You have placed your husband's life in my hands."

"What?" She gasped and clutched her throat.

"Citizen Valentin!" Alexandre snapped.

The platoon leader responded with a crisp salute.

"Bring Gabrielle de Polignac and her husband."

"Yes, Citizen!" He saluted again and soon returned with Gabrielle and Jules.

Gabrielle, dirty and haggard, barely glanced at Viviane but curtsied in front of Alexandre. Five months imprisonment had taught her the meaning of humility.

"I have kept my end of the bargain, Monsieur—"

"That's *Citizen* Alexandre," Valentin straightened and thrust out his chest. "Usin' titles and such is against the law now. Everyone's equal under the new law, ain't that right, Citizen Alexandre?"

"You are free." Alexandre waved them off, ignoring the strutting soldier.

"Thank you, Citizen, thank you!" Jules bowed before Alexandre several times then grabbed his wife's hand, giving the keening Viviane a wide berth. They hurried toward the prison gates and disappeared into the evening shadows.

"Not even a backward glance," Alexandre said. "They leave you here to rot and don't even thank you for saving their wretched necks." He clucked sympathetically. "That's precisely the kind of ingratitude that started this revolution."

Viviane glared up at him, teeth clenched. "What do you care?"

"Citizen Valentin." Alexandre kept his eyes on Viviane. "Escort this woman to her cell. No harm comes to her, is that understood?"

"Alexandre—" Salomé grabbed his arm and spun him toward her.

"Patience Salomé." Alexandre turned away. Salomé fell silent but spit at Viviane's feet as Valentin dragged her into the prison.

Alexandre turned to the deserted streets as a cool, evening breeze whipped his shaggy hair around his head. "Come and save her, Philippe. Come and die for her."

⚜

Louis, erstwhile King of France, stared with glassy eyes at his two remaining children. At the door stood a guard whose red, Phrygian cap half-covered his eyes.

"Ten minutes." The guard held up six fingers before slamming the door behind him. Louis shook his head at the man's stupidity and focused on the real problem. *Ten minutes.* Ten minutes to say a lifetime's worth of words. Ten minutes to enshrine himself in their memories. The last ten minutes of his life.

"I-I love you all so much." Tears spilled over his cheeks. Charles, his only surviving son and heir, folded his hands as though praying.

"Don't let them kill you, *Papa*. Don't be dead." He threw his chubby arms around his father's neck. Marie-Thérèse, his eldest daughter, fell to her knees screaming. "No, Papa! No!"

"Do not fear children," Louis managed. "We shall meet again in God's kingdom. You will see me again."

He untangled himself from his wailing children and turned to his wife. *Ten minutes.*

"Marie?" His voice was hoarse. She came forward, her face stained with tears and they sat together on the bed. "So much to say now that there is no time." He averted his eyes.

They had been kept apart during their imprisonment but, in that time, Louis had found a measure of peace.

Marie bit her lip and ran her hands down her skirt. "I have not been a good wife to you." She lowered her voice as she confessed. "I—I have wronged you in many ways, and for that, I am truly sorry."

He took her hand in his. "Forgive me for not leading as a king and husband should."

"No." Her shoulders quivered. "You have done nothing wrong." She pressed her handkerchief against her nose. "I thought that I could win on my own. I thought that I could save us all. Oh Louis, I have so many regrets!"

"Marie." Louis slipped his arm around her shoulders.

"Say you forgive me!" Her eyes begged for his mercy. "Forgive my infidelities, m-my wrongs."

He leaned forward and kissed her. "I forgive you. I too have many regrets. My fear of disappointing you kept me from being the man I should have been."

She bowed her head and wiped her eyes. She was broken. "But now at last we have spoken."

"Yes." He lifted her chin to meet his gaze. "At last we have spoken."

The door flew open. Six burly soldiers marched in and grabbed his arms. "I love you all!" Louis shouted the words. "My children, I love you."

"Papa, don't die."

"No!"

The crashing door cut off the broken family's wails, but Marie could hear the chanting of the throng as her husband was pushed forward, heckled by the maddened people of Paris.

"Blood, blood, blood!" The chant penetrated the prison's thick stone walls.

She gathered her children in her arms, covering their ears as best she could. "God, have mercy on his soul. Have mercy on us all."

A hush came over the crowd and she could hear the grinding squeak of the guillotine's blade as it was pulled upward. She imagined her husband's prostrate body, his neck outstretched beneath the biting edge of the knife.

"Louis." Tears slid down her cheeks. "I am so sorry."

Then a massive roar swept over the crowd as ululating cries of bloodthirsty joy burst from thousands of savage hearts. It was done. The king, her husband, was dead.

⚜

Philippe pulled the cowl of his cloak closer around his face and affected the shuffling gate of a drunk. He had left his horse tied to a tree on the other side of the Seine, knowing that he would attract less attention on foot. The streets of Paris were crawling with the Revolutionary Guard, soldiers who burst into random homes and herded their occupants into wooden carts destined for Temple Prison or worse.

He shuddered and pressed his body closer to the wall, marveling at how much had changed. Everywhere, men and women skulked about, avoiding each other's eyes. Philippe shook his head. Their revolution had failed to bring freedom. Fear ruled Paris. That fear was embodied in a man named Maximilien Robespierre.

A sudden roar pulled him to a stop. "Blood, blood!" The echoes were faint but loud enough to be heard. Someone had just been executed—legally murdered by the will of the mob. He quickened his pace, and turned for the one place in Paris where he might find a friend.

Alexandre would expect him to ride directly toward the Temple but, as much as Philippe's heart begged him to do just that, his mind argued that to do so would be to play the game on his enemy's terms. He needed to even the odds.

He needed Jacourt, but he had no idea where he could be found—or even if he was still alive. Friends of the nobility were being executed daily and Jacourt had made no secret of his affection for Philippe Égalité. Only one man in Paris might be willing to tell him where the soldier was.

The Revolutionary Guard stalked the streets all around him. He was sure that Alexandre's Moustiquaires were on high alert, but he had one advantage. After his break with Alexandre, Philippe's father had overseen the modernization of Paris's sewers. The Duke had charged the director of the project to involve his teenage son in the planning phase. Philippe had spent years poring over maps and charts of the subterranean world and knew the tunnels as well as the builders themselves.

He glanced around, saw that he was unobserved, and tugged at a stubborn sewer grate. "Come on, give." His biceps rippled underneath his sleeves. The approaching tramp of soldier's boots caught his attention. *The Guard!*

"Give!" Finally, the heavy stone yielded to his strength and Philippe slid it to one side. He glanced below, coughed as he inhaled the paralyzing stench of sewage and grabbed the first rung of the slimy ladder. He steadied himself, replaced the cover and allowed his eyes time to adjust to the gloom. He braced himself, then climbed down until he felt wet stones beneath his feet.

He stifled a cough and hurried to his right. It was time to talk to Lafayette.

⚜

Marie-Antoinette huddled alone in a corner of the cold, gloomy cell of the *Conciergie*, a building dedicated to those awaiting execution. She had been separated from her children just after Louis's execution. They remained in the Temple, a thought which brought a miniscule ray of comfort to her tortured heart. Perhaps, if they had not been brought here with her, they were somehow destined to survive the madness.

She cried out, but her scream was swallowed up by hundreds of others that bounced off the unfeeling walls around her.

Darkness.

Darkness pervaded the very air; it gnawed away like a ravenous wolf at her soul. She thought to pray, but why should a holy God answer? Her lovers were all gone, her dearest hopes were crushed. She had overheard talk that von Fersen had escaped to Austria where he hoped to convince her brother to declare war on France but she cast the thought out of her mind. She was beyond hoping for miracles.

A muffled voice sounded outside and she pulled herself up, determined to meet her fate as a queen.

Keys jangled in the lock. The door opened to admit a gaunt and pale Robespierre. Evidently, his rise to power had not brought him much joy. He carried a torch in his hand and beyond him waited a sea of guards. The sight made her knees weak.

"Wait outside!" The guards retreated and he slammed the door shut.

"What do you want?" Marie clenched her shaking hands into fists at her sides.

He did not answer but came closer.

She remained motionless. He encircled her, inhaling the scent of her hair and clothes.

"You have lost." With a single finger, he traced a curved line across her throat.

Marie pushed him aside. "We have both lost."

He grabbed her arms and manhandled her into a corner of the room. "I have power!"

Marie shook him off. "And you abuse it as much as I did. Hundreds are imprisoned or killed each day because of you. The people now fear *you* as much as they hated *us*."

She lifted her chin. "I was a queen, and you took away my crown; a wife, and you killed my husband; a mother, and you deprived me of my children." Her eyes drilled into his skull. "My blood alone remains: take it, but do not make me suffer long."

He eyed her for a long moment. "You were right." He pulled off his wig and raked his fingers through his thin hair. "As long as one of us is alive, the other will be haunted. Death alone can free us both."

"You will not be enslaved for long." Marie's lips thinned in a small smile. "The people of Paris will soon see you for the monster you are, and their revenge will be terrible indeed. You have sown the seeds of death, and you will surely reap a full harvest!"

"Guards!" Robespierre covered his ears with both hands. "Take her away!"

✦

General Lafayette, commander of the National Guard, stared in speechless horror at the man before him. Speechless because, underneath the muck and grime, he recognized the face of Philippe Égalité—a man that had become France's most wanted fugitive. Horror because of the ghastly stench that emanated from every fiber of Philippe's body.

"Are the sewers *that* filthy?" He clamped a hand over his nostrils.

"Worse," Égalité said. "Instead of murdering innocents, Robespierre would be better served cleaning out the gutters."

"Shh, not so loud, my friend." Lafayette raised a finger in warning. The two were alone in the outhouse that was conveniently located behind the General's quarters at the Paris barracks. Égalité had climbed up the narrow ladder that descended into the public sewer line underneath the outhouse and had concealed himself in the eaves of its roof, confident that Lafayette would come to the privy sooner or later. The general shuddered to think of what the man had seen while he waited. As soon as he had begun to sit down, the prince-turned-fugitive had dropped onto his unsuspecting shoulders.

"Criticizing Robespierre is now illegal?"

"Not only illegal; it is suicidal," Lafayette could hold his breath no longer. He released his nose. After a moment, he continued. "To speak against him or his government is to bring death to yourself and those that you love."

"Surely the king is working to stop him," Philippe said.

Lafayette started to lay his hand on Philippe's shoulder compassionately but thought better of it at the last minute. "I am afraid, my friend, that the king is dead." He bowed his head.

Philippe recoiled. "Dead! But how is that possible?"

"Shh!" Lafayette looked over his shoulder. "He was executed only this morning. His wife will be next. Everywhere, people are being accused of horrible crimes against the state. For once I am glad I am not a moneylender." He shrugged and managed a small smile. "If you owe a man money, you accuse him of being a conspirator. The man gets arrested, guillotined and—*voilà*—you are now debt free!" His smile faded. "This is what Robespierre has done to our country."

"*Mon Dieu.*" Philippe wiped his grimy brow.

Lafayette nodded. "That is exactly what Robespierre seeks to become—a god. As far as politics and religion are concerned, he has succeeded. Although I command the Guard, I too am also watched. You were wise to come to me in this rather, um, unusual manner."

"I am desperate for your help." Philippe leaned forward. "My wife is being held in the Temple. I need to locate Jacourt. Is he still alive?"

Lafayette pressed his lips into a thin line. "He is alive. I can take you to him but I must warn you that if your wife is in the Temple..." He shook his head, not wanting to say the obvious.

"I know." Philippe lowered his head. "Get me to Jacourt and I will take care of the rest."

Lafayette looked at him for a long moment. "Many of my aristocratic friends have been cast into mass graves. I hope that I will not count you among them."

Philippe did not answer. The soldier straightened his shoulders and nodded. "Wait here." He undid the latch on the privy.

"Where are you going?"

"To get you some clothes and a bucket of water. In case you did not know it, *mon ami,* you stink!"

⚜

Geneviève waited in the shadowed hallway of Temple Prison until she was certain that Alexandre was not in his apartment. The light of a few candles glowed faintly underneath its door. With each step, the fear that clung like weighted shackles to her feet, gnawed away at her will. She gritted her teeth. *I must do this.*

The thin door in front of her loomed like a mighty wall, ready to crush her beneath its weight. Or perhaps she cringed from the weight of her own guilt. She licked her cracked lips and rapped on the door twice. No response.

Run!

"No." She planted her feet. "If I do not do this now, I never will." She mustered her courage and knocked again. This time, the door swung open.

"Alexandre?" A woman stepped forward, one arm resting lightly upon her swollen belly.

"Hello, Salomé."

Salomé stared at her mother. Her mouth opened and closed as she struggled to voice the words that tumbled about in her heart.

"Hello, daughter." Geneviève tried again. "I've come—"

"How dare you?" Salomé found her voice at last. "How dare you show your face to me? Whore! Murderer!"

"Salomé, please." Her mother wilted beneath her verbal attack. "I've come to apologize."

"Apologize?" Salomé's voice cracked. "You *murdered* my father. You abandoned me and as good as killed your husband with a lie. All because some louse of a man promised you somethin' better." She laid her hands across her belly and sagged against the wall.

"Daughter, let me help you!" Geneviève reached for her arm, realizing that Salomé was experiencing the first stage of labor.

"Don't touch me!" Salomé jerked away.

"I want to apologize for everything."

"Now you come to apologize?" Salomé spat the words out from between clenched teeth. Beads of sweat dotted her forehead and her face twisted with pain. "As if I could *ever* forgive a dog like you."

Geneviève blanched and fell backward. "I know I've done wrong, child." She clutched her chest. "I wanted to come to you so many times, but I just couldn't find the courage."

Salomé sucked in air and stared at her with accusing eyes. "You should've stayed away. My mother died the day my father did."

She slammed the door in her mother's face. Geneviève stared after her, her heart too broken to weep. She waited, hoping against hope that her daughter would relent but the muffled sobs she heard through the door were Salomé's tears for herself, and not for the woman she could never forgive.

At length, Geneviève turned away. She wandered the darkened streets, giving no thought to time. Daylight found her at the heart of the city, but she did not feel the crowds that shoved by. She did not hear the jubilant cries that celebrated the death of Marie-Antoinette. She did not see the gory head of the queen as it was lifted triumphantly above the masses or notice the white shrouded corpse as it was tossed into a common grave.

She could only feel the cold caress of the Seine as she stepped off its banks and waded, unnoticed, into the water. She could only smell the rotting scent of decay that seemed to emanate from her own soul. She could only taste the bitter tang of death as she opened her mouth and pressed on into the river's dark bosom. The waters covered her head and still she walked on. Then the darkness opened its arms and Geneviève knew no more.

Chapter Twenty-Seven

August 1793. Third Precinct, Paris.

Robespierre brooded alone in his bedroom. The shuttered windows allowed a few pinpoints of light to penetrate the gloom, but the dictator's eyes were closed. He pressed the white linen clothing taken from the body of Marie-Antoinette to his nose and inhaled. Her scent lingered long after her soul had taken flight.

He began to weep. "Why did you have to die?" When her beautiful head had fallen into the waiting basket, his life had lost all sense of meaning.

From outside, the faint roar of the masses reached him as yet another collaborator against the state fell beneath the guillotine's blade. He held the life of the nation in his hands. A king and queen had fallen before him. No one was immune. He had become the master of life and death as he had once sworn he would.

How many of his political opponents had he authorized to be killed today? A hundred? A thousand?

It did not matter. Nothing mattered. *She* was dead.

"If you had to die," he sobbed, "no one else deserves to live." His tears stopped. He perked up his head, riveted by the thought.

What were the wretched masses but worms beneath his feet? Ants to be crushed underneath the powerful heel of ruthless imagination? *They do not deserve to outlive her.*

Anticipation made his spine tingle. Marie was, regrettably, dead. But she needed a monument, a shrine to commemorate her brief life.

"A tribute to her greatness." He tapped his chin with one finger, awed by the magnitude of his plan. *Yes!* One by one, he would extinguish the putrid larvae who squiggled about Paris's streets, spawning generation after generation of filthy vermin who crawled about in their own excrement.

What were they but commoners? They were incapable of appreciating Marie's true worth! He would slaughter them beneath the guillotine until the land itself could no longer accommodate the piles of their dead, bloated bodies. He would raise a memorial of corpses to the queen that he had immortalized in a tragic death.

Robespierre's mind flitted to Alexandre, the pious wretch whose usefulness had expired when his beloved Marie drew her last breath. Alexandre would be the first to die.

"Augustin." Robespierre rubbed his hands together, a crooked smile on his lips. He had found a reason to live. "Come at once brother. We have work to do!"

⚜

"Are you sure there is no other way?" Jacourt leaned forward, his gaze intent on Philippe. The darkness of night shrouded the abandoned fisherman's warehouse on the banks of the Seine in which they were cloistered. Lafayette, who had arranged the meeting, listened to the plan that Philippe had proposed in grim silence.

"It is the one thing he will not expect." Philippe tapped the table between them with his finger. "If any of you see another way..." He shrugged.

"Viviane's safety is all that matters." Philippe inhaled a deep breath through his nose, then exhaled through his mouth. "How many men can you raise?"

Jacourt shook his head. "Not enough. You see where I live." He gestured at the tattered walls around them. "I am a wanted criminal because I am your friend. Most of the men loyal to me have been hunted down and killed. I can muster forty, maybe fifty at most."

"It will be enough." Philippe hoped his voice sounded confident. "Alexandre has sworn her safety, but I know that he lies. Viviane carries my child. She is therefore too tempting a target. He will seek to exterminate our entire bloodline." He folded his arms across his chest. "Once she is free, I will need you to get her out of France."

"Leaving the country now will be difficult." Jacourt stroked his chin. "But assuming we succeed, where should we go?"

"England is still too close," Philippe said. "Alexandre's assassins could find her even there."

"America." Lafayette broke his silence. "I have fought there, as you know, and there is no country outside of France in which I would rather live. It is a land of opportunity. She will be protected until it is safe to return. As commander of the National Guard, I can see that your passage out of France is unhindered."

Philippe nodded. "So be it." Their eyes met.

"We have a plan," Lafayette said.

"There is one more thing." Philippe placed a hand on Jacourt's arm. "I left something for my wife near the roots of a white pomegranate tree at the abandoned *Château de Versailles*. She calls it the Bride Tree. Take her there before you leave the country."

"It will be done." Jacourt gave a strong nod.

Philippe gripped both of their hands. "I thank God for you, my friends."

"When will you strike?" Jacourt raised an eyebrow.

"Tomorrow at dawn."

The captain touched the hilt of Philippe's sword. "May the God of battle give you victory."

"Amen." Lafayette closed his eyes for a moment. "Amen."

⚜

Simon peered at Viviane through the small aperture in the door of her cell. The woman was curled in a fetal position on the stone floor, arms folded protectively over her belly. Her back was toward him, but he doubted she slept.

"Your instructions are clear?" Alexandre spoke in a low tone.

Simon nodded. "Once Égalité shows up, she is to be released. When he is safely in chains, I go after her, have a little fun with the beauty and then gut her!"

"I wouldn't put it quite so crudely, Simon." Alexandre shook his head. "But see that both she and the child are dead."

His lieutenant paused. "Didn't you promise by the saints that she would be safe?" He glanced at his friend and blinked. He would not hesitate to swear or even blaspheme a little but to willfully violate an oath sworn by heaven was a different matter.

"Oaths can be broken for the greater good." Alexandre did not meet his gaze.

"Alexandre." Simon grabbed his friend's forearm. "You and I are devoted to the Church. You cannot break that oath."

Alexandre lifted his face to Simon's. "I no longer serve Mother Rome."

Simon stared at him blankly, then the corners of his mouth curved in an attempted smile. "This is no time for jokes, Alexandre."

"I am not joking. As soon as Philippe and his wife are dead, Salomé and I will leave France."

"What?" Simon recoiled. "What madness is this?"

"I doubt the Moustiquaires will be needed in the new order." Alexandre continued as though his lieutenant had not spoken. "But if so, I entrust them to you."

Simon's eyes blazed. "Everythin' we have done has been to establish Rome's control over France. We've given twenty years of our lives to this cause and now you want to walk away?" He scoffed. "Your lust for Salomé has driven you mad!"

Alexandre's face reddened. "I've given up more than you can ever know. But now I'm making a new life for myself, one in which I will decide my fate. In any case, I'm not asking for your opinion. Follow my orders. Kill the woman and kill her child!"

He spun on his heel and stalked off.

Simon stared after him, blind rage pulsing through his veins. Not only had Alexandre betrayed him by choosing to abandon their mission when he would be most needed, but he had also turned his back on the Church!

He considered his options. The betrayal could never be forgiven and, now that he knew of Alexandre's plans, he also would be guilty in the eyes of God and the Church if he did nothing to stop it. His mind flashed back to a moment twenty years ago that had seemed strange as a boy, but now seemed almost prophetic.

Cardinal Rezzonico gripped his wrist moments before he boarded the ship that would carry him to an abandoned dock along the Mediterranean coastline of France. From there he would find his own way to Paris and then Alexandre.

"You, Simon, shall be the eyes of Rome," Rezzonico had intoned. "Alexandre has great potential for good or evil. See that he does not stray from the path. If he does, you must do as the Levites did to those who abandoned the calling of God. Strike him down and your soul will be cleansed from whatever sins you commit."

Simon's fingers twitched as they dropped to the dagger at his side. Rezzonico's warning had been clear. *"Fail me,"* the cardinal had continued, *"and you will be eternally damned."*

Simon spun and pounded his fist against the wall. Alexandre had betrayed him. He deserved to die. Simon knew his sins outweighed the virtues of his soul. Since Alexandre had chosen the path of rebellion, he had no choice but to kill his own friend if he hoped to escape the fires of hell.

The torment in his heart raged on but, in his mind, there issue was decided. He slid the dagger from his belt.

⚜

Philippe pressed his body against the outer wall of the Temple, mentally calculating the minutes until dawn. The gray mist, rising from the ground, and the mud he had plastered onto his face and hands concealed his body from the soldiers who marched on the ramparts above.

Now Jacourt! He tightened his grip on his pistols, his pulse slamming in his throat. As if in answer to his mental command, the deafening roar of a pair of small range canons shattered the predawn stillness.

The ground lurched beneath his feet. Philippe covered his face to protect it from flying debris. The canons thundered again and the gates of the Temple were reduced to rubble.

Pandemonium exploded within the prison. Shouts of alarm were indistinguishable from the screams of the wounded and dying. A final salvo exploded in the heart of the castle itself, sending an entire section of the building crashing to the ground.

"Time to go." Philippe drew his pistol and dagger, leaving his longsword sheathed, and dashed into the smoking interior. The destruction had been more devastating than he had hoped. The six balls had not only smashed through the gates but had crushed some of the key support beams of the main courtyard. Everywhere, holes—caused by collapsing walls—grinned like toothless skeletons. He ran forward, focusing on the most difficult part of his mission: finding Viviane.

"Viviane!" He raised his voice over the cacophony of sound that swelled around him. A National Guard soldier sprouted in front of him taking aim at his head. Philippe did not hesitate. He pulled the trigger on his pistol, thrust the falling body out of his way, and snatched up the dead man's musket. He had not come this far to die. Not without saving his wife.

A group of crackling muskets poured fire upward. Philippe grunted with appreciation. The first wave of Jacourt's men had caught up with him. About twenty soldiers now jogged alongside him while the other half covered their assault with withering fire from outside. Philippe deflected a cut aimed at his chin and ran his sword through an attacker while breathing a prayer of thanks for Lafayette who had supplied them with weapons and powder.

"Viviane!" Their attack was born of desperation and its success depended upon speed and surprise. Within minutes, Alexandre would mount a counterattack and, if they were not already out of the fortress, they would all die.

The group sprinted into a large hall with two different staircases that spiraled upward to the prisoners' cells. As planned, his men split into four small groups, each charged with releasing any female prisoner they found. This would be where the fighting became brutal. Philippe kicked in a doorway that blocked off a staircase, thankful for the years of hard labor that had turned his flesh into steel.

"Follow me!" He sprinted up the stairs, into the darkness.

⚜

Alexandre leapt out of bed at the first salvo of the cannons and quickly buckled his sword belt around his waist. He had slept fully dressed, somehow knowing that he would face Philippe today.

"Will you be alright?" He jerked the cinch tight as he called over his shoulder to Salomé.

"Go." She moaned and flapped a hand his direction. "I'll be fine." Her face was pale and sweaty. He frowned as his gaze swept over her body. Her eyes were red from a sleepless night filled with cramping that had grown more frequent and intense in recent hours. At first, they had both feared for the baby but there had been no blood.

She cried out as the pain struck again.

Alexandre shook his head, calling himself every sort of a fool for not securing a midwife.

"Alexandre?" Salomé's knuckles turned white as she gripped the chair by their bed with sweaty hands. "I think... I think..."

He glanced from her to the door then back to her again. She needed him now, but the prison was under attack.

"Oh God." Salomé's words were a ragged cry of agony. "Help me!"

"I'll be back." Alexandre had to shout to be heard over the second blast of the canons. *Canons?*

He kissed her roughly and slammed the door behind him.

Salomé writhed on the thin mattress. "Help me!"

But he was gone.

⚜

"Viviane!" Philippe's eyes darted around in search of his wife. He could hear the guns of the defenders ringing out and realized they were organizing a counterattack. He blocked an opponent's lunge.

"Sir!" A voice called from his left. It was Henri, Jacourt's second-in-command. "I think I've found something."

Philippe slammed his knee into his opponent's chest and sent him spiraling over the railing to the floor below.

In an instant, he was at the man's side.

"Viviane?" He peered through the guard's opening.

"Philippe?" She sat up and stared at the door.

"Get this door open!" He thrust his bloodied blade at the lock.

Henri slipped the musket off his shoulders, pointed it at the lock and pulled the trigger. Before the echo had faded away, Philippe had grabbed hold of the bars and ripped the door off its hinges.

Then she was in his arms.

"I'm sorry." She clung to him, wrapping her arms around his neck. "I never should have left."

"It is forgotten, my love." He pressed his lips against her golden hair. Tears of gratitude spilled over his eyes. "Thank God!"

"Sir, we have to go. Now." Henri's voice brought him back to the moment.

"Here." Philippe pulled a cloak and hat, emblazoned with the colors of Jacourt's dragoons, from a bag on his back. He threw the cloak around her shoulders and placed the hat on her head.

"They'll expect to see a woman, not a soldier. Keep your head down and stay in the center of the dragoons."

"And you?" She clutched his arm.

"I will follow. Now go!"

He placed his hand in the small of her back and pushed her to the center of his small band. They streamed down the stairs and were joined by two of the other groups returning from a fruitless search. They had passed through the courtyard and were halfway to the gate when Philippe heard Alexandre's voice rip through the air.

"There they are! Cut them off!"

Philippe's heart sank. *So close.* "Get her through the gates!"

Viviane spun around. "Philippe?" She pushed past the dragoons that separated them.

He stared at her, memorizing every detail of her face, and crushed her lips with his own in a final embrace. The world faded out of their sphere of consciousness as, for a few moments, their love drowned out the clamor of war. Philippe pulled back, knowing he had to let her go.

"Go!" He pushed her back into the arms of his friends. "I will always love you."

Viviane screamed and beat her fists on those who dragged her away. "No, let me go! I cannot leave him!" Her screams became a jagged sob.

Jacourt's men on the outside of the gates encircled her in a protective shield.

"Send another round in." The captain's face was set in a grim line. "It will buy us time."

The dragoons rolled the cannons forward and aimed them at the walls.

"I will always love you!" Philippe's voice soared over the battered gates, seconds before the firing canons surged forward and the prison walls erupted in a hurricane of stone and dust.

⚜

Alexandre regained his feet slowly, coughing as he stared at the devastation around him. Everywhere, smoky fires burned, ignited by the exploding cannonballs. The ravaged courtyard had been transformed into a scene from hell itself. Philippe had also been thrown by the blast, but he stood and lurched forward.

"Alexandre!" He wiped dust out of his eyes.

"So, you've finally arrived." A cruel smile played across his adversary's lips. "I thought you were defeated the night of your arrest. I wanted to kill you when we destroyed the Bastille, but," he shrugged, "here you are, in my domain and under my power."

Philippe drew his sword. "You've failed, Alexandre."

Alexandre laughed and gestured at the seething soldiers that extracted themselves from heaps of rubble and began to surround the two contestants. "Failed? You'll soon be dead!"

Triumph shone in Philippe's eyes and he shook his head. "My wife is no longer under your control. Your deceit and cruelty brought her to this prison but now she is free. I will live on through her."

Alexandre's long black blade flew out of its sheath. He leapt toward Philippe and, with all the might of his arms, swung the sword downward. Philippe dropped to one knee and raised his own blade in a parry while slipping his dagger from his boot with his left hand. Alexandre saw the motion, but he was already committed.

The shock of contact almost ripped the sword from Philippe's arms. Alexandre's momentum carried him forward and, instead of recoiling, Philippe threw himself within his enemy's reach, burying his dagger into his opponent's side.

Alexandre howled as the edge of the blade slid against his ribcage and snapped inside his body. Before Philippe could strike again, the mob of soldiers grabbed his arms and pinned them behind his back.

Alexandre lurched to his feet, and pressed his hands against his side. "Fool!" He cried out in pain as he slammed his left fist into Philippe's abdomen. "I would kill you where you stand if I didn't want all of Paris to witness your execution."

"Simon." He gritted his teeth as he called his lieutenant. There was no answer. He clamped his hand against his side as he tried to slow the steady flow of black blood.

"You!" Alexandre pointed to the nearest soldier. "Escort this man under heavy guard to the *Place de la Révolution*. Tell everyone that Philippe Égalité, will be executed in three hours." The soldier saluted and left with the remaining soldiers. Alexandre watched them leave, then groaned as he sank to the ground, left alone in a world of smoke and ashes.

Chapter Twenty-Eight

August 1793. Place de la Révolution, Paris.

"*Allez, allez!* Move along!" A soldier of the National Guard snapped his riding whip across Philippe's shoulders. The sharp edges split the fabric of his shirt and drew twin streams of bright blood from his flesh. "Not so noble now, are we?"

Philippe remained silent. His stoic response to the man's cruelty seemed to infuriate him further and the soldier flung a stream of spittle into Philippe's face as he shoved him into a cell that reeked of moldy straw and feces.

"Look at 'im." He slammed the cell door shut and grabbed another guard's shoulder. "Who'd have thought that the mighty Prince Philippe would die like a common murderer?"

"Father." Philippe closed his eyes and leaned back against the jagged wall. "Watch over her. Watch over our child."

"No need to pray." One of the guards sneered and pounded his fist against the iron bars. "You'll be seein' the Big Man soon enough!"

Laughter followed their receding footsteps, but Philippe's mind had gone beyond the reach of their ridicule. *Viviane. Our child.* Tears of joy slid down his cheeks. *They are free.*

⚜

The door to his bedroom stood ajar. Alexandre frowned, knowing that he had left it closed. He peered around the corner and felt his heart stop.

Salomé lay sprawled on the bed, her deathly white face contrasting sharply with the pool of bright blood that covered the sheets around her. Alexandre's eyes darted around the room.

Simon stood between a large willow basket and the bed, wiping blood—Salomé's blood—from the cruel edge of his dagger.

"Simon!" He rushed toward the giant. "What have you done?"

"Alexandre?" Salomé's faint voice cut through the red haze that had fogged his mind. In a heartbeat he was at her side, kneeling and clasping her small hand. She smiled up at him weakly.

"You're a father." She whispered motioning to the large basket that lay next to the giant. He stared at it, unable to move.

"Go and see," Salomé urged. He rose slowly and peered inside. Two infants slumbered peacefully, wrapped in a woolen blanket.

"Two?" He gaped at Salomé, his jaw slack.

"Both girls." A wan smile slid across her lips. Alexandre's blood-stained hands trembled as he reached into the basket. He paused and looked at their mother.

"Go ahead."

Alexandre picked them up, painfully conscious their frailty in contrast to his powerful arms. He laid a soft kiss on each bald head, then cautiously put them back on the soft blanket that lined the basket.

"I was in the hall when I heard her screamin'." Simon spoke up for the first time, dagger still in hand. "I came in and saw that it was her time."

"He delivered our daughters." Salomé's head fell back on the pillow. "Who would have thought," she yawned, "that Simon... would be... our... midwife?" Her eyes closed and she drifted into sleep.

Alexandre wrapped Simon in a tight embrace. "Forgive me. And thank you."

"Don't thank me, Alexandre," Simon said.

"And why not?" Alexandre held his friend at arm's length. "Were it not for you—"

Simon's next words turned him to stone. "Don't thank me because I came to kill you."

⚜

Viviane pulled her horse to a halt and glared at Jacourt. "Captain."

He wheeled his horse around and glanced at their surroundings. They had shed their Dragoon uniforms but there was no concealing the fact that they were a military entourage. They were near the warehouse where he had met Philippe and, while few people ventured into this part of the docks, discovery was always a possibility.

"Madame Égalité?" He edged his horse closer.

"I cannot do this. I will not leave my husband." Viviane's shoulders trembled as she spoke.

The older man dipped his head. "I commend your loyalty, Madame, but it was your husband's express order that I take you out of France. Arrangements have been made and I will keep my word if it means taking you on the ship by force. I respect him too much to fail him."

She bit her lip. "At least, let me be there for him… in his final hours. I beg you. It's my fault he's been captured. I-I need to do this."

She looked at him, her eyes pleading her cause. The soldier knew that he could not deny her this request. "As you wish. But you must follow my orders to the letter."

Viviane grabbed his hands. "Thank you."

Jacourt wheeled his horse around. "Dragoons, to me!"

⚜

"Cardinal Rezzonico ordered *you* to kill *me*?"

Alexandre tried to process the mind-numbing revelation. Another thought shoved its way forward. It was not only his own life at stake, but that of his wife and their children. "Who are you, exactly? Not an orphan from Italy?"

He needed to keep Simon talking until his slowly descending fingers could wrap around the hilt of the knife at his belt.

Simon sighed and backed away. "Yes, I am an Italian orphan. That much of my story is true. What you don't know is that, like you, I was adopted by Cardinal Rezzonico before I could walk. Like you, I trained all my life for this mission. You and I were deliberately kept apart but Rezzonico often made me watch you when you were trainin' or studyin'. I learned your habits. I learned the way you think. The goal was that I should be Rome's eyes in France."

Alexandre's mind sped back to the night he had received the letter from the Vatican urging him to strike. "You slipped the note from Rezzonico under my door?"

Simon nodded. "Before I was sent to join you in Paris, Rezzonico warned me that if you strayed—as you have—I was to take your life on pain of my immortal soul. He couldn't allow someone who possesses your skills and knowledge to remain unchecked on the continent. Think of what could happen if the world knew that Rome had toppled a kingdom!"

Simon's face darkened. "God knows he probably intends to kill us both when this is over anyway." His eyes shifted to the sleeping woman. "But when I saw Salomé, when I helped her bring the little ones into the world..." His voice cracked. "I don't want them to be like us: fatherless!"

He let the dagger in his hand clatter to the floor. "I can't do it. I won't do it."

Alexandre eased his hand away from his knife. "Your soul?"

"I'll take my chances." Simon folded his arms across his broad chest. "Maybe God is more merciful then they make him out to be."

His friend nodded. "It was a cruel choice but I am grateful. With this wound, killing me would've been easier than it seems."

"What wound?" Simon's eyes now moved to the torn shirt Alexandre had tied around his waist.

Alexandre groaned. "Part of Philippe's blade has gone in too deep to get out."

"Let me see." Simon's experienced fingers gently probed at the wound.

"It's bad." He clucked his tongue. "I can't get it out."

Alexandre locked eyes with his friend. "It's working its way in deeper, slicing through my insides." They both fell silent for a moment, knowing what that meant.

Alexandre broke the quiet with a bitter laugh. "Ironic, isn't it? I'll be killed by the very man that I will execute today."

Simon's face twisted. "Everythin' about us is ironic. We were children, trained to butcher men." He jerked his head toward the sleeping woman. "Will you tell your wife? She deserves to know."

Alexandre sighed. "Not yet. Let her enjoy this moment of happiness. I'll tell her when the time comes." He stole over to where his daughters still slumbered.

"Get out of France while you can," Simon said. "Enjoy whatever time you have left with your family."

"What about you?"

The giant shrugged and flashed a smile. "When the pope seizes control of this place, I'll get a woman, or two, and settle down."

"Settle down?" Alexandre raised an eyebrow. "You?"

"If I'm not dead first." Simon chuckled then fell quiet. He motioned toward Salomé. "I'll leave you both alone."

"Stay close."

Simon nodded and slipped out the door as Alexandre tenderly kissed his wife back to consciousness.

"Hmm...?" Her eyelids flitted as a slow smile spread across her face.

"We must name her." Alexandre pointed to the girl on the right. They had chosen the name Renée in the event they had a girl, but the extra arrival had been a surprise.

"What—" She sat up and paused to wipe her eyes. "What do you want to call her?" They leaned over the basket together.

"Victoire." Her husband said after a moment.

Salomé's lips curved upward. "Victory. It is a good name."

"Simon will remain with you." He flinched while rising and her eyes flew to his side.

"You're hurt." She touched his arm.

"It is nothing." He brushed aside her concern with a lie.

She tilted her head, her eyes moving from his side to his face. "Do you have to go?"

"Philippe dies today." That was answer enough.

She pressed her lips against his hand. "Be careful."

He nodded once, kissed both sleeping girls on the head and left.

"Do you still want me to go after Viviane?" Simon propped his foot against the wall.

Alexandre shook his head. "She's too heavily guarded. Watch over my family while I am gone."

He clasped his lieutenant in his arms. "*Grazie, mio fratello.* Thank you for this extension of my life, however short it may be."

"If I end up in hell," Simon's smile was faint, "I'll kill you."

Chapter Twenty-Nine

August 1793. Place de la Révolution, Paris.

The streets outlying *la Place de la Révolution* overflowed with violently ecstatic crowds. Throngs of jeering, cursing revolutionaries surged around a raised dais on which a mammoth guillotine, bearing a fluttering tricolored flag, towered above the crowd. *This* was the indisputable absolute monarch, an unfeeling sovereign who cut down kings like wheat and maintained its rule with the point of an iron blade.

The sinking sun splattered a fresh coat of red over the guillotine's already crimson edge. Around the stage, a sea of blue, white and red flags surged over the banisters of the surrounding buildings. Hundreds of yards away from the murderous machine, effigies of Philippe de Valence writhed like tormented demons in the flames of massive bonfires that had been lit by the swarming, riotous crowds.

A haze of smoke swirled past the towering spires of Notre Dame Cathedral, blotting out the light of the setting sun. To Alexandre, it was as though God himself had turned his face from the anarchy that man had unleashed upon his creation. But Alexandre no longer cared about God's opinion. Today, he would take vengeance from the hands of God and place it where it belonged—in his own hands.

He thrust his fists into the air and howled with savage triumph, ignoring the searing pain in his chest that each motion produced. He was dying. Every twitch of a muscle, each beat of his heart drove the jagged shard deeper into his torso. Any moment could be his last. *Not before Philippe dies.* His bared his teeth in a savage grin.

"He dies today!" His voice punched through the air with the force of a cannonball.

The masses echoed him, baying like savage dogs for the death of a man they had once claimed to love. "He dies today!"

"What shall I do with him?" Alexandre thrust his hands skyward again, feeding on their violent energy. The question was purely rhetorical. "What shall I do with the man who wanted to be your king?"

"We have no king!" The sound reverberated like the clamor of a million stampeding horses. "No king but the people!"

"What shall I do with him?" He swung his arms wide as if pulling them all into his embrace. "What is your will?"

"Kill him, kill him!"

They screamed their rancid hatred, ripping off their ragged clothes and thrusting hoes, knives and swords in the air. Their jubilation found its source in the fact that, not only was it a noble who was condemned, but a man who had once stood as a contender for the crown. The blood of kings ran in Philippe's veins. His blood must therefore be spilled to purge the nation of the evil that lingered within.

"Blood, blood. We want blood." The single cry became a chant and the chant swelled into a tidal wave of sound that no one could resist.

Alexandre's eyes flashed with triumph. He pulled the executioner's mask down over his face. This was his time. This was his moment.

"Bring out Philippe de Valence!"

⚜

Robespierre watched Alexandre from the back of a pale horse. "Is everything prepared for the lunatic's arrest?" He swung his head toward Augustin. They were surrounded by fifty of the National Guard who maintained a perimeter around the Robespierre brothers, giving them a special view of the evening's proceedings.

"Yes, Maximilien." Augustin shifted uneasily in his saddle. "As soon as the execution is over the soldiers will arrest him at your command."

"And if his men are interspersed in the crowd? Nothing must go wrong." Robespierre frowned.

"We have another hundred soldiers stationed on all sides, ready to put down any resistance." Augustin cleared his throat. "Calm yourself."

"Calm?" Robespierre glared at his brother. "I want him dead! I want them all... dead!"

He gestured toward the masses. "Look at them." He threw his head back and snorted. "They are nothing more than teeming cockroaches. They do not deserve to outlive Marie."

"Maximilien!" Augustin grabbed his brother's arm. "Be quiet or someone will hear you."

His brother's frown deepened but he lapsed into silence. Robespierre did not seem to notice that the pendulum of public opinion which had pushed him to the pinnacle of glory had quickly reversed its course. His brother had become inured to death, indiscriminately ordering the slaughter of over a thousand ordinary citizens in only a few months. Now he was planning something that would make what he had done thus far look like child's play.

Augustin shivered.

⚜

Viviane stood in the frontline of the spectators, one trembling soul in a multitude of screaming demons. Immediately to her left stood Jacourt. Most of the remaining dragoons were interspersed in the crowd just behind them, while others assumed hidden positions in the empty balconies and rooftops of the adjoining buildings. None wore uniforms. All military-grade weapons were concealed beneath their clothes but Jacourt had permitted them to keep their daggers and short swords visible.

Viviane, following Jacourt's strict commands had tied up her flowing hair, concealing it beneath a red Phrygian bonnet—a cap commonly worn by supporters of the revolution. Her face was hidden deep within the cowl of a nondescript cloak. *God, please save him!*

Her heart twisted as Alexandre pulled the mask over his face. "Bring out Philippe de Valence!"

The crowd shrieked with bestial glee as, from its rear, a solitary figure was led toward the dais. *Philippe!*

The guards shoved him forward. He stumbled into the arms of the jeering crowd. Instantly they ripped the shirt off his back, swinging fists and clubs across his muscled shoulders.

"Bring him forward." Alexandre rushed toward the edge of the dais. He would not let the masses cheat him of his final victory.

The soldiers grabbed their victim from the savage arms of the spectators and, slamming their own fists against the back of his neck, they moved him onward. The catcalls, profanity and refuse hurled upon the rejected prince grew more abusive with each step he took toward the guillotine.

"Traitor!"

"You thought you would rule over us!"

Viviane's heart palpitated. *I must go to him.* Even as the thought crossed her mind, she felt Jacourt's iron grip on her forearm.

"Don't let his sacrifice be in vain." The aged soldier bowed his head to speak in her ear. "He loves you enough to die for you. Honor him by staying alive."

She froze, numbed beyond words. *He's coming closer.* The crowd's clamor was deafening. *Closer.* Beads of salty sweat trickled down her forehead, stinging her eyes. He mounted the stadium, placing one trembling foot in front of another. Then he turned toward her.

"Philippe!" She choked back a ragged sob. She couldn't help herself. His face was a mass of battered welts and bruises. His left eye had swelled completely shut and his lips had been reduced to a mass of bloody pulp. Her cry had been swallowed up by the crowd's roar of approval, but somehow Philippe seemed to have heard her voice.

His right eye searched the crowd, stopping only when it rested on the hood that covered her face. Did she imagine it or did those bleeding lips which had once kissed her so tenderly curve into a slight smile?

"Behold the man!" Spittle flew from Alexandre's mouth as his mocking laughter spilled over the crowd. "The man whose death spells the end of the oppression for us all. It is better for

Philippe to die than to have tyranny crush us under its heel. Are you with me?"

"Kill, kill!" The frenzied mob vented their rage. Their piercing screams dripped blind hatred.

The words throbbed like war drums in Viviane's skull. *Could these possibly be the same people who once screamed his praises?*

"God, no." Tears fell like rain from her red-rimmed eyes. "God, I beg you to stop this."

But God was silent.

In that silence, one man's frenzied rage cried out for revenge. Philippe was stretched out on the wooden platform, his face upturned toward the sky. Alexandre strode over to his enemy and slowly removed the mask as an expectant hush rolled over the crowd.

"No more masks, Philippe." He tossed it aside. "The time for pretense is over. I have won!"

Philippe's one eye rolled upward. He mustered his remaining strength and, though his words were faint, they reached Viviane's ears. "You h-have lost. Y-your day is... f-finished. My life g-goes on... Viviane is f-free."

Alexandre spat on Philippe's upturned face, then turned on his heel and stormed to the cord that held the guillotine's blade suspended.

Viviane could not breathe. *God, spare him. I can't live without him.* Philippe turned his head toward her. His eye rested upon her, speaking words that no human ear could discern.

Alexandre reached for the rope.

I will always love you. Philippe's unvoiced words reached her heart, turning her knees to water.

Setting his shoulder, Alexandre grasped the cord between firm hands.

You are my life.

A whimper escaped Viviane's trembling lips. She wrung her fingers together, clutching them against her chest.

I will never leave you. I will never abandon you.

Alexandre jerked the rope. She heard Philippe's final intake of breath.

"Freedom!" His cry of victory erupted from a soul that had fulfilled its destiny. "Freedom!"

Then the blade fell.

Chapter Thirty

August 1793. Place de la Révolution, Paris.

Alexandre stepped to the edge of the dais, triumphantly lifting Philippe's head by its blood-spattered curls. A sharp wind swirled down, heralding a swiftly-approaching summer storm, and sprayed his face with the blood of his victim. His lips twisted in a savage grin as the deafening shouts of the frenzied throng seemed to make the very buildings tremble.

Robespierre barked out an order. Under the darkening sky, the contingent of fifty soldiers began to shove their way toward the elevated platform.

Viviane's eyes were locked on the small, gruesome object that dangled from Alexandre's fingers. A spray of Philippe's blood had splashed against her face and she touched it in stunned disbelief. "No, no, no, no!"

An ominous rumble of thunder echoed from the skies. Viviane screamed until her throat, raw and bruised, refused to emit another sound.

Her mind rebelled against what her eyes knew to be true. *It's not real. It's a nightmare. I've gone mad.* Anything was possible—anything but the reality that Philippe was... *dead.* The word ripped into the core of her being, producing an anguish more punishing than she could have ever imagined. *Dead.*

But the knife of grief that lacerated her very soul was too real, the sudden void in her heart too tangible for his death to be a lie. *He is dead.* She buried her face into the old soldier's shoulder whose tears also spattered the ground.

⚜

Alexandre turned around, hearing someone clamber onto the stage behind him. It was Drouet, the Moustiquaire who had identified Louis on the night of his arrest. The rising wind whipped the man's ragged clothes tightly against his body.

"A fine thing you've done, Alexandre." He shouted above the cacophony of thunder and ecstatic masses. "A victory for us all."

Alexandre was about to reply when movement from his left caught his eye. A horde of soldiers marched toward him, led by Robespierre. His gaze swept over the jubilant crowd. Literally hundreds of the Guard were all making their way in the direction of the platform. He spun around, his throat suddenly dry. More approached from the rear. *They're surrounding me.*

"Drouet." He gripped the man's shoulder. "Get to the Temple. Tell Simon to take my wife and children to our Paris shelter. He'll know the one I mean. Tell him to take the documents we buried. If I do not come to him by sunset, it means I am dead in which case he must get Salomé and the children out of France. Do you understand?"

Drouet nodded as Alexandre's eyes swiveled back to Robespierre. The man almost looked happy. He picked out the faces of a few of his men scattered among the crowd. *Thirty or forty. Much too few for a fight.*

"Repeat your orders!" Alexandre cracked his fingers and felt for his daggers and pistols.

More soldiers.

"Get to the temple." The words spilled out of Drouet's mouth. "Warn Simon. Flee to shelter. He must take the woman and children out of France if you're not back by sundown."

"Good!" Alexandre drew his sword. "Now get out of here." He realized he was squinting and glanced upward. Billowing clouds roiled above the turbulent scene, blotting out the sun and turning the afternoon sky as dark as night.

Drouet dropped off the back of the platform and began shoving his way through the tightly packed spectators, just as Robespierre reached the bottom of the stage. The lawyer slid off his horse and, backed by twenty of his guard and Augustin, clambered up to Alexandre. Scudding, dark clouds now completely blackened the sky.

"Citizens of Paris!" Robespierre held up a gloved hand and bellowed over the whistling wind. Torches, illuminated by the large bonfires, cast flickering spots of light around the mob.

Gradually, the shouts began to die down as the people recognized Maximilien Robespierre, the man who had risen from their ranks to the very pinnacle of power. This man had promised freedom, but had enslaved them to a greater fear than they had ever known.

Loathing crept over their faces, and some of the more brazen spat on the ground. Hundreds in the throng had lost loved ones who, by one word from this man's mouth, had been condemned to the guillotine. Their silence was born of fear not respect.

"This man," Robespierre thrust a fist under Alexandre's nose, "is no true patriot! He is the leader of a band of instigators who are plotting, at this moment, against the state. In the name of the government of France I declare that this Alexandre and his followers are conspirators against our nation. We will hunt them down. We will arrest, torture and exterminate them until their very memory has been wiped from the face of the earth. Anyone found offering food or shelter to these terrorists will share their fate. Arrest him!"

His words were punctuated by a violent clap of thunder. The soldiers around him surged forward and, at that moment, utter chaos erupted.

Shouts of protest exploded from hundreds who had fought with Alexandre at the Bastille.

"He saved us at the Bastille!" Some bellowed out the words.

Others shouted, "Leave him alone!"

Those closest to the platform threw themselves forward, viciously attacking the guards nearest Alexandre. "Remember the Bastille!"

"Moustiquaires, to me!" Alexandre hurled Philippe's head at Robespierre who drew back in revulsion. Lightening split the sky above as the bonfires on the ground cast garish light on the unfolding apocalypse.

The Moustiquaires closest to the stage drew their knives and began hacking away at the soldiers around him, joining the revolutionaries loyal to Alexandre. The National Guard, surprised by this onslaught, turned to face this new threat while Robespierre and Augustin stared in stupefied awe at the violence they had unleashed. Out in the screaming, struggling masses, the bonfires hungrily licked at the smashed debris and the bodies of the dying. Fire spread from one building to another, sending a column of eerie light over the carnage. Spewing columns of thick smoke curled heavenward, filling the air with the stench of charred human flesh.

"Death to Robespierre!" A voice rang out and soon others picked up the cry. "Death, death, death!"

Maximilien recoiled as men hacked each other to bloody bits all around him. "Augustin." He tripped over a hand that had been severed from its owner's arm. "Save me!"

Augustin's ashen face appeared at his side. "Come brother, we must flee."

"Death! Kill the tyrant!"

The chants were growing louder as the crowd exploded into a full riot.

Augustin clutched his brother's shoulder and glanced around him. To his right he saw a slight opening off the stage and, tugging at Robespierre's arm, he dragged his brother toward it.

⚜

Jacourt was the first to notice the reinforcements who punched their way through the crowd, swords rising and falling like scythes as they indiscriminately cut down anyone who stood in their way. Screams of pain, fury and death rose on all sides as the ground became slick with blood.

"Dragoons!" The old soldier drew both his sword and pistol. "To me!" He had to get Viviane out of this chaos before a stray bullet or sword thrust took her life. "Circle formation!"

His men formed two concentric circles with Jacourt and Viviane at its core. The outer line neutralized immediate threats while the inner circle replaced holes punched into the line when a dragoon fell.

"Left flank, forward!" Jacourt pointed with his sword. They moved as one unit, slowly cutting their way to the nearest side street that led to the banks of the Seine. *Fifty yards... forty...*

They were about thirty yards away when a detachment of the National Guard, noticing the organized formation, broke off from the main body and swung toward them.

⚜

Alexandre fought desperately to reach Robespierre, but the pain inside his chest slowed his motions and hindered his reflexes. Despite the mob's unexpected support, his Moustiquaires were being slaughtered.

Robespierre. If I kill him, it stops! The thick smoke and raging fires had spread to the base of the stage, scorching buildings and transforming the square into a scene from hell.

Through the smoke, he glimpsed Augustin pulling his brother off the scaffold.

"Robespierre, stay and fight!" His lungs burned and a fit of coughing drove him to his knees. Blood and phlegm spewed out of his mouth. He pushed himself upright and gripped his sword.

A blur of motion.

Alexandre spun and raised his sword in a defensive reflex. *Too late.*

The butt of a musket smashed into his chest, then pummeled his stomach.

"Ugh!" He flew backward, smashing his head against the bloody base of the guillotine. His vision blurred. The noise of battle seemed to fade as though an invisible conductor had signaled the musicians of his entourage to lower their volume. Alexandre struggled to rise but another vicious blow struck his temple.

Black.

⚜

The National Guard had almost reached the dragoons' outer perimeter when Jacourt's men, hidden in the balconies of the apartments lining the square, opened fire. Despite the dense smoke that blocked their vision, more than a dozen of the Guard lay sprawled on the ground when the volley ended. The attacking Guard stopped and looked upward, searching for their hidden opponents.

"Double-time, dragoons, double-time!" Jacourt's voice rolled out above the crashing thunder and booming gunfire. His men sped up, trying to take advantage of the confusion, but the

Paris militia quickly recovered and responded with their own fire.

Dragoons on the outer line were mown down by the withering barrage. Screams rose to the dark skies above as their guns slid from nerveless fingers. The dragoons on the inner circle sent rounds of crackling musket balls into the Guard's ranks as Jacourt, Viviane and a small retinue of ten men slipped into the darkness of an alley leading to the Seine.

A shout of rage echoed off the massive buildings and encompassed the square. The people, armed with fiery torches, knives and guns rushed forward to attack the blue-coated soldiers of the Guard.

"*Vive la France!*" The rallying cry passed from mouth to mouth as they ripped the National Guard to pieces, wreaking vengeful havoc on the men who had slaughtered hundreds of innocents moments before. The carnage seemed to only inflame their bloodlust and they smashed forward, heedless of their own losses as they chased the retreating soldiers.

"*Vive la République!*" They surged forward. "Death to Robespierre and his militia!"

The crush of the oncoming masses was too great for the Guard. The line of soldiers bent like the arc of a great bow, trying desperately to resist the fury of the people. Then the crowd gathered itself and rushed forward with a unified roar, overrunning the line and crushing the remaining soldiers beneath their feet.

⚜

Simon peered through a crack in the overlapping boards of the shanty's wall, and stared at the rain-soaked street below. They had taken refuge in the upper floor of an abandoned shack near the docks. Years before, he and Alexandre had stored food, weapons, and false identity cards for male and female Moustiquaires under the floorboards. They had left everything as they had found it, trusting that the building's unpleasant atmosphere would keep intruders away. A quick check had confirmed that everything was in order. All that remained was to wait and pray that, somewhere in the darkness, Alexandre still lived.

Behind him, a bone-weary Salomé nursed her two infants on a pile of straw. They had made the difficult trip to the safehouse in the gloom and wet of the still-overcast sky. Most of the city had gone to the *Place de la Révolution* making the threat of discovery remote but Simon kept his weapons close, ready to turn them on anyone who even looked at them twice. They had heard echoes of the tumult in the square and, on occasion, a terrified survivor darted past them. Anarchy ruled Paris.

"Are you alright?" Simon kept his back to Salomé.

"As good as can be expected." Her voice was tired and he frowned. The move could not have been easy so soon after giving birth and the possibility that Alexandre was dead surely preyed upon her mind.

"What is this place?"

"Alexandre and I created it a few years ago." Simon cracked his neck. "We called it Safehouse because we wanted a safe place in case things went wrong with our plans."

"To overthrow the king?"

He hesitated. It was time she knew the truth—the full truth. "To bring France under the control of the Vatican."

Silence filled the room.

"Who are you both? Really?" Salomé asked the question in a quiet voice.

Simon sighed. "We are orphans, trained from childhood to be assassins." He cleared his throat. "Can I turn around?"

Salomé made him wait a moment then said, "Yes."

Simon faced her. "For over twenty years we have been working to bring down the government of this country so our masters in Rome can put their own man into power."

He slid forward. "I know it's hard to accept but Alexandre could not have told you."

"You don't have to justify his actions to me." Salomé folded her hands in her lap. "It doesn't matter now." She glanced away, but not before he saw the tears glimmering in her eyes. "He never loved me anyway—not since Viviane got her claws in him."

Simon's brow crinkled. "He never loved Viviane."

Her head snapped toward him. "What do you mean?"

Simon hesitated, but only for a moment. "Years ago, Alexandre fell in love with a woman who could have been your twin sister." He chuckled softly. "He always was closemouthed, but this was one secret he couldn't keep. At least, not from me."

His smile faded. "Philippe sabotaged their relationship. Alexandre became obsessed with settlin' the score. He'd never talk about it afterward. Not to me and, apparently, not even to you." He held her gaze. "Believe me, there was no love in his heart for that woman."

Salomé's eyes widened. "All this time I feared she had him wrapped in her claws."

"No, he just couldn't let go of his past." Simon grimaced. "He couldn't let go of Juliette, or his hate, but that didn't mean that he didn't love you."

She fell silent, pondering the implications of his words. Finally, she spoke.

"I'm not leavin' without knowin' he's dead." She put her daughters in their basket and struggled to her feet.

"What do you mean?" A sinking feeling rose in Simon's heart. "We can't go out there, not now!"

"No, *we* can't," Salomé raised her chin. "But *you* can."

"I can't leave you alone, woman!"

"Then we will never leave France at all."

Simon sucked in his breath. "Alright," he said through clenched teeth. He walked over to the floorboard he had ripped up and pulled out two wrapped pistols from a chest hidden below.

"I know that you can use these." He shoved them toward her. "Each is already loaded." If anythin' comes through that door while I'm gone, shoot it."

"Alright." Salomé nodded and took the guns from Simon's outstretched hands.

⚜

He returned within the hour, calling out her name before opening the door. His deep voice jolted Salomé from an uneasy sleep. Simon's dripping hair framed a grim face and she clutched at her heart.

"He's dead?"

The giant shook his head, sending water spraying over the room. "No, but he soon will be." His shoulders slumped. "They dragged him a little way from the guillotine and left him for dead."

She rose hurriedly, ignoring the pain that sliced through her abdomen.

"I have to go to him!" She shoved the pair of pistols into her belt. "Stay here and I will go."

Simon grabbed her wrist. "Not on your life. It's a war zone out there. We'll take everything we need with us and go to him together."

She gently picked up her daughters, and placed one in the first of two cloth slings while he gathered their supplies. When everything was in order, she placed the other child in the makeshift cradle that hung around his neck.

"Let's go." He opened the door.

⚜

Simon picked his way around the mangled corpses that littered the public square. Here and there smashed wooden carts and other debris still smoldered despite the steady showers that fell from a stormy heaven. Not far from his right, Salomé waited with both children underneath the sheltering arches of a nearby house. Except for the dead, the square was largely deserted but Simon still cast wary glances over his shoulder as he hurried toward the place where he had last seen Alexandre.

A hundred yards from the guillotine, his friend lay sprawled on the ground, face turned toward the rumbling skies. Rain sloshed into his open mouth.

"Alexandre?" Simon rushed to his side. He shook the leader's shoulder. "Alexandre!"

Alexandre's eyelids fluttered briefly then opened. "Simon?" He coughed. "Where... is Salomé?"

"She's here. I'll take you to her." He eased his arms under Alexandre's body and made his way toward the arch. A sob ripped through Salomé's throat at the sight of her husband. "Alexandre!"

His head tilted slightly toward her and Simon gently propped him against the wall. "I'll wait over there." He pointed to the far side of the building. "Call if you need me."

Salomé slid next to him. "Oh, my love!" She kissed his face, then his head. "My poor love."

"Salomé?" He reached for her. Deep gashes crossed his face and chest.

"Yes?"

"I'm dying."

She pressed his broad palm against her wet cheeks, kissing his fingers. "Don't say that, Alexandre. Please... don't say that!"

"Philippe's blade," he fell silent and gasped for breath, "is killing me." His blood-shot eyes rolled toward her. "Where are my... daughters?"

"They are here, my love. Look." Salomé placed the two squalling girls into their father's slack arms.

"Victoire." He wheezed, a faint smile slipping over his face. "Renée." She heard the fluid gurgling around his lungs. "Be good to your mother."

"Call Simon." His eyes fluttered closed.

Hearing Salomé's anxious call, Simon hurried over.

"Leave tonight." Alexandre's voice grew insistent. "Take my family... to America. Bring them back when... safe. Last orders."

Simon knelt beside him. "As you wish, my friend."

"All the Moustiquaires are dead." Alexandre coughed twice. "You are free Simon. Free... to choose your own fate."

Alexandre kissed the heads of his children and Salomé handed them to Simon.

"A few moments, please," she whispered. He nodded, took the children, and left them alone.

"Salomé." His voice was growing fainter and she leaned close. "...So much to say. So... sorry I never told you the truth."

"It's alright, my love." She leaned against him, her heart splintering into countless shards of pain. "It's alright."

He began coughing uncontrollably, spurting bright blood onto her face and eyes. Salomé cradled his head in her arms, ignoring the crimson splashes. Her fingers curled into tight fists behind his head as her hot tears sluiced through the stain of his blood.

"Do... something for me." Alexandre coughed again.

"Anythin'!"

"Avenge me. Finish... what we started. Destroy Philippe's family. They... must not... prevail. If they... come to power, my death is for nothing."

His voice was weak, but the words burned in her mind.

"Alexandre, I swear that this is not over." Her voice hardened. Philippe had struck the fatal blow and now, his entire family would pay the price. "I will look for Viviane until I die and, if I fail, our daughters will continue our fight."

"Salomé?" Alexandre's chest rose and fell rapidly. "There's something you... must know."

She sniffled and dabbed blood from his mouth with her sleeve. "What is it?"

"I love you."

"You love me?" She choked on the words that she had longed to hear him say.

"I really love... you."

Salomé kissed him tenderly, smoothing back the hair that had fallen into his face. "Not as much as I love you."

Alexandre touched her lips with his finger. The corners of his lips curved upward in a faint smile. He inhaled sharply, eyes wide, as his body convulsed. Then, with a groan, he slumped against the wall... and breathed his last.

Chapter Thirty-One

August 1793. Mediterranean coastline of France

Horses' hooves thundered along the dirt road that snaked upward from the Mediterranean coastline to Paris. Cardinal Rezzonico leaned forward over his mount's shoulder, urging the animal on, as a triumphant smile touched his lips. Seeing that his attempts to forge a European alliance against continued French aggression had failed, Pope Pius had at last given him the authorization to rally loyal Catholics throughout the country in a counter-revolution against its secular government.

"Faster!" He twisted in his saddle to shout at the small contingent of Swiss mercenaries who rode behind him. Too much time had already been wasted. The path directly ahead twisted around a sharp bend and the cardinal slowed his mount for the turn, then jerked on the reins of his protesting horse.

"Stop. Stop!" His heart plummeted as his own men milled around the corner. It was too late. Three full divisions of French soldiers blocked the road and, in effort to avoid a head-on collision, the Swiss slammed into each other, raising a whirlwind of dust and blood.

The French leader's derisive laugh rang in Rezzonico's ears. "And they thought to invade France with this bunch of clowns!"

The troops around him echoed his laughter. Cardinal Rezzonico rode forward shaking with rage.

"Who dares impede a servant of the Holy Church?" Beads of nervous sweat dotted his brow.

"I dare, old man." The leader of the band edged his prancing stallion closer to the prelate.

"And who are you?" The irate priest narrowed his eyes.

"Napoléon Bonaparte." The man doffed his hat. "Don't worry, you will have plenty of time to think about my name when you are in prison."

Cold fear snaked around Rezzonico's heart. "W-what do you mean?"

"I know that you have come to incite rebellion against the new government of France."

"How could—"

Napoléon cut him off with a contemptuous snort. "Sometimes the ones we trust the most are the ones who are the first to betray us."

Rezzonico stared at him as truth sank into his mind. Pius! The duplicitous pope was the only one who had known of the cardinal's true purpose. Pius had betrayed him, no doubt misinterpreting Rezzonico's ambition as a threat instead of an asset.

"Do not fear, *mon Cardinal*." Napoléon threw back his shoulders and laughed again. "You will soon see your precious Holy Father."

A chill ran down Rezzonico's spine. "What are you going to do?"

Napoléon's eyes bored into Rezzonico's skull. "First, I will go to Rome. Then I will crush Pius's armies. Finally, I will bring him back to France in chains."

Rezzonico shuddered. "You would make a prisoner of a pope?" Despite Pius's treachery, the thought of such sacrilege made the aged cardinal cringe.

"I will destroy any man who opposes me—as you will soon learn." Napoleon turned to his men. "Kill the guards and take him away!"

The cardinal's mind reeled as he was dragged from his horse and bound in heavy chains. "God's curse be upon you, Napoléon!" The priest shouted over the panicked screams of his men. "You will end your days defeated and alone—an object of scorn before the entire world!"

"Away with him!" The general slammed his hat back on his head. "I have no time for fools."

Augustin paced the floor of his brother's *salon*, wiping sweat from his brow with trembling fingers. "We should leave, Maximilien. This will be the first place they'll look for us. We can still escape to Arras."

Robespierre appeared not to have heard his brother. He slumped in his chair, clutching a piece of lace from the dress Marie had worn to her execution.

"Maximilien are you listening?"

"I am listening." Robespierre shook his head and released a deep sigh. "There is no point in running. All of France knows my face. I would be stopped within moments. I refuse to share Louis's humiliation."

He kissed the blood-spattered lace. "No. You can run, but I will join her. We will be together, if not in life... then in death." He rose and retrieved a pistol from his drawer. His yellow eyes swiveled to Augustin's.

"Maximilien, you can't take your own life!" Augustin's face went white with horror.

"Go, brother." Robespierre cocked the hammer. "This is not a road that you must walk."

Augustin swallowed hard, as the clatter of weapons and soldiers' boots sounded outside their apartment. *Too late!*

He shook his head. "I've always been at your side. I won't leave you now."

Robespierre met his gaze. "Thank you. Our father's name will live on because of what we have done."

Bitterness, love and fear swirled within Augustin's heart. He knew that the events leading to this day had been motivated by personal revenge and lust, not anything as noble as enshrining their father's memory. But he had been Maximilien's shadow for so long that the thought of outliving his brother seemed somehow profane.

A wan smile crossed Maximilien's face. He pulled the trigger.

The door to the *salon* crashed open. Startled by the noise, Maximilien's hand jerked backward, sending the bullet into his jaw instead of his brain. He collapsed, screaming on the floor as soldiers of the National Guard, led by General Lafayette, poured into the room with muskets trained on the two brothers.

"Citizen Robespierre." Lafayette held up a sealed document and cast a contemptuous glance at the man who writhed in a puddle of blood on the floor. "By order of the National Assembly, government of France, you are hereby condemned to execution without trial."

He turned to Augustin. "I have no orders for your arrest, sir. You are free to go."

Augustin glanced at his moaning brother whose outstretched fingers grasped at his feet.

"I am as guilty as he." Augustin looked the general in the eye, a sense of peace spreading through his heart. *This would make our father proud.* "I share his virtues; I want to share his fate. I also ask to be charged."

Lafayette inclined his head and saluted. "So be it." He waved his men forward. "Take them both."

The soldiers roughly grabbed Robespierre who, at the last moment, lost hold of Marie's scrap of lace. One of them pressed it into Robespierre's hand. He pressed the handkerchief against the steady flow of blood. "Thank you, Monsieur," he said softly. "Thank you."

✦

The guards led them through the battered doors and into the ravaged public square. Scenes of death marred the streets. Those who saw the pair of brothers being led to the guillotine harangued them with mocking words. Their scorn brought back his first meeting with Marie that fateful day in Rheims. Robespierre had sworn that all of France would tremble at the sound of his name.

He had kept that promise. He would die, but the world would remember the man who had risen from obscurity to place France under a reign of terror.

Forced into a supine position, Robespierre strained to roll his eyes toward the dreary skies. He knew that his chances of attaining heaven were remote at best. His fondest hope was that Marie waited for him in hell.

"Death," he closed his eyes, "is only the beginning of immortality."

Chapter Thirty-Two

The storm yielded to a steady rain that fell from an overcast sky, turning the dirt road into a muddy quagmire. Jacourt's men pressed on with blood streaming from the garish wounds they had received in their violent escape. Five of the men whose blistering fire from the balconies had saved their lives, joined them. The entire group trudged along in bone-weary silence.

Fulfilling his promise to Philippe, the captain had led the group back to the outskirts of the Versailles compound. Viviane had not said a word in the four hours since they had left the square, but he believed her heart still silently screamed its outrage at an unjust world that had snuffed out the light of her husband's life.

Jacourt had sent a few scouts ahead to ensure Viviane's safety on the deserted grounds. They had returned with nothing to report. He now held up his fist and the remnants of his tattered band of dragoons slid to a weary halt. Viviane rode up beside him.

"Take all the time you need. We'll wait for you here." He patted his horse's neck. "Philippe said he left something buried for you among the roots of a white pomegranate tree." He paused. "I hope whatever you find brings you peace."

⚜

Viviane spurred her horse forward, oblivious to the tears that fell from heaven. She rode by the broken gates, numbed by the destruction that surrounded her. After the executions of Louis and Marie-Antoinette, revolutionary mobs had descended like locusts upon the palace grounds, hacking down some trees and burning others. The hand of death was omnipresent. As were memories of Philippe.

The palace rose before her, alone and empty, like a mother bereft of her children. She slid off the back of her horse, tossed the reins over the blackened stump of a once-glorious palm tree, and turned to descend the Hundred Steps that were now covered with grime and ashes.

Her heart convulsed as she remembered the night when she had abandoned Philippe to run down these stairs with Alexandre. The heavy hand of guilt grabbed her soul with scorching fingers.

She leaned against the slick railing, seeing afresh the pain in Philippe's eyes when Alexandre taunted him with the knowledge of what they had done.

And yet he loved me still.

Her steps turned up the long dirt path toward the round pool where she had chosen to leave with Alexandre. "I didn't deserve his love!" She staggered forward, reeling as each sight revived a painful memory. Her tears mingled with the rain and, when she glimpsed the Bride Tree, her heart stopped.

It had been cut down to a stump. Gone were its waving majestic branches and the heavy lobes of fruit. Like her, it was now a brutalized shadow of what it had once been.

Viviane sunk to her knees. "Why?" She raged to a God who had turned his face away. "Why do you steal all that is good in the world? My father, my mother, my husband—everyone who loved me is dead!"

Bitter tears poured down her face and she slammed her fists against her breasts. "*I'm* the one who sinned! *I* abandoned him without a word. He came to save *me*. Why kill him and let me live?"

Blind rage flooded her mind. She thrust both hands heavenward screaming out a pain that words could not express. "You say you are a just God." Spittle flew from her mouth. "Well, where is your justice now?"

Viviane jerked wet hair away from her lips. "I tried to serve you. You took my father and still I believed. I still prayed, I obeyed and still," she grabbed a handful of sharp gravel and squeezed it, "still you persecute me by taking the man whose love meant more to me than life itself!"

Anger melted into an overwhelming rush of despair. "Just kill me God." She let the gravel drop from her fingers. "I can't outlive him. I can't raise..." Her words melted into a strangled moan. "I can't raise his child... without him."

She spread out her hands, feeling only the renewed sense of her guilt, the brutal pain of his loss and the profound emptiness of her religion. "Where are you God?" She glared at the heavens. "Are you even listening? Do you care?"

No response.

"Talk to me!"

Silence.

Heartbroken, she slumped forward, laying her pain at the foot of the tree. Time lost its meaning as minutes blended into hours, but the surging whirlpool of emotion sucked her in, keeping her prostrate.

At length, the irony of her situation broke through the fog of her sorrow. She, a woman who had committed one wrong after another, demanded an audience with a holy God. Why should he answer? Hadn't she left a litany of bad decisions behind her?

Her mind flashed through the tragedies that had led up to this moment. If only she hadn't jumped out of the carriage that night in Paris, Olivier, the carriage driver, would still be alive. If only she hadn't given the mute child a coin, he might have escaped the carriage that claimed his life.

If only she hadn't given herself to Alexandre, she would have avoided a lifetime of regret. If only she hadn't run off, Philippe could have found a solution to deal with Alexandre's threat. Now, her husband was dead because *she* had felt compelled to save them all by herself.

Viviane crumbled under the weight of her guilt. It was her foolishness that had murdered the man she loved. "I'm sorry!" She screamed the words over and over, choking on her own saliva. "I don't deserve to live. I am unlovable."

I LOVE YOU.

The voice was quiet—so quiet that she almost missed it. When the words did sink into her consciousness, some part of her grief-stricken mind thought it was Philippe's voice. She pushed herself up, pulling mangled strands of hair out of her face.

"Philippe?" Irrational hope flared within her.

I LOVE YOU.

The voice was louder now. Her eyes darted around but she saw no one. Her spine tingled with an indescribable fear. She slammed her eyelids shut, overcome by the presence of someone she could not see.

"God?" She choked back a sob. "Kill me, please! My mother, my husband, all dead because of me." Her wails, born of a vindictive conscience that pointed accusing fingers at her stubbornness, rose to overcast skies.

She was as guilty of Philippe's murder as was Alexandre. "It's all my fault!"

I FORGIVE YOU.

Chills ran through her body.

Forgiveness? The thought burned in her mind. Philippe had forgiven her betrayals. He had loved her unconditionally despite everything she had done.

But he was dead.

She caught her breath as she remembered his kisses, the light of joy in his eyes whenever he looked at her. Not once had he reprimanded, not once had he brought up the past. What was it he always said? *It is forgotten.*

"How?" She breathed, not daring to hope. "What forgiveness could there be for me?"

I WANT YOU TO KNOW THE TRUTH.

Truth. Her eyes flew open and she stared in mesmerized silence at the stump in front of her. A tendril of desperate, fragile hope sprouted in her heart. *Truth.* Philippe's words, spoken so long ago by this very tree, suddenly crowded her mind. *You have a heart that will pursue truth relentlessly.* Could it be that the truth she had sought for so long was contained in the words he had written?

Viviane crawled to the foot of the tree and began scrabbling at the soil, throwing aside handfuls of gravel. The rain had stopped but had loosened the earth. After a few moments, her hands touched something hard in the loose soil. She eased it out.

She held a wooden box that, when opened, revealed a familiar book. She rose and walked to the bench where she had met Philippe each day for three weeks. The ghost of a smile touched her lips as she wiped her hands as best as she could. *How I have changed since those days.* When her hands were clean, she reverently opened the simple, leather-bound volume.

> My love Viviane,

The words, scrawled on the first page, caught her eyes.

> When you read this, I will be gone.

She sucked in her breath. Philippe had known that he was going to die. How?

> I do not want you to hold yourself responsible for my death. It had to be this way.

Viviane felt the burn of fresh tears. He had written this *after* she had left Lussan to return to Paris. She wiped her eyes with the back of her hand and continued reading.

> God has planned my life for the moment that is now ahead of me. I do not run from the challenge but go toward it. I do this willingly because, in my death, you will find a new life.

She could not help it. "I don't want a life without you." She wailed, putting the book aside and burying her face in her hands. "What good is life if you're not in it?"

When the well of her tears had at last run dry, she picked up the book again.

> My purpose is to die for you. Do not blame yourself, for I do not blame you. The words in this book will guide you and our son in the days ahead.
>
> Everything is forgotten. Everything is forgiven.
>
> I will always love you. I will never leave you. I live on through you.
>
> Philippe.

She closed the book, placed it back in the box and clasped it to her wet chest.

I FORGIVE YOU.

The voice spoke from within, echoing Philippe's words. It comforted her, wooing her into a sweet embrace of unfathomable warmth and light.

MY GRACE IS SUFFICIENT. DO YOU BELIEVE THIS?

"God!" She gasped, crying out with every part of her broken heart. "I believe. I believe!"

The floodgates of her broken spirit flew open and a tidal wave of peace washed over her soul. She stood upright, pressing the book against her chest, as the stones of her guilt were rolled away. Olivier, Germain, Alexandre—in a moment, every accusing voice of her past that had tormented her mind was silenced.

"I'm forgiven." She whispered the words, tasting their intoxicating power. A ray of evening sunlight ripped through the scudding clouds and tenderly caressed her face. "Forgiven."

Warmth flooded her entire being. Awe at the reality of this experience sent tingles rippling up and down her spine. Philippe had known that he would die, but had come to Paris willingly, holding nothing against her. This knowledge did not assuage her grief, but the assurance that he had forgiven her and the understanding that God's grace was greater than her sins, eradicated the guilt that she had carried for so long.

She made her way toward the stump of the Bride Tree, guided by a solitary ray of evening light. It silhouetted a green shoot that had begun to push its way up from among the gnarled roots.

"New life." Viviane stood, rooted in place, and drank in the sight before her. Suddenly, the pieces fell together in her mind. She *was* the Bride Tree. Like it, she had been cut down by evil, but Philippe's words of life had restored her. His death had opened a gateway to a spiritual awakening—a new life replete with the power of grace. Her hands shifted to her belly. His love had created a new life that swelled within her even now.

YOU ARE MINE.

"Yes, Father." She whispered the words, a spark of joy burgeoning past the pain in her heart.

At last she understood the wonder of Philippe's relationship to God. His own love for her had constantly reached beyond her frailties, just as the grace of God had reached beyond her shadowed past. With it, he had taken a mountain of guilt and ground it into dust beneath her feet.

Viviane wiped the corners of her eyes. She could never forget the role she had played in Philippe's death, but perhaps it was better that way. Remembering the extent of her mistakes could only amplify the power of his love. She would remember but *he* had chosen to forgive... and forget. *It is forgotten.*

A fresh evening breeze softly ruffled her hair. She touched her belly, feeling their child stir within her womb. *I live on through you.* Hope surged within her as the future became clear.

"A new life, Philippe." She tilted her head back and spoke to the sky above. "One day our child will return to France. He will restore the fallen house of Valence."

She closed her eyes as the light danced upon her face. "You died as a commoner, but he will take his place as a king." She hugged the book to her heart again. "This I swear."

⚜

Salomé wept bitter tears as the small frigate, *Espérance,* began the long voyage to America. Simon stood next to her, as forlorn as she. The only sound, aside from the lapping of the waves, was the contented gurgling of her daughters in the basket at her feet.

"We must plan our revenge." Her voice was as strong as iron.

"Salomé." Simon touched her arm. "All the killin' in the world won't bring Alexandre back. We have no idea where Viviane has gone and to spend your life lookin' for her seems a waste."

She rounded on him, eyes blazing. "A waste? Alexandre asked me to finish what we started. If we don't exterminate Philippe's family then they could bring back the monarchy. Alexandre would have died in vain!" She clenched her teeth.

"I swore that they would die, and heaven help me if I don't keep that promise!"

His eyes took in her radical determination. "What will you do?"

She held his gaze. "I want you to train my daughters. Train them to kill."

"What?" Simon's incredulous snort caused a few of the sailors to cast curious glances in their direction.

Salomé clutched the front of his shirt. "Teach them everythin' that you know."

"Teach a girl to kill?" Simon shook his head. "No, Salomé. I've been down that road. It's no life for a boy, let alone a girl. A child deserves more than that."

"Simon, listen to me." Her voice became pleading. "Philippe killed him. While that woman and her child breathe, Alexandre's spirit will roam the earth callin' for revenge. The war between my seed and hers must go on until one of us is broken by the other."

He turned away. She grabbed his shoulder, pulling him back to her. "How can you, who loved him as a brother, deny this last request?"

"Because it's not what he would've wanted." Simon pounded a fist on the ship's railing. "Even if he asked you to finish it, that doesn't mean you should involve his daughters. If you want to kill Philippe's family, fine! But leave your children out of it."

Salomé stepped back, releasing him. "With or without your help, my girls will carry on this war. I will see to it that they hate the aristo and her child as much as I do. They will blame Philippe for their father's death. With every breath they take, they will curse the name of Valence."

Her eyes narrowed. "With your help, we can finish what Philippe started years ago. Ask yourself: did Alexandre deserve to die?" She lifted her chin. "Do his children deserve to be fatherless—as you were?"

He lowered his head and clutched at the railing as his emotions warred within his heart. Alexandre had wanted nothing more than to be a father to his children. It was Philippe's blade that had robbed him of that right, condemning his daughters to the same fate that he and his friend had faced.

He sighed. "No, they don't."

"Then help me avenge their father." She grew quiet. "As soon as I am healed, I will pay you with whatever physical comforts you desire."

He recoiled, sickened by her offer. Salomé was rapidly reverting to her old ways, using her body to manipulate men. It wouldn't work on him.

"I'll do it." He rubbed the back of his neck. "But only out of respect for Alexandre's memory. As to payment—don't even think about it. Whatever I do, I do for him."

Salomé jerked her head downward in a stiff nod then gazed out at the water as the sea breeze whipped through her hair. "I can never love again, Simon. I am married to revenge."

"A poor match that will make." Simon frowned then inhaled through his nose and breathed out through his mouth. "Nothin' will be done without a good solid plan." *What would Alexandre come up with?*

"What should we do?" Salomé twisted her head in his direction.

He paused as an idea flickered in his mind. "We'll keep our ears open for news from France," he said. "The day will come when Viviane will return to claim her late husband's estate. If her child is a boy, he will undoubtedly unite the royalists in a play for the throne."

She remained expressionless. "The news will take a long time to reach American shores."

"Which is why we will return to France when this madness is over." Simon pointed to the receding shoreline.

Salomé remained silent for a long moment before agreeing. "So be it." She picked her daughters up with a swish of her bedraggled skirts and together they faced the setting sun. Its crimson rays turned the water into a sea of lapping flames.

"We will wait in the shadows, my daughters." She kissed each child's head. "But one day, we will step into the light and strike our fatal blow." She clenched her jaw. "This I swear."

⚜

General Lafayette watched as Viviane stepped onto the boarding plank and slunk aboard the Hermione. He grimaced. It was the first time the girl would leave her native soil but there was no joy in this departure, only the knowledge that everything she loved would remain on a land ravaged by war and uncertainty. There had been no time to seek Philippe's body or bury Viviane's mother, but he had promised that he would do whatever he could for them both.

The general now called Jacourt to one side.

"The child she carries," Lafayette nodded toward Viviane, "could very well be the future King of France."

Jacourt cocked his head to one side. "Such a child must be protected at all costs."

"*Exactement,*" Lafayette agreed. "That is why I am ordering you to accompany her to Virginia."

He pulled a sheaf of papers from his breast pocket. "These documents will grant you access to Secretary of War, General Henry Knox who will conduct you to the presence of my good friend, General Washington."

"You are ordering me to go to America?" Jacourt took a step backward.

Lafayette's eyes bored into Jacourt's skull. "I am ordering you to save the future of France. Her marriage to Philippe de Valence is recorded in the official records of the Church and their offspring is legitimate. The darkness that is swallowing France will not be stopped by Robespierre's death. He has left an ineffective government and our internal divisions refuse to heal. This child may be the only hope for our nation."

Lafayette coughed. "If she bears a son, he *must* return to France and claim his throne." He tapped the papers against Jacourt's chest. "Keep them safe until that time comes and teach the child what it means to be a king."

"And if it is a girl?"

Lafayette sighed. "The law does not allow a woman to inherit the throne." His expression was grim. "For the sake of France, pray that she bears a son."

Jacourt gave a crisp salute, then joined Viviane at the ship's stern as cries of "weigh anchor" drifted over the water.

"I have been ordered to accompany you, Madame." Jacourt smiled and tipped his hat.

A weak smile crossed Viviane's lips. "I will be glad of your company." She was silent for a few moments, then spoke again. "It's strange."

"What is?" The soldier folded his arms across his chest as the maritime wind played games with his graying hair.

Viviane clutched the boat's railing. "When Philippe was alive, I longed to have the same peace that he always possessed. Now, he is gone, and I face an uncertain future in a new land whose language and people I don't know. But I feel no fear, only an assurance that God will one day bring me back to my home."

Jacourt studied her face. "I have not known you for long, Madame, but I can see that you found more than a book at Versailles. You found peace."

"Yes, I did," she said. "I will always mourn my loss, but I feel somehow that Philippe's death has made God more real in a way that I can never explain." She shook her head. "His book is filled with messages for our child. Instructions on how to behave, what kind of words to say and a detailed description of how we met."

Viviane sobered. "It's almost as though he knew for the past four years that he would die."

"He can never die." The soldier's eyes shifted to France's shoreline. "He was a hero. A coward will perish a thousand times, but a hero?" He looked upward. "A hero is immortal."

"I know that now." Viviane's eyes dropped to her swollen belly where new life grew. "One day, Philippe will return to France. He will bring it out of the darkness and usher in a new age of glory."

Epilogue

August 1812. Château de Versailles, France

Viviane sat astride a white mare, eyes blazing with maternal pride as she looked at the young man whose matching white stallion danced beside her. Her son had been named King of the French that morning at a restored Versailles. A thousand emotions crashed in exuberant harmony within her as she glanced at this shrine of hallowed memories. Philippe's body had never been found, but she believed that the greatest tribute to his memory was the restored Bride Tree whose heavy, fruit-laden branches perfumed the summer air with the rich scent of life.

Viviane smiled at the aged Lafayette. The war hero proudly positioned his guards behind the king as they made their way toward Paris.

How Jacourt would have loved to see this day! Her eyes watered as she remembered the elderly soldier who had died in America a few months before she had received Lafayette's letter inviting them to return to France.

"Philippe," she called softly, her silver-streaked hair fluttering in the wind.

"Mother?" Her son's gentle voice, so reminiscent of his father's, rose above the cheering throng that lined the streets.

"You have your father's book?"

He winked at her mischievously. "Right over my heart." He smiled and patted his chest. "I had Johnson, the American leatherworker, create a sort of holster to attach it to that metal breastplate you insisted I wear."

She looked askance at the slight bump underneath his white cloak and wondered how she had not noticed it before.

His brown eyes followed her gaze. "I thought it only proper that I carry a part of Father with me when riding into Paris for the first time."

"He would be honored to know how much you value his writing." Viviane laid a hand on her son's arm.

She had replaced the book's worn leather cover with a more durable one of heavy bronze before they left America, praying that the words it contained would protect and guide her son for the rest of his life. Knowing he carried it over his heart comforted her. It was a sort of spiritual shield that she knew he would need in the days to come.

The procession inched forward, and her heart overflowed with joy as she saw the genuine smiles that wreathed the faces of the people. Reports of the rise and fall of Napoleon, the general who had seized power after Robespierre's demise, had reached them in America. It seemed that France was at last ready to welcome the House of Valence to the throne.

She had warned her son to never trust the smiles of his subjects and insisted that he wear a metal breastplate beneath his clothes the day of his inauguration. It appeared that her maternal worries had been in vain.

"Our time has come, Philippe." Viviane reined in her horse and allowed her son to ride forward alone into the glorious light of his destiny.

⚜

Salomé's brow furrowed in concentration as her daughter, Renée, pushed her way through the massive crowds that lined the tree-studded route to Paris. She grunted softly in approval as the girl positioned herself on the other side of the road, ensuring that no obstructions would hinder her view of her target: the queen-mother.

"You remember your instructions?" She spoke in hushed tones to Victoire, her other child. The twins were identical reproductions of her younger self but, whereas her head was now silver and her cheeks wrinkled, their hair was coal-black and their skin was smooth.

"*Oui, maman,*" Victoire said. "The son is mine. The mother belongs to Renée and to you."

"You only have one shot." Salomé lowered her brows and then released them.

"Don't worry, Mother." The young beauty tossed her head. "I will aim for his heart and that is where my bullet will strike."

Salomé released her breath in a speculative *humph*. Victoire possessed her looks but lacked the same ruthless courage. Maybe the devil hadn't snatched her soul as he had taken Salomé's years before. Renée, on the other hand, possessed both a killer's instinct and a ruthless will to do what was necessary. That was why she had entrusted the real prize, Viviane, to Renée and herself. Renée would not let her down.

Renée was born for this task. Hadn't Simon himself said so? She shook her head and grimaced. They had lost Simon to a strange illness about a year ago.

No more thoughts of the dead. Not today.

Age had cursed her with a wandering mind, but today she would focus. Today would end the horrible emptiness that had gnawed at her relentlessly for the past twenty years. Today... she would die.

"Let's go." Salomé slowed her gait to a shuffle as the royal cavalcade swung around the bend.

Victoire stepped back into the outer fringe of the crowd, putting some distance between herself and her mother, her fingers lightly resting on the butt of the pistol that pressed hard and cold against her hip.

"I'm comin' Alexandre." Salomé whispered the words.

The armed guards who rode behind the king would be too quick for her aged legs to outrun, but the knowledge that her daughters would escape was consolation enough. Simon's rugged training, first in the Kentucky frontier and then in the forests of France, had transformed innocent girls into lethal assassins. While he had worked on their bodies, she had molded their minds. She had taught them about their father and ingrained his dying request to "finish what he had started" into their every waking thought.

As they grew, they had developed a relentless hatred for the House of Valence, blaming Philippe for their troubles. The girls knew the cost of today's assassination but, like their mother, they did not shrink from their duty. Salomé licked her lips, savoring the taste of vengeance.

The entourage pressed closer, horses moving at an even trot. Salomé slowed her ragged breath to an even rhythm. *Timin'. Simon said it's all in the timin'.* She waited until she could hear the jangle of the horses' harnesses.

A convincing scream rose above the crowd's acclaim as Victoire pretended to lose her balance and stumbled directly into the path of the young king's horse.

"Stop!"

"Someone help her!"

Cries of alarm rose on all sides. Philippe jerked his rearing horse to an abrupt halt. *Now!* Salomé screamed inside her skull.

The confusion had worked perfectly to her advantage. The king's eyes, as well as the eyes of those closest to him, were locked in immobilized panic on Victoire while Renée closed in from the other side.

She caught a glimpse of motion as her daughter subtly slid her pistol free. Trained by a master assassin, both girls ignored the emotion of the moment and coolly awaited her signal. Philippe leapt down from his still-snorting horse. He rushed toward Victoire whose struggles and cries of pain masked her furtive attempts to better grip the gun's smooth stock.

Salomé slipped forward, making her way behind the screen of concerned onlookers until she stood across from Viviane, keeping her head bowed.

"Are you alright?" Salomé could hear the king's voice as he bent over her daughter. "Madame, can you hear me? Are you hurt?"

"Philippe?" It was Viviane's voice, calling out to her son as she began to make her way toward him. She had not seen Salomé... yet.

Now! It must be now!

"Philippe, I think—"

Salomé bared her teeth in a vicious smile as she shoved her way past the man in front of her, ripped her own pistol free, and took aim at the woman's chest. Viviane gaped at this phantom from her past.

"Salomé!" Her hands flew to her mouth.

"Long live... the... king!" Salomé shouted the signal. She heard the twin roar of her daughters' guns, saw Viviane jerk forward as Renée's bullet smashed into her lower back and then—with a scream of rancid hate that had defied two decades—Salomé pulled the trigger.

To Be Continued

The story is not over! Look for *When Stars Burn Down*, the thrilling conclusion to *Bride Tree* in 2019. Subscribe to the author's email list for updates and exclusive plot previews.

Sign up now at: www.jprobinsonbooks.com.

Author's Notes:

Jesus said, "Behold, I stand at the door, and knock: if any man hear my voice, and open the door, I will come in to him, and will sup with him, and he with me." (Rev. 3:20). It is worth noting that Christ was not speaking to the sinner but to the Church.

In the 2,000 years since Christ's departure, two groups have consistently been at odds within the ranks of Christianity: those who wish to be transformed into Christ's image and those who desire only religious formalism and the power it brings. Like Viviane, who chose the charm of Alexandre over the humble character of Philippe, the Church opted for alluring creeds and rituals instead of a living encounter with Christ.

Salomé's relationship to Viviane—a hatred that spans generations—gives us a glimpse of a conflict between the two groups that has spanned millennia. This conflict has influenced politics and shaped world history. Like the Bride Tree, truth was cut down by reason and formal religion, but I am thrilled to write that hope has risen, shining like a beam of light on a gloomy day, as the promise of the Lord's coming draws near. Scriptures, such as Malachi 4:5-6 and Joel 2:25, promise a restoration of truth to all who have ears to hear.

Dear reader, regardless of your religious affiliation or if you have no spiritual inclination, open the door of your heart to Jesus Christ, the Way, the Truth and the Life. Like Viviane, begin the journey on your knees before the rugged tree of Calvary. I pray that, as she did, you will experience the transforming love that will make you a bearer of the life of Jesus Christ. I pray that you also will become part of the restored Bride Tree.

"And I will restore to you the years that the locust hath eaten, the cankerworm, and the caterpillar, and the palmerworm, my great army which I sent among you."
Joel 2:25 KJV

Historical notes:

The French Revolution was a defining moment in the history of France and of the world but, despite its magnitude, my vision for *Bride Tree* was to create a story around the central theme of the Revolution—not to chronicle its events. With that said, the excessive luxuries of the upper classes and the misery of the poor were much as I described. Painstaking research was conducted to provide an accurate picture of French society to modern readers. I have, however, modified several historical elements.

There is no evidence that the Roman Catholic Church was behind the French Revolution; that is a fictional spin that I have created to add dimension to the plot. It is not my intent to harm or defame any individual or organization. There is historical evidence for strong tension between the governments of France and the Vatican in the pre-and-post revolutionary time periods. It is my intent to capture the turbulent relationship between the popes of Rome and the leaders of France during the late 18th century in this novel.

To date, I have not come across definitive evidence supporting a love-interest between Maximilien Robespierre and Queen Marie-Antoinette, however such a relationship has been purported. The exchange of letters is a dramatization of a factual account known as the "Affair of the Necklace."

Robespierre did become obsessed with life and death after the execution of Marie-Antoinette, and was primarily responsible for the brutal murder of an estimated 40,000 people. Ultimately loathed by the very people who once championed him as "The Incorruptible," he was guillotined along with his brother, Augustin. Augustin did choose to die with his brother, despite being given the opportunity to keep his life.

Philippe de Valence is a fictitious character whose life is loosely based on Philippe-Joseph, Duke of Orléans and Chartres. The real Philippe was a noble who did indeed lay aside his title in support of the common man and took the surname of Égalité. He did not, regrettably, display the moral integrity shown by my fictitious character and endured a difficult marriage with Adélaide de Bourbon. Ultimately, after having voted in favor of the death of King Louis, the real Philippe Égalité was also executed by guillotine—a victim of his noble blood, family ties, and the fear that gripped France during the Reign of Terror.

For the sake of simplicity, I altered several key dates. King Louis XVI was executed on Jan 21, 1793 and his wife was killed on October 16, 1793. Philippe Égalité's son, who was born prior to his father's execution, came to power in 1830 and not in 1812. It is my fervent hope that the alterations to the historic record will not obscure the literary enjoyment and the spiritual lessons hidden within *Bride Tree*.

About the Author

JP Robinson began writing as a teen for the Times Beacon Records newspaper in New York. He holds degrees in both English and French is a teacher of French history. He is known for vivid, high-adrenaline plots laced with unexpected twists.

Born to praying parents who were told by medical doctors that having children was impossible, JP Robinson's writes to ignite faith in a living God.

Connect with JP via his website: www.jprobinsonbooks.com

Also by JP Robinson

Twiceborn
Secrets of Versailles I

Versailles is the center of European power but the court of King Louis XIV is also a hotbed of intrigue and political manipulation. Despite the rigid structure of Angélique's upbringing, temptation proves stronger than her principles. Her children, Antoine and Hugo, are ripped apart by their mother's shadowed past.

Years later, Antoine is caught in a web of intrigue when his jealous brother—now a powerful member of the clergy—accuses him of treason and threatens to destroy the woman he loves.

But Hugo has bigger plans than just his brother's downfall. He ignites a plot that threatens to bring the Kingdom of France to its knees, little suspecting the cataclysmic forces his actions will unleash.

Tears will fall, blood will flow and, in the end, only one man will remain standing.

Meet characters, watch trailers and more:
www.JPRobinsonBooks.com

Praise for Secrets of Versailles

"...Had me on my toes guessing in suspense what was going to happen. It was exciting and I had a hard time putting it down. I kept finding myself wondering what would happen in each chapter when I was doing other things. —EF

"Robinson has a clear talent for weaving an intricate plot, along with a bold flair for the dramatic." —NK

"Lush detail." —BG

"An epic drama." —KK

"Drew me in from the first page!"—AE

"When I finished, my first thought was, 'when's the next one coming out?' It was that good." —RS

"From start to finish, he draws you in and you won't be able to put the book down."—LR

Made in the USA
Columbia, SC
05 June 2018